William Howie Wylie

Thomas Carlyle

The man and his books. Illustrated by Personal reminiscences, table-talk, and

anecdotes of himself and his friends

William Howie Wylie

Thomas Carlyle

The man and his books. Illustrated by Personal reminiscences, table-talk, and anecdotes of himself and his friends

ISBN/EAN: 9783337057626

Printed in Europe, USA, Canada, Australia, Japan

Cover: Foto ©Raphael Reischuk / pixelio.de

More available books at **www.hansebooks.com**

THOMAS CARLYLE.

The Man and His Books.

*ILLUSTRATED BY PERSONAL REMINISCENCES,
TABLE-TALK, AND ANECDOTES OF
HIMSELF AND HIS FRIENDS.*

By WM. HOWIE WYLIE.

LONDON
MARSHALL JAPP AND COMPANY
1881

"A true Great Man; great in intellect, in courage, affection and integrity; one of our most lovable and precious men. Great, not as a hewn obelisk; but as an Alpine mountain,—so simple, honest, spontaneous. . . . Unsubduable granite, piercing far and wide into the Heavens; yet in the clefts of it fountains, green beautiful valleys with flowers!"

PREFACE.

THIS attempt to give an account of Thomas Carlyle and his Works that might be of some slight service as a guide to the study of his writings was printed before the appearance of the posthumous *Reminiscences* edited by Mr Froude. These throw much new light on the early life of their Author, some chapters of which had previously been obscure; but this fresh information does not materially affect what appears in the following pages. For the first time, however, it is now possible to state with precision that Carlyle went to the Grammar School at Annan in 1806, and to Edinburgh University in 1809. In 1814 he was usher at Annan, in 1816 schoolmaster at Kirkcaldy, and in 1818 he took pupils at Edinburgh. In 1822 he became the private tutor of Charles Buller, and after his marriage he lived for eighteen months near Edinburgh before removing to Craigenputtoch. Into one misapprehension respecting the burnt MS. of the *French Revolution*, I was beguiled by the report of Mr Milburn, of America, whose statement I accepted as a correction of my own previous information ; the latter now turns out to have been accurate. It was the MS. of the first, not of the second, volume that was destroyed by fire.

It will be observed that I have had the good fortune to discover what I believe to be a hitherto unknown Poem by Carlyle; and the reasons for ascribing the piece to him have now received an accession in the account which he gives in the posthumous *Reminiscences* of his father's connection with the building of the Bridge at Auldgarth.

To Mr Boehm, A.R.A., the friend of Carlyle, my best acknowledgments are due for his kind and courteous permission to allow the use of his Statue-Portrait of the subject of this volume, and also of the Medal designed by him to commemorate the Eightieth Birthday of the immortal Sartor. These works of art were thought highly of by him whose features they so truthfully delineate ; and I shall be content and grateful if my endeavour to pourtray the same subject should commend itself to the reader as not altogether unworthy the companionship of Illustrations so full of genius and of life.

W. H. W.

March 9, 1881.

CONTENTS.

APPENDIX.

Mrs Carlyle.

The Arched House—Birthplace of Thomas Carlyle.

THOMAS CARLYLE.

CHAPTER I.

THE COUNTRY OF THE CARLYLES—WHAT SCENERY OWES
TO NOBLE LIVES—THE ANCIENT HOUSE OF CARLYLE
—A CARLYLE BROTHER OF THE BRUCE—THE LORDS
OF TORTHORWALD—LORD SCROPE AT ECCLEFECHAN—
DECLINE OF THE FAMILY—THE FARMERS OF HODDAM.

FIFTY years ago the words, "Thomas Carlyle, Nutholm,"
painted by a village artist on a rustic cart as homely as
his letters, would not have been likely to attract any
particular notice from the passing pilgrim who had just
emerged from the pastoral valley of the Clyde into that
comparatively level, well cultivated, and sylvan country
from which you first descry the sparkling waters of the
Solway.   Yet it was with a positive thrill that, on a
summer day a little more than twenty years ago, two
young students from Edinburgh, making their first tour
on foot into England, read the name on that old, battered
cart, as it went jolting painfully past a clump of pines, in
whose shade they had lain down to rest, away from the
heat of the noonday sun.   That name was the first strong
reminder that we were now actually on the confines of a
region which we had greatly desired to see.   It told us

that we must be nearing the village where, five years before the dawn.of the present century, there was born to a humble, but industrious, intelligent, and God-fearing couple—members of that peasant class which has furnished Scotland with a majority of her greatest names— a son who was destined to grow up into an illustrious guide and inspirer of men.   From these hedges of thorn guarding our path, Thomas Carlyle, as a boy, had probably gathered the sprigs of "may" in the early summer, and the ripe, if not luscious, fruit in the late autumn.   In this very fir wood, who knows, he may have played with his schoolmates, or rested, book in hand, on his lonely rambles.   These very fields and lanes may have witnessed his eager converse with his student friend Edward Irving, when there was "nothing but joy, health, and hopefulness without end" in their young hearts.   Such were the reflections suggested by the sight of that name on the old country cart.   A new glory diffused itself over the landscape; for were not these the scenes in the midst of which had been nurtured the greatest of all the living sons of the Scottish soil?

How the charm would be lessened that we find in the scenery of our native land, how much less potent would be·the influence of that scenery in the formation of character, were it not for such associations as these! Without the moral interest derived from humanity, the physical beauty and grandeur would count for comparatively little; even the most splendid prospects in nature assert but a limited power over the mind until they have been linked to the story of noble lives.   What are the fields, however good for growing corn, that have been hallowed by no memories of martyr and hero? the rivers that are songless but for their own natural music? the mountains that are no more associated with human life than are the clouds which mantle round their summits? Even the sky-cleaving peaks that rise from the Yosemite Valley, and the groves of that marvellous region, must, after all, be comparatively tame, since, with all their material magnitude, they have no story to tell about man. The figure of Columba, emerging from the mists of a venerable antiquity, glides with us as we sail among the Hebridean isles, and the grey old evangelist and his school of the prophets rise upon our view as we cast anchor under the Cyclopean walls of Elachnave, or set foot on the sacred soil of Iona; the savage gloom of Glencoe is deepened by the song of Ossian, which comes moaning down every corrie, like the sighing of the night-wind among the hills; a whole west country, from Elderslie to Lochryan, is transfigured by the memories of Wallace, and Bruce, and Burns; and, go where you may in the land of Walter Scott, every hill, and valley, and stream has felt the touch of the magician's wand. Not merely for their natural loveliness do we visit those lakes on whose woody shores dwelt Southey and Coleridge, De Quincey and Arnold, Wilson and Wordsworth. Sheffield, with its clang of hammers, and thick smoke curtain, looks less grim when we think of Ebenezer Elliott and James Montgomery. Byron and Kirke White deepen the romance of Sherwood Forest, and send a pathos through Wilford Grove; the whole of woody Warwickshire becomes like fairyland at thought of Shakespeare; even the dull banks of the sleepy Ouse are glorified by the Farmer of St Ives and the Bedford Tinker—the one the doer of the greatest deeds, the other the dreamer of the grandest dream, that fill with so much meaning the name of England.

Although the man who was to add a fresh charm to the lovely shire in which the Bruce was born, and where Burns found his grave, did not appear in the world till the eighteenth century was nearly ended, the name he bore had long been one of the most illustrious in Annandale. The Carlyles, indeed, were among the very oldest families in that richly-storied province of Scotland; and before they came thither, they had been one of the most powerful houses in Cumberland, where, at the time of the Norman Conquest, they possessed large estates. The history of the Carlyle family is a subject in which its most distinguished member naturally felt a keen interest, and on which, as we have reason to know, he had bestowed considerable attention—so much, indeed, that a rumour was at one time current to the effect, that he was collecting materials for a history of the House.* The

---

* "That Mr Carlyle descended from this grand stock, there can be no sort of doubt, but his genealogical tree was too imperfect to establish the connection. In a letter to a kinsman some years ago, Mr Carlyle related how, when Nicholas Carlisle, the antiquarian, paid them a visit, while searching for materials for a family history, his father and uncle gave the distinguished visitor audience in a field where they were busily engaged in ploughing."—*The Globe Newspaper*, Feb. 5, 1881. The castle of Torthorwald, the chief seat of the Carlyles, is supposed to have been built in the thirteenth century. It has been placed in the second class of Border castles, not because of its size, but on account of its strength and accessory defences, in which respect it was not exceeded by some of the first-class fortresses. It is supposed to have been last repaired about 1630. "An ancient man now (1789) living at Lochmaben," writes Capt. Grose, "remembers the roof of this building on it." Mr M'Dowall, writing in 1872, says: "The appearance of the ruin at the present differs little from the picture of it given by Grose, the

Annandale Carlyles trace their descent from Crinan, Abthane of Dunkeld, whose son, Maldred, married Beatrice, daughter of King Malcolm II. About 1124, Robert de Brus, who had come into Scotland with David I., received a grant of Annandale from his royal friend and patron; and his grandson, also named Robert, on entering upon his inheritance, was created Lord of Annandale, or, as it was then called, Estrahannent. Under this third of the Scottish Bruces, and about the year 1185, the Carlyles held lands in Annandale. They also owned property in Cumberland, deriving their surname, in all probability, from the ancient capital of that picturesque region. By the daughter of the king, Maldred had a son, named Uchtred; and the eldest son of the latter was Robert of Kinmount. Uchtred's second son, Richard, received the lands of Newbie-on-the-Moor from his grandfather. Eudo de Carlyle, grandson of Richard, witnessed a charter to the monastery of Kelso, about 1207. The next head of the Carlyle family, Adam, had a charter of various lands in Annandale from William de Brus, second lord of the district, who died in 1215. Gilbert, son of Adam, who had joined in the disastrous Baliol revolt, swore fealty to Edward I. in 1296.

Sir William de Carlyle, grandson of Gilbert, rose so high in the favour of his liege lord, Robert, Earl of Carrick, that the latter gave him his daughter Margaret in marriage; thus the head of the house of Carlyle became brother-in-law to the greatest and best of the

---

lapse of eighty-two years having made scarcely any impression upon it." The parish of Torthorwald, which contains the three villages of Torthorwald, Collin, and Rowcan, lies near the foot of Nithsdale, and is separated from Dumfries parish by Lochar Water.

Scottish monarchs, the famous Robert the Bruce. This is attested by a charter of the Patriot-King bestowing upon them the lands of Crumanston, in which the wife of Sir William is designated "our dearest sister." It is further confirmed by a charter in which Sir William de Carlyle's son received a grant from his royal uncle of the lands of Colyn and Roucan, near Dumfries; the recipient is designated "William Karlo, the King's sister's son." Sir William Carlyle of Torthorwald was slain at the fatal battle of Lochmaben, when Edward III. of England was engaged setting up the perfidious puppet Edward Baliol on the Scottish throne; and it is well worthy of note that, in the same engagement, there fell Sir Humphrey de Bois of Dryfesdale, supposed to be an ancestor of Hector Boece, the historian, and Sir Humphrey Jardine, the head of that Annandale house which in the present century produced Sir William Jardine, the eminent naturalist. Few battle-fields can boast of an incident like this.

At the battle of Neville's Cross, Thomas Carlyle of Torthorwald fell while gallantly defending the person of the young King David; and when the latter was ransomed from his captivity in England, nine years afterwards, he displayed a grateful recollection of Carlyle's services; a charter, signed by the King, October 18, 1362, conveyed the lands of "Coulyn and Rowcan to our beloved cousin Susannah Carlyle, heir of Thomas de Torthorwald, who was killed defending our person at the battle of Durham, and to Robert Corrie, her spouse, belonging formerly to our cousin William de Carlyle." When the daughter of James I. crossed to France in 1436 to be married to Louis the Dauphin, William

Carlyle was one of the train of knights who attended the Princess Margaret. It was this Carlyle who gave a bell for the parish kirk of Dumfries, which is not only still extant, but which, according to the worthy historian of the burgh of Dumfries, Mr William M‘Dowall, was employed till about twenty years ago in "the secular duty of warning the lieges when fires broke out in the burgh." It hangs on the bartizan of the Mid Steeple, and bears a Latin inscription, which, when Englished, runs thus: "William de Carlyle, Lord of Torthorwald, caused me to be made in honour of St Michael. The year of our Lord 1433." In 1455, at the battle of Langholm, which sealed the doom of the rebellious house of Douglas, one of the leaders of the victorious royal army was Sir John Carlyle of Torthorwald, who, along with the head of the house of Johnstone, took Hugh, Earl of Ormond, prisoner, for which service he received from the King a grant of the forty-pound land of Pettinain in Clydesdale. Ennobled in 1470, he sat as Lord Carlyle of Torthorwald* in the parliament of 1475 ; and he was subsequently sent on an embassy to France, in recompence for the great expense attending which he received several grants of land from the Crown in 1477, though one of these grants was revoked by the succeeding monarch, James IV. After the battle of Pinkie and the engagement at Annan, among the landholders of Annandale who were driven to

---

* If the Prime Minister who, when it was too late, offered a small titular distinction to Thomas Carlyle had been acquainted with the history of the country which for a time he was permitted to rule, perhaps it might have occurred to him that it would have been more seemly to suggest to Her Majesty the revival of this ancient title in favour of the greatest of all the Carlyles, instead of insulting him with the offer of a G.C.B.

swear allegiance to Edward VI. we find the Lord Carlyle,
with 101 followers; next to whom on the record comes
Irving of Coveshaw, with 102 followers, who may have
been a progenitor, for aught we know, of Thomas Carlyle's bosom friend, Edward Irving.

In 1570, when the friends of Mary Stuart in Dumfriesshire were assailed by an English force under Lord
Scrope, Lord Carlyle was one of the leaders who mustered
his followers and took part in the battle, in which he was
taken prisoner. Lord Scrope's account of the engagement opens with the statement that on entering Scotland
he encamped at " Heclefeaghan," by which his lordship
did his best to reproduce on paper the troublesome name
of Ecclefechan—the village destined to be made for ever
memorable as the birth-place of Thomas Carlyle. When
we come to the momentous struggle of the seventeenth
century, which has been nowhere described with so much
of insight and graphic force as in Carlyle's *Cromwell*, we
find that the Irvings of Bonshaw and of Drum, as well
as their relations in the burgh of Dumfries, espoused the
Royalist and anti-Presbyterian side; but as to the part
played by the Carlyles at that period the local records
are silent. The family had apparently degenerated, or
at least fallen into decay. In 1580, their peerage passed
to a daughter of the house, Elizabeth, who carried the
family estates over to a Douglas. The eldest son, Sir
James Douglas, was created Lord Carlyle of Torthorwald
in 1609, and by his son the title was resigned in 1638 to
the Earl of Queensberry, who had acquired the estate.
A George Carlyle, from Wales, turned up as a claimant
of the estate, and got it, too, by a decree of the House
of Lords in 1770. It was thought that in him also lay

the right to the peerage, but after dissipating his estate at Dumfries, which he accomplished in a few years, he vanished into Wales. A professor of Arabic at Cambridge, the Rev. Joseph D. Carlyle, who died in 1831, was said to be the next heir; and it is worthy of note that a branch of the family, the Carlyles of Bridekirk, who also fell upon evil days, had for their male representative that minister of Inveresk whose *Autobiography* has sufficient vitality as a picture of manners to preserve the memory of the Rev. Alexander Carlyle as perhaps the crowning example of the Scottish " Moderate."

No one who has read the family history of the Gladstones, who declined from the position of territorial magnates of old renown in Lanarkshire to that of humble burgesses in Biggar, and who have again risen by the force of character and genius to a place second to that of no family in Britain, will regard our story of the Dumfriesshire Carlyles as an impertinence, though we are unable directly to connect the greatest man who has ever borne the name with the ancient lords of Torthorwald. He was of the same stock, beyond question; and, if all the truth were known to us to-day, it might be found that he had as good a claim as any to such a preface as this to the story of his life. In the opening years of the seventeenth century we discover Carlyles among the merchant burgesses of Dumfries, one of them figuring as Bailie (Alderman) William Carlyle in the municipal records; and we have only to enter such a burial-ground as that of Hoddam, on the roadside, a mile and a-half to the south of Ecclefechan, to find from the gravestones that Carlyles have for many generations been settled as farmers in the district. When we visited the place, the

first inscription that met our eye was in memory of a
Thomas Carlyle who died at Eaglesfield in 1821; and
near it was the memorial of a still earlier Thomas Carlyle
of Sornsisyke, who died in the last century, two years
before the philosopher was born. This quaint little City
of the Dead, not more than 35 feet square, is shrouded
by a thorn hedge on one hand and a strip of dark firs on
the other. It was quite by accident that we lit upon it,
and not without some difficulty that we discovered an
entrance. Once within the enclosure, nothing outside
was to be seen but a patch of blue sky overhead. There
is no church near to remind you of the living—amid
the old tombstones, thickly planted, you are alone
with the dead. No more skilful chisel than that of the
rustic mason has been employed; but when we read the
inscriptions that connected the peasants sleeping beneath
our feet with the most kingly Scot of our century, the
spot became more impressive in its primitive simplicity
than the stateliest mausoleum. Greater than the proud-
est lord of Torthorwald is he who sprang from the ranks
of the homely farmers of Hoddam.

CHAPTER II.

BIRTH OF CARLYLE AND DEATH OF BURNS—BIRTH-PLACE
AND PARENTAGE—ANECDOTES OF HIS FATHER AND
MOTHER.

THE month of December 1795, which was darkened by
national distress consequent on a failure of that year's
harvest, and by political agitation of excessive violence
resulting from the stringent Sedition Bill passed by the
dominant party to restrict the expression of public sentiment, is perhaps even more memorable as having witnessed the one meeting in the struggle of public life that
took place between the two greatest Scotsmen of the
period. While Robert Burns was upholding with his pen
the cause of freedom as represented by the Liberal leader
Henry Erskine, Walter Scott was voting in the Parliament
House at Edinburgh for the reactionary Dundas. But
what we now care most to remember was the sore trouble
that had entered the humble home of the poet at Dumfries. For four months the life of his youngest child,
"a sweet little girl," as he described her in a letter written
on one of those sad December days to Mrs Dunlop, had
been trembling in the balance; his own health was giving
way; poverty held him in its grip so tightly that he was
obliged to write to a friend for the loan of a guinea; and
in the anxious, sleepless hours of the night he was
incessantly asking himself, "What will become of my

poor wife and bairns when I am taken away?" Ere seven months had come and gone after that bleak December, the "awkward squad"—aptly symbolising a nation that knew not the value of the gift till it was gone —had fired their farewell shots over the grave of Burns. It was while the great light of the Scottish nation was flickering to extinction at Dumfries that its successor dawned in a still humbler domicile in an obscure hamlet not more than sixteen miles distant from the burgh in which Burns breathed his last. Thomas Carlyle was born at Ecclefechan,* in the parish of Hoddam, on Tuesday the 4th December 1795.†

He was the first child of James Carlyle and Margaret Aitken, who had been married on the 5th March in the same year. Like Hugh Miller, his father was originally a stonemason, and at the time of his son's birth he had reached the mature age of thirty-seven—the very same age as that of the poet who was then dying at Dumfries. There is a slight discrepancy in the statements that were published during Mr Carlyle's lifetime, both as to the precise position occupied by James Carlyle when he became a father, and also as to his residence at that date. According to the account that might fairly enough

---

* It has been stated in some of the newspaper obituaries of Carlyle that this village was also the birth-place of Dr Currie; but the biographer of Burns, born in 1756, first saw the light at Kirkpatrick-Fleming, in the same county of Dumfries, of which parish his father was then the minister.

† The coincidence is worth noting that the still surviving Leopold von Ranke, who has performed for English history a service akin to that which Carlyle rendered to German history, was born in Thuringia in the same month of the same year as his Scottish contemporary—Dec. 21, 1795.

be deemed the best accredited, since it came from the pen of a personal friend of Carlyle's, and was printed in a volume which he had himself authorised, he was born "in the parish of Middlebie, about half a mile from the village of Ecclefechan," and it is added that "his father was a small farmer in comfortable circumstances."* But there is every reason to believe that the father, presently to become a small farmer and by and by a pretty extensive one, was at the date of his marriage still following his original occupation as a stonemason, being also a bit of an architect, and that at the time of Thomas's birth his parents were resident in the village. James Carlyle had come into possession of two small one-storeyed cottages in Ecclefechan, between which a lane ran conducting to some houses at the back, and over this lane he thriftily threw an arch, thus connecting the cottages, besides adding a storey to their height. He let the ground floor to a baker, and, with his young wife, occupied one-half of the top floor, containing two rooms. It was in the smaller of these, the room immediately over the arch, a mere cupboard, nine feet by five, that Thomas Carlyle (according to this story) was born. To this day nothing is changed in the inner or outer aspect of the house, which is now inhabited by the gravedigger of the village and his family.†

The father was the second of five brothers, sons of Thomas Carlyle, tenant of Brownknowe, a small farm

---

* Biographical Memoir by Thomas Ballantyne, prefixed to *Passages selected from the Writings of Thomas Carlyle.* London : Chapman & Hall. 1855. P. 1.

† *The Biographical Magazine.* No. 1, June 1872. London : Trübner & Co.

in Annandale, all of whom, it is said, followed the same occupation of stonemason; and who have left behind them, in the locality, a reputation for great strength, as well as eccentricity of character. "The Carlyles were like no other people," we have been told by more than one person who knew them. Strongly marked were their features, both of mind and body; and to intellectual powers and moral force, much above the average, they would seem to have united a pugilistic tendency, and even a "fractiousness," to borrow a native term, that sometimes developed itself in peculiar forms. "Pithy, bitter-speaking bodies, and awfu' fechters," is the description of them given by one neighbour; and the sentence gathers up in a few words the most of the opinion that has been handed down by their contemporaries to the present generation, and which is found floating to-day all over Annandale. Of the five brothers, James appears to have been the most notable, both in respect to his skill as a mason, and his general sagacity, as well as in some other respects. The local traditions regarding him, indicate a character in many ways akin to that of his illustrious son. "What a root of a bodie he was!" exclaimed one old lady of Ecclefechan who had known him well; "Ay, a curious bodie: he beat this warld. A spirited bodie; he would sit on no man's coat tails. And sic stories he could tell! Sic sayings, too! Sic names he would give to things and folk! Sic words he had as were never heard before!" He was a great reader as well as a great talker. "It was a muckle treat to be in his house at nicht, to hear him tell stories and tales. But he was always a very strict old bodie, and could bide no contradiction." Mr Ballantyne describes him as "a man possessing great force of character, of an earnest, religious nature, and much respected throughout the district, not less for his moral worth than for his native strength of intellect." He seems to have had many of the good qualities, the intelligence, earnestness, and moral purity, that shone conspicuous in the father of Burns; and we have sometimes thought, that in delineating the peasant-saint of Alloway, which he did with signal power,* Carlyle had the figure of his own father vividly before his mind. But the elder Burns, we should say, though he could be stern on occasion and was of a sombre temperament, had a gentleness and a quiet dignity that did not pertain to the more active-minded, self-assertive, and even rather contentious Borderer. Annandale, we must bear in mind, had been for many centuries the arena of incessant warfare; and the fighting quality, brought to a high pitch of perfection in all the old families of the "Debateable Land,"† descended with much of its mediæval vigour to the eighteenth century Carlyles. Truth to tell, there seems to have been in Carlyle's father at least a touch of what his son found, and describes so well, in a second Ayrshire worthy, "Old

---

* Sublimer in this world know I nothing than a Peasant Saint. Such a one will take thee back to Nazareth itself; thou wilt see the splendour of Heaven spring forth from the humblest depths of the Earth, like a light shining in great darkness."—*Carlyle's Essay on Burns.*

† *The Debateable Land* is the title of a Dumfriesshire local history, or historical pamphlet rather; said to be a valuable little work in its way, manifesting considerable research. It was written by a Thomas Carlyle, described as "of Waterbeck." No student of the history of England and Scotland needs to be told the origin of the name which gave a title to his pamphlet.

Sulphur Brand," the irascible father of Boswell, known in the Parliament House at Edinburgh as Lord Auchinleck, and who, being a staunch Whig, proved more than a match even for Dr Johnson, when the two got on politics at his lordship's seat in Ayrshire.

Of Carlyle's father, many anecdotes are still current at Ecclefechan. Some of these, as we might expect, are apocryphal, especially a set of stories that represent him and his brothers as noted pugilists; it is just possible, however, there may be a grain of truth in the anecdote that, while working as a mason, he, in order to evince his contempt for a "pup" (that is, a dandy) who was passing, let fall upon him, from the top of the ladder, a huge mass of mortar. A venerable native of Ecclefechan (alive and resident in Glasgow the other day), who is old enough to remember him, tells of the unfailing regularity, and almost soldier-like strictness of discipline with which the rustic patriarch marshalled his family into the front pew of the gallery in the Burgher Kirk, where they worshipped; and one little incident she relates is not without significance. The windows of the meeting-house being destitute of blinds, many of the congregation were inconvenienced on the warm summer days by the burning rays of the sun. A proposal was made to procure blinds, and a subscription started. The collectors called on old Carlyle, and stated their case, expressing a hope that he would give something. "What!" he exclaimed, " you want siller to shut God's blessed licht out o' His ain house? Na, na, I'll give you nothing for sic a purpose. If you had wanted more licht it would have been a different matter, and I micht have given you a subscription." So the collectors had to go away as they came. Another story, though homely and even grotesque, illustrates his hatred of all deceit. One of his children—there were nine in all—was about to be married, and the young folks concluded, in view of the festive occasion, that it would be seemly to have the doors and walls of the house adorned with a coating of paint. But the father refused to listen to this proposal, holding that it was better to let the old walls remain in their native integrity than to pollute them with what he regarded as the brush of falsehood. The rest of the household, however, remained resolute in their determination, and gave the painters instructions to proceed with the work, meanwhile bringing all their batteries of persuasion to bear on their father, in which effort they were probably assisted by the gentle mother. The combined pleadings, however, were all urged in vain. On the appointed day came the painters, whereupon the old man, who had planted himself in the doorway of his domicile, demanded to know what had brought them thither. "To pent the hoose," they replied. "To pent the hoose!" he exclaimed; "ye can just slent the bog (that is, retrace your steps) wi' yer ash-backet feet, for ye'll pit nane o' yer glaur (mud) on my door."

As he advanced in life, he became more decidedly religious, and one proof of this was furnished by the gradual mellowing of his disposition. Mr Carlyle once told a friend that his father had a special fondness for reading theology, and that John Owen was his favourite author. "He could not tolerate anything fictitious in books," said his son, "and walked as a man in the full presence of Heaven, and Hell, and the Judgment." Mr Carlyle thought his father, all things considered, the best

man whom he had ever known. On one occasion he
said to a friend, "He was a far cleverer man than I am,
or ever will be." At another time he described him as
one who, "like Enoch of old, walked with God." He
was much in the habit of using old-fashioned words and
phrases, with which he had become familiar in his reading
of the puritan divines; there was a rare pungency, too, in
his speech; and "his pithy sayings," according to one
writer, "occasionally prickly and sharp, ran through the
countryside." Edward Irving, while paying a visit to the
family, was greatly impressed with the bright and vivid
phraseology of the old man; and, after conversing for a
while with the sire, he turned to the son, saying, "I
have often wondered where you acquired that peculiar,
original, and forcible manner of expressing your ideas.
I have discovered that it is an inheritance from your
father." The old man died in 1832, at the age of
seventy-four. He had four sons—Thomas, James, Alexander, John Aitken, the last named well known as Dr
Aitken Carlyle, the translator of Dante's *Inferno*—and
five daughters. In one of the opening years of the
century, he entered on the occupation of the farm of
Mairhill, in the parish of Hoddam, and at the end of
his lease he removed to Scotsbrig, in the parish of
Middlebie, a farm consisting of two or three hundred
acres; it is now occupied by Mr Carlyle's only-surviving
brother James.

If Irving was right, as he seems to have been, in the
notion that the father had talents which had been trans-
mitted to the son—a talent for the laying on of nicknames
that would stick being one that evidently came from that
source—it may be asserted with equal, if not greater,

confidence, that Carlyle owed very much that was best, in his nature and even in his writings, to his mother. She was her husband's second wife; for James Carlyle, at the age of thirty-two, had married a distant cousin of his own, Jannet Carlyle, the daughter of a small farmer. But this first wife died in 1792, in her twenty-fifth year, leaving no children. About three years afterwards, the widower—who had meanwhile built for himself the quaint little dwelling known as "The Arched House"—married Margaret Aitken, a native of Whitestanes, in the parish of Kirkmahoe. Her parents, though belonging to the upper section of the working class, were not in such circumstances as enabled them to keep their family at home; and so Margaret was sent out to domestic service. She could read, but, like most of the members of her class at that time, and even down to a much later period, she was not able to write. It is a remarkable fact that, like Janet Hamilton the Coatbridge poetess, she taught herself writing when she was well advanced in life, with the care of a large family resting upon her; and she did so with the sole object of being able to correspond with her eldest son. All the accounts we have got of this woman go. to prove that, though originally a domestic servant, she was, in the best sense of the word, a lady. In person she was a little woman, of a slender make, and endowed with the gift of beauty. As a housewife she was careful and hardworking, and an admirable manager; but in her the qualities of Martha were blended with those of the meditative Mary: for she was a great reader, deeply religious, and endowed with a very sweet temper, in which last-named respect she furnished a contrast to her fiery and, at times, tempestuous husband. The quality of her mind, both as to its strength and independence, is sufficiently attested by the fact—the most remarkable we know concerning her—that it was she who first suggested to her son that new theory as to the character of Cromwell which he was the first to lay before the world. It was through her spiritual instincts, we are told, that she had discovered that the then prevailing estimate of the Protector was incorrect; and more than this we do not require to know, in order to feel that her son was indeed justified in indulging that tone of personal self-gratulation which may be detected in one of his aphorisms, to the effect that no able man ever had a fool for a mother. To strength of brain she united a most winsome tenderness of heart; and there can be no doubt that Carlyle's delicacy of insight, and poetic sensibility, were inherited from his mother. While he was fond of dwelling on her virtues, he would confess that she was "entirely too peaceable and pious for this planet;" and he was wont humorously to deplore some sad results of her enjoining non-resistance upon him at school. His love for her amounted to a kind of worship, and tradition has handed down many touching little anecdotes—that about her learning to write being one of the number—which go to prove that the affection of the son was recriprocated to the full.

When we know that it was she who suggested that vindication of Cromwell, which many regard as his greatest, and which is certainly his most satisfactory work, we are not surprised to be told that, though most of the subjects upon which her son wrote were new to her, she read all his books with great care, and particularly read and re-read his *French Revolution*. One of his college friends, like himself an Ecclefechan man, used often to call on Mrs Carlyle and get an early reading of her son's latest book, which, with filial attention, was always forwarded to her at the earliest possible moment. This gentleman would read the book aloud to the old lady, doing his best, no doubt, to help her over the difficulties; for it was her frequent, if not invariable, salutation, "I hae gotten anither o' Tam's buiks, but I can mak' naething o't." We suspect, however, that she generally contrived to master them. It is said that she was at first somewhat disturbed by the new religious views she met with in the books, but when she found that her son was in earnest, and steadfast, she cared for no more. The first anecdote that we remember to have heard concerning Carlyle, was one relating to the visit he paid to his mother, for the purpose of spending a few days with her before he set off for Germany to procure materials for his Life of Frederick. On the morning when he had to take his departure, a little group of friends—all of whom, we fear, must now be gone—were gathered on the railway platform at Ecclefechan to see him off. On entering the booking office he happened to put his hand into his coat pocket, where he discovered something bulky, of whose presence he did not seem to have been aware. He at once took it out, and on unfolding the mysterious parcel, he discovered it to contain some nice home-made Dumfriesshire bannocks, which his mother—just as when he was a little boy at school—had stowed away in his pocket, that he might use them on his journey. The discovery was too much for him. The simple circumstance had transported him to the days of childhood; and when his friends came forward to grasp his hand, his eyes were

suffused with tears, and his voice trembled.   One of the
two saddest visits he ever paid to Scotsbrig was in the
last hours of 1853, when his venerable mother was laid in
the grave.   She died on Christmas Day.   She had survived
her husband twenty-one years.

CHAPTER III.

ETCHINGS OF ECCLEFECHAN — VILLAGE CULTURE AND GREAT MEN—THE HOME TRAINING OF CARLYLE—HIS MOTHER'S LESSON—HOW HIS FATHER DIED—ANECDOTES OF HIS CHILDHOOD.

FEW writers of even a professed autobiography have given a fuller, and none a more vivid, history of their early life than Carlyle supplies in the second book of *Sartor Resartus*. The more narrowly we investigate the subject on the spot, the plainer does it appear that those wonderful opening selections from the paper bags of Diogenes Teufelsdröckh are not only a spiritual record of the childhood of Thomas Carlyle, but that they are also a scrupulously faithful picture of the actual scenes and society in the midst of which he was reared. Under the thinnest possible veil, woven by richly humorous fancy, we find portraits of his parents in Father Andreas and Gretchen; and Entepfuhl is a picture of Ecclefechan as accurate as if it had been written for a guide book or a gazetteer. Mrs Oliphant, as the biographer of Edward Irving, visited the place not so many years ago; and she gives a graphic view of the scene where "the low grey hills close in around the little hamlet of Ecclefechan, forgotten shrine of some immemorial Celtic saint; a scene not grandly picturesque, but full of sweet pastoral freedom and solitude; the hills rising grey against the sky, with.slopes of springy turf, where the sheep pastured, and shepherds of an antique type pondered the ways of God to man." But more lovingly minute are the etchings of the village and the surrounding country that have been executed by the superb artist who spent there the happy years which were as ages, when the young spirit, "awakened out of Eternity," had not yet learned what is meant by Time—when "as yet Time was no fast-hurrying stream, but a sportful sunlit ocean."

Each sentence in the opening chapters of the second book of *Sartor* is the fruit of the impressions made "in those plastic first-times, when the whole soul is yet infantine, soft, and the invisible seed-grain will grow to be an all overshadowing tree." We are told how the village stood, as it still stands, "in trustful derangement, among the woody slopes;" and "the little Kuhbach gushing kindly by, among beech-rows, through river after river, into the Donau," is the burn that runs down the centre of the single street that forms Ecclefechan. When we saw it upwards of twenty years ago, on a midsummer day, it seemed rather a sluggish little stream; and it was crossed in the village by a multitude of bridges. It was open at that time; but since then the greater part of it has been covered over,* doubtless to the sanitary advan-

---

* This was effected, at his own sole cost, by Dr Arnott, a son of a native of the village, over whose grave, in the south-east corner of the parish churchyard, there is a headstone with the following epitaph :—"Sacred to the memory of Archibald Arnott, Esq., Kirkconnell Hall; born 1772, died 6th July 1855. Dr Arnott was for many years surgeon of the 20th Foot, and served in Egypt, Maida, Walcheren, throughout the Peninsular War, and in India. At St Helena he was the medical attendant of Napoleon Bonaparte, whose esteem he won, and whose last moments he soothed. The remainder of his most useful and exemplary life he spent in the retirement of his native place, honoured and beloved by all who knew him."

tage and the convenience of the inhabitants; though the good work has involved a sacrifice of the picturesque charm which the burn had for Carlyle in his early days. The pilgrim to his shrine will be pleased to note that, in front of the tenement in which he was born, the streamlet still flows in an open channel; and traces may be seen on its margin of the ash and beech trees with which it was formerly fringed.

Though so many of the lines in Carlyle's picture of the place are as true to-day as they were eighty years ago, some others, like that of the gushing Kuhbach, have been either altered or wholly blotted out. The swineherd's horn, and the spectacle of the " hungry happy quadrupeds starting in hot haste " to answer its welcome morning call, to say nothing of their humorous but orderly return in the evening, when each, " topographically correct," trotted off " through its own lane to its own dwelling," are no longer to be heard or seen. The last swineherd of Ecclefechan long since doffed for ever his " darned gabardine and leather breeches, more resembling slate or discoloured-tin breeches," and now sleeps peacefully in the same kirk-yard with the bright-eyed boy who was to send the memory of him down through the ages. The *Postwagen* that used to wend through the village northwards from London to Glasgow " in the dead of night, slow-rolling under its mountains of men and luggage," and which passed " south-wards visibly at eventide," has given place to the railway train. And the woodman's axe has been laid years ago to the root of the grand old tree, so long the pride of the villagers, which stretched " like a parasol of twenty ells in radius, overtopping all other rows and clumps;" but there are many people yet alive who remember the time when, under its shadow, "in the glorious summer twilights," the elders of the hamlet sat talking, just as they had done when little Thomas was one of their most attentive auditors, "often greedily listening," as he himself tells us, to their stories and debates, while "the wearied labourers reclined, and the unwearied children sported, and the young men and maidens often danced to flute-music." The annual cattle fair, however, "undoubtedly the grand summary of Entepfuhl's child-culture," though now shorn of much of its pristine glory, as is the case with all similar institutions in this age of railways, still gathers into a field close by "the elements of an unspeakable hurly-burly;" and looking out and up from any point of 'vantage in the hollow where the village lies we see how faithful remains the word-picture of the "upland irregular wold, where valleys, in comflex branchings, are suddenly or slowly arranging their descent towards every quarter of the sky."

Such were the scenic and social environments of Carlyle in his childhood. We may add that the village was then, what it has latterly ceased to be, a seat of the gingham manufacture; so that eighty years ago the population was composite, including a large proportion of men and women who wrought at the loom. Indeed, there is an old tombstone in the churchyard, in memory of a Robert Peal, who lived in Ecclefechan, and who died in 1749 at the age of 57, concerning whom the local tradition asserts that he was either the great-grandfather or the great-grand-uncle of Sir Robert Peel; and it is further stated, by the same authority, that the ancestors of the great statesman, once weavers in Ecclefechan, removed to Lancashire to engage in the cotton trade.* Now the population, which numbers about 900, is exclusively agricultural. The older one-storeyed cottages were for the most part built by Carlyle's father and uncle; and as they are regularly whitewashed once a year, on the approach of the annual fair, they have a much tidier appearance than one is accustomed to find in villages farther north. The winsome aspect of the hamlet is enhanced by the more modern tenements being faced with the red sandstone that abounds in the district. This outward neatness is not the only token which tells the stranger passing through from the north that he is leaving Scotland behind him. The country has become more level, the verdure richer; if you ask your way at any roadside cottage, ten to one but you are answered in the dialect of Cumberland or of Lancashire by an English tongue, which wags cheerily to the music of pattens on the clean stone floor; the very tavern signboards proclaim that England is near by intimating " *ale* and spirits "—an inversion of the Scotch order—or by leaving out altogether what in Scotland is the leading article.

A man's parentage and early surroundings, according to Carlyle's view, are the grand factors in determining the nature of his life; and we have his own authority for concluding that his early position was, in both respects, " favourable beyond the most." Certain sapient editors, with the spirit of provincial self-complacency that is

---

* " There is a short cross street in the village which used to be known as Peal's Wynd, where lived an old lady, Betty Peal, who is said to have been the recipient of Sir Robert Peel's bounty, on the ground that she was considered by him to be a relative."— *Scotsman Newspaper*, Feb. 11, 1881.

nowhere found to such perfection as in a metropolis, have remarked that few educational advantages were to be found in the obscure hamlet where Carlyle was born. The mere mention of his name might have led them to pause before expressing such an opinion; and they had forgot the case of Burns, whose opportunities, from their point of view, were smaller still. The scholar whose university was the stony farm of Mount Oliphant, who had studied men merely in a few clachans and farm-houses of Kyle, did he not become the interpreter of Scotland to herself and to the world? The two greatest female writers of England were village bred; and almost the same may be said of Shakspeare himself. We have seen how fortunate Carlyle was in his parentage; and the impression already made is deepened by the definite facts relating to his personal history that are revealed in *Sartor*. The home training of the child was, no doubt owing to the father's temperament, rather too stoical; but for the mother's unfailing gentleness, the severity of the paternal discipline might have proved more than the child could bear. Even as things were, the limitations imposed were productive of evil results which the victim himself clearly perceived. " My active power was unfavourably hemmed-in ; of which misfortune how many traces yet abide with me !" Perhaps he failed to realise the whole extent of the misfortune. It is evident that James Carlyle, who, as we have seen, married rather late, was an exigeant husband. That is indicated in the picture of the anxious wife watching over him, hovering round him, eager to anticipate his slightest wish and to avert his anger: "assiduously she cooked and sewed and scoured for him "—words that have a good deal of meaning. The father was a pious man;

but before time had mellowed him his piety was of a somewhat different sort from that of the mother. His attendance at church partook of the character of parade-duty, "for
which he in the other world expected pay with arrears,—
as, I trust, he has received." But the mother, "with a
true woman's heart, and fine though uncultivated sense,
was in the strictest acceptation religious." She rendered
an altogether invaluable service to her boy by teaching
him, "less by word than by act and daily reverent look
and habitude, her own simple version of the Christian
Faith." For any defects in the parental training Carlyle
was not the man to whimper. Instead of being disposed
to quarrel with his upbringing, he was devoutly thankful as
he looked back upon it, and saw that even out of its
excessive austerity good had come. In an age that has
witnessed a sad and often disastrous relaxation of parental
control, the words in which Carlyle congratulates himself
on his rigorous training cannot be too earnestly pondered.
The bond of obedience imposed upon him was, he tells
us, strait and inflexible. " I was forbid much : wishes in
any measure bold I had to renounce." Often he shed
bitter tears as the lessons were administered which taught
him how Freewill comes in painful collision with Necessity. But, if his father erred, it was on the right side ;
for, in the habituation to obedience, " it was beyond measure safer to err by excess than by defect." That habit
laid for him "the basis of worldly discretion, nay of morality
itself." It was "the root of deeper earnestness, of the
stem from which all noble fruit must grow." Tender and
true are the last loving touches in the picture of the
domestic culture which left its mark indelibly on Thomas
Carlyle. " Above all, how unskilful soever, it was

loving, it was well-meant, honest; whereby every deficiency was helped."

How faithfully the son returned that love! He was never weary of sounding the praises of the father who had been so sternly faithful; and when he mentioned his mother's name, even when he was a grey old man of more than fourscore, his tones melted with tender emotion. One day in London, when he was within a few months of eighty, Carlyle was walking in company with an American stranger who had that day called to see him. They approached a street-crossing. When half way over, Carlyle suddenly stopped, and stooping down kicked something out of the mud, at the risk of being run over by one of the many carriages that were rushing past. With his bare hands he brushed the mud off and placed the white substance in a clean spot on the curbstone. "That," said he, in a tone as sweet and in words as beautiful as his companion had ever heard, "is only a crust of bread. Yet I was taught by my mother never to waste, and above all bread, more precious than gold, the substance that is the same to the body that the mind is to the soul. I am sure the little sparrows or a hungry dog will get nourishment from that bit of bread."* Thus did he bear in his heart till his last days on earth the homeliest lesson he had learnt from the lips of his mother.

It is a fact worth noting that the last time Carlyle ever saw his father was on his journey from Craigenputtoch to London, when he went to the modern Babylon with the MS. of *Sartor* for the purpose of getting into print. "I

---

* "Thomas Carlyle at Home," by Clarence Winthrop Bowen, in *The Independent* (New York), Sept. 9, 1875.

came upon my fool's errand," said he once to Milburn, the blind Methodist preacher from America, "and I saw my father no more, for I had not been in town many days when tidings came that he was dead. He had gone to bed at night as well as usual, it seems; but they found in the morning that he had passed from the realm of Sleep to that of Day. It was a fit end for such a life as his had been. He was a man at the four corners of whose house there had shined through the years of his pilgrimage, by day and by night, the light of the glory of God. Like Enoch of old, he had walked with God; and at the last he was not, for God took him." And, after a pause, he added: "If I could only see such men as were my father and his minister,—men of such fearless and simple faith, with such firmness in holding on to the things that they believed, and saying and doing only what they thought was right, in seeing and hating the thing that they felt to be wrong,—I should have far more hope for this British nation, and indeed for the world at large."

Some of the anecdotes of Carlyle's childhood are significant as well as amusing. It is evident that he was precocious. "In some fifteen months," baby Thomas "could perform the miracle of—Speech !" Even earlier than that he seems to have begun to realise the great truth that Silence is Golden. He was " noted as a still infant, that kept his mind much to himself; above all, that seldom or never cried. He already felt that time was precious; that he had other work cut out for him than whimpering." A profound impression seems to have been made upon his mind by his investiture in his first short-clothes of yellow serge; "or rather, I should say, my first short-cloth, for the vesture was one and indivisible, reaching from neck to

ankle, a mere body with four limbs,"—a fashion of child
attire that long obtained in that and other parts of Scotland, though now probably quite extinct. Very pretty is
the picture of his suppers on the orchard wall, whither on
the evenings he was wont to carry forth his porringer of
bread and milk : having either got up himself by climbing,
or been assisted by his father. " There," he says, " many
a sunset have I, looking at the distant western Mountains, consumed, not without relish, my evening meal.
Those hues of gold and azure, that hush of World's
expectation as Day dies, was still a Hebrew Speech for
me ; nevertheless I was looking at the fair illuminated
Letters, and had an eye for their gilding." He was on
friendly terms with all the cattle and poultry, thereby
acquiring "a certain deeper sympathy with animated
nature." The sense of humour was awakened within him
by the " touching, trustful submissiveness to man " of the
poor pigs obeying the summons of the swineherd ; and
the swallows, " snug-lodged in our cottage lobby," with
the little bracket fixed by his father plumb under the nest
(for cleanliness' sake), were loved by him from the heart,
so that the bright, nimble creatures taught him many a
precious lesson. He was about eight years old when it
first struck him that the stage coach "could be other than
some terrestrial moon, rising and setting by mere law of
nature, like the heavenly one ; that it came on made
highways, from far cities towards far cities ; weaving them
like a monstrous shuttle into closer and closer union." A
city child of the same age would probably have known
that fact earlier ; but to how few would the reflection have
come that arose in the mind of this little rustic in Annandale ? His imagination was stirred—" and a historical

tendency given him," a fact specially worthy of note—by the narrative habits of his paternal grandfather (though in *Sartor* he ascribes these to Father Andreas). The old man had been of an adventurous turn, had travelled even as far as London; and eagerly the child "hung upon his tales, when listening neighbours enlivened the hearth." With amazement he began to discover that Ecclefechan "stood in the middle of a Country, of a World; that there was such a thing as History, as Biography; to which I also, one day, by hand and tongue, might contribute." Thus, at the tender age of eight, the Vindicator of Cromwell and the most brilliant historian of the French Revolution got the first glimpse of the work that had been given him to do.

CHAPTER IV.

THE BOY BOOKWORM—HIS FIRST SCHOOLMASTER—CLAS-
SICAL LESSONS AT THE MANSE—THE HINTERSCHLAG
GYMNASIUM AT ANNAN—AT BURNS'S GRAVE.

BEFORE the first-born of James Carlyle had entered his
second year, the improving circumstances of the father
enabled him to move from the small house over the
Arch, or "Pend," as it is called in Scotland, to a more
commodious dwelling—a two-storeyed cottage, away from
the coach road, in a lane which used to be called
"Matthew Murray's Close," but which is now known
as "Carlyle's Close." In this house all the other eight
children were born, and here Thomas was brought up.
After undergoing a number of changes, the tenement
has at length become the village butchery, or "slaughter
house," as they phrase it in the North. Almost from his
infancy Carlyle was a great reader. In a cottage close by
there lived until a year or two ago an aged woman, Mrs
Milligan, who, when a girl, had often nursed Thomas, and
"given him many a ride upon her back;" and, according
to her testimony, which agreed with that of other contemporaries, he was always a thoughtful and studious child,
who mixed little with the village children, or even with his

own brothers or sisters, having a greater relish for the
society of his grandfather and other grown up people, and
who was fond of roaming about the fields and hills, always
with a book in his hand. In *Sartor* he himself tells us
that he could not remember ever to have learned
reading; "so perhaps had it by nature." What printed
thing soever he could meet with, he read; and all his
pocket money, never more than copper, he laid out on
stall literature, by which is signified, we presume, those
penny chap-books that were then the sole literature for
the people; which, as they accumulated, he with his own
hands sewed into volumes. "By this means was the
young head furnished with a considerable miscellany of
things and shadows of things: History in authentic
fragments lay mingled with fabulous chimeras, wherein
also was reality; and the whole not as dead stuff, but as
living pabulum, tolerably nutritive for a mind as yet so
peptic." He was early noted for his extraordinary
memory. At the age of five he could repeat the heads
and particulars of any sermon he heard, a greater feat, in
those days of "painful" preachers and long sermons,
than it would be in our more superficial time. As a
boy he exhibited considerable ability as an orator, and
on one occasion, at some local public discussion, he
astonished the audience, including even his own father,
by an extraordinary burst of eloquence.

Of his schoolmasters, using the word in its technical
sense, he does not speak very respectfully. "Of the
insignificant portion of my education which depended
on schools, there need almost no notice be taken." He
must have been little more than an infant when he was
sent to the parish school, then taught by a poor dominie

of the "stickit minister" genus, one William Gullen by name, whose portrait makes a pathetic passage in *Sartor*, and the sad story of whose life might be worth telling, had it been preserved in an authentic form. According to the local tradition, he seems, like too many of his kind, to have been harshly used by the parish minister; and this is so far borne out by Carlyle's account of him— "a down-bent, broken-hearted, under-foot martyr," who, if he did little for his pupil, had at least "the merit of discovering that he could do little;" and whom we are bound to think of respectfully, since he had the insight to discern the powers that were lying waiting development in the little Carlyle, whom he pronounced "a genius." Without hesitation, he declared that he was fit for the learned professions, and must be sent to the Grammar School, and one day to the University. The struggling dominie, it is said, was driven, by the persecution of the minister, to emigrate to America, and no more was ever heard of him at home. The schoolhouse is still standing, close to the churchyard, facing the Hoddam Road—a long cottage-like building, in a tolerable state of repair, said to have been built with the stones of the ancient church of St Fechan, from which the village derives its name. More than twenty years have elapsed since a more commodious schoolhouse was erected, and the old one now serves the purpose of a poorhouse for the reception of "casuals."

Carlyle was only in his eighth year when he was transferred to the Academy, or Grammar School, of Annan, where his father had once been a pupil, and upon which he bestows the significant name of "the Hinterschlag Gymnasium." According to all accounts, it must have well deserved the unsavory title, for the master, even at that period of educational brutality, was distinguished for the unmerciful severity of his punishments. Adam Hope was his rather inappropriate name; he knew syntax enough, "and of the human soul thus much—that it had a faculty called memory, and could be acted on through the muscular integument by appliance of birch rods." Hope was also the teacher of Edward Irving, and it is only doing justice to his memory to say, that Irving used to ascribe to his tutor's severity the scholarship which his own disposition would not have led him to acquire. He often had his ears pinched by the master till they bled. Young as he was, it would seem that Carlyle had acquired the elements of Latin before going to Annan, having been assisted in the task by a student son of the Secession minister of Ecclefechan, who taught a class in his father's manse when he was at home during the University recess. There is a local tradition that it was the mother who insisted on her eldest boy having the advantage of this classical training. Old James wished little Thomas to "gang and work," which set the child book-worm a-crying bitterly. He told his mother that he wanted to keep to his "buiks;" and her gentle influence prevailed, against the paternal decision, in securing for her first-born the greatest wish of his heart. It is a story that has been repeated in many a humble Scottish home. Young Johnston, the minister's son, was wont to tell in after years how he discovered that the boy (not yet eight years old) had been privately studying his Latin Rudiments with great industry, but that his grammar and construction were in a chaotic state. After three months' drill, however, little Thomas had succeeded in grasping the intricacies of both, and could translate Virgil and Horace with an ease that astonished his tutor.*

The precocity of the child is attested by the marvellously distinct impression which he retained of that "red sunny Whitsuntide morning," when, trotting the six intervening miles, full of hope, by his father's side, he entered the main street of Annan, "and saw its steeple-clock (then striking eight) and jail, and the aproned or disaproned burghers moving in to breakfast." A little dog was rushing past, in mad 'terror, with a tin kettle which some human imps had tied to its tail ; this, and all the other details of the scene, fix themselves in his memory, and are reproduced nearly thirty years afterwards with the quaint fidelity of a Dutch painter. The bullies of the school were cruel to the little boy from Ecclefechan, taking advantage of "his small personal stature," and also of the unwillingness to fight which his mother had succeeded in planting in him as a fundamental principle of action; and he wept so often under their tyranny "that he was nicknamed the Tearful, which epithet, till towards his thirteenth year, was not quite unmerited." At rare intervals, however, "the young soul

---

* A surviving friend of Mr Johnston's writes :—"Carlyle continued to retain a warm affection for Mr Johnston, who, for a considerable time, occupied a Presbyterian pulpit in Jersey City, New York. They frequently corresponded, and Mr Johnston received a copy of every work Carlyle produced. He watched the tendencies of Carlyle's religious views, sometimes with regret, and sometimes with pleasure. When he forwarded his 'Letters and Speeches of Oliver Cromwell,' Mr Johnston wrote, thanking him, and complimenting him for his thorough appreciation of the soundness of the Calvinistic principles ; but following this great work came his biography of John Sterling, which completely demolished Mr Johnston's hopes concerning the soundness of his old pupil's religious views."

burst forth into fire-eyed rage, and, with a stormfulness under which the boldest quailed," he asserted his rights, in defiance of his mother's law.

Even in his purchasing of chap-books before he left home, it is hardly possible that he could have observed with strictness the rigid rule laid down by his father against all works of fiction; but, under the milder sway of the cooper in whose house he lodged at Annan, the paternal injunctions were no doubt set aside with even greater freedom, for he tells how "he remembered few happier days than the one on which he ran off into the fields to read *Roderick Random*, and how inconsolable he was that he could not get the second volume." "To this day," he added, "I think few writers equal to Smollett"—an estimate that may be ascribed, in part at least, to the sweet memory of that day in which he drank the stolen waters. So far as the school was concerned, his time at Annan, according to his own report, was utterly wasted, the teaching being purely mechanical; but he "went about, as was his wont, among the craftsmen's workshops, there learning many things," and he also got good from "some small store of curious reading"— probably including that fragment of the forbidden Smollett —which he found at the house where he lodged. It confirms our faith in the strictly autobiographical character of *Sartor* when we learn that it was actually a cooper's house, the cooper being a relation of his father's.

It is, perhaps, not unworthy of note that one of Carlyle's school-fellows at Annan was Thomas Burns, a nephew of the poet, who subsequently became parish minister of Monkton, in Ayrshire, and died at Dunedin, where he was Free Church minister and Chancellor of the University of Otago, in 1871. While at Monkton he betrayed a dislike to any mention of his illustrious uncle being made in his presence. The good man came to know better as the years went by; and at the antipodes he enjoyed the lustre that was reflected upon him from the chief of Scottish song. It was probably during the Annan days that Carlyle went to Dumfries to see the grave of Burns. This glimpse of his boyhood, a picture that must henceforth be treasured in the Scottish heart, he gave to an American visitor a few years ago during a walk from Chelsea to Piccadilly. He told of his early admiration of Burns—how he used to creep into the churchyard of Dumfries, when a little boy, and find the tomb of the poet, and sit and read the simple inscription by the hour. "There it was," said he, "in the midst of poor fellow-labourers and artisans, and the name—Robert Burns!" At morn, at noon, and eventide, he loved to go and read that name. Thus were thoughts dimly suggested to the mind of the boy, that quickened and grew, till at length, in his manhood, they found expression in what was the first—and seems likely to be the last—worthy and all-sufficing exposition of the life and works of the Scottish bard.

CHAPTER V.

THE SECESSION KIRK—CARLYLE'S PORTRAIT OF DR LAW-
SON — LETTER TO A PASTOR'S WIDOW — ANOTHER
LINK WITH BURNS.

CARLYLE's parents were Nonconformists; and it was in
the Secession Church at Ecclefechan, of which his father
and mother were members, that he received such nutriment as the Scottish pulpit was destined to bestow upon
him in his early years.   Those who know what that particular branch of the Church was at the dawn of our century,
and especially the character of its leading lights, will have
no difficulty, as they read his works, in discerning the
permanent mark which this part of his youthful culture
left upon his mind and heart.   It was a Church which
had its origin in the attachment of the best part of the
Scottish nation to two things without which a true Church
is simply impossible—purity of doctrine and life, and
freedom of administration.   Its chief founders were
Ebenezer and Ralph Erskine, the former of whom, along
with three other parish ministers, had been expelled from
their ministerial charges by the General Assembly in 1733
for their faithful protest against the worldly policy which
had degraded the doctrine and the life of the Established
Church, besides annihilating the rights of the people by
the infliction of the tyrannical Law of Patronage.   In
1747 the new communion, which, however, represented

the old spirit of the Scottish people, was unhappily broken into two sections by a difference of opinion with respect to the burgess oath, which imposed on all who swore it a pledge "to profess and allow the true religion presently professed within this realm, and authorised by the laws thereof." Some held that the swearing of this oath was virtual approval of the Establishment with all its corruptions; others maintained that the oath referred only to the true religion as professed, but did not involve any approval of the mode of its settlement by the State. The controversy led to a separation. The party which objected to the taking of the oath formed itself into the General Associate Synod; the other section retained the original title of Associate Synod. The former body were popularly styled the Anti-Burghers, the latter the Burghers—names that remained in use long after they had ceased to represent any living reality.

The church at Ecclefechan belonged to the Burgher branch of the Secession. Its pastor, the Rev. John Johnston, was a notable man, an excellent scholar, and in every other essential respect the model of what a Christian minister ought to be. He had studied theology under Professor Brown of Haddington; and he was himself the first classical tutor of a carpenter's son in Peeblesshire, who made his mark on the spiritual history of Scotland as Professor Lawson of Selkirk. The lines in *Sartor* that may be construed as bearing at least some reference to the church which Carlyle attended with his parents are few, but they are impressive. "The highest whom I knew on earth I here saw bowed down, with awe unspeakable, before a Higher in Heaven: such things, especially in infancy, reach inwards to the very core of your being; mysteriously does a Holy of Holies build itself into visibility in the mysterious deeps; and Reverence, the divinest in man, springs forth undying from its mean envelopment of Fear."

The United Presbyterian Church,* in which all sections of the Seceders are now happily included, is represented at Ecclefechan to-day by a handsome Gothic edifice, situated close by the churchyard, with a square clock tower—the most conspicuous object in the village; but it was in a rude little meeting-house, in no wise differing from the cottages of the peasantry, and which the pilgrim may still see standing by the roadside as he walks from the railway station to the village, that the young soul was impressed with the awe to which he has given such memorable utterance.

More fully, both in conversation and in letters, did Carlyle, down to his closing years on the earth, testify to the depth and duration of that hallowed influence. Oftener than once he was heard to declare, "I have seen many capped and equipped bishops, and other episcopal dignitaries; but I have never seen one who more beautifully combined in himself the Christian and the Christian gentleman than did Mr Johnston." To the blind preacher Milburn, from America, he said (in 1860) that "it was very pleasant to see his father in his daily and weekly relations with the minister. They had been friends from youth. That minister (he must have said the

---

* "We had the pleasure of visiting the locality in the month of August last, and found several relatives of Mr Carlyle, all in comfortable circumstances, and mostly connected with the United Presbyterian Church."—*Thomas Carlyle: the Man and Teacher.* By David Hodge, M.A. Ardrossan: Arthur Guthrie. 1873.

minister's son) was the first person that ever taught me
Latin, and I am not sure but that he laid a very great
curse upon me in so doing. I think it is likely I should
have been a wiser man, and certainly a godlier one, if I
had followed in my father's steps, and left Greek and
Latin to the fools that wanted them."*

When the summer communions came round there often
stood by the village pastor's side, in the pulpit at Ecclefechan, his old pupil, now the learned and pious Professor from the little Secession Academy at Selkirk; and
that these occasions were not forgotten by at least one
youthful hearer has been put beyond dispute by the testimony of Carlyle himself. When the late Dr John Mac-
farlane, of Glasgow, latterly of Clapham, published his
memoir of Lawson, he sent a copy of the book to the
aged philosopher at Chelsea, and received (in 1870) an
acknowledgment which was probably the most fondly-
cherished guerdon for what had been his labour of love.
"Your *Biography of Dr Lawson*," wrote Carlyle, "has
interested me not a little, bringing present to me from
afar much that it is good to be reminded of; strangely
awakening many thoughts, many scenes and recollections
of forty, of sixty years ago—all now grown very sad to
me, but also very beautiful and solemn. It seems to me
I gather from your narrative and from his own letters a

---

* *Thomas Carlyle: His Life, his Books, his Theories.* By Alfred
H. Guernsey. New York, 1879. Milburn, who dictated the recollections of his conversations with Carlyle to Mr Guernsey, makes
Carlyle say that his father was "an elder of the Kirk," and that his
pastor was "minister of the parish." The reporter must have
forgotten the exact words that were really used by Carlyle. The
report throughout is evidently a very free one, though bearing the
marks of general authenticity.

perfectly credible account of Dr Lawson's character, course of life, and labours in the world; and the reflection rises in me that perhaps there was not in the British Island a more completely genuine, pious-minded, diligent, and faithful man. Altogether original too, peculiar to Scotland, and, so far as I can guess, unique even there and then. England will never know him out of any book —or, at least, it would take the genius of a Shakspere to make him known by that method; but if England did, it might much and wholesomely astonish her. Seen in his intrinsic character, no simpler-minded, more perfect 'lover of wisdom,' do I know of in that generation. Professor Lawson, you may believe, was a great man in my boy circle; never spoken of but with reverence and thankfulness by those I loved best. In a dim but singularly conclusive way I can still remember seeing him, and even hearing him preach (though of that latter, except the fact of it, I retain nothing); but of the figure, face, tone, dress, I have a vivid impression (perhaps about my twelfth year, *i.e.*, summer of 1807-8); it seems to me he had even a better face than in your frontispiece —more strength, sagacity, shrewdness, simplicity, a broader jaw, more hair of his own (I don't much remember any wig); altogether a most superlative steel-grey Scottish peasant (and Scottish Socrates of the period); really, as I now perceive, more like the twin brother of that Athenian Socrates who went about, supreme in Athens, in wooden shoes, than any man I have ever ocularly seen. Many other figures in your narrative were, by name or person, familiar to my eyes or mind, in that far-off period of my life."

Not unworthy to be ranked with this is the letter

addressed in 1868 to the widow of a United Presbyterian minister, who had edited a volume of her husband's sermons, and sent a copy to Carlyle. "Your gentle, sad, and modest gift," he replied, "is mournful and affecting to me. I received it with thanks, and it shall be among my precious things. Well do I understand your desolate feelings; and what pious beauty was in the noble labours you undertook for the sake of him that is gone; the fruit of which is this book, which I doubt not will be a spiritual benefit to many. May it be a blessing to many; as to yourself, I cannot doubt, it has already been! An admirable work; and a difficult, and at last a successful —possible perhaps to you alone of the living! I know well what of solacement and sacred assuagement to a bitter sorrow must have been in it, and much approve of your courageous wisdom, and still augur well of you. Human sympathy, alas, cannot help; only time and devout reflection—and above all, strenuous employment in doing what remains to be done. Only once did I see the loved partner whom you have lost; but I marked deeply in him the features of a faithful, steadfast, and piously high-minded man,—as indeed I had been taught to expect by what my dear, sincere, and pious mother often said of him. Your loss, I see how immense it is, and how vain is speech upon it. I will only say, may you have comfort springing from your own faithful, brave, and loving soul, inspired (we may well say) from a higher source."

Dean Stanley, in a sermon preached in Westminster Abbey on the day following Carlyle's death, asserted that Carlyle "still clung, amidst all the vicissitudes of his long existence," to "the Church of Scotland." The

Dean is so intimately conversant with Scottish ecclesiastical history, that he ought to have perceived the misleading tendency of such a phrase. It may not be out of place here to note that Dean Stanley, in his entertaining *Lectures on the History of the Church of Scotland*, describes Burns as "the prodigal son of the Church of Scotland," and alleges that "the kindly and genial spirit of the philosophic clergy and laity saved him from being driven, by the extravagant pretensions of the popular Scottish religion, into absolute unbelief." The lecturer does not seem to have known the fact, that what the poet really thought of "the philosophic clergy" of the Establishment was placed beyond all doubt by the selection he made at Dumfries, when he took seats for himself and his family in the Secession Kirk, of which the Rev. William Inglis was pastor. When Burns was asked by some one, in a taunting tone, why he condescended to listen to the preaching of a Seceder, he replied, "I go to hear Mr Inglis because he preaches what he believes, and practises what he preaches." We have been told by a grandson of Mr Inglis, of a circumstance not noticed in any of the biographies of Burns. Mr Inglis was the Christian pastor who attended the poet on his death-bed; and to him Burns "expressed the deepest penitence for his immorality, and for his profane and licentious writings." This fact our informant had from his father, who, when a youth, frequently saw Burns. Mr Inglis, though he had been settled in his ministerial charge at Dumfries as early as 1765, performed all its duties till 1810, and was able to preach till the time of his death, in 1826. Though he was an Anti-Burgher, it is not improbable that he may have had amongst his occasional hearers the lad in the neighbouring village, who was, so many years afterwards, to give the world an imperishable portrait of Lawson of Selkirk. If this was the case, that old Dumfries Seceder is doubly worthy of remembrance, since it fell to his lot to preach the gospel needed by all men—and that in lowly meeting-houses, upon which the world hardly bestowed a look, or, at the utmost, only a glance of scorn—to Robert Burns and Thomas Carlyle.

CHAPTER VI.

THOUGH the Ecclefechan boy must have spent the greater
part of six years in the native town of a contemporary
who was to be his first friend, outside the domestic
precinct, Carlyle had entered his fourteenth year before
he met Edward Irving. That in so small a town he had
got earlier glimpses of him, is extremely probable; but
they did not come together till 1809. In the exquisitely
tender obituary of his friend, a tribute that stands unrivalled in the whole compass of our prose literature,
written for the *Fraser* of January 1835, he says:—"The
first time I saw Irving was six-and-twenty years ago, in
his native town, Annan. He was fresh from Edinburgh,
with College prizes, high character and promise; he had
come to see our Schoolmaster, who had also been his.
We heard of famed Professors, of high matters, classical, mathematical, a whole Wonderland of Knowledge:
nothing but joy, health, hopefulness without end, looked

out from the blooming young man."* That meeting was freighted with momentous issues for Carlyle. " But for Irving, I had never known what the communion of man with man means." And it was through Irving that he was to meet the future partner of his life, the true helpmate to whom, when his work was nearly done, he ascribed all of worth that he had been able to achieve in the world.

It was not long after that first meeting till Carlyle followed Irving to the "Wonderland." He was but a boy of fourteen when, in 1810, he matriculated at Edinburgh. His extreme youth may account, in part at least, for the scantiness of the information that we possess respecting his student life at the University, and also for the comparative faintness of the impression which the literary and social characteristics of the city seem to have made upon him. It was, perhaps, the most brilliant epoch in the history of the Scottish capital. The whole atmosphere of the place was richly charged with intellectual ozone. The charm of its social life at that period has been depicted in such works as Mrs Fletcher's *Autobiography;* its literary and political activity is reflected with even greater vivacity in the kindred masterpieces of Lord Cockburn. The great Tory rival of the *Edin-*

* Irving had just taken his M.A. degree. All accounts concur in representing him as perhaps the noblest-looking youth in Annandale. Allan Cunningham said he could not enter a village but he caught the admiring attention of both old and young. "Once, when a boy," said a resident in Annan to Irving's earliest biographer, poor Washington Wilks, "I went to Ecclefechan Fair with my father; every one was looking at a very tall young man, with a pony. I asked my father who it was, and he said, 'Irving, the tanner's son, that's training to be a preacher.'"

burgh Review had been started in the year preceding that in which Carlyle entered the city of Sir Walter Scott and Jeffrey; the *Lady of the Lake* was but newly issued from the press. Brougham had not long left for London; but Harry Erskine, a purer patriot and a greater lawyer, as well as the most brilliant wit of his day, was still adorning the Scottish bar. Old Henry Mackenzie, author of *The Man of Feeling*, and of the first critical essay recognising the genius of Burns, remained as a relic of the generation which had Hume and Robertson among its central figures, and was still able to enliven the conversation with reminiscences of men and manners gone by. Old Sir Harry Moncreiff, the successor of Dr John Erskine as leader of the Evangelicals, was reminding visitors to the General Assembly of Jupiter among the lesser gods; and the polished and persuasive Alison, father of the coming historian of Europe, was worthily representing the "church of deportment" in the city of John Knox. Mrs Grant of Laggan and Mrs Elizabeth Hamilton were each centres of most agreeable society, in which one was sure to find the ladies listening to the brilliant talk of the little dictator who was controlling the public taste and policy through the lately-invented medium of the great Whig Review. In the University, Dr Thomas Brown, most poetical of philosophers, was just stepping into the chair vacated by Dugald Stewart; Playfair, the tutor of Lord John Russell, was the professor of Natural Philosophy; and Leslie, who, the year before, had issued his *Elements of Geometry*, was teaching mathematics.

But the seat of the most popular poetry and the most influential criticisms of the time does not seem to have stirred the blood of the singular boy from Ecclefechan. It is no doubt true that, when he addressed the students as their Lord Rector in 1866, he spoke kindly of his "dear old *Alma Mater*," and told how, fifty-six years before, he had entered the city "with feelings of wonder and awe-struck expectation." These feelings, however, he does not appear long to have retained; and they had certainly vanished when he was writing *Sartor*. There he gives a description of his University almost less flattering than the account of his school experiences in his native village and at Annan. "Out of England and Spain," says Teufelsdröckh, "ours was the worst of all hitherto discovered Universities." The professors, "stationed at the gates, to declare aloud that it was a University, and exact considerable admission fees," he pictures as no better than the "hide-bound pedants" and "mechanical Gerund-grinders" of Dumfriesshire, concerning whom he had already declared that, in a subsequent century, teachers quite as effective "will be manufactured at Nürnberg out of wood and leather." In the above-mentioned address he did not name one of his old teachers; and it was only too evident that he hurried over the subject of his own connection with the place as quickly as possible. It was the opinion of some of his contemporaries, the ready victims of exuberant eloquence, that Brown was the superior of his predecessor; but this estimate was not shared by Carlyle. The only Edinburgh Professor of that day he names in any of his writings is Dugald Stewart—"a name venerable to all Europe," he says, "and to none more dear and venerable than ourselves." Of Brown, on the other hand, he never spoke in private except under the derisive title of "Miss

Brown," or " the little man who spouted poetry." Even the most enthusiastic admirers of Stewart's successor acknowledged that his manner was strongly marked by affectation, and that while his poetry (as Dr Gregory observed) was too philosophical, his philosophy was too poetical. Carlyle turned away from his too liquid and musical diction with disgust. Against Playfair it is well known that he bore a grudge, and not without a cause; for, after having worked hard in that professor's class, the certificate he got was exceedingly cold and reserved. As Lord Rector, Carlyle counselled the students to be diligent in their attention to what their teachers told them; but, according to all accounts, he had not himself observed this rule very strictly in the case of some at least of his own professors. Though we hear of his having secured one honour, he was far too discursive a reader to be one of the model prize-taking class of students. Indeed, he is said to have been the most omnivorous reader who ever passed within the portals of the University. In *Sartor* the library is described as " small" and " ill-chosen;" but he adds that from its chaos he " succeeded in fishing up more books, perhaps, than had been known to the very keepers thereof." These, indeed, did not suffice to satiate his craving for books; and it is alleged that, after having exhausted the University library, he did the same by several circulating libraries in the city, including the one which had been founded by Allan Ramsay. Yet it would be a mistake to suppose that he was not a real student, though he failed to concentrate his attention upon any one special subject or set of subjects, and left the University without a degree. Nay, it is likely that he profited more than most by the culture which the place afforded. "What vain jargon of controversial metaphysics, etymology, and mechanical manipulation, falsely named science, was current there, I, indeed, learned better, perhaps, than the most. Among eleven hundred youths, there will not be wanting some eleven eager to learn. By collision with such, a certain warmth, a certain polish, was communicated; by instinct and happy accident, I took less to rioting than to thinking and reading, which latter, also, I was free to do." In the same passage of *Sartor* he states that he learned, on his own strength, to "read fluently in almost all cultivated languages, on almost all subjects and sciences." Almost in the same words, he told the students in 1866 that what he had found the University do for him was, that it taught him to read "in various languages and various sciences," so that he could go into the books that treated of these things, and try anything he wanted to make himself master of gradually, as he found it suit him. In spite of the vast extent of his reading, it was probably from the outset discriminative; and as he began to discover the province in which he could study and work to most purpose, it no doubt became more so. His teachers, with one exception, do not seem to have very clearly perceived either his merits or his drift. Leslie, who possessed some qualities akin to those of the erratic and thoroughly independent pupil, was the only one of all the professors who formed the opinion that Carlyle was a youth of extraordinary capacity. Believing that he possessed a genius for mathematics and natural philosophy, Leslie exhorted him to devote himself to the cultivation of science.

This advice ran counter, not indeed to his own growing inclinations, but certainly to the purpose of his parents, whose fondly-cherished wish it had been to see their son a minister. To the students in 1866 he said, "Pursue your studies in the way your conscience calls honest. Count a thing known only when it is stamped on your mind, so that you may survey it on all sides." To this he added, "Gradually see what kind of work you can do; for it is the first of all problems for a man to find out what kind of work he is to do in this universe. In fact, morality, as regards study, is, as in all other things, the primary consideration, and overrides all others. A dishonest man cannot do anything real; and it would be greatly better if he were tied up from doing any such thing." Herein, doubtless, he was but repeating in words what he had himself wrought out in his own personal action half a century before; and the inquiries which he pursued in the spirit of stern fidelity to conscience, led him to abandon the design that had been formed for him by his parents, and into which he had probably never personally entered with completeness of sympathy. Filial piety, we cannot doubt, prolonged the struggle in his own spirit. It is said that, at the close of his arts curriculum, extending over four years, he went through the greater part of the course of study prescribed for aspirants to the ministerial office; nay, there is a dark tradition that he went farther in his theological course— so far, indeed, that it had been arranged in what church he was to appear as a "probationer"; but this must be pure fiction. He had, perhaps, taken two or three "partial sessions," as they are locally termed, in the Theological Hall of the University; but he had not so much as entered the Secession Academy. One thing is certain. A day came, when he finally concluded that his vocation, about which he had not yet succeeded in making up his mind, did not, at all events, lie in the direction of the pulpit. What he might turn to, was, as yet, far from being plain to him; but one thing was clear enough—he could not be a minister in a Church of the Westminster Confession, or indeed in any other Church then existing. There were many then, and it is to be feared the number has gone on increasing ever since, who did not allow themselves to be troubled by scruples of conscience. But he was not content to undertake the task of pretending to throw light upon the pathway of other men, while he was still himself stumbling on in the darkness. He realised the worse than absurdity of the blind presuming to become the leaders of the blind. He would not add another unit to the already too numerous host who, in hollow-sounding pulpits, were teaching the world lessons which they had not first mastered themselves, or, perhaps, teaching what they actually in their secret heart disbelieved. This decision, when it was intimated to his parents, caused them no small amount of sorrow; his father, especially, seems to have taken it greatly to heart. The watchful mother, with a keener insight, had probably foreseen what was coming, and her loving heart would therefore be prepared for the blow when it came. But the father found it hard to accept the bitter disappointment. A story is told, on what seems to be good authority, of a neighbouring farmer one day finding old James sitting on a gravestone in the churchyard near his home in a very despondent frame of mind, and learning on inquiry that the cause of his grief was, the receipt, that day, of the intelligence from his son in Edinburgh, that he had finally determined not to become a minister.

The sorrowing father, though he knew it not at the time, had reason to be grateful that he had a son capable of arriving at such a decision. The severity of the struggle through which Carlyle had passed in reaching that resolve is, perhaps, at least partially indicated in the reply which he gave forty years afterwards to the question of the blind preacher from America, already named. Milburn, bolder than most people in the enjoyment of their sight, ventured to ask Carlyle whether his dyspepsia was hereditary or acquired. "I am sure I can hardly tell," was the reply. "I only know that for one or two or three-and-twenty years of my mortal existence I was not conscious of the ownership of that diabolical arrangement called a stomach. I had grown up the healthy and hardy son of a hardy and healthy Scottish dalesman; and he was the descendant of a long line of such; men that had tilled their paternal acres, and gained their threescore years and ten—or even, mayhap, by reason of strength, their fourscore years, and had gone down to their graves, never a man of them the wiser for the possession of this infernal apparatus. And the voice came to me, saying, 'Arise, and settle the problem of thy life!' I had been destined by my father and my father's minister to be myself a minister. But now that I had gained man's estate, I was not sure that I believed the doctrines of my father's kirk; and it was needful I should now settle it. And so I entered into my chamber and closed the door, and around me there came a trooping throng of phantasms dire from the abysmal depths of nethermost perdition. Doubt, Fear, Unbelief, Mockery,

and Scorn were there; and I arose and wrestled with
them in travail and agony of spirit. Whether I ate I
know not; whether I slept I know not; I only know
that when I came forth again it was with the direful persuasion that I was the miserable owner of a diabolical
arrangement called a stomach; and I have never been free
from that knowledge from that hour to this, and I suppose
that I never shall be until I am laid away in my grave."

That this struggle, which so shook him to the very
centre of his being, had a prejudicial effect on his bodily
health, may be granted as a most likely thing; but it is
only reasonable to suppose that the vast amount of reading
this Scottish Scaliger went through in his boyhood, and
which at Edinburgh amazed all the librarians as a phenomenon without parallel in their experience, must have
tended to undermine his naturally vigorous constitution.
The chronic dyspepsia that was to accompany him henceforth through life was, we may rest assured, not the result
of one spiritual conflict confined to a brief period of time;
it must have been the gradual work of years. Had he
not been gifted with a more than ordinary share of the
vitality inherent in his race, it is hardly possible to conceive
that a youth, who had been almost constantly reading from
his very infancy, and who at nineteen had probably read
more books than all the professors in Edinburgh put
together, would have survived such a terrible strain,
imposed at that period of life when the body, as well as
the mind, is in a formative state. "You cannot," he told
the Edinburgh students, when he was an old man, "if
you are going to do any decisive intellectual operation—
if you are going to write a book—at least I never could—
do it without getting decidedly made ill by it." He had

begun early to realise that fact, when he was crushing the reading of years into months. Nor is it at all unlikely that inattention to diet, perhaps partly the result of limited means, may have had something to do with the physical evil that was to dog his footsteps through all the remaining days of his earthly pilgrimage. Not without significance is the acknowledgment in *Sartor*, that his upbringing had been "too frugal;" and the impression made by these words is deepened when we find it delicately hinted that "even pecuniary distresses" were not wanting in the lowly home, and that it was in "an atmosphere of Poverty and manifold Chagrin" that the brave young soul struggled onwards. To an American visitor, in 1875, when speaking of his admiration of Goethe, he said that he was filled with an intense desire, when he was a young man, to visit him. "But," he added, "his parents were too poor to send him to Germany, and he received, instead, a few precious letters from the great poet."

This view of the limitations imposed by poverty receives support from one little glimpse, apparently quite authentic, into Carlyle's mode of life while attending the University. It is furnished by a gentleman who, when he published the reminiscence, was one of the representatives of the city of Sydney in the Parliament of New South Wales. "When coming from the West Indies to England, I met on board a Dr Nicholson, who in course of conversation informed me that he was a student with Mr Carlyle at the Edinburgh University, and that they lived together in lodgings, along with another young student, and that the whole three slept in the same bedroom. Dr Nicholson added, that Mr Carlyle took the dux prize in the mathematical class, and that their other bedroom companion took the second prize; but he observed, that while Mr Carlyle seemed to master the subject without much effort or application, the other lad laboured at his problems with desperate zeal, sometimes sitting up all night at the task. I happened to mention this (about 1869) to Mr Carlyle, who remembered Dr Nicholson well, and described him accurately. He also remembered their residence in Edinburgh; but he said that Dr Nicholson was greatly deceived if he thought he mastered his mathematical difficulties with ease, or that it did not cost him much exertion. He said that he laboured most intensely at the study of mathematics, and that he has gained nothing in this world worth speaking about without the hardest of labour."* The fact that a sharer of his humble lodging could be so much in the dark as to his modes of working, is an indication of the self-contained nature of young Carlyle; and therefore we need not be surprised to find few reminiscences of his student life by personal acquaintances either at Edinburgh or near his father's home, where he spent each of the long summer vacations that extend in the Scottish Universities from April to November. There is but one anecdote of that period of his life which throws much light on his College work. To some congenial friend, most likely his first classical tutor, Mr Johnston, he so far unbosomed himself, on returning to Ecclefechan at the close of a session, as to intimate, with justifiable exultation, that the *Principia* of Newton were " all prostrate at his feet!" He may have been irregular in his application to the work of his

---

* *Observations on the Public Affairs and Public Men of England.* By David Buchanan. Sydney : 1871.

classes, turning to it only at intervals, and then with desperate energy; but this was a great thing for a youth to be able to say who left the University in his nineteenth year.

It is hardly necessary to add, that Carlyle never entered into the social life of the University. None of its associated societies, formed for the cultivation of oratory, is able to boast that his name stands on its list of members; though the Dialectic, which had been founded in 1787, included at the time more than one fellow-student from his own district of country, and had among the rest Macdiarmid, who became a journalist of note at Dumfries. If he was too young to become connected with these debating clubs, there was a social bar, as well as that of youth, to hinder his admission to the Speculative Society, which had, and probably still has, a standard of gentility to maintain. But even if the door had been open, Carlyle would not have chosen to enter; for the testimony of each of the few contemporaries who had any knowledge of him, goes to show that he was lonely and contemplative in his habits. When his University career had come to a close, we see the solitary youth, already with a stamp of sadness on his countenance that was never to leave it in this life, turning to his native hills. There, free at last from the " neck halter " which had " nigh throttled him, till he broke it off," he will in solitude face the problem that yet remains to be solved.

CHAPTER VII.

A NEW plan of life had to be formed, and it was no easy task getting under way. It was, doubtless, only as a tentative that he turned to the occupation of school-master. When he went home to Annandale from the University, or soon thereafter, the post of Mathematical Teacher in the Burgh School of Annan, where he himself had been a pupil, happened to become vacant; and for this he presented himself as a candidate, receiving the appointment after a competitive trial, which is said to have taken place at Dumfries. The young man who had mastered Newton's *Principia*, and who knew himself to be the superior of his teachers in the Metropolitan University, must have felt the stirrings of a lofty ambition within him. Yet we cannot doubt that he gratefully accepted the work that offered itself, even though it was but that of the pedagogue in an obscure provincial town, yielding small honour in the eye of the world, and, "at best, bread and water wages," as is stated by Teufelsdröckh. Nor, although it is hinted in *Sartor* that the work "was performed ill, at best unpleasantly," are we inclined to accept this view of the result as other than fictitious; for the young man was in earnest, and, in spite of the transcendentalism that had already begun to dominate his being, he cherished a reverence the most profound for all learning, and especially for the branch he had been appointed to teach to his successors in the school at Annan. More than thirty years afterwards, conversing one autumn day in a little company in Yorkshire, at a time (1847) when the Education controversy was waxing furious, he went in strongly for education in any or all forms, "saying, among other characteristic things," as we are told by one who was present, "that the man who had mastered the 47th proposition of Euclid, stood nearer to God than he had ever done before." So that this new mathematical master at Annan must have been cheered at his work by the reflection, that it was indeed of a sacred character.

It must be confessed, however, that it is difficult to gather from such materials as are available, any definite notion of Carlyle as a schoolmaster. Even the dates are somewhat obscure. It would seem, from all we can learn, that he remained in his Annan situation only two years, if so long; and it is certain that, having been recommended by his friend Professor Leslie, he was, in 1816, appointed Rector of their Burgh School by the Town Council of Kirkcaldy. At this date Edward Irving had been four years the teacher of what was called "The Subscription School," a genteel private academy for the superior families in the same Fifeshire burgh—a place noted for its great length, and as the birthplace of Adam Smith. Though Mrs Oliphant makes no allusion to the circumstance of Carlyle's advent and residence in Kirkcaldy, beyond saying that he came to be the master of a school "set up in opposition" to Edward Irving's ;* there can be no doubt that the two friends were now brought more closely into contact, and that, in the little Fifeshire seaport, their intercourse strengthened that attachment which has caused some writers to speak of them as David and Jonathan. They were frequently seen walking together on the beach.

There is some significance in the local tradition that Carlyle, in spite of the contemptuous picture he has drawn of the Hinterschlag Gymnasium at Annan, was himself too much given to the evil practice of acting on the memory through the "muscular integument." In this respect he resembled his friend Irving; and stories are still current at Kirkcaldy respecting the severity of the discipline which they both administered. One of these has been related by Mrs Oliphant. A joiner, the deacon of his trade, a man of great strength, appeared one day at the door of Irving's schoolroom, while shrieks were resounding from within, with his shirt-sleeves rolled up to his elbows and an axe on his shoulder, and with dreadful irony inquired, "Do ye want a hand the day, Mr Irving?" We are also told of the strong indignation that was excited among the mothers of the pupils on more than one occasion by the excessive punishment of their

---

* This remark is calculated to convey a distinctly false impression, for it was at Irving's instigation, and with a view to be near him, that Carlyle had exchanged Annan for Kirkcaldy. An anonymous writer says :—"Kirkcaldy seems at this time to have been, in educational matters, entirely under Annan influences, since there were no less than six teachers in it all hailing from that place. Whether they were all as firm believers in the efficacy of the birch rod as Irving, tradition says not."

children. Alexander Smith, indeed, who had apparently devoted some little attention to the matter, asserted in the *Argosy* of May 1866 that Carlyle was actually chased out of the "Lang Toun" by the angry matrons, his severity having risen to a pitch which they could no longer endure. For the accuracy of these statements we cannot vouch; and, even if they had a substratum of truth, it is not unlikely that they came to be considerably exaggerated during their repetition as the years went by. We may safely conclude, however, that Carlyle in school was a rigid disciplinarian; nor should we be disposed to question the justice of the remark, made by more than one critic, that this was the earliest exhibition of a quality which was destined in after days to exert a prejudicial influence on his practical teaching of men. He had set up an ideal standard of excellence to which the poor bairns of Kirkcaldy must attain; and, in his impetuous insistence upon this, he betrayed a want of consideration for the weakness of the large number of pupils who could not possibly reach the master's ideal. A gentleman of Kirkcaldy informs us that Carlyle was little known to the public generally during his residence there, "being then, as afterwards, moody and retiring in his disposition." The school in which he taught was situated in the Kirk Wynd. It has been incorporated in a line of warehouses for the storage of flax, belonging to Mr Swan, Provost of the burgh, who is now the only surviving pupil of Mr Carlyle. Though using the schoolroom for storing purposes, he has kept it unaltered out of respect for the memory of his old teacher—"an act of hero-worship," says Alexander Smith, "for which the present and other generations may be thankful." The school, we are told, is wonderfully roomy and commodious for the time in which it was built. In the September of 1874 Carlyle revisited the town in which he had been a schoolmaster fifty-six years before, and it was with his old pupil, now the chief magistrate of the burgh, that he made his home. One evening, at Mr Swan's fireside, " he fell back on his reminiscences of St Andrews University and its professors in the days when he himself was a teacher in Kirkcaldy. The wondrous tenacity of his memory showed itself in these old-world allusions, for he recounted many names and incidents with freshness and vivacity, with now and again a touch of loitering wonder about what had come of all these lives ?"*

It was in the summer of 1818 that Irving gave up his school at Kirkcaldy and removed to Edinburgh ; and in the same year Carlyle also retired finally from the scholastic profession, having found that it was not the work to which he could devote his life. Not long after the two friends had betaken themselves to the city, we find Irving (in 1819) writing thus out of the " cloudy regions of uncertainty and unsuccess," in which they were both enveloped : " Carlyle goes away to-morrow, and Brown the next day. So here I am once more on my own resources, except Dixon, who is better fitted to swell the enjoyment of a joyous than to cheer the solitude of a lonely hour. For this Carlyle is better fitted than any one I know. It is very odd, indeed, that he should be sent for want of employment to the country ; of course, like every man of talent, he has gathered

---

* "A Night with Carlyle" in the *Fifeshire Journal*, by its editor, Mr William Hodgson.

around this Patmos many a splendid purpose to be fulfilled, and much improvement to be wrought out." The writer proceeds to represent Carlyle as saying, "I have the ends of my thoughts to bring together, which no one can do in this thoughtless scene. I have my views of life to reform, and the whole plan of my conduct to new-model; and withal I have my health to recover. And then once more I shall venture my bark upon the waters of this wide realm, and if she cannot weather it, I shall steer west and try the waters of another world." "So he reasons and resolves," says Irving; "but surely a worthier destiny awaits him than exile."

Irving himself, not long afterwards, was only prevented from seeking an outlet for his powers in a distant land, after he had made a farewell tour round the coast of Ayrshire, by the letter from Dr Chalmers which heralded an opening at home; and it is a further coincidence worthy of being remembered in this connection that a trivial incident, at the last moment, saved Robert Burns from becoming an exile, when "hungry ruin had him in the wind," and he had actually secured a steerage passage in the first ship that was to sail for the West Indies from the Clyde. Had Carlyle gone to the United States, as appears to have been for at least a little while an incipient purpose in his mind, what would the issue have been to himself and to the world? However idle, it is hardly possible to refrain from speculating on the problem. His was a home-loving nature, however, that could not possibly regard with complacency the idea of leaving his native country; we have seen a letter he wrote to a valued friend, a brother Scotsman of distinguished merit in the field of philosophy, who had been invited to a chair at Harvard, and one of the first of several reasons urged by Carlyle against the acceptance of the invitation was the fact that it would involve " expatriation." The patriotic sentiment thus expressed at a recent date was probably not less strong in the heart of the writer when he was a young man ; for had he not his parents still in the Annandale home where he had been nurtured ? And, moreover, was he not feeling, with added emphasis as each day went by, that his calling lay in a direction that would make the literary resources of the old country more than ever essential to the performance of his life-work? During the four years he had spent as schoolmaster at Annan and Kirkcaldy, he had been applying himself assiduously not only to mathematics—it was at that period he translated the greater part of Legendre's *Geometry* *—but also to the study of

---

* *Elements of Geometry and Trigonometry, with Notes.* Translated from the French of A. M. Legendre. Edited by David Brewster, LL.D. With Notes and Additions, and an Introductory Chapter on Proportion. Edinburgh : Oliver & Boyd. 1824. Pp. xvi. and 376. It will be observed that Brewster's name alone was inserted in the title-page, though his connection with the book was merely nominal, as he appears to have done nothing for it beyond writing a preface of a page and a half. Carlyle received £50 for his work. He was always proud of his essay on Proportion, which is a clear and compendious exposition in three theorems with corollaries. " I picked up a notion," says Professor De Morgan in his *Paradoxes*, " which others had at Cambridge in 1825, that the translator of Legendre was the late Mr Galbraith, then known at Edinburgh as a writer and teacher, but it turns out that it was quite a different person, and one destined to shine in quite a different walk. It was a young man named Thomas Carlyle. He prefixed from his own pen an ingenious essay on Proportion, as good a substitute for the fifth book of Euclid as could be given in speech, and quite enough to show that he would have been a distinguished teacher and thinker in first principles ; but he left the field imme-

the language and literature of Germany; and in proportion as he began to feel the work of tuition irksome, and
the school experiment hopeless, he must also have felt
that a new country, requiring the manual worker rather
than the man of letters, the farmer instead of the philosopher, was no fitting place for him.

It had at length become clear to him that Literature
was his true vocation. Able and accomplished as he had
proved himself to be in the field of mathematics, his
strong bent was not for science or scientific research. He
did indeed become a candidate, we are told, for the
chair of Astronomy in Glasgow University; and it has
been suggested that the mutilated note with " huge blot "
given in *Sartor* is a sardonic memorial of an actually
existing document received by Carlyle in connection with
this candidature. There is certainly such a stamp of
reality upon it as forbids the notion that it is purely
imaginary, and has no connection with the career of
Teufelsdröckh's editor while he was getting under way.
The Inkblot was, we can well believe, some self-important
personage of established repute and influence, perhaps
connected with the Western University; and, on the
whole, we cannot regret that he was so " tied-down by
previous promise " that he felt himself unable, " except
by best wishes," to forward the views of the young man
from Ecclefechan who aspired to teach astronomy in St
Mungo's town. It was just as well that " the cruel
necessity" was laid upon the Inkblot of " forbearing, for the
present, what were otherwise his duty and joy, to assist in

---

diately." Meritorious as it was, the larger part of the issue of this
work is said to have remained in the publishers' hands as dead
stock ; and the volume is now rarely to be seen.

opening the career for a man of genius, on whom far higher triumphs are yet waiting." This compliment was indeed a prophecy; but, before the triumph came, there had to be the strenuous labour, with meek acceptance of much preliminary drudgery, without which no veritable triumph is ever secured in this world. No Westminster Confession barred the entrance to the Priesthood of Letters; but the wolf had to be kept from the door by the candidate for admission, and this involved the necessity of accepting such work as he could obtain. He was poor and had to earn his bread. Nor was this the only difficulty that had to be surmounted; he was but an apprentice, and must slowly learn his trade. He had to find out the kind of work he was best fitted for—the portion of the vast field that he might cultivate with most advantage. His first attempt, strange to say, was a story! Had it been a poem, as is usually the case with literary tyros, we need not have been so much surprised. It appeared in the twelfth number of *Fraser's Magazine*, published in the February of 1831; so that although it is believed to be the first thing he wrote, it was not the first of his writings which procured the honour of print.* The earliest essays in authorship of Carlyle that reached the public were a number of articles on topographical and biographical subjects written for Brewster's *Edinburgh Encyclopædia*. These had for their subjects Lady Mary Wortley Montagu, Montaigne, Montesquieu, Montfaucon, Dr Moore, Sir John Moore, Necker, Nelson,

---

* An account of the story, with quotations, was given in *Fraser* for June 1879, the last number edited by Mr William Allingham, who, no doubt, personally received the information from Mr Carlyle.

Netherlands, Newfoundland, Norfolk, Northamptonshire, Northumberland, Mungo Park, Lord Chatham, William Pitt. They are to be found in the fourteenth and two succeeding volumes of Brewster's work, the first of the three bearing the date 1820, and the last 1823. Most of the articles are distinguished by the initials " T. C.," but they are all credited to Carlyle in the list of the authors of the principal articles prefixed to the encyclopædia on its completion. None of these essays have ever been republished; and, although it has been said that "they give but faint, uncertain promise of the author's genius and of those gifts which made his later works as individual as a picture by Albert Dürer or Rembrandt," they are certainly not altogether destitute of the characteristic traits of their author's subsequent work. Indeed, when we take into account the nature of the publication for which they were prepared, along with the youth and inexperience of the writer, as well as the standard of taste at the time, they must be considered strikingly indicative of original power, as well as of the patient research, industry, and minute attention to details which few authors have ever exhibited to the same degree as Carlyle. Though an encyclopædia did not offer any scope for imaginative work, but rather imposed a strict exclusion of it, we find here and there in the articles a play of fancy that lights them up very pleasantly, and gives token that the compiler is no ordinary hack of the Grub Street species. The humour, and the peculiar style of expression that we now regard as Carlyle's own, are both exemplified, for example, even in the article on Newfoundland, where we might least expect to find them. There is no mistaking the pen that describes one of the few Newfoundland authors, Mr. Anspach, as " a clerical person, who lived in the island several years, and has since written a meagre and very confused book, which he calls a history of it." This is by no means according to the regulation pattern for topographical articles in a work of reference, even to-day; still less was it in the conventional mode of sixty years ago. Other germs of the remarkable style that was by-and-by to become familiar to the world may be detected in some of the other articles, especially in that on Montesquieu. The philosopher's theory as to the influence of climate on race and history is refuted in a manner thoroughly characteristic, with a nervous vigour and a confidence that are truly astonishing in so young a writer; and it has been justly remarked by an able critic that, in the vivid picture of Montesquieu as a cheerful and benign sage, talking with the peasants under the oak at La Brède, it is not difficult to recognise the author of *The French Revolution.* Of Necker we are told that he combined, " in a singular union, the fervour of the stripling with the experience of the sage ;" and in some of the other biographical articles there are strokes of equal felicity. Those who have said that these brief encyclopædia essays gave small indication of their author's future brilliance have not noted with sufficient care the points that distinguish them from the productions of the rest of Brewster's contributors, nor have they made sufficient allowance for the limitations imposed by the nature of the work in which they appeared. It must ever be regarded as creditable to Sir David Brewster that he had the prescience to discover the ability which led him to invite the untried Carlyle to become one of the writers for his *Encyclopædia,* and that he had sufficient confidence in the young man's judgment to allow its free exercise in criticisms that were thoroughly original and expressed in a tone of the utmost confidence.*

To the same period belong a couple of critical articles contributed to the *New Edinburgh Review* in 1821-22, the one on Joanna Baillie's *Metrical Legends,* the other on Goethe's *Faust,* neither of which has been republished. In 1823 he began some slight experiments in verse ; and, although he seems to have felt that his strength did not lie in that direction, so that these trials were not pursued with any great earnestness of purpose, he succeeded in producing at least three pieces that are marked by genuine poetic power, two of these being also invested with an autobiographic interest. The *Tragedy of the Night Moth* bears the impress of one of the many dark hours through which he had to pass in the years of painful endeavour and of waiting for his proper work, when he was oppressed with gloomy apprehensions of failure :—

---

* When, after the lapse of more than forty years, Carlyle came to Edinburgh to address the students as Lord Rector, the Principal of the University was Sir David Brewster. "Seeing him sit beside the venerable Principal," wrote Alexander Smith, in the happiest of all the sketches of that memorable day, "one could not help thinking of his earliest connection with literature. Time brings men into the most unexpected relationships. When the Principal was plain Mr Brewster, editor of the *Edinburgh Cyclopædia,* little dreaming that he should ever be Knight of Hanover, and head of the Northern Metropolitan University, Mr Carlyle—just as little dreaming that he should be the foremost man of letters of his day, and Lord Rector of the same University—was his contributor, writing for said *Cyclopædia* biographies of Voltaire, and other notables. And so it came about that, after years of separation and of honourable labour, the old editor and contributor were brought together again—in new relations."

> Poor moth ! thy fate my own resembles :
> Me too a restless asking mind
> Hath sent on far and weary rambles,
> To seek the good I ne'er shall find.
>
> Like thee, with common lot contented,
> With humble joys and vulgar fate,
> I might have lived and ne'er lamented,
> Moth of a larger size, a longer date !

The *Adieu* strengthens the impression that poor Teu-felsdröckh's Blumine was no merely imaginary maiden, but a reality, who did indeed announce the dawn of Dooms-day as she said, in a tremulous voice, to her unhappy victim, " They were to meet no more." So he turns his sorrow into song :—

> Hard fate will not allow, allow,
> Hard fate will not allow ;
> We blessed were as the angels are,—
> Adieu forever now,
> My dear,
> Adieu forever now.

Of the poetical fragments, however, the most spon-taneous is the little gem, *Today*, a genuine poetic birth; though *The Sower's Song* also is a lyric that deserves to live. The poems are all saturated with German feeling, and may have been written while Carlyle was studying the poetry of Schiller, whose Life he was shortly about to publish. By this time he had thoroughly familiarised himself with German literature, the paper on *Faust* being apparently his initial venture in the field wherein he was to win his first laurels. His brother was studying in Germany, and the letters he received from Dr Carlyle heightened the already keen interest which he felt in the language and literature of that country.

In spite of his being now a man, we know almost as

little of his life in Edinburgh during this second sojourn there as we do of the first, when he was only a boy. Irving, after his return from Kirkcaldy, had resumed attendance at the University; and it is thought that Carlyle may have done the same, since we find him speaking of 1819-20 being "well onward in my student life at Edinburgh." It has also been suggested that the crowning feats in the voracious use of the University Library are connected with this period. Under the lead of Irving a Philosophical Society was set on foot, specially intended for the students who had completed their arts course; and Carlyle was one of its members. But it was short-lived. Carlyle's lodgings were in Bristo Street; and one surviving contemporary, a college acquaintance in the habit of visiting him in the evenings, testifies that he "always found him a queer-spoken fellow." The dialogues between Irving and Carlyle are said to have left their mark in the memory of casual hearers, as they were likely to do; but none of these hearers have given us the opportunity of sharing their privilege. We are only told that Irving usually stood on the defensive in support of the orthodox views, and that Carlyle was "always eloquent," and always on the other side. Carlyle's principal resort was the Advocates' Library, of which he says, "Lasting thanks to *it*, alone of Scottish institutions." He read literature of every description, from romance to the most abstruse theology. As he seems to have maintained himself by literary work, it is probable that he wrote some things for the press that have never been heard of; otherwise, his living must have been a poor one, and we need not wonder that he speaks in *Sartor* of "those obstructed, neglectful, and grimly-forbidding years," during which no work in the right direction was to be had, "whereby he became wretched enough." His natural stillness of manner, "which did but ill express the keen ardour of his feelings," was probably at this time aggravated into a seeming hardness, made more offensive to those who did not know him by "the panoply of sarcasm" wherein he had striven to envelop himself for reasons pathetically explained in the confessions of Teufelsdröckh. There is an anecdote that bears out this view. On a Saturday afternoon, some time in 1822, Edward Irving introduced to a friend's house at Paisley a stranger of shy and gruff demeanour, who spoke little, and who was otherwise not prepossessing. No name had been mentioned, and the members of the household concluded that he was some stranger who had been picked up on the road by Irving, and brought with him to tea. They only learned who the "gruff" stranger was when one of the family had him pointed out to her, years after, as Thomas Carlyle.

CHAPTER VIII.

THE PIONEER OF GERMAN LITERATURE IN BRITAIN—
HIS LIFE OF SCHILLER—TRANSLATION OF GOETHE'S
"WILHELM MEISTER"—ATTACKS BY JEFFREY AND
DE QUINCEY—LETTER FROM GOETHE—CLOSE OF
JOURNEY-WORK—CHARLES BULLER—TRIBUTE TO HIS
OLD PUPIL.

ACCORDING to the dictum of Bulwer Lytton, it was Colé-
ridge who first made England aware of the riches of
German philosophy and German song, and to him, we
are told, must be ascribed the merit of originating whatever influences the higher spirit of German genius has
exercised upon the English mind. This statement
ought to have been qualified by mention of William
Taylor of Norwich, who published his version of Bürger's
Lenore (the recitation of which led to the production of
that of Sir Walter Scott) as early as the year following
the one in which Carlyle was born, and who by his subsequent translations " did much in the beginning of the
century to reveal to cultured Englishmen the mine of
intellectual wealth that lay awaiting them in the regener-
ated German literature."* While according the meed of

---

* *German Life and Literature.* By Alexander Hay Japp, LL.D.
A work that should not be overlooked by any student of Carlyle,
respecting whom it contains some acute and admirably-sustained,
as well as incisive, criticism.

praise that is due to these pioneers (and also to De Quincey) in the good work of opening up that mine to English readers, it must still be asserted that the great and popularly effective pioneer was Thomas Carlyle. The review of Goethe's *Faust* in that *New Edinburgh* which did not live long enough to belie its name, was the first fruits of a knowledge greatly exceeding even that of Coleridge, and which was united to a perseverance and steady power of working that were conspicuous by their absence in the Seer of Highgate. This article was followed in 1823 by the first part of the *Life of Schiller*, which appeared under the title of "Schiller's Life and Writings" in the *London Magazine* for October of that year. No name was attached to the contribution; but those who were in the secret of its authorship, and who had made the personal acquaintance of Carlyle, or at least knew him to be a young man, were deeply impressed with its indications of power. They predicted great things from a writer who, in youth, exhibited such noble simplicity and maturity of style, and who had conceptions of criticism that were rare indeed in those times. The second part of the sketch of Schiller appeared in the number of the magazine for January 1824, and the third part in the numbers for July, August, and September of the same year. The vivacious Aberdonian who edited the *London*, that John Scott who fell in a duel with Lockhart, at which the latter officiated by proxy, had gathered round him a staff of brilliant writers—De Quincey and Hood, Hazlitt and Lamb, Croly and Cary, besides Carlyle's fellow-Borderer, honest Allan Cunningham; yet, even amongst the writings of these exceptionally capable men the memoir of the German poet by the quite unknown Scottish youth was received with special marks of favour, to such an extent indeed that the publishers of the magazine felt encouraged to reprint it in the form of a book in 1825.

Before this, however, Carlyle had made his *debût* as a "Maker of Books" by the publication, in 1824, of a translation of *Wilhelm Meister's Apprenticeship*, which was issued from the press of Messrs Oliver & Boyd, of Edinburgh, and was his first book, if we except the translation of Legendre's *Geometry*, which Charles Lamb would probably have classified with those printed volumes he did not consider to be books at all. The name of the translator was not given on the title-page ; and this has suggested the reflection that he may have had some misgivings as to how his countrymen would receive a work so repugnant in many ways to English notions of taste, and even of morality—a work in which, more than once, Goethe has grossly violated his own axiom, that "there are some things which, though all know them, should yet be treated as secrets, because it favours modesty and good morals." Carlyle's translation was the first introduction of Goethe to the English people. Though its sale was at first very slow, its reception by the general body of readers was more favourable than that accorded to it by the professional critics. Both De Quincey and Jeffrey, who well knew who the translator was, fell upon it with almost savage delight, the attack of the former appearing in the pages of the *London Magazine*, where just then Carlyle's sketch of Schiller was in course of publication The editor of the *Edinburgh Review*, who was really as incapable at the time of forming a just conception of the work of Goethe as he had proved himself sixteen years before to be of appreciating the poetry of Wordsworth, only succeeded in demonstrating his own ignorance. "After the most deliberate consideration," he set out by pronouncing the work "eminently absurd, puerile, incongruous, and affected," and "almost from beginning to end one flagrant offence against every principle of taste and every rule of composition." But the article which opened with this unqualified denunciation, closed with an admission that proved the onslaught in the initial sentences to have been written before the book had been read by its censor. "Many of the passages to which we have now alluded are executed with great talent, and we are very sensible are better worth extracting than those we have cited. But it is too late now to change our selections, and we can still less afford to add to them. On the whole we close the book with some feeling of mollification towards its faults and a disposition to abate, if possible, some part of the censure we were impelled to bestow upon it at the beginning." As for the translator, Jeffrey condescended to say that he was "a person of talents," proved to be such "by his preface;" and the reviewer graciously added that every part of the work also demonstrated that he was "no ordinary master, at least of one of the languages with which he has to deal." It is only charitable to ascribe the qualification to an unwonted access of modesty in the critic, who was ignorant of the language in which the book was written by its author. De Quincey knew better what he was about, though he spared neither Goethe nor his translator; and those who have ascribed the Opium-Eater's adverse criticism to "one of his fits of ill-humour" can hardly themselves have bestowed on the work he criticised a sufficient amount of attention to justify their expression of an opinion. The fact must not be passed over without notice that Carlyle's translation of *Wilhelm Meister* gives in a perfectly unmodified form passages that do not appear in any other English translation, not even in Bohn's, where they are either given partially or wholly omitted. The alternative is forced upon us, which Dr Japp has suggested, "that Mr Carlyle was either all too faithful to the text of his author, or all too little concerned for that English domestic purity which others had found was not likely to profit by such suggestions from German literature." It is worth while noting that the *Monthly Magazine*, a periodical honourably distinguished for its careful attention to foreign literature, declared that the translation was "executed in a masterly way," and with "much strength, originality, and raciness about it, which cannot fail to please the reader." The verdict of the critics caused the demand for the book to become lively; and it is probable that the attacks furthered this end even to a greater extent than the two favourable notices which the work received.*

---

* The second appeared in *Blackwood*, whose critic, with greater discernment than the editor of the Whig review had exhibited, said : "The translator is, we understand, a young gentleman in this city who now for the first time appears before the public. We congratulate him on his very promising *debût*, and would fain hope to receive a series of really good translations from his hand. He has evidently a perfect knowledge of German. He already writes English better than is at all common, even at this time; and we know no exercise more likely to produce effects of permanent advantage upon a young mind of intellectual ambition." Dr Maginn, at a later date, complained that Goethe had been translated from "the Fatherlandish dialect of High Dutch to the Allgemeine Mid Lothianish of Auld Reekie," and that Carlyle was seeking to acclimatize "the roundabout, hubble-bubble, rumfustianish (*hübble-bubblen, rümfüsteanischen*), roly-poly, gromerly of style, dear to the heart of a son of the Fatherland."

The *Life of Schiller*, published in book form by Taylor and Hessey, in London, in 1825, established itself at once as a public favourite, passing rapidly through several editions. But more grateful to the author than even this success at home, the first that had come to lighten his struggling pathway, was the publication in the poet's own country of a German translation of the work, with a highly laudatory introduction by Goethe himself. The young Scottish pupil of the sage of Weimar had taken the master's heart by storm. With unerring instinct Goethe perceived that this man was to be his interpreter to the English-speaking nations of the world; nor was it merely on his own account that he hailed his advent with grateful joy. He saw that German literature would now have justice done it in England. He wrote to Carlyle, making inquiry as to his occupations, etc., the commencement of a correspondence that ceased only with the death of Goethe; and he had a bust of Carlyle executed and set up in his study, that he might have always before him the image of the living countenance of his great Scottish expositor.

The good fortune that visited Carlyle at this turning-point in his life is associated with a name that occupies a position of honour and mournful interest in the political history of our century. Through the suggestion of his faithful friend Edward Irving, who had now entered on that ministry in London, the brilliancy of which at its beginning was only equalled by the tragic gloom of its close, Carlyle in 1823 became the private tutor of Charles Buller. This took him away from Edinburgh to London, and a twofold influence was now at work stimulating his literary activity. Though he did not fail to do justice to his pupil, he had a good deal of spare time on his hand ; and as there was no longer any pressing necessity to write for money, he was free to devote his leisure to the kind of work which had the greatest attraction for him, and in the performance of which he felt that he could do full justice to his powers. Thus he had secured at length a vantage-ground which some have sought for a lifetime to reach, but have never attained. Besides, residence in London brought him into contact with men who both stirred his literary impulse into greater activity and were able to provide or help him to the medium through which he might speak to the public. Now he gave up hack-work, and his life as a man of letters, in the true sense of the term, began. Brief as was his first sojourn in London, it was laden with blessing for him and had momentous issues that coloured the whole of his after life. His last piece of compulsory work had now been finished, though it did not appear till 1837, when it was issued by genial William Tait of Edinburgh, in four volumes, under the title of *Specimens of German Romance.* " This was a book of translations," said Carlyle himself thirty years afterwards in the preface to a republication of some of them, " not of my suggesting or desiring, but of my executing as honest journeywork in defect of better. The pieces selected were the suitablest discoverable on such terms : not quite of *less* than no worth (I considered) any piece of them ; nor, alas, of a very high worth any, except one only. Four of these lots, or quotas to the adventure, Musäus's, Tieck's, Richter's, Goethe's, will be given in the final stage of this series: the rest we willingly leave, afloat or stranded, as waste driftwood, to those whom they may farther concern." The *Specimens*, which included *Wilhelm Meister's Wanderjahre*, the sequel to the *Lehrjahre*, were as well received by the public as the translator's two former works. Earnest wishes were expressed from all sides that he would devote his whole attention to the cultivation of German literature, so that gradually its choicest flowers should be transplanted from their native into the English soil. This, however, he declined. He was to be much more than a mere transplanter of foreign flowers—more than a conduit through which the literary waters of Germany should flow to freshen the English soil. That part of his service was over; new and higher work was about to be begun. Yet the function which he had been fulfilling during those days of journey-work at Edinburgh was not one to be despised; and the memory of it, if less thought of in his own country than the greater achievements of his after life, was fresh in Germany that day when the tidings flew all over the Fatherland that Thomas Carlyle was dead. "Not only England, but Germany also, is indebted to him," said the *Berliner Tageblatt*, "since he first thoroughly understood the beauties of German literature and made them known to his fellow-countrymen." "Thomas Carlyle," wrote the *Börsen Courier*, "was the man who discovered to Englishmen the heretofore hidden intellectual treasures of German poetry. He made known to them Goethe's wonderful *Wilhelm Meister* in an excellent translation. His was the first foreign hand that penned the biography of a German poet. He wrote the *Life of Schiller*, and all England was full of enthusiasm, in the twenty years during which these works appeared, for the great Weimar epoch with which Carlyle had so familiarised himself." This reference to the enthusiasm in

England brings to mind the account which Sir Walter Scott has given of the intoxication that was excited amongst his Edinburgh contemporaries by their first draught from the general literature of Germany; but it was as nothing compared with the fuller and deeper enthusiasm that pervaded the succeeding generation when they had the privilege of reading those translations that first made the name of Carlyle known to his countrymen. With pardonable pride, the leading Edinburgh journal recalls the work which he began in that city sixty years ago. " His function as guide of his countrymen into the new world of German poetry and thought is by no means the least of his claims to remembrance. It is difficult to realise the magnitude of the revolution he effected. At a time when the flippant criticism of the *Edinburgh Review* marked the general ignorance, and when only Coleridge and De Quincey in their own mazy fashion had dropped a few hints of the undiscovered literary continent, the young Carlyle rose and measured German thought and literature, and especially Goethe, in their true significance for the modern world."*

With his pupil Charles Buller, Carlyle formed a friendship that lasted until the lamented death of the younger of the two in 1848. Not only did Carlyle prepare him for Cambridge, where he achieved a success that he always attributed to his tutor, their intimate connection was continued after the pupil entered Parliament. This was evident from the strikingly original views on pauperism, emigration, and colonisation which the young statesman so effectively advocated in the House of Commons,

---

* *The Scotsman Newspaper*, Feb. 7, 1881.

and many of which have since his death been embodied in practical legislation. In everything to which Charles Buller put his hand, it was easy to trace the influence of his illustrious teacher ; and when he died at the early age of 42 none of the numerous tributes to his memory moved the heart of England like the one uttered by Carlyle :—

" A very beautiful soul has suddenly been summoned from among us ; one of the clearest intellects and most aërial activities in England, has unexpectedly been called away. Charles Buller died on Wednesday morning last, without previous sickness, reckoned of importance, till a day or two before. An event of unmixed sadness, which has created a just sorrow, private and public. The light of many a social circle is dimmer henceforth, and will miss long a presence which was always gladdening and beneficent ; in the coming storms of political trouble, which heap themselves more and more in ominous clouds on our horizon, one radiant element is to be wanting now.

" Mr Buller was in his forty-third year, and had sat in Parliament some twenty of those. A man long kept under by the peculiarities of his endowment and position, but rising rapidly into importance of late years ; beginning to reap the fruits of long patience, and to see an ever wider field open round him. He was what in party language is called a ' Reformer,' from his earliest youth ; and never swerved from that faith, nor could swerve. His luminous sincere intellect laid bare to him in all its abject incoherency the thing that was untrue, which thenceforth became for him a thing that was not tenable, that it was perilous and scandalous to attempt maintaining. Twenty years in the dreary weltering lake of parliamentary confusion, with its disappointments and bewilderments, had not quenched this tendency, in which, as we say, he persevered as by a law of nature itself, for the essence of his mind was clearness, healthy purity, incompatibility with fraud in any of its forms. What he accomplished, therefore, whether great or little, was all to be *added* to the sum of good ; none of it to be deducted. There shone mildly in his whole conduct a beautiful veracity, as if it were unconscious of itself ; a perfect spontaneous absence of all cant, hypocrisy, and hollow pretence, not in word and act only, but in thought and instinct. To a singular extent it can be said of him that he was a spontaneous clear man. Very gentle, too, though full of fire ; simple, brave, graceful. What he did, and what he said, came from him, as light from a luminous body, and had thus always in it a high and rare merit, which any of the more discerning could appreciate fully.

" To many, for a long while, Mr Buller passed merely for a man of wit, and certainly his beautiful natural gaiety of character, which by no means meant *levity*, was commonly thought to mean it, and did for many years hinder the recognition of his intrinsic higher qualities. Slowly it began to be discovered that, under all this many-coloured radiancy and coruscation, there burnt a most steady light ; a sound, penetrating intellect, full of adroit resources, and loyal by nature itself to all that was methodic, manful, true ;—in brief, a mildly resolute, chivalrous, and gallant character, capable of doing much serious service.

" A man of wit he indisputably was, whatever more,

amongst the wittiest of men. His speech, and manner
of being, played everywhere like soft brilliancy of lambent
fire round the common objects of the hour, and was,
beyond all others that English society could show, entitled
to the name of excellent, for it was spontaneous, like all
else in him, genuine, humane,—the glittering play of the
soul of a real man. To hear him, the most serious of
men might think within himself, ' How beautiful is
human gaiety too ! ' Alone of wits, Buller never made
wit ; he could be silent, or grave enough, where better
was going ; often rather liked to be silent, if permissible,
and always was so where needful. His wit, moreover,
was ever the ally of wisdom, not of folly, or unkindness,
or injustice ; no soul was ever hurt by it ; never, we
believe, never, did his wit offend justly any man, and
often have we seen his ready resource relieve one ready
to be offended, and light up a pausing circle all into
harmony again. In truth, it was beautiful to see such
clear, almost childlike simplicity of heart co-existing with
the finished dexterities, and long experiences, of a man
of the world. Honour to human worth in whatever form
we find it ! This man was true to his friends, true to
his convictions,—and true without effort, as the magnet
is to the north. He was ever found on the right side ;
helpful to it, not obstructive of it, in all he attempted or
performed.

" Weak health ; a faculty indeed brilliant, clear, prompt,
not deficient in depth either, or in any kind of active
valour, but wanting the stern energy that could long
endure to *continue* in the deep, in the chaotic, new, and
painfully incondite—this marked out for him his limits ;
which, perhaps with regrets enough, his natural veracity

and practicality would lead him quietly to admit and stand by. He was not the man to grapple, in its dark and deadly dens, with the Lernæan coil of social Hydras; perhaps not under any circumstances: but he did, unassisted, what he could; faithfully himself did something —nay, something truly considerable;—and in his *patience* with the much that by him and his strength could not be done let us grant there was something of beautiful too!

" Properly, indeed, his career as a public man was but beginning. In the office he last held, much was silently expected of him; he himself, too, recognised well what a fearful and immense question this of Pauperism is; with what ominous rapidity the demand for solution of it is pressing on; and how little the world generally is yet aware what methods and principles, new, strange, and altogether contradictory to the shallow maxims and idle philosophies current at present, would be needed for dealing with it! This task he perhaps contemplated with apprehension; but he is not now to be tried with this, or with any task more. He has fallen, at this point of the march, an honourable soldier; and has left us here to fight along without him. Be his memory dear and honourable to us, as that of one so worthy ought. What in him was true and valiant endures for evermore—beyond all memory or record. His light, airy brilliancy has suddenly become solemn, fixed in the earnest stillness of Eternity. *There* shall we also, and our little works, all shortly be."*

---

* *The Examiner Newspaper*, Dec. 2, 1848.

CHAPTER IX.

HIS MARRIAGE—JANE WELSH OF HADDINGTON—ANECDOTE
OF HER CHILDHOOD—EDWARD IRVING—HER ANCES-
TORS—WELSH OF AYR AND JOHN KNOX'S DAUGHTER
—HER LETTER TO SIR GEORGE SINCLAIR—CHARLOTTE
CUSHMAN'S PICTURE OF MRS CARLYLE—HER HUSBAND
ON THE QUEEN OF THE WORLD.

IT was in 1826 that Carlyle took the most momentous,
as it also proved the most fortunate, step of his life. It
would be difficult to name another equally eminent man
of letters, in any land, who was so perfectly happy in his
marriage.   To his wife, in perhaps the most touching
inscription that has been placed by a husband over the
tomb of his departed helpmate, he ascribed all his
success; and there is every reason to believe that this
was no more than the simple truth.   Jane Welsh was,
in every respect, a woman worthy to be the wife of
Thomas Carlyle.   Richly gifted in all those qualities of
heart that form the first essential, she was not less
distinguished for vigour of intellect, and for a richly
varied culture and a refinement of nature that caused
her to be regarded, by those in the best position for
judging, as one of the most remarkable women of her
day.   Born at Haddington in 1801, she was the only

child of Dr John Welsh, a medical practitioner in that town, and of Grace Welsh, of Caplegill, Dumfriesshire, his wife. In her girlhood she had Edward Irving for a tutor; and it was through Irving that Carlyle became acquainted with her. While yet a mere child, she had overheard domestic discussions with respect to her future training, in which her father expressed the resolution to have her educated like a boy, since she was his only child; the mother, on the contrary, hoping "for nothing higher in her daughter than the sweet domestic companion most congenial to herself:" and who that has read can ever forget the charming story, that touches at once the spring of laughter and of tears, how the child, her ambition roused, secretly acquired a copy of the *Latin Rudiments*, and, after conning it for many days alone, suddenly from her place of concealment under the table, when the good doctor was sitting at leisure after dinner, burst forth in breathless steadiness with her first lesson, "*Penna, pennæ, pennam!*" The wish of both the parents was realised. Recommended by Professor Leslie, of whom it is pleasant to remember that he made himself the early patron of both Carlyle and Irving, the latter, who had just gone to Haddington to be master of the Mathematical School in the birthplace of John Knox, was chosen by Dr Welsh to become the teacher of his little girl, then aged nine years. Tutor and pupil became fast friends—the friendship existing "unbroken," as Mrs Oliphant informs us, "through all kinds of vicissitudes; even through entire separation, disapproval, and outward estrangement, to the end of Irving's life." While in Edinburgh, after the Kirkcaldy teaching days were over, Irving met once more his precocious little pupil at

Haddington, now a beautiful and vivacious young lady; and, though he had no right to be jealous, since he had formed an attachment elsewhere, we are not surprised to learn that he could not conceal the mortification with which he heard falling too warmly from the young lady's lips the praises of the friend whom he had himself introduced to Dr Welsh's hospitable home. When his little ebullition was over the fair culprit turned to leave the room; but had scarcely passed the door when Irving hurried after her, and called, entreating her to return for a moment. When she came back, she found the simple-hearted giant standing penitent to make his confession. "The truth is, I was piqued," said Irving; "I have always been accustomed to fancy that *I* stood highest in your good opinion, and I was jealous to hear you praise another man. I am sorry for what I said just now—that is the truth of it;" and so, not pleased, but penitent and candid, he let her go.*

Mrs Carlyle's ancestors, like those of her husband, had been settled for centuries in Dumfriesshire, and were persons of distinction, many of them having risen to positions of eminence in the Church. As early as 1488 we find a Nicholas Welsh the Abbot of Holywood; Dean William Welsh was Vicar of Tynron in 1530; soon after the latter date, Dean Robert Welsh was vicar of the same parish; and John Welsh, vicar of Dunscore, took office in the Reformed Church in 1560. After the last-named, arose the greatest member of the family, in the person of another John Welsh, the celebrated Reformer, and son-in-law of John Knox. The father of this eminent man, of

---

* *The Life of Edward Irving,* by Mrs Oliphant.

the same name, was Laird of Colliston, and owned other estates in Dunscore and Holywood. Of a romantic and adventurous disposition, young Welsh, when a mere boy, ran away from his father's house, and joined a band of Border robbers; but he did not stay long in their company, and soon presented himself at the door of an aunt, Mrs Forsyth, in Dumfries, through whose good offices he was reconciled to his father. At the early age of twenty-two this stirring boy had settled down as a devoted Christian minister, in the parish of Kirkcudbright; in his twenty-eighth year he had his famous controversy with the Commendator of Sweetheart Abbey, in which he maintained the cause of Protestantism with such signal success, that the King bestowed upon him a glowing eulogium; and seven years thereafter, that is, in 1605, he was the leader of the famous Aberdeen Assembly, which met in defiance of the same monarch, when James was seeking to subvert the Presbyterian constitution of the Church of Scotland. Condemned to death, Welsh's sentence was commuted to transportation; and after sixteen years of exile in France he was suffered, on his health failing, to return in 1622 to England. But the King would on no account allow him to cross the Border when he wished to get the benefit of his native air, His Majesty declaring that "it would be impossible to establish Prelacy in Scotland if Welsh were permitted to return." James even debarred him from preaching in London till informed that he could not long survive, and when the preacher at length obtained access to a pulpit he discoursed with his wonted fire and eloquence, but, on returning to his lodging, expired within two hours. This faithful witness was a lineal ancestor of Mrs Car-

lyle ; indeed, the estate of Craigenputtoch, which came
to Carlyle though his wife, had been the property of the
old minister of Ayr. We can hardly wonder, then, that
Carlyle should at one time have thought of writing
Welsh's life, though he ultimately gave up the project ;
and the fact that his wife's most distinguished ancestor
married Elizabeth Knox * probably did not tend to
lessen the interest with which Carlyle studied the character and career of her father, the great Reformer, the
essay on *The Portraits of John Knox* being the last
work he gave to the world. Welsh would have been
a subject not unworthy even of the pen that restored
Oliver Cromwell to the English people. When the
late Rev. James Young, of Edinburgh, informed Carlyle
that he was engaged upon a memoir of Welsh, he
received cordial encouragement to prosecute the task.
"Welsh's Biography," wrote Carlyle (8th September
1862), "if he could be made conclusively intelligible, as
at least the public Church-History of his time could by

---

* This worthy daughter of a worthy sire, by means of some of
her mother's relations at Court, obtained access to the Royal
Solomon when her husband lay dying in London, and petitioned
the King to grant him permission to return to Scotland. His
Majesty asked her who was her father. "John Knox," she
replied. "Knox and Welsh," exclaimed the King, "the devil
never made such a match as that." "It's right like, sir," said
Elizabeth, "for we never speered (asked) his advice." Again she
urged her request, that he would give her husband his native air.
"Give him his native air !" replied the King ; "give him the
devil !" "Give that to your hungry courtiers," said Mrs Welsh,
offended at his profaneness. At last he told her, if she would
persuade her husband to submit to the bishops, he would grant her
prayer. Mrs Welsh, lifting her apron, and holding it to the
monarch, replied, "Please yer Majesty, I'd rather kep (receive)
his head there."—*M'Crie's Life of John Knox.*

right pains, might be a very acceptable book ; the anti-Presbyterian procedure of King James, and scenes one has seen, of 'all the women gathered weeping on Leith Sands,' I think at two in the morning, 'as Welsh and consorts lifted anchor for exile,' etc., etc., represent a vivid state of things in what has now fallen altogether blank to common Scotch readers. Mr David Laing printed somewhere, not many years ago, certain letters from Welsh in his exile—('I dwine and dee !' was a phrase in one of them)—which to me were considerably instructive as to his affairs, and him. Mr Laing, you are no doubt aware, is worth all living aids put together in regard to such a matter. I fear, however, there will be a great scarcity of real documents as to Welsh. At Ayr, I suppose, there will be nothing ;—unless, perhaps his old kirk is still head uppermost, in an *indisputable* way ? In Dumfriesshire, (in Glenesland, Upper Nithsdale), you will still find the name of Colleston sticking to a patch of the property which was his father's ; but, except that, and perhaps some inferences (of small moment) deducible from that, I doubt nothing more whatever." In reply to this letter, Mr Young wrote :—" Your fear that there will be a great scarcity of documents is, I am happy to inform you, without foundation. On the contrary, there is an exuberance of materials, and one great difficulty I have felt is how best to arrange and compress them." The phrase of Welsh's at the parting on Leith Sands which dwelt in Carlyle's memory is to be found, probably, in *Row's History* or *Melville's Diary ;* but, in spite of the suggestive reminiscence of his correspondent, Mr Young had not the tact to quote it, but preferred to give his own feeble paraphrase of the story.

That Mrs Carlyle was worthy of the noble stock from which she came, and that she possessed not a little of the ready wit of brave Mrs Welsh of Ayr, has been attested by all who knew her. Among her other gifts was that of writing a letter in no wise inferior to the choicest productions of her husband in the epistolary line. Of this we find an example in a playful communication to Sir George Sinclair, written in 1860, shortly after her husband had gone north on a visit to the baronet at Thurso Castle :—

"5 Cheyne Row, Chelsea, August.

" My dear Sir,—Decidedly you are more thoughtful for me than the man who is bound by vow to 'love and cherish' me; not a line have I received from *him* to announce his safe arrival in your dominions.

" The more shameful on his part, that, as it appears by your note, he had such good accounts to give of himself, and was perfectly *up* to giving them.

" Well! now that *you* have relieved me from all anxiety about the effects of the journey on him, he may write at his own 'reasonably good leisure.' Only I told him I should not write till I had heard of his arrival from himself; and he knows whether or no I am in the habit of keeping my word—to the letter.

" A thousand thanks for the primrose roots, which I shall plant so soon as it fairs! To-day we have again a deluge, adding a deeper shade of horror to certain household operations going on under my inspection (by way of 'improving the occasion' of *his* absence)! *One* bedroom has got all the feathers of its bed and pillows airing themselves out on the floor! creating an atmosphere of down in the house, more choking than even 'cotton-fuzz.' In another, upholsterers and painters are plashing away for their life; and a couple of bricklayers are tearing up flags in the kitchen to seek 'the solution' of a non-acting drain! All this on the one hand; and on the other, visits from my doctor resulting in ever new 'composing draughts,' and strict charges to 'keep my mind perfectly tranquil.' You will admit that one could easily conceive situations more ideal.

"Pray, do keep him as long as you like! To hear of him 'in high spirits' and 'looking remarkably well' is more composing for me than any amount of 'composing draughts,' or of insistence on the benefits of 'keeping myself perfectly tranquil.' It is so very different a state of things with him from that in which I have *seen* him for a long time back!

"Oh! I must not forget to give you the 'kind re-membrance' of a very charming woman, whom any man may be pleased to be remembered by as kindly as *she* evidently remembered *you!* I speak of Lady William Russell.* She knew you in Germany, 'a young student,' she told me, when she was *Bessy Rawdon.* She 'had a great affection for you, and had often thought of you since.' You were 'very romantic in those days; oh, *very* romantic and *sentimental,*' she could assure me! Pray, send me back a pretty message for her; she will like so much to know that she has not remembered you 'with the reciprocity all on one side.'

"I don't even send my regards to Mr C., but—

"Affectionately yours,

"JANE W. CARLYLE."

---

* The mother of the present Duke of Bedford—a lady of rare gifts

Surely that is a very pretty letter, with a fine arch humour breathing through every line of it, under which you can see lurking a tender, yearning affection for the absent husband, and as much of intellectual vigour and good common sense as of heart. Edward Irving, we may rest assured, did not exaggerate when he used to speak of Jane Welsh's intellect as the most powerful he had ever seen in a woman.

In the memoirs of Charlotte Cushman, an actress who was descended from, and not unworthy of, one of the most distinguished of the Pilgrim Fathers of New England, there is a vivid account of Mrs Carlyle, whom the fair American first saw at the house of Miss Jewsbury, but afterwards often met in her own house in Cheyne Row. She is described as "that wonderful woman, who was able to live in the full light of Carlyle's genius and celebrity without being overshadowed by it; who was, in her own way, as great as he, and yet, who lived only to minister to him." Thus Miss Cushman describes their first interview:—"On Sunday, who should come self-invited to meet me but Mrs Carlyle? She came at one o'clock and stayed until eight. And such a day I have not known! Clever, witty, calm, cool, unsmiling, unsparing, a *raconteur* unparalleled, a manner *un*-imitable, a behaviour scrupulous, and a power invincible—a combination rare and strange exists in that plain, keen, unattractive, yet unescapable woman! O, I must *tell* you of that day, for I cannot write it!" The picture of the domestic scene at Cheyne Row, at tea-time, is remarkably graphic.

---

and accomplishments who, until the time of her lamented death, at an advanced age, continued to be the centre of perhaps the most intellectually brilliant circle in the society of London.

Then Carlyle would talk like no other mortal that ever was made. "Meanwhile his wife, quiet and silent, assiduously renewed his cup of tea, or by an occasional word, or judicious note, struck just at the right moment, kept him going, as if she wielded the mighty imagination at her pleasure, and evoked the thunder and the sunshine at her will. When she was alone, and herself the entertainer, one became aware of all the self-abnegation she practised, for she was herself a remarkably brilliant talker, and the stories of quaint wit and wisdom which she poured forth, the marvellous memory which she displayed, were, in the minds of many, quite as remarkable and even more entertaining than the majestic utterances of her gifted husband. It was said that those who came to sit at his feet remained at hers." Some good stories are told of the clever way in which she would prevent her husband, when absorbed in the labours he had assigned to himself, from being intruded upon by bores and lion-hunters. She had an excellent judgment in literary matters; Charles Dickens held her critical faculty in the highest esteem, and was in the habit of frequently asking her advice. She also possessed considerable artistic skill as well as taste; when her husband conceived the notion of sending to Goethe a birthday present as a token of gratitude and affection on the part of himself and a few other British disciples of the master at Weimar, it was Mrs Carlyle who designed the seal chosen for the memento. Occasionally she did a little writing on her own account; in her husband's *Life of John Sterling,* there is a reference to a piece from her pen, entitled, "Watch and Canary Bird," and we learn, from one of Dickens's letters to John Forster, dated immediately after her death, that she was engaged upon a novel, of the philosophico-analytic sort, when that event happened.*

The gratitude felt by Carlyle for the precious gift he had received in such a wife was expressed in many indirect and touching ways. The thought of his mother might have sufficed to make him, what he always was, full of a knightly courtesy to all women; but this was no doubt deepened by his happy experience as a husband, in which he had seen realised the ideal that he sketched with so much of tender grace and beauty in one of his letters written after his helpmate was gone. "I have never doubted the true and noble function of a woman in this world was, is, and forever will be, that of being Wife and Helpmate to a worthy man; and discharging well the duties that devolve on her in consequence, as mother of children and mistress of a Household, duties high, noble, silently important as any that can fall to a human creature: duties which, if well discharged, constitute woman, in a soft, beautiful, and almost sacred way, the Queen of the World, and, by her natural faculties, graces, strengths, and weaknesses, are every way indicated as specifically hers. The true destiny of a Woman, therefore, is to wed a man she can love and esteem; and to lead noiselessly, under his protection, with all the wisdom, grace, and heroism that is in her, the life prescribed in consequence." †   The sentiment so charmingly expressed

---

* "Those of her school companions who still survive say, that she was the only girl in the Latin class of the burgh school, that she was very clever, and was generally at the head of it. One school companion who still lives, remembers that he and his class fellows were continually reproached by the Rector for 'letting a lassie beat them.'"—*Standard Newspaper*, Feb. 7, 1881.

† The letter (of date 9th Feb. 1871) from which this is excerpted

in this passage found utterance on some other occasions in forms that were quaintly humorous—as, for example,

---

was addressed to Mr Robert Lawson, a medical student at Edin-burgh, in answer to a request that Mr Carlyle would state his opinion on the subject of the admission of female medical students to the classes in the University and the clinical teaching in the Infirmary—a question which had raised a furious controversy, then at its height. "It is with reluctance," replied Carlyle, "that I write anything to you on this subject of Female Emancipa-tion, which is now rising to such a height; and I do it only on the strict condition that whatever I say shall be private, and nothing of it get into the Newspapers. The truth is, the topic for five-and-twenty years past, especially for the last three or four, has been a mere sorrow to me; one of the most afflicting proofs of the miserable anarchy that prevails in human society; and I have avoided thinking of it, except when fairly compelled; what little has become clear to me on it I will now endeavour to tell you." After laying down the principle that woman's true function is that of wifehood, he continues :—"It seems furthermore indubitable that if a woman miss this destiny, or have renounced it, she has every right, before God and man, to take up whatever honest em-ployment she can find open to her in the world; probably there are several or many employments, now exclusively in the hands of men, for which women might be more or less fit;—printing, tailoring, weaving, clerking, etc., etc. That Medicine is intrinsic-ally not unfit for them is proved from the fact that in much more sound and earnest ages than ours, before the Medical Pro-fession rose into being, they were virtually the Physicians and Surgeons as well as Sick-nurses, all that the world had. Their form of intellect, their sympathy, their wonderful acuteness of observation, etc., seem to indicate in them peculiar qualities for dealing with disease; and evidently in certain departments (that of female diseases) they have quite peculiar opportunities of being useful. My answer to your question, then, may be that two things are not doubtful to me in this matter. 1st, That Women, any Woman who deliberately so determines, have a right to study Medicine; and that it might be profitable and serviceable to have facilities, or at least possibilities, offered them for so doing. But, 2d, That, for obvious reasons, Female Students of Medicine ought to have, if possible, Female Teachers, or else an extremely select kind of men; and in particular that to have young women present among young men in Anatomical Classes, Clinical Lectures, or in that chivalrous defence of what all other biographers had considered the crowning blunder of Dr Johnson's life. Carlyle could see no matter for ridicule in the marriage with the good Widow Porter, even though she was old enough to be the Doctor's mother. Rather in her love and pity for Johnson, and in his love and gratitude, he saw something that was most pathetic and sacred: "Johnson's deathless affection for his Tetty was," he declares, "always venerable and noble." Well might the husband of Jane Welsh regard as sacred that institute of marriage which had worked so well for him!

---

generally studying Medicine in concert, is an incongruity of the first magnitude, and shocking to think of to every pure and modest mind. This is all I have to say, and I send it to you, under the condition above mentioned, as a Friend for the use of Friends."

CHAPTER X.

IN HIS MOORLAND HOME——THE LIFE AT CRAIGENPUTTOCH
——LETTERS TO GOETHE, DE QUINCEY, AND CHRISTO-
PHER NORTH——PROPOSED "BOG SCHOOL" OF PHILO-
SOPHERS——EARLY PILGRIMS——WRITES THE "MISCEL-
LANIES"——HIS DEMOLITION OF JEFFREY——THE ESSAY
ON BURNS.

THERE is a story of Carlyle's boy-days, told us by a friend who spent his youthful years in the same neighbourhood, which may be mythical, but ought to be true, since it certainly answers to all that we know of the character and circumstances of the persons concerned. According to this local tradition, little Thomas had built in a retired nook of his father's farm a kind of hut for himself to study in; but as his father preferred that he should go to work instead of devoting himself exclusively to his "buiks," he sent the Laird (Mr Sharpe of Hoddam),* who happened to be calling, to order the boy to remove his hut off the ground. But the boy rose to the occasion, slammed the door on the Laird's face, and took himself to his literary studies, careless of the consequences. The

---

* Of the same line to which Charles Kirkpatrick Sharpe, called by Scott "the Scottish Horace Walpole," belonged, and which is now extinct. Matthew Sharpe of Hoddam was the friend and correspondent of David Hume; perhaps it was he who went to evict "oor Tam" from the Hut. If not, it must have been his successor.

resolute character of James Carlyle's eldest son has thus far carried him on in the path which he had so early marked out for himself; but it has been a path beset by obstacles, and wherein there has hung over him at every moment the threat of eviction. Now at length the difficulties have been removed out of the way. The little boy of the hut threatened by Sharpe of Hoddam is at length himself a Laird, free to fashion his own life, so far as that is possible for mortal. His wife's dowry, sufficient if not large, has delivered the struggling son of the peasant-farmer from the necessity of earning his bread. The days of compulsory drudgery, with birch-rod among the urchins in the school and at hack-work for the publishers, are happily ended; and he may at last shape his course in a manner consistent with his sense of personal dignity and the most efficient use of the powers with which he has been endowed.

He had already tasted the sweets of London life. "Under its ink-sea of vapour, black, thick, and multifarious as Spartan broth," he had in 1824 renewed his intercourse with Edward Irving, and met for the first time some men of note whom he was to know better in the coming years. As he had remembered so vividly certain features in the main street of Annan that met his curious gaze that morning he entered it for the first time, as a child of eight, so were there images in his mind that he had carried away with him from his first sojourn in the metropolis; and twenty-six years afterwards, when he sat down to write the *Life of John Sterling,* one of these that came back with special force was the spectacle of the Spanish Refugees, "the Trocadero swarm, thrown off in 1823," who, to the number of fifty or a hundred, perambulated, "mostly with closed lips, the broad pavements of Euston Square and the regions about St Pancras' new Church." Charles Buller's Scotch tutor must have marked them well; and the fact that he saw them will preserve their memory. "Old steel-grey heads, many of them; the shaggy, thick, blue-black hair of others struck you; their brown complexion, dusky look of suppressed fire, in general their tragic condition as of caged Numidian lions." That and many another strange sight had the young Caledonian seen in London streets, not without deep interest, as his life-like etchings attest; men of intellect, also, he had met—John Stuart Mill, we believe, amongst the number. But, in the mean time, he did not think of settling in London, great as its attractions were to the man fired by literary ambition. For a little while, after his marriage, he seems to have resided at Comely Bank, in the immediate vicinity of Edinburgh, within easy reach of the libraries and publishers, and enjoying the society (which even the leaders of London life might have envied him) of such neighbours as De Quincey and Sir William Hamilton. At this time he was completing those translations from the German which William Tait published in 1827.

In 1828, the young couple resolved to fix their abode on their own property, and accordingly betook themselves to Craigenputtoch, a farm lying in a wild solitude on the southern shore of Loch Urr, among the granite hills of Nithsdale. Out of the world in one sense; yet, after all, not so many miles from Burns's Ellisland, on the silver Nith, only fifteen miles from the town of Dumfries, and even within a comparatively manageable distance (about a day's journey on foot) from Carlyle's native village, where both father and mother were still alive to welcome their son.

It was in this mountain-home that Carlyle was to spend the next six years of his life—in deep meditation on the great problems with which he had been so long wrestling, but which still remained unsolved. Here he would enter at last on his course as an original writer, and achieve much while he prepared for the doing of more. The first picture of the place, his mode of life and the purposes he was cherishing, is given in a letter (of date 25th September 1828) addressed to Goethe at Weimar, and which was first printed in the preface to the German translation of Carlyle's *Life of Schiller*, published at Frankfort in 1830. "You inquire," writes Carlyle, "with such warm interest respecting our present abode and occupations, that I am obliged to say a few words about both, while there is still room left. Dumfries is a pleasant town, containing about fifteen thousand inhabitants, and to be considered the centre of the trade and judicial system of a district which possesses some importance in the sphere of Scottish activity. Our residence is not in the town itself, but fifteen miles to the north-west of it, among the granite hills, and the black morasses, which stretch westward through Galloway, almost to the Irish Sea. In this wilderness of heath and rock, our estate stands forth a green oasis, a tract of ploughed, partly enclosed and planted ground, where corn ripens and trees afford a shade, although surrounded by sea-mews and rough-woolled sheep. Here, with no small effort, have we built and furnished a neat, substantial dwelling; here, in the absence of a professional or other office, we live to cultivate literature according to our strength, and in our own peculiar way. We wish a joyful growth to the roses and flowers of our garden; we hope for health and peaceful thoughts to further our aims. The roses, indeed, are still in part to be planted, but they blossom already in anticipation. Two ponies which carry us everywhere, and the mountain air, are the best medicines for weak nerves. This daily exercise, to which I am much devoted, is my only recreation; for this nook of ours is the loneliest in Britain, six miles removed from any one likely to visit me. Here Rousseau would have been as happy as on his island of St Pierre. My town friends, indeed, ascribe my sojourn here to a similar disposition, and forbode me no good result. But I came hither solely with the design to simplify my way of life, and to secure the independence through which I could be enabled to remain true to myself. This bit of earth is our own : here we can live, write, and think, as best pleases ourselves, even though Zoilus himself were to be crowned the monarch of literature. Nor is the solitude of such great importance; for a stage-coach takes us speedily to Edinburgh, which we look upon as our British Weimar. And have I not, too, at this moment, piled upon the table of my little library a whole cart-load of French, German, American, and English journals and periodicals—whatever may be their worth? Of antiquarian studies, too, there is no lack. From some of our heights I can descry, about a day's journey to the west, the hill where Agricola and his Romans left a camp behind them. At the foot of it I was born, and there both father and mother still live to love me. And so one must let time work. But whither am I wandering? Let me confess to you I am uncertain about my future literary activity, and would gladly learn your opinion concerning it; at least, pray write to me again, and speedily, that I may feel myself united to you. The only piece of any importance that I have written since I came here is an *Essay on Burns.* Perhaps you never heard of him, and yet he is a man of the most decided genius; but born in the lowest ranks of peasant life, and through the entanglements of his peculiar position was at length mournfully wrecked, so that what he effected is comparatively unimportant. He died in the middle of his career, in the year 1796. We English, especially we Scotch, loved Burns more than any poet that had lived for centuries. I have often been struck by the fact that he was born a few months before Schiller, in the year 1759, and that neither of them ever heard the other's name. They shone like stars in opposite hemispheres, or, if you will, the thick mist of earth intercepted their reciprocal light."

In the preface which Goethe wisely lit up with this memorable fragment of autobiography (and which was, furthermore, illustrated with two engravings, representing Carlyle's residence among the Scottish hills), the great German poet remarks that Burns was not unknown to him; and very warmly does he commend Carlyle for the pains he has been at in realising the life and individuality, not only of Schiller, but of all the German authors whom he had introduced to the English-speaking world. That these efforts of Carlyle's had been immediately fruitful is proved by the facts which he was able to communicate, in another letter to Goethe, in the December of 1829. "You will be pleased to hear," he writes, "that the knowledge and appreciation of foreign, and especially of German, literature spreads with increasing rapidity wherever the English tongue rules; so that now at the antipodes, in New Holland itself, the wise men of your country utter their wisdom. I have lately heard that even in Oxford and Cambridge, our two English Universities hitherto looked upon as the stopping-place of our peculiar insular conservatism, a movement in such things has begun. Your Niebuhr has found a clever translator at Cambridge, and at Oxford two or three Germans have already enough employment in teaching their language. The new light may be too strong for certain eyes; yet no one can doubt the happy consequences that shall ultimately follow therefrom. Let nations, as individuals, only know each other, and mutual jealousy will change to mutual helpfulness, and instead of natural enemies, as neighbouring countries too often are, we shall all be natural friends." Amongst the various records of the intercourse that brought Craigenputtoch into such intimate relations with Weimar, not the least pleasant are several graceful messages in verse from Goethe to Mrs Carlyle, which have been included in the collected edition of the poet's works.*

In the December of the same year in which he sent to Goethe the graphic view of his life and surroundings at Craigenputtoch, he wrote a letter to De Quincey, wherein

---

* It has often been asserted that Carlyle became personally intimate with Goethe in Germany prior to the writing of the above letters; but the truth is, that Carlyle had not, as yet, visited Germany at all. The originator of the fiction, we suspect, must have been James Grant, of *Random Recollections* notoriety. While there was some excuse for the ignorance he betrayed in 1841, there is none for the recent repeaters of his idle story, since Carlyle himself, in the second appendix to his *Life of Schiller*, expressly informed his readers that he "never saw" Goethe.

some striking lines are added to the picture. We cannot
be too grateful for the fortunate preservation of this epistolary gem, which might so readily have fallen aside
beyond all chance of recovery amid the frequent flittings
to and fro of the strangely-gifted being to whom it was
addressed. We are told by De Quincey's biographer
that Carlyle, "with that generous interest in what is
original and excellent which has so honourably distinguished him throughout his long career, had, in common
with many others, asked after the 'Opium-Eater' whose
contributions had drawn so much attention to the *London
Magazine*, and had met him, while he was on visits to
Edinburgh, at the houses of Mr John Gordon and others."
Hearing that De Quincey had come to Edinburgh at this
time, he sent him the following letter, which reflects, in
its playful mirth, the sunny influences that were now
resting on the hitherto storm-tossed Sartor in the happy
haven to which he had been brought among his native
hills :—

"Craigenputtoch, 11th December, 1828.

"My dear Sir,—Having the opportunity of a frank, I
cannot resist the temptation to send you a few lines, were
it only to signify that two well-wishers of yours are still
alive in these remote moors, and often thinking of you
with the old friendly feelings. My wife encourages me
in this innocent purpose : she has learned lately that you
were inquiring for her of some female friend ; nay, even
promising to visit us here—a fact of the most interesting
sort to both of us. I am to say, therefore, that your
presence at this fireside will diffuse no ordinary gladness
over all members of the household ; that our warmest
welcome, and such solacements as even the desert does

not refuse, are at any time and at all times in store for one we love so well. Neither is this expedition so impracticable. We lie but a short way out of your direct route to Westmoreland ; communicate by gravelled roads with Dumfries and other places in the habitable globe. Were you to warn us of your approach, it might all be made easy enough. And then such a treat it would be to hear the sound of philosophy and literature in the hitherto quite savage wolds, where since the creation of the world no such music, scarcely even articulate speech, had been uttered or dreamed of ! Come, therefore, come and see us ; for we often long after you. Nay, I can promise, too, that we are almost a unique sight in the British Empire ; such a quantity of German periodicals and mystic speculation embosomed in plain Scottish *Peat-moor* being nowhere else that I know of to be met with.

" In idle hours we sometimes project founding a sort of colony here, to be called the ' Misanthropic Society ;' the settlers all to be men of a certain philosophic depth, and intensely sensible of the present state of literature ; each to have his own cottage, encircled with roses or thistles as he might prefer ; a library and pantry within, and huge stack of turf-fuel without ; fenced off from his neighbours by fir woods, and, when he pleased, by cast-metal railing, so that each might feel himself strictly an individual, and free as a son of the wilderness ; but the whole settlement to meet weekly over coffee, and there unite in their *Miserere*, or what were better, hurl forth their defiance, pity, expostulation, over the whole universe, civil, literary, and religious. I reckon this place a much fitter site for such an establishment than your Lake

Country—a region abounding in natural beauty, but blown on by coach-horns, betrodden by picturesque tourists, and otherwise exceedingly desecrated by too frequent resort; whereas here, though still in communication with the manufacturing world, we have a solitude altogether Druidical—grim hills tenanted chiefly by the wild grouse, tarns and brooks that have soaked and slumbered unmolested since the Deluge of Noah, and nothing to disturb you with speech, except Arcturus and Orion, and the Spirit of Nature, in the heaven and in the earth, as it manifests itself in anger or love, and utters its inexplicable tidings, unheard by the mortal ear. But the misery is the almost total want of colonists! Would *you* come hither and be king over us; *then* indeed we had made a fair beginning, and the 'Bog School' might snap its fingers at the 'Lake School' itself, and hope to be one day recognised of all men.

"But enough of this fooling. Better were it to tell you in plain prose what little can be said of my own welfare, and inquiry in the same dialect after yours. It will gratify you to learn that here, in the desert, as in the crowded city, I am moderately active and well; better in health, not worse; and though active only on the small scale, yet in my own opinion honestly, and to as much result as has been usual with me at any time. We have horses to ride on, gardens to cultivate, tight walls and strong fires to defend us against winter; books to read, paper to scribble on; and no man or thing, at least in this visible earth, to make us afraid; for I reckon that so securely sequestered are we, not only would no Catholic rebellion, but even no new Hengist and Horsa invasion, in anywise disturb our tranquillity. True, we have no society; but who has, in the strict sense of that word? I have never had any worth speaking much about since I came into this world: in the next, it may be, they will order matters better. Meanwhile, if we have not the *wheat* in great quantity, we are nearly altogether free from the *chaff*, which often in this matter is highly annoying to weak nerves. My wife and I are busy learning Spanish; far advanced in *Don Quixote* already. I purpose writing mystical *Reviews* for somewhat more than a twelvemonth to come; have Greek to read, and the whole universe to study (for I understand less and less of it); so that here as well as elsewhere I find that a man may '*dree his wierd*' (serve out his earthly apprenticeship) with reasonable composure, and wait what the flight of years may bring him, little disappointed (unless he is a fool) if it bring him mere *nothing* save what he has already—a body and a soul—more cunning and costly treasures than all Golconda and Potosi could purchase for him. What would the vain worm, man, be at? Has he not a head, to speak of nothing else—a head (be it *with* a hat or without one) full of far richer things than Windsor Palace, or the Brighton Teapot added to it? What are all Dresden picture-galleries and magazines *des arts et des métiers* to the strange painting and thrice wonderful and thrice precious workmanship that goes on under the cranium of a beggar? What *can* be added to him or taken from him by the hatred or love of all men? The grey paper or the white silk paper in which the gold ingot is wrapped; the gold is inalienable; *he* is the gold. But truce also to this moralising. I had a thousand things to ask concerning you: your employments, purposes, sufferings, and pleasures. Will you not write to

H

me? will you not come to me and tell? Believe it, you are well loved here, and none feels better than I what a spirit is for the present eclipsed in clouds. For the present it can only be; time and chance are for all men; that troublous season will end; and one day with more joyful, not deeper or truer regard, I shall see you 'yourself again.' Meanwhile, pardon me this intrusion; and write, if you have a vacant hour which you would fill with a good action.   Mr Jeffrey is still anxious to know you; has he ever succeeded?   We are not to be in Edinburgh, I believe, till spring; but I will send him a letter to you (with your. permission) by the first conveyance. Remember me with best regards to Professor Wilson and Sir W. Hamilton, neither of whom must forget me; not omitting the honest Gordon, who I know will not.

"The bearer of this letter is Henry Inglis, a young gentleman of no ordinary talent and worth, in whom, as I believe, *es steckt gar viel.* Should he call himself, pray let this be an introduction, for he reverences all spiritual worth, and you also will learn to love him.—With all friendly sentiments, I am ever, my dear sir, most faithfully yours,   T. CARLYLE."

So there was no small grudge lurking in the soul of Goethe's translator and prophet on account of that severe castigation of *Wilhelm Meister* which De Quincey wrote a little more than three years ago! We may rest assured that no one perceived more clearly than Carlyle himself the merit of that criticism; and, with the generosity of a large nature, that has neither time nor inclination for petty quarrels, he would be ready to forgive—probably did not bestow a second thought, except one of mirth, upon—the touch of spleen that might be perceptible in the vigorous onslaught of his critic. The only opponent who had power to make him angry for a little while was the man who, being really ignorant, yet pretended to know; and such a character could not be justly ascribed at any time, to the marvellous scholar and man of genius who was playfully invited by the greatest of his contemporaries to come and be king of the new school to be founded in the moors of Nithsdale.

A third glimpse of the gladsome, though secluded, life in that mountain home—with its stern yet tender beauties, congenial to the spirit and genius of the recluse—is furnished by Carlyle himself in a letter, of date 19th December 1829, addressed to Professor Wilson. The author of the *Noctes* had promised to spend some days at Craigenputtoch at the approaching Christmas season; and Carlyle writes to remind him that the promise is "not forgotten here." He and Wilson had met only once—in the house of John Gordon, a favourite pupil of the Professor's; and, when we take the slightness of their acquaintance into consideration, it will be perceived that Carlyle was not merely genial, but positively exuberant, in his friendly hospitable overtures. "Come, then," he exclaims, "if you would do us a high *favour*, that warm hearts may welcome in the cold New Year, and the voice of poet and philosopher, *numeris lege solutis*, may for once be heard in these deserts where, since Noah's Deluge, little but the whirring of heath-cocks and the lowing of oxen has broken the stillness. You shall have a warm fire and a warm welcome; and we will talk in all dialects, concerning all things, climb to hill-tops, and see certain of the

kingdoms of this world,* and at night gather round a
clear hearth, and forget that winter and the devil are so
busy in our planet." The writer then proceeds to give,
in detail, information as to the links that connect the
place with the busy world of man from which they have
escaped. There is a mail-coach nightly to Dumfries
passing close by, and two stage-coaches every alternate
day to Thornhill, from each of which places they are
fifteen miles distant, with a fair road and plenty of
vehicles procurable in both towns. "Could we have
a warning, we would send you down two horses; of
wheel carriages (except carts and barrows) we are still
unhappily destitute." But perhaps Christopher, noted
as a great pedestrian—he thought nothing of a walk from
Oxford to London in his student days—would be disposed to do without horses and carriages or stage-
coaches either. "Nay, in any case, the distance"—
that is, from Dumfries or Thornhill—"is but a morning walk, and this is the loveliest December weather
I can recollect of seeing." It is added, that "we
are at the Dumfries Post Office every Wednesday and
Saturday." The seclusion could hardly have been more

---

* It was on one of these Galloway hills a shepherd told an
English tourist that he would see "sax kingdoms." When they
got to the summit, asked to prove this extraordinary statement by
the sceptical Southerner, he pointed out in succession—Cumberland,
in England; the Isle of Man, once a sovereignty in the families of
Derby and Athole; the coast of Ireland; and the ground on which
they were standing, part of Scotland. "Yes, that makes four,"
said the Englishman; "but you have two more to show me."
"That's true, sir; but don't be in a hurry. Just look up aboon yer
head, and that is by far the best of a' the kingdoms—that, sir,
aboon is Heeven. That's five; and the saxth kingdom is below
yer feet, and to it I hope ye'll never gang; but that's a point on
which I canna speak wi' ony certainty."

complete in any part of the British Island south of the Grampians. "I have not seen one *Blackwood*, or even an Edinburgh newspaper, since I returned hither. Scarcely have tidings of the *Scotsman-Mercury* duel reached me, and how the worthies failed to shoot each other, and the one has lost his editorship, and the other still continues to edit." That ridiculous duel, fought between Charles Maclaren, the geologist, who was also the conductor of the *Scotsman*, and Dr James Broune,* editor of the *Caledonian Mercury*, had happened on the 12th November; but the news of it took close upon five weeks to travel to Craigenputtoch, so that the laughter of all Scotland over the incident must have been clean exhausted before Carlyle had his guffaw, with sardonic commentary on the fact—which he, perhaps, regarded as slightly calamitous—that neither of the combatants had succeeded in slaying the other. A delicate compliment

---

* Broune, who was an LL.D., seems to have been a versatile creature. Originally a schoolmaster and then a preacher in his native county of Perth, he passed advocate in 1826; took to writing for Constable, edited the ancient *Mercury*, then started *North Britain*, and contributed to the seventh edition of the *Encyclopædia Britannica*. He is remembered as the author of a *History of the Highlands and the Highland Clans*, and in Edinburgh as the exposer of the West Port Murders, a feat accomplished a couple of years before he called out Maclaren, one of the least belligerent of men. The poor LL.D. wore himself out soon, dying at 48. He is all the more entitled to brief notice here, since we find him again alluded to by Carlyle in his reminiscences of Sir William Hamilton, contributed to Professor Veitch's Life of the great metaphysician. Broune was no doubt the newspaper editor, "the author of some book on the Highlands," who was known in Edinburgh society by the sobriquet of Captain Cloud, "from his occasionally fabulous turn." The poor "Captain," who turned up at literary parties frequented by Carlyle, about 1832-3, had evidently been an object of some slight interest to Sartor.

closed the epistle to Wilson. Mrs Carlyle, he was told,
" still hopes against hope that she will wear her Goethe
brooch this Christmas, a thing only done when there is a
man of genius in the company." But Christopher North
never saw Craigenputtoch, and, indeed, Carlyle and he
never met but once after the first introduction. " Either
want of opportunity, or other circumstances," says Mrs
Gordon in the Life of her father, "prevented the
continuance of personal friendship." When the professor
received that charming letter, so brimming over with the
humanities, he had read a certain essay, now known to
all the world, on Burns, which had appeared that very
year in the great Whig review; yet in the *Noctes* for
April 1829, there is a colloquy on Burns, in which
Carlyle is not so much as named, or even alluded to,
while the Shepherd is allowed to say, " You've written
better about Burns yoursel', sir, *nor onybody else breathin'.*
That you hae—baith better and aftener—and a' friends
of the poet ought to be grateful to Christopher North."
In the instalment for April 1830, there is a panegyric of
the *London Magazine,* put into the mouth of De Quincey,
in which the "chief supporters" of that periodical are
specified, down even to Reynolds, and "the most amiable and ingenuous Aytoun"—not the author of the *Lays
of the Scottish Cavaliers;* but not a syllable is said of
Carlyle and his *Life of Schiller.* In August of 1834,
North says :—" Goethe's idolators—mind ye, I exclude
Thomas Carlyle and Hayward, and all minds of *that
order and stamp*—are, of course, not Christians, and use
a heathenish lingo worse than the unknown tongue." In
the index to the four volumes of the *Noctes,* we may note
in conclusion, Carlyle's name does not appear.

Though neither De Quincey nor Wilson were able to visit Craigenputtoch, many friends, and also strangers desirous of seeing the new teacher who had so profoundly touched their spirits, found their way thither from time to time; so that even in his mountain fastness Carlyle was not altogether cut off from the world. In the letter to Wilson, he makes incidental allusion to the circumstance that "an Oxonian gigman" was coming to visit him in an hour; and such pilgrims from afar were no uncommon phenomena at the farm. Of course, there would be long stretches of time when the young couple had the place all to themselves, and the only variety given to the day would be supplied by the long walk taken together over the moors, or the ride on horseback to some more distant part of the vast domain beyond their little estate which they might no less call their own, so far as the enjoyment of its picturesque aspects was concerned. Sometimes there would be the unexpected arrival of an old friend or a new pilgrim, and one of the domestics, or Mrs Carlyle herself, would be obliged hastily to mount a pony and go forth in search of provisions to meet the unlooked-for demand. But even when these calls upon their hospitality were least frequent, the time would not hang heavy upon their hands; for much work was being done in that plain apartment of the farm-house—now shewn with so much pride to visitors—in which, as the crowning effort of those quiet years, the immortal *Sartor* was written. It has been too much the habit to speak and even write of the time spent on the Dumfriesshire moors as if it were merely a period of preparation and waiting; it was, in fact, a time of splendid achievement. From his settlement here dates the beginning of Carlyle's course as an original writer. It was at Craigenputtoch that he wrote the essays which constitute much of his very finest work; and here also he began and finished the most creative effort of his genius. From the letter to De Quincey it would be perceived that its writer was then in friendly communication with the other leading assailant of Goethe; and this reminds us that Carlyle was now enrolled on the staff of the *Edinburgh Review.* The year following his marriage was the one that witnessed his admission to Jeffrey's company by the appearance in the 91st number of the " Blue and Yellow " of that article on Richter which now stands first in the initial volume of his *Critical and Miscellaneous Essays.* The publication of this essay was the beginning of a connection which lasted for about four years, terminating with the publication of the article entitled *Characteristics* in 1831, in the 108th number of the *Edinburgh.* As we shall see presently, the six or seven years that were chiefly spent at Craigenputtoch also produced much good work of a kindred sort for other reviews as well as for *Fraser's Magazine;* and, although it might be true when he wrote his letter to Goethe in the September of 1828 that "the only piece of any importance" he had produced in his mountain solitude was the *Essay on Burns,* even that achievement of this epoch of his life sinks into a position of minor importance when we recollect that the Nithsdale hermitage was the birthplace of *Sartor Resartus.* This, in the coming years, will be what Scotch divines are in the habit of calling the grand " outstanding " fact in connection with Craigenputtoch. Long after our century has ended, pilgrims from many a land will visit that moorland shrine as they go to look at the bridge in Bedford town on which, it has been thought, stood the prison where John Bunyan wrote his *Pilgrim;* and they will regard it as much more than the seed-bed of future achievements, though it is doubtless true that, besides being rich in fruit, the years of retirement in that wilderness formed a preparation for the work that was yet to be performed in the mighty Babel on the banks of the Thames. " There he unravelled the tangled skein of his thoughts. There he laid up stores of knowledge, of health, of high resolutions for the work lying before him. There, in a solitude peopled only by books and thoughts and the companionship of his wife, and converse with some congenial stranger, he laid the sure foundations of a life which was destined to be so complete."*

The article on Jean Paul was followed up in the next number of the *Edinburgh* by the essay on *German Literature*, of which it has been said that it "at once entitled the young reviewer to a place among the first critics of the age"—a remark that might have been expressed in stronger terms without exaggeration of the truth. It entitled him to a place above them all. How these articles, especially the second, came to be accepted by the Editor, is a problem we cannot pretend to solve. Not only did they run counter to the views of Jeffrey and the other members of the Whig circle gathered around him ; the second of these articles, as Mr Ballantyne pointed out in his brief sketch of Carlyle, actually dared to attack " the prince of critics " for his abuse of Goethe, and, furthermore, asserted the claims of genius in a fashion that must have been deemed flat rebellion by the habitués of Holland House. In his article on *Wilhelm*

---

* *The Times Newspaper*, Feb. 7, 1881.

Meister, Jeffrey had poured contempt upon the German authors for their alleged bad taste, which he ascribed to the assumed fact that they did not enjoy the privilege of moving in good society. "Their works smell," he said, "as it were, of groceries—of brown papers filled with greasy cakes and slices of bacon—and fryings in back parlours. All the interesting recollections of childhood turn on remembered tit-bits, and plundering of savoury store-rooms. . . . The writers as well as the readers of that country belong almost entirely to the plebeian and vulgar class. Their learned men are almost all wofully poor and dependent; and the comfortable burghers, who buy entertaining books by the thousand at the Frankfort Fair, probably agree with their authors in nothing so much as the value they set on those homely comforts to which their ambition is mutually limited by their poverty, and enter into no part of them so heartily as those which set forth their paramount and continual importance." Thus, to an old cuckoo-cry raised against the Germans by the French, "at once their plunderers and their scoffers," the superficial writer who was controlling the public taste of Britain added a vulgar sneer at poverty— the outcome of a spirit which may have been contracted, along with his mincing attempts at English pronunciation, in the London drawing-rooms of the aristocratic Whigs. Such a theory as the one formulated against the German authors came with a bad grace from a critic who had planned his Review in a " flat " of what was then the most unsavoury town in Europe, who had at the outset "culti-vated literature on a little oatmeal," and the furnishing of whose house when he entered on his married life did not cost more than fifteen pounds. The recluse of Craigenputtoch, reared in the same hardy school as Burns, made short work of the snobbish theory that authors who live in mean houses, and are unfamiliar with "the polish of drawing-rooms," must therefore think and write in a mean style. He might have insinuated a contrast between German poets then living who were the familiar companions of princes, and the British poets who deemed themselves in Elysium if permitted once a brief accidental interview with the poorest creature who ever wore the name of king; but he took higher ground. "Is it, then, so certain," he asks, in one of the noblest passages he ever wrote, "that taste and riches are indissolubly connected? That truth of feeling must ever be preceded by weight of purse, and the eyes be dim for universal and eternal Beauty, till they have long rested on gilt walls and costly furniture? To the great body of mankind this were heavy news; for, of the thousand, scarcely one is rich, or connected with the rich; nine hundred and ninety-nine have always been poor, and must always be so. We take the liberty of questioning the whole postulate. We think that, for acquiring true poetic taste, riches, or association with the rich, are distinctly among the minor requisites; that, in fact, they have little or no concern with the matter. Taste, if it mean anything but a paltry connoisseurship, must mean a general susceptibility to truth and nobleness; a sense to discern, and a heart to love and reverence, all beauty, order, goodness, wheresoever or in whatsoever forms and accompaniments they are to be seen. This surely implies, as its chief condition, not any given external rank or situation, but a finely-gifted mind, purified into harmony with itself, into keenness and justness of vision; above all, kindled into

love and generous admiration. Is culture of this sort
found exclusively among the higher ranks? We believe
it proceeds less from without than within, in every rank.
The charms of Nature, the majesty of Man, the infinite
loveliness of Truth and Virtue, are not hidden from the
eye of the poor; but from the eye of the vain, the cor-
rupted and self-seeking, be he poor or rich. In old ages,
the humble Minstrel, a mendicant, and lord of nothing
but his harp and his own free soul, had intimations of
those glories, while to the proud Baron in his barbaric
halls they were unknown. Nor is there still any aristocratic monopoly of judgment more than of genius: for
as to that *Science of Negation*, which is taught peculiarly
by men of professed elegance, we confess we hold it
rather cheap. It is a necessary, but decidedly a subordinate accomplishment; nay, if it be rated as the
highest, it becomes a ruinous vice. . . . . . Are the
fineness and truth of sense manifested by the artist
found, in most instances, to be proportionate to his
wealth and elevation of acquaintance? Are they found
to have any perceptible relation either with the one or the
other? We imagine, not. Whose taste in painting, for
instance, is truer and finer than Claude Lorraine's? And
was not he a poor colour-grinder; outwardly the meanest
of menials? Where, again, we might ask, lay Shakspeare's rent-roll; and what generous peer took him by
the hand and unfolded to him the 'open secret' of the
Universe; teaching him that this was beautiful, and that
not so? Was he not a peasant by birth, and by fortune
something lower; and was it not thought much, even in
the height of his reputation, that Southampton allowed
him equal patronage with the zanies, jugglers and bear-

wards of the time? Yet compare his taste, even as it respects the negative side of things; for, in regard to the positive and far higher side, it admits no comparison with any other mortal's,—compare it, for instance, with the taste of Beaumont and Fletcher, his contemporaries, men of rank and education, and of fine genius like himself. Tried even by the nice, fastidious and in great part false and artificial delicacy of modern times, how stands it with the two parties; with the gay triumphant men of fashion, and the poor vagrant linkboy? Does the latter sin against, we shall not say taste, but etiquette, as the former do? For one line, for one word, which some Chesterfield might wish blotted from the first, are there not in the others whole pages and scenes which, with palpitating heart, he would hurry into deepest night? This too, observe, respects not their genius, but their culture; not their appropriation of beauties, but their rejection of deformities, by supposition the grand and peculiar result of high breeding! Surely, in such instances, even that humble supposition is ill borne out. The truth of the matter seems to be, that with the culture of a genuine poet, thinker or other artist, the influence of rank has no exclusive or even special concern. For men of action, for senators, public speakers, political writers, the case may be different; but of such we speak not at present. Neither do we speak of imitators, and the crowd of mediocre men, to whom fashionable life sometimes gives an external inoffensiveness, often compensated by a frigid malignity of character. We speak of men who, from amid the perplexed and conflicting elements of their everyday existence, are to form themselves into harmony and wisdom, and show forth the same wisdom to others that exist along with them. To such a man, high life, as it is called, will be a province of human life, but nothing more. He will study to deal with it as he deals with all forms of mortal being; to do it justice, and to draw instruction from it: but his light will come from a loftier region, or he wanders forever in darkness; dwindles into a man of *vers de société*, or attains at best to be a Walpole or a Caylus. Still less can we think that he is to be viewed as a hireling; that his excellence will be regulated by his pay. 'Sufficiently provided for from within, he has need of little from without:' food and raiment, and an unviolated home, will be given him in the rudest land; and with these, while the kind earth is round him, and the everlasting heaven is over him, the world has little more than it can give. Is he poor? So also were Homer and Socrates; so was Samuel Johnson; so was John Milton. Shall we reproach him with his poverty, and infer that, because he is poor, he must likewise be worthless? God forbid that the time should ever come when he too shall esteem riches the synonym of good! The spirit of Mammon has a wide empire; but it cannot, and must not, be worshipped in the Holy of Holies. Nay, does not the heart of every genuine disciple of literature, however mean his sphere, instinctively deny this principle, as applicable either to himself or another? Is it not rather true, as D'Alembert has said, that for every man of letters, who deserves that name, the motto and the watchword will be FREEDOM, TRUTH, and even this same POVERTY; that if he fear the last, the two first can never be made sure to him?"

The richness of their information and the depth of their thought must have constituted the sole reason for the acceptance of articles containing such unwelcome revolutionary sentiments as these. They came like fresh moorland breezes, laden with the fragrance of the heather, into the close, sickly atmosphere of the crowded city. But, though his editorial tact was sufficient to cause Jeffrey not to reject contributions so valuable, the acceptance must have been made with a wry face; and we have sufficient grounds for concluding that he failed to perceive, at least with the clearness that is possible to any reader to-day, how completely they annihilated very much that he himself had written. Could he have foreseen the terrible force of the contrast that would be visible in after days, between the shallow conventionalities that flowed from his own pen, and the strong original criticism of this new writer who was actually at the pains to ascertain, and who had the courage to speak, the truth, it is scarcely possible that his virtue would have sufficed to grant admission to the essays of Carlyle. If he had even half-realised their real nature and potentiality, in reference to his own reputation, his acceptance of them would have been an act of self-denying heroism without a parallel in the history of "able editors." There is, however, abundant evidence to show that he did not apprehend their significance. It has been said, and not without some reason, that Jeffrey "had the courage to recant notions when he came to think them wrong, and the moral principle always to prefer truth to consistency;" but, on the other hand, we have the mournful assurance from his own pen, that he did not comprehend Carlyle, and that, so far as he did perceive his drift, he did not like him. "I fear Carlyle will not do," he writes to Macvey Napier, his successor in the editorship in 1832, "that is, if you do not take the liberties and pains with him that I did, by striking out freely, and writing in occasionally. The misfortune is, that he is very obstinate, and, I am afraid, very conceited." And then the ex-dictator adds, with a compassionate sigh, "It is a great pity, for he is a man of genius and industry, and *with the capacity of being an elegant and impressive writer.*" Four years had elapsed since the publication of the essay on *German Literature;* and all that this "prince of critics" can see, even now, in the shaggy recluse of Nithsdale is a "person of talents," who seems to have "the capacity" of becoming by-and-by, if he would only listen to the good advice of Jeffrey and Macvey Napier, "an elegant and impressive writer!" A worse turn for Jeffrey's memory was surely never done, than when this unfortunate private epistle of his was disinterred from the repositories of his successor; but we at least may forgive the indiscretion, since it makes the whole case of Carlyle's connection with Jeffrey so clear to us to-day.

The third contribution of "the very obstinate and very conceited" contributor was the best article on its particular subject that has yet been written, and the noblest on any subject which the *Edinburgh Review* has ever been honoured to convey to the world. The *Essay on Burns* appeared in the 9th number, in 1828. The contrast between this and Jeffrey's own article on the same subject, published in 1809, is, if possible, even more striking than that between the Goethe article of the editor and the essay in which one of its main contentions was so effectively disposed of. The general scope and tendency of Jeffrey's critique is indicated by the passage in which he says "that the leading vice in the character of Burns, and the cardinal deformity indeed of *all* his productions "—including, we suppose, the *Cottar's Saturday Night*, *Tam o' Shanter*, the *Vision*, and all his lyrics —"is his contempt for prudence, decency, and regularity, and his admiration of thoughtlessness, oddity and vehement sensibility; that he represents himself as a hair-brained sentimental soul, constantly carried away by fine fancies and visions of love and philanthropy, and born to confound and despise the cold-blooded sons of prudence and sobriety; that he is perpetually making a parade of his thoughtlessness, inflammability, and imprudence, and talking with much complacency and exultation of the offence he has occasioned to the sober and correct part of mankind; that this odious slang infects almost all his prose and a very great proportion of his poetry, and communicates to both a character of immorality at once contemptible and hateful; and that his apology is to be found in the original lowness of his situation, and the slightness of his acquaintance with the world."* Even Henry Mackenzie, writing in 1786, had formed a truer conception of the new-fledged poet than this, and had been enlightened enough to rebut the charge that Burns's works breathed a spirit of libertinism and irreli-

---

* It is impossible not to recall the words of the poet describing how he "listened, and trembled, in blasting anticipation, at the idea of the degrading epithets that malice or misrepresentation might affix to his name," and how he foresaw the "future hackney scribblers, who, with the heavy malice of savage stupidity," would exultingly assert "that Burns, notwithstanding the *fanfaronade* of independence to be found in his works, was quite destitute of resources within himself to support his borrowed dignity, dwindled into a paltry exciseman, and slunk out the rest of his insignificant existence in the meanest of pursuits, and among the lowest of mankind."

gion. "We shall not look upon his lighter Muse," said the *Lounger*, "as the enemy of religion, of which in several places he expresses the justest sentiments, though she has sometimes been a little unguarded in her ridicule of hypocrisy." The tide of calumny, swollen by an editor whose motives were pure and kindly, but whose judgment was not strong enough to resist the prevalent prejudice and do justice to the Bard; still further increased by such articles as those of Walter Scott in the *Quarterly* and Jeffrey in the *Edinburgh*, was at length turned back by Carlyle, who gave the interpretation of Burns that is now accepted universally by all persons of good sense and good feeling. The continued acceptance of that interpretation is placed beyond doubt, not because of the charming style in which the essay is written, but because its force and beauty as a composition are, if possible, surpassed by the truth of its substance. It has been urged by some of Carlyle's censors that he seems to think that real knowledge of mankind is to be derived rather from the imagination than from the understanding, and some one has said that he seldom gives a complete view of any man whom he attempts to pourtray—that his portraits, if powerful, are partial, and powerful just because they are partial. We cannot imagine a more groundless complaint; and how very wide of the mark it is may be discovered by a critical study of this essay on Burns. Read all that has been written by and about the poet, spend years in gathering the traditions respecting him which yet linger in his native province, recall every fragment of information you may have derived from that now nearly exhausted company of witnesses who personally knew the man; and after you have done all this, you will be constrained to say that no more complete and just, as well as striking, delineation of the Ploughman-Bard is possible than we find in Carlyle's Essay on his great countryman. It has been the theme of universal praise, and of the thousands of essays, articles, and orations that have been written since 1828 on the same theme, it may perhaps be said without injustice to them or the truth, that not one of them has escaped reproducing, either consciously or unconsciously, the ideas and the feelings that were first uttered in his matchless Essay by Carlyle.

Even Jeffrey himself was no exception to the rule. He felt, if he did not expressly own, the constraining power of the essay. Nearly ten years after it was published, we find him sitting down at Craigcrook to study anew the life and works of Burns. The result is such as might have been expected if he had never seen them before. He tells Empson that he has read them "not without many tears." "What touches me most," he continues, "is the pitiable poverty in which that gifted being (and his noble-minded father) passed his early days—the painful frugality to which their innocence was doomed, and the thought, how small a share of the useless luxuries in which *we* (such comparatively poor creatures) indulge, would have sufficed to shed joy and cheerfulness in their dwellings, and perhaps to have saved that glorious spirit from the trials and temptations under which he fell so prematurely. Oh my dear Empson, there must be something *terribly* wrong in the present arrangement of the universe, when those things can happen, and be thought natural. I could lie down in the dirt, and cry and grovel there, I think, for a century, to save such a soul as Burns from the suffering, and the contamination, and the *degradation* which these same arrangements imposed upon him; and I fancy that if I could but have known him in my present state of wealth and influence, I might have saved, and reclaimed, and preserved him, even to the present day. He would not have been so old as my brother judge, Lord Glenlee, or Lord Lynedoch, or a dozen others that one meets daily in society. And what a creature, not only in genius, but in nobleness of character, potentially, at least, if right models had been put *gently* before him. When I think of *his* position, I have no feeling for the *ideal* poverty of your Wordsworths and Coleridges; comfortable, flattered, very spoiled, capricious, idle beings, fantastically discontented because they cannot make an easy tour to Italy, and buy casts and cameos; and what poor, peddling, whining drivellers in comparison with him!" There is not a word here about that "very obstinate" and "very conceited" fellow from Craigenputtoch; but of one thing we may rest assured—this noble letter to Empson would never have been written if the lessons taught by Carlyle had not sunk deep into the heart of Jeffrey. Less worthy was the attempt of the old editor of the *Edinburgh* to appropriate some of the credit due to the writer of the epoch-making essay. In one of his letters, written in 1838, but not published till after his death, Charles Sumner says :—" I observed to Lord Jeffrey, that I thought Carlyle had changed his style very much since he wrote the article on Burns. 'Not at all,' said he; 'I will tell you why that is different from his other articles— *I altered it.'*" Some living critics have professed to find in this story a confirmation of what they had always thought, but which none of them, so far as we are aware, had ever expressed till Sumner's letter was printed. A careful study of Carlyle's writings does not support the theory. Jeffrey may possibly have cut something out; we are certain he put nothing of his own in. There is not a sentence in the essay that does not bear, both as to its form and substance, the signet mark of Carlyle; moreover, he was not the man ever to put his name to any bit of work, however microscopic, that was not his own.

By no writer has the essay been more accurately described than by one of Burns's later and most competent editors, Alexander Smith, who declares that it "stands almost alone in our literature as a masterpiece of full and correct delineation." The same authority gives as the main reason why it occupies this position of pre-eminence, the fact that Carlyle has succeeded so admirably in detecting the unconscious personal reference in the literary productions of the Scottish Bard. He "makes this line or the other a transparent window of insight, through which he obtains the closest glimpses of his subject." One other reason is doubtless to be found in the fact that the essayist's own birth and upbringing were, in so many respects, akin to those of the poet; so that personal experience quickened the sympathy, without which there can be no true comprehension of the life of our fellow-man, and thus provided windows of insight, even more transparent than the poet's verse.

CHAPTER XI.

IN his letter to Professor Wilson, Carlyle had said, "I have some thoughts of beginning to *prophesy* next year, if I prosper; that seems the best style, could one strike into it rightly." The articles he was writing for the *Edinburgh*, the *Foreign Quarterly*, and *Fraser* represented by themselves an amount of literary activity that might have sufficed, without any further prophetic business, to engross the years in which they were produced; but there is reason to believe that simultaneously he had been, from the very outset of his settlement at Craigenputtoch, occupied also with *Sartor Resartus*. True, he has himself told us that it was "undoubtedly written among the mountain solitudes in 1831;" but we apprehend this meant no more than that it was completed in that year. It is said to have been re-written more than once, which we can very well believe; and several years (five, according to some authorities) were at least partially devoted to its composition. These stories about its genesis are quite likely to have more than a grain of truth in them; thus much is certain, that its mental production was not the work of one solitary year, even though that year had been crushed full of the most strenuous toil directed exclusively to the one end. It must ever be regarded as one of the most striking facts in the literary annals of this nation, that *Sartor*, completed in 1831, could not get itself published in book form, at least in its native country, till 1838! Its birth, therefore, as a printed book, was even a more protracted agony than its completion in a written form—a circumstance that must appear all the more remarkable to any one who is at the trouble to look back and note what kind of literature was being poured from the English press during those seven years in which this new candidate was kept standing at the gate. Yet we need scarcely marvel that the publishers looked askance at a work that bore no resemblance to any printed book extant at that hour in the English tongue. It would probably be a hard task to get a publisher to-day for anything so completely novel in style and substance; and the chances against the acceptance of such a violent departure from the conventional standards were still greater fifty years ago. In that very year which saw *Sartor* ready for the press, the *Edinburgh Review* had felt itself compelled to give Carlyle notice to quit, the essay entitled *Characteristics*, richly laden with the loftiest thought expressed in the noblest language,*

---

* "It is a grand article, fuller of high thought than anything of the like sort ever seen in the *Edinburgh Review* before or since, and more closely packed with Carlylese ideas, or the germs of them, than any of its author's pages elsewhere—germs subsequently to be seen full-blown in *Sartor Resartus* and his later books, and expanded

having proved too much for its feeble digestion. If an article in the *Sartor* vein frightened Professor Napier, who, to do him justice, must be called a very good friend to Carlyle, how much greater was the excuse for the publishers who declined to undertake the task of launching an entire volume, written in the same unheard-of, volcanic style; wherein more than the wildest liberties of the most daring poet were taken by an author who yet had cast his work in the mould of prose; added to which flagrant departure from the standards of the still reigning Addison, were the sky-piercing flights of imagination, mingled in the oddest way with reflections that seemed vulgar in their exceeding homeliness. It was a new experiment in more than language; and, apart from its substance, the form was sufficient to frighten even the professional "taster" who had discernment enough to perceive that its author must be a man of genius. There would be a suspicion as to the sanity of the writer haunting the mind of the least conventional of this class of men; the majority would have no doubt whatever that he must be mad. Not without some natural touches of scorn, Carlyle has told how the publishers "to a man, with that total contempt of grammar which Jedediah Cleishbotham also complained of, 'declined the article.'" When he did ultimately get

---

upon the nodosities and angularities of the mature oaken Carlylese style; such, for example, as his oft-repeated lamentation that the 'Godlike has vanished from the world;' that a Byron finds occupation in 'cursing his day;' a Shelley in filling the earth with 'inarticulate wail,' as if of forsaken infants; a Hazlitt in digging wells that yield desert sand, but no water; and a sceptical Frederick Schlegel gives his life to doubt, and returns at the end of it to Catholicism, like a child who has roamed all day over a silenced battle-field, going back at night to the breast of its dead mother."—*The Scotsman Newspaper*, Feb. 7, 1881.

it out in book form, in 1838, he appended a grimly-humorous set of " Testimonies of Authors," which many readers no doubt regarded as purely fictitious ; but when reprinting these, thirty years afterwards, he prefixed a note, wherein it was intimated, *inter alia*, that they actually contained " some straggle of real documents."   The first " taster " cited admits, as Jeffrey had done in the *Edinburgh* a few years before, that the editor of *Sartor* is " a person of talent," but complains of his " want of tact," and also of the heaviness of his wit, which "reminds one of the German Baron who took to leaping on tables, and answered that he was learning to be lively."   He wants to know if the work is really a translation.   The leading bookseller, echoing his taster, thinks that " only a little more tact is required" by the writer to produce " a popular as well as an able work."   We cannot say whether the newspaper criticism is authentic ; but the *Sun* points out a sentence in the work " which may be read either backwards or forwards, for it is equally intelligible either way ; indeed, by beginning at the tail, and so working up to the head, we think the reader will stand the fairest chance of getting at its meaning."   The author had most likely sent the manuscript to Edinburgh, in the first instance ; and the gossips have always concluded that there must have been at least a couple of rejections there—a notion sure to be inferred from the circumstance that two of his three previous books (we do not count *Legendre*) had been issued by two separate firms in the Scottish capital.   Then the wider field of London was next tried, with no better result, till at length the disgusted author "gave up the notion of hawking his little manuscript book about any further."   So he wrote in 1832, adding that for a long time it had lain quiet in a drawer waiting for a better day. "The bookselling trade seems on the edge of dissolution; the force of puffing can no further go, yet bankruptcy clamours at every door; sad fate! to serve the Devil, and get no wages even from him! The poor Bookselling Guild, I often predict to myself, will ere long be found unfit for the strange part it now plays in our European world; and will give place to new and higher arrangements, of which the coming shadows are already becoming visible." It helps to mitigate the rigour of our judgment against the rejectors of the volume to learn that such a man as John Stuart Mill, who was by this time a personal friend of Carlyle's, at first shared their incapacity to appreciate the book. "Even at the time when our acquaintance commenced," says Mr Mill, "I was not sufficiently advanced in my new modes of thought to appreciate him fully; a proof of which is, that on his showing me the manuscript of *Sartor Resartus*, his best and greatest work, which he had just then finished, I made little of it; though when it came out about two years afterwards in *Fraser's Magazine* I read it with enthusiastic admiration and the keenest delight."

Its publication in that periodical during 1833-34 is said to have been effected through the friendly help of Dr John Carlyle, physician to the Duke of Buccleuch. The reception accorded to it by the readers of "Regina" cannot be described as favourable; and the painful fact was frankly acknowledged in a paragraph tagged on at the close: "Here can the present editor, with an ambrosial joy as of over-weariness falling into sleep, lay down his pen. Well does he know, if human testimony be worth aught, that to innumerable British readers likewise, this is a satisfying consummation; that innumerable British readers consider him, during those current months, but as an uneasy interruption to their ways of thought and digestion; and indicate so much, not without a certain irritancy and even spoken invective. For which, as for other mercies, ought not he to thank the Upper Powers? To one and all of you, O irritated readers, he, with outstretched arms and open heart, will wave a kind farewell." The publisher, it is said, had reported to the author that the magazine was getting into trouble because of the articles. The most of its readers seemed to be pretty much of the same mind as the indignant nobleman who inquired of Mr Fraser when " that stupid series of articles by the crazy tailor" were to end, as his patience was all but exhausted. Only two subscribers had written in a contrary sense, the one a Roman Catholic priest at Cork, the other " a Mr Emerson, in America;" about the latter of whom Carlyle was to learn more presently.

The truth is that America was much quicker than his own country in recognising the genius of Carlyle. Youth is more open-minded and receptive than old age; and not seldom the Republic of the West has been before the mother country in true perception of the merit of new authors as they have arisen in the Old Home. Beyond the sea the fugitive works of De Quincey and Charles Lamb were collected with pious care, from our own magazines and newspapers, years before they could be obtained in England; and other cases might easily be named in which the daughter's loving appreciation has rebuked the mother's cold neglect. Less under the sway of the conventional standards which he set at defiance, the students of the United States were not so apt as those of Britain to resent the audacities of the editor of Teufelsdröckh. Carlyle's articles in the *Edinburgh* and other reviews had instantly attracted earnest attention, and elicited the most cordial praise, on the other side of the sea. In the *North American Review*, so early as 1835, we find its proprietor and editor, Alexander H. Everett, venturing the opinion that their author is "destined to occupy a large space in the literary world;" and in the following year, 1836, *Sartor* received at Boston the honour denied it as yet in England. Heralded by the appreciative review of Everett, and superintended in its passage through the press by a young man of kindred genius, Ralph Waldo Emerson, who wrote an introduction for it, the book commanded an immediate popularity; and the name of Carlyle was familiar all over the Western world before it had become much known in England. "We have heard it insinuated," wrote Mr Everett in 1835, "that Mr Carlyle has it in contemplation to visit this country, and we can venture to assure him that, should he carry this intention into effect, he will meet with a cordial welcome." Pressing invitations had been sent to him by Emerson and other leading writers to pay their country a visit; and he actually had a mind to accept—was, indeed, on the point of arranging for the voyage—when an unhappy accident to a certain manuscript volume of his, of which we shall hear anon, thrust the plan aside for the time being, and the opportunity— or the compliant mood rather—never came back again. But he never forgot that day when, equally to his amazement and delight, there came to him from Boston a copy of his first great work in the form of a book, and along with it a kindly letter enclosing a cheque for a handsome sum in payment of the right to publish *Sartor* in America. Often, in conversation, would he revert to that incident; and in the note appended in 1868 to the edition of *Sartor* in his collected works, after relating how the "questionable little book" could not for more than seven years appear as a volume in England, "and had at last to clip itself in pieces, and be content to struggle out, bit by bit, in some courageous magazine that offered," he adds that the first English edition, of 1838, had had "the way opened" for it by "an American or two American."* It ought to be added that the *Miscellaneous Essays* were also issued in book form in the United States before they had assumed that shape in England; nor will it be out of place to insert here a note of the fact that the first money Carlyle ever received for his *French Revolution* also came from America. In 1838, conversing with Charles Sumner, he said, " the strangest thing in the history of literature was his recent receipt of fifty pounds from America, on account of his *French Revolution*, which never yielded him a farthing in Europe, and probably never would." In this expectation Mr Carlyle was happily disappointed, for the work named must have been a source of large pecuniary profit during the more than forty years that intervened

---

* When it at last came out as a book in England, it was stated on the title-page to have been "reprinted for friends." One of the most interesting letters in the *Correspondence of Macvey Napier* is one written by Carlyle in 1831, where, speaking of *Sartor*, he says : " All manner of perplexities have occurred in the publication of my poor book, which perplexities I could only cut asunder, not unloose; so the MS., like an unhappy ghost, still lingers on the wrong side of Styx ; the Charon of —— Street durst not risk it in his *sutilis symba*, so it leaped ashore again."

between its publication and his death. From oral state
ments heard from his own lips at a later date than
Sumner's visit, it would appear that he received further
payments from America for the *French Revolution*; he
had got as much as £130 from that source when the
work had "brought him no penny" in England. It
was always a source of regret to his American friends
that he never carried out his early purpose to visit the
United States; and, in view of some things written by
him in later years, we are, perhaps, justified in the conclusion that the loss was more his own than theirs. At
one time we heard it stated by visitors from America
who had been conversing with him about their country,
that he had hinted the existence of some plan in his
mind that would prove the reality of the gratitude which
he cherished for the early recognition he had received
in America when he was still struggling against the *vis
inertia* of the old country.*

---

* On his seventy-second birthday, Mr Emerson was visited by a
company of Methodist ministers, and Carlyle having been spoken of
in course of conversation as no friend of the United States during
the great Civil War, Mr Emerson replied :—"Let me tell you,
friends, what is a little secret. He is a very good friend of the
Americans, and has testified it lately by an act which is not to be
made public until he dies and his will appears. But some of our
best men and women have made his acquaintance. He is a man
of the world. He does not belong to this or that country only, but
by his broad genius and talent of satire, which he throws about him,
he is cosmopolitan ; but his aims are as good as can be. I think
Mr Carlyle really sympathises with us. I remember his scolding
a little in the war, but not afterwards. I have been in constant correspondence with him ever since 1833 or '34, I think. I
have a hundred letters from him running along that period, and
his sympathies are with us. Mr Norton, of Cambridge, has preserved every word in his memory of his personal conversations with

The last, as it is also the fullest and most valuable, account of the life at Craigenputtoch is supplied by the American friend who wrote the introduction for the Boston edition of *Sartor*. Emerson's first visit to Britain was made forty-seven years ago, when he was in his thirtieth year, and he has himself put upon record two facts—first, that he had then felt himself greatly indebted to the men of Edinburgh, Scott, Jeffrey, Playfair, and De Quincey; and, secondly, that he came to Scotland chiefly that he might see the faces of three or four writers, of whom Carlyle and De Quincey were two. Landing in the Thames, he was soon on the Clyde, penetrated into the Highlands, and on his way back he took the coach from Glasgow to Dumfries, whence he proceeded to the farm of Craigenputtoch to deliver a letter to its Laird which he had brought with him all the way from Rome, and which was probably from the Laird's brother, Dr Aitken Carlyle. That first meeting of the two sages took place in the August of 1833. How the American visitor walked and talked with Carlyle—the latter at one moment expatiating on the talent shown by his pig, and the next discoursing on the immortality of the soul—Emerson has himself related in a pleasant chapter of one of his books, published many years afterwards:—" No public coach passed near it, so I took a private carriage from the inn. I found the house amid desolate heathery hills, where the lonely scholar nourished his mighty heart. Carlyle was a man from his youth, an author who did not need to hide from his readers, and as absolute man of the world,

---

Mr Carlyle, and I have insisted that he should write them down to be saved. There is great wit in his talk. He despises every kind of meanness, every kind of selfishness and of petty sin."

unknown and exiled on that hill-farm, as if holding on his own terms what is best in London. He was tall and gaunt, with a cliff-like brow, self-possessed, and holding his extraordinary powers of conversation in easy command; clinging to his northern accent with evident relish; full of lively anecdote, and with a streaming humour, which floated everything he looked upon. His talk playfully exalting the familiar objects, put the companion at once into an acquaintance with his Lars and Lemurs, and it was very pleasant to learn what was predestined to be a pretty mythology. Few were the objects and lonely the man, 'not a person to speak to within sixteen miles except the minister of Dunscore;' so that books inevitably made his topics.

" He had names of his own for all the matters familiar to his discourse. *Blackwood's* was the 'sand magazine;' *Fraser's* nearer approach to possibility of life was the 'mud magazine;' a piece of road near by that marked some failed enterprise was the ' grave of the last sixpence.' When too much praise of any genius annoyed him, he professed hugely to admire the talent shown by his pig. He had spent much time and contrivance in confining the poor beast to one enclosure in his pen, but pig, by great strokes of judgment, had found out how to let a board down, and had foiled him. For all that, he still thought man the most plastic little fellow in the planet, and he liked Nero's death, ' *Qualis artifex pereo !*' better than most history. He worships a man that will manifest any truth to him. At one time he had inquired and read a good deal about America. Landor's principle was mere rebellion, and *that* he feared was the American principle. The best thing he knew of that country was, that in it a man can have meat for his labour. He had read in Stewart's book, that when he inquired in a New York hotel for the Boots, he had been shown across the street, and had found Mungo in his own house dining on roast turkey.

"We talked of books. Plato he does not read, and he disparaged Socrates ; and, when pressed, persisted in making Mirabeau a hero. Gibbon he called the splendid bridge from the old world to the new. His own reading had been multifarious. *Tristram Shandy* was one of his first books after *Robinson Crusoe*, and Robertson's *America* an early favourite. Rousseau's *Confessions* had discovered to him that he was not a dunce ; and it was now ten years since he had learned German by the advice of a man who told him he would find in that language what he wanted.

" He took despairing or satirical views of literature at this moment ; recounted the incredible sums paid in one year by the great booksellers for puffing. Hence it comes that no newspaper is trusted now, no books are bought, and the booksellers are on the eve of bankruptcy.

" He still returned to English pauperism, the crowded country, the selfish abdication by public men of all that public persons should perform. 'Government should direct poor men what to do. Poor Irish folk come wandering over these moors. My dame makes it a rule to give to every son of Adam bread to eat, and supplies his wants to the next house. But here are thousands of acres which might give them all meat, and nobody to bid these poor Irish go to the moor and till it. They burned the stacks, and so found a way to force the rich people to attend to them.'

K

"We went out to walk over long hills, and looked at Criffel, then without his cap, and down into Wordsworth's country. There we sat down, and talked of the immortality of the soul. It was not Carlyle's fault that we talked on that topic, for he had the natural disinclination of every nimble spirit to bruise itself against walls, and did not like to place himself where no step can be taken. But he was honest and true, and cognizant of the subtle links that bind ages together, and saw how every event affects all the future. 'Christ died on the tree; that built Dunscore kirk* yonder; that brought

---

* "In that Kirk, in Burns's day, there laboured a Mr Kirkpatrick, a Calvinistic clergyman of the old school, whose public teaching was in inverse ratio and dismal antithesis to his private benevolence. He was a blameless and good man; but his doctrine made Burns, not unaccustomed to the habit, to 'blaspheme an octave higher,' and to cry out, 'From such conceptions of my Creator, good Lord deliver me.'"—*Gilfillan's Life of Burns.* The minister seems to have taken a petty revenge on his critic. Burns had got up a library in the parish, but, in the account of the place which the Rev. Mr Kirkpatrick supplied for Sir John Sinclair's great statistical work on Scotland, this fact, so creditable to the poet, was deliberately suppressed. Gilfillan, sketching Burns's Nithsdale home, says:—"A few miles from Ellisland, to the northwest, lies a fine undulating country, stretching towards the little village of Dunscore; on the south are the hills of Irongray, a bold and rugged range; in the valley at their feet, in the centre of a wood, stands the monument erected by Sir Walter Scott to Helen Walker, the prototype of Jeanie Deans; and in the midst of these lies Craigenputtoch, the property and once the dwelling-place of Thomas Carlyle—a gloomy place, we are told, with its dark firs around and melancholy moors behind, reminding visitors, who are also readers, of the pine-shadowed and moated castle where Maturin describes his dark Knight of the Forest keeping his state, and conversing at the portals with those doomed ones who came to consult him and inhale all hell through his half-shut vizor, as

'Rolls the rich thunder of his awful voice'

in that

'Infernal colloquy sublime,'

you and me together. Time has only a relative existence.'

"He was already turning his eyes towards London
with a scholar's appreciation. London is the heart of
the world, he said, wonderful only from the mass of
human beings. He liked the huge machine. Each
keeps its own round. The baker's boy brings muffins to
the window at a fixed hour every day, and that is all the
Londoner knows or wishes to know. on the subject. But
it turned out good men. He named certain individuals,
especially one man of letters, his friend, the best mind he
knew, whom London had well served."

Though it had been so long utterly rejected at the outset by the publishers in the country where it was written,
and for some years after its appearance failed to make an
adequate impression save on the minds of a select few,
the book that will henceforth be associated with Carlyle's
sojourn among the grim hills of Nithsdale gradually grew
in favour with the English public, and came at last to be
regarded as the greatest work of its author, perhaps the
greatest of our century. The estimation in which it was
held by the man who wrote it was silently but impressively indicated when, placing it out of its chronological
order, he made it the first volume of his collected works.
"Written in star fire and immortal tears," it has been
called by some the *Pilgrim's Progress* of the nineteenth
century; and as a picture of the conflict of the human
soul battling with the haggard spirits of Doubt and Fear,

---

and who remained his vassals and victims for ever more." Pilgrims
to this shrine of Sartor may, perhaps, be reminded of the saying of
Carlyle, that the enthusiastic minister of Dundee "painted with a
big brush."

as these present themselves to so many under the changed conditions of modern society, it has certainly never been equalled. To classify this book would be no easy task. As we have already seen, it is a real, though veiled, autobiography—much more authentic, indeed, than a large number of the works that expressly call themselves by that name ; but it is also a romance, still more an exposition of its author's mystic philosophy, and, most of all, a poem, though not written in verse. It gives expression to the ultimate thought of Carlyle on those great problems of Religion and Life that he endeavoured to work out for himself in the shadow of the mountains, whither he had turned in quest of a faith that should take the place of the one he had lost. As he made that search with the earnestness of a nature that was Knox-like in its intensity, and recorded the results in a form that unites the tenderness and melody of a Scottish ballad with a stately grandeur of style that not one of the great masters of English prose has ever surpassed, we can hardly wonder that the book should often lay hold of other spirits, especially such as are in a state of unrest, with a force that makes their opening of *Sartor* the beginning of a new epoch in their lives. How many on both sides of the sea will find a record of their own experience in the words of the blind Methodist preacher, Milburn, when he exclaims, " Ah, Thomas Carlyle, you have much to answer for, in sending adrift upon the fog-banks such raw and inexperienced boys as I was when your mighty genius found me out. Many a day of miserable doubt and night of morbid wretchedness have you caused me. Yet, for all that, I owe you more and love you better than any author of the time.

Sartor Resartus first fell in my way while I was living in Washington, and I much question if Christopher Columbus was more transported by the discovery of America, than I was in entering the new realm which this book opened to me. Everything was novel, huge, grotesque, or sublime: I must have read it twenty times over, until I had it all by heart. It became a sort of touch-stone with me. If a man had read *Sartor*, and enjoyed it, I was his friend; if not, we were strangers. I was as familiar with the everlasting 'nay,' the centre of indifference, and the everlasting 'yea,' as with the side-walk in front of my house. From Herr Teufelsdröckh I took the Teutonic fever, which came nigh costing me so dear." And happily the number is not few of those who can add, in the words of the same writer, "Years have passed since he led me forth to the dance of ghosts, and I have learned to read him with a less feverish enthusiasm ; but, I believe, with a more genuine appreciation of his rare and extraordinary powers. He did me harm, but he has helped me to far more good. With all his defects, to me he stands first among the men of this generation."* Even those for whom the spiritual guidance of John Bunyan still suffices, gladly acknowledge the help they have received from Teufelsdröckh, as to the conduct of their lives—the high practical value of the lessons he communicates on domestic and social duty, on culture and work, on fidelity to conscience, courage, and morality; and, if they lament the vagueness of his teaching in its reference to Christianity, they are yet consoled by the all-pervading purity of its tone as well as by the sublime

---

* *Ten Years of Preacher-Life*, by William Henry Milburn. 1859.

hopefulness that illumines the page when, emerging from the "everlasting No" which threatened to engulph the pilgrim after he had lost the faith of his fathers, he attained at length to the "everlasting Yea" of heroic work and duty, and was able to say, "The universe is not dead and demoniacal, a charnel-house with spectres; but God-like, and my Father's."

To all who have read it without adverse prepossessions, and in the sympathetic spirit that is essential to the proper understanding of any author, *Sartor* seems invariably to have proved one of the most wholesomely stimulating of books. Both Maurice and Kingsley acknowledged that it did them a greater service than any other work they ever read; and the latter sought to extend its influence by expounding its fundamental lessons in more than one of his novels, more especially in *Yeast* and *Alton Locke.* The saintly Thomas Erskine of Linlathen, who was wont warmly to recommend its perusal to his friends, found precious nutriment in it for a spiritual nature of rare strength and refinement. In the year of its publication as a book, we find him writing to his sister, "I thought you would like *Sartor;* the chapter on natural supernaturalism, Book iii. chap. 8, is a wonderful thing." To Erskine it appeared good "to be brought in contact with a mind like Carlyle's, so unconventional in all matters;" and he declared, "I love the man. He has a real belief in the invisible, which in these railroad and steam-engine days is a great matter. He sees and condemns the evil and baseness of living in the lower part of our nature instead of living in the higher." Similar testimonies from eminent Christian teachers of our time might easily be multiplied. While these men have regarded its author with veneration as a prophet recalling the Church to a sense of forgotten truths, and awakening it from a false reliance on the merely mechanical use of dogma, there have been other classes of readers who have admired this wonderful book for its philosophy, or its humour, or its literary style ; and it is worthy of note that in many of the busy hives of manufacturing industry it has been long a favourite with the more thoughtful working-men. These have been attracted not merely by the keen sympathy which it exhibits with the "toil-worn craftsman," but by the realism which pervades it from the first page to the last, by its suggestions of radical reform in the organisation of society, and the fraternal spirit of pity for the weak and wayward which distinguishes it so pleasantly from some of the author's later works.

That there has been, on the other hand, not a little adverse criticism of the work, both on account of its teaching and style, must be hereafter shewn ; but, meanwhile, we hasten to close that portion of the record which relates to the epoch of Carlyle's life that is associated with the lonely farm house in which *Sartor* was born. How fruitful that period had been, the reader will perceive who duly weighs, besides numbering, the essays written at Craigenputtoch, not only for the periodicals already named, but also for the *Westminster Review*, to which Carlyle had begun contributing in 1831. Life had been varied, of course, during the performance of all this work by occasional visits to Edinburgh, and latterly to London in search of a publisher for *Sartor*. In 1832-33 the little household transferred itself to Edinburgh for the winter, and entered into the mild dissipations of the season, attending pleasant literary parties at Captain Hamilton's, and also, amongst others, at the house of Sir William, his brother. It was at the hospitable board of the metaphysical baronet that Carlyle, one evening, astonished both host and company by resolutely refusing to take more for his supper than one potato; that being "an epoch," as Carlyle himself explains, " when excellent potatoes yet were." He was present at the Royal Society on the evening when Sir William read his famous paper on Phrenology, which so completely demolished George Combe, and, as we might expect, Carlyle was a cordially approving auditor. In the April of 1833, the Carlyles returned to their moorland home. But the time was approaching when, for the reasons stated to Emerson, they must bid that home farewell. Carlyle was now contemplating work that could not possibly be achieved in solitude. He who would write a history of the French Revolution must have the best libraries within easy reach. And so it came about that, on one of the opening days of July 1834, Carlyle was writing to Sir William Hamilton, telling him that "the hope of ever seeing him at Craigen- puttoch had now vanished into the infinite limbo." The epistle was dated from the writer's London home. The two friends, the greatest Scottish thinkers of their generation, never met again, though mementoes occasion- ally passed between them. "From the ever-silent whin- stones of Nithsdale to the mud-rattling pavements of Piccadilly, there is but a step;" and now that step had been taken. We are on the threshold of a fresh epoch in the career of the patient toiler, who at length is recognised on all hands as one of the foremost of the literary leaders, if not the first, of his time.

One point, however, remains to be noted before we close the record of the life in Nithsdale. To Carlyle, we cannot doubt, one of the sweetest features of that life had been the opportunity it furnished of enjoying, from time to time, the society of his venerated parents, and of ministering, personally, to their happiness as their years declined. When the time came for his departure to distant scenes, he could not repeat what he had said in his letter to Goethe six years before. The mother, indeed, still lived to love him; but his good old father was gone. We have already seen how bitterly Carlyle lamented his absence from home at the time his father died, and how the occasion of that absence—a visit to London in the futile hunt after a publisher for *Sartor*—added a new sting to the mortifying early story of that book; a sting which was still felt acutely by him, even after he had himself become an old man. There can be no doubt, however, that in the years immediately preceding the death of his father, the son's residence in the vicinity had often brought them together, to their great mutual comfort. With all his relatives, indeed, even in later years, and down to the time of his death, he preserved a close and most affectionate intimacy; and of the way in which he entered into their affairs, sympathising keenly with them in all their trials, and doing his best to further their interests, we have one affecting and profoundly impressive token before us. The first visitation of our country by cholera has made 1832 one of the best remembered dates in the domestic history of the nineteenth century; and nowhere did that year make a more indelible impression than in the town of Dumfries. So severely was it stricken, beyond any town in the kingdom in proportion to its size, that many communities, in England as well as Scotland, joined in a subscription to assist it in fighting the merciless foe. As many as forty-four deaths took place in a single day. The scenes witnessed in the burgh, according to the local historian, were such as it had never witnessed before, though often in the olden times had it been desolated by the fiends of war. What added to the horror, when the disease was at the worst, for days a canopy of black clouds hung over the town, like a funeral pall let down from heaven, to intimate that it was doomed to utter destruction; and in an atmosphere so dense that they could hardly breathe, the people gave themselves up for lost. It was on the 4th of October that this ghastly "cholera cloud" was dispersed at last by a tremendous thunderstorm, which sounded "like voice of judgment from the sky;" but though the atmospheric change sent a ray of hope into hearts that had been crushed beneath the grief and terror of the previous weeks, it was the middle of November before the fell destroyer stayed his hand. Upwards of a thousand persons had been attacked; and nearly seven hundred perished in that burgh of Dumfries and the suburb on the opposite bank of the Nith.* It was in the very midst of this dreadful visitation that Carlyle wrote the following letter to a brother of his mother's resident in the devoted town; and even those who may be most disposed to question the speculative views of the author of *Sartor Resartus*, will admit that there is here such evidence of

---

* For a detailed account of this visitation, the severity of which arose no doubt from the situation of the town, and its previous total neglect of all sanitary law, see the *History of the Burgh of Dumfries*, by William M'Dowall. 1872.

practical piety, of a faith capable of sustaining the soul under the severest of earthly trials, as may well excite their admiration, if not their envy also, and at least mitigate the rigour of their censure. The letter was addressed to "Mr John Aitken, mason, Friars' Vennel, Dumfries :"—

"Craigenputtoch, 16th October, 1832.

"My Dear Uncle,—Judge if I am anxious to hear from you! Except the silence of the Newspapers I have no evidence that you are still spared. The Disease, I see, has been in your street : in Shaw's ; in James Aitken's ; it has killed your friend Thomson: who knows what farther was its appointed work! You I strive to figure in the meanwhile, as looking at it, in the universal terror, with some calmness, as knowing and practically believing that your days and the days of those dear to you, were now, as before and always, in the hand of God only ; *from* whom it is vain to fly ; *towards* whom lies the only refuge of man. Death's thousand doors have ever stood open ; this indeed is a wide one, yet it leads no further than they all lead.

"Our Boy was in the town a fortnight ago (for I believe, by experience, the infectious influence to be trifling, and quite inscrutable to man ; therefore go and send whithersoever I have *business*, in spite of cholera); but I had forgot that he would not naturally see Shaw or some of you, and gave him no letter; so got no tidings. He will call on you to-morrow, and in any case bring a verbal message. If you are too hurried to *write* in time for him, send a letter next day 'to the care of Mrs Welsh, Templand, Thornhill ;' tell me only that you are all spared alive !

"We are for Annandale after Thornhill, and may possibly enough return by Dumfries. I do not participate in the panic. We were close beside cholera for many weeks in London : 'every ball has its billet.'

"I hear the disease is fast abating. It is likely enough to come and go among us; to take up its dwelling with us among our other maladies. The sooner we grow to compose ourselves beside it the wiser for us. Man who has reconciled himself *to die* need not go distracted at the *manner* of his death.

"God make us all ready; and be His time ours! No more to-night.—Ever your affectionate

"T. CARLYLE."

The Mrs Welsh named in this letter was the mother-in-law of Mr Carlyle, who had retired in her widowhood to Templand. Her husband had died at Haddington in 1819, and was succeeded in his practice there by a younger brother, Dr Benjamin Welsh. Some of the older inhabitants of Thornhill and its vicinity preserve a vivid recollection of Mrs Welsh, whom they describe as an old lady of singular beauty and a charming manner. She often had the company of her daughter and son-in-law, who would come over from Craigenputtoch to pass a few days, or even weeks, with her; and memories of the immortal Sartor abound in the district, one of the still surviving inhabitants, a professional gentleman, shewing with pride a copy of Count D'Orsay's portrait of Carlyle received from his wife.

———0———

CHAPTER XII.

HIS LONDON HOME — THE CHARM OF CHELSEA — ITS LITERARY MEMORIES—SARTOR ON THE PLATFORM— LECTURES ON GERMAN HISTORY, THE HISTORY OF LITERATURE, REVOLUTIONS OF MODERN EUROPE, AND HERO-WORSHIP — SKETCHES OF HIS ORATORY BY LEIGH HUNT, GOSSIP GRANT, CHARLES SUMNER, AND MARGARET FULLER—HISTORY OF THE FRENCH REVOL- UTION—HOW THE MS. OF THE SECOND VOLUME WAS BURNED AND RE-WRITTEN.

WHEN Carlyle had got the length of speaking so freely, especially to a visitor whom he had never seen before, of his purpose to " flit" from Nithsdale, we may be sure that his mind was made up on the subject ; so in a few months from the date of that conversation with Emerson, the hermit of Craigenputtoch had struck his tent and moved away to pitch it in the great Babylon on the banks of the Thames.   There he took up his abode in the house No. 5 (now re-numbered 24) Cheyne Row, Chelsea, where he continued to reside down to the day of his death —that is, for the long space of forty-seven years.   He was now verging on forty, and, in spite of the longevity of the race from which he sprang, it is scarcely possible he could have anticipated that the larger half of his earthly pilgrimage was yet to come, and that for well on to half a century he would be a dweller in this new Chelsea home.   Nor is it easy to conceive of any spot

in all the vast and varied expanse of the mighty city,
unless it be, perhaps, some of the pleasant hermitages
on the Northern heights about Hampstead or Hornsey
Rise, that would have better suited the new citizen of
London who was destined soon to become known to the
whole English-speaking populations of the world as "the
Sage of Chelsea."* Of course, this may be in some
degree a fancy, springing from the fact that ever since we
first heard of him, it was the fashion to employ the above
familiar sobriquet; yet, those who know London best,
will probably concur in the notion that the site he chose
in that summer of 1834, and to which he ever afterwards
clung with all the tenacity of his home-loving nature, was,
indeed, the most appropriate on which he could have hit.

This nook near the river, lying between Chelsea
Hospital and Cremorne, is the richest in literary associations of all the suburbs of London. Here dwelt the
author of *Utopia*, more than three hundred years ago,

---

* This title, almost oftener applied to Carlyle for many years in
the newspapers than his proper name, roused the patriotic ire of
Professor Blackie, who, in one of his characteristic addresses, rebuk-
ing Cockney presumption, spoke of "that strong, deep-mouthed,
shaggy-bseasted Titan, Thomas Carlyle, who, though now among
the Southerns generally known as the 'Chelsea Prophet,' is literally
a sturdy Dumfries peasant, and has no more to do with Chelsea than
I have to do with Cheltenham." If the sobriquet was incongruous,
Carlyle's own countrymen were not themselves free from blame in
the matter, since they used it no less habitually than did the
English. They had better reason, perhaps, to resent the phrasing
of the tribute to Carlyle's memory which appeared the week after
his death in *Punch*, where he was apostrophized as

"England's philosopher! old Chelsea's sage!"

And yet the most intensely patriotic Scot must own that the substitu-
tion of Ecclefechan or Craigenputtoch for Chelsea would not be
unattended with difficulty.

and here he held frequent discourse with his friend Erasmus; while from the days of Sir Thomas More, down to our own, it has continued to be a favourite home or haunt of eminent men of letters, in this respect surpassing any other spot that can be named in the British islands. The great essayists of Queen Anne's time, Swift, Addison, and Steele, were familiar figures in this suburb when Carlyle's house was being built; Boyle, Locke, and Arbuthnot knew the region well; so did Goldsmith and the Walpoles. Old Sir Hans Sloane has left his name linked with the oldest square and the finest street in the district, while his body lies within a stone's-throw of Carlyle's house, in the little, closely-packed parish churchyard. A noble plane tree and the remains of a fine Cedar of Lebanon on the other side of Carlyle's house indicate the site of the Botanic Gardens founded so long ago as 1674 by the Society of Apothecaries—a little plot of ground shut in on the landward side by lofty walls, within which much good work has been, and still continues to be, done. The tomb of Bolingbroke is to be seen across the water in that ancient church of St Peter's from which Battersea, by familiar processes of the vulgar tongue, derives its name; and close by the church, in the sleepy little High Street, that might be a bit of a country town, you see the schoolhouse that was founded by the great statesman's grandfather, Sir Walter St John, with his arms over the gateway and underneath them the inscription, "Rather Deathe than false of Faythe." Quiet, indeed we might almost say somnolent, picturesque in a high degree, with charming outlooks on park and river, Chelsea abounds in quaint, antique houses and dignified, heart-moving associations, and, with the help of the river and the trees and gardens, preserves even to the present hour a sort of fresh country air about it. The low tone of the red-brick terraces is cool and grateful to the artistic eye. There is nothing new and showy, no air of "rawness and recency," to use a characteristic phrase of Dr Chalmers's, about this suburb; and each old house has a history. Even in Lawrence Street, now peopled by very poor folk, you may find traces of the mansion in which Smollett found a retreat for himself, his wife, and his little daughter, when he settled down as a literary worker in London. This bore the name of Monmouth House in those days; a detached villa, with a garden extending behind it, of which Smollett has himself given a description in *Humphrey Clinker*, it derived its name from the fact that it had been occupied in Queen Anne's time by that Duchess of Buccleuch who became Duchess of Monmouth by her alliance with the unfortunate son of Charles II. It is a singular coincidence that the great Scottish humourist of the eighteenth century should have written *Ferdinand Count Fathom* and his *History of England* within a few yards of the very spot where the still greater Scottish Master of Humour in the nineteenth century wrote all his greatest books except *Sartor*. No. 119 Cheyne Walk, a humble two-storeyed brick house, was the residence of the Shakespeare of English art in his latter years, chosen by the great painter that he might give himself up to the enjoyment of the soft effects upon the still reaches of the Thames (effects which probably were part of the attraction that drew Carlyle thither too). Turner added to the house a balcony that is still extant, and it was in that house the forlorn old man—mean and miserable, in spite of his greatness as a painter—passed away from earth. At No. 4 Cheyne Walk, Maclise, the artist, lived and died. Leigh Hunt, who was attracted thither by Carlyle's influence, resided in Upper Cheyne Row, within a stone's-throw of Carlyle's house—a convenient distance when duns or tax-collectors were pressing, and the generous Scot, after the manner of his "canny" countrymen, had to come to the rescue. In 1877 good Mrs Senior died in Cheyne Walk, cut off in the very midst of her devoted labours on behalf of the prisoners and the poor; and Frances Power Cobbe still lives there, while for a little space towards the close of her life it was also the home of that greatest of all the female authors of England who was taken from us in the same year as Carlyle. William Bell Scott, the brother of David, true poet as well as artist, is an old resident in the Walk; and for a short period it could boast of Whistler as a denizen, one memorial of his Chelsea days that is not without interest, whatever its real value, being a portrait by him of his most illustrious neighbour. Till within a year or two of Carlyle's decease there lived in the same King's Road region another octogenarian writer, not without merit in his lines of playwright and archæologist, the vivacious Planché, who seemed as if he would never grow old; and nearer still to Carlyle's house, though included in the Brompton district, is the residence of his friend Mr Froude. The erudite Mrs Sommerville was once a resident in the same suburb; and among the poets who have their abode in the region at present we may name Dante Rossetti, who resides at No. 16 Cheyne Walk, and the Hon. Leicester Warren, son of Lord de Tabley. That Carlyle was not insensible to the literary associations of the region is proved by the letter which

L

he wrote at the very outset of his London life to Sir William Hamilton, in which he said: "The house pleases us much; it is in the remnant of genuine *old* Dutch-looking Chelsea; looks out mainly into trees. We might see at half a mile's distance Bolingbroke's Battersea; could shoot a gun into Smollett's old house (at this very time getting pulled down), where he wrote *Count Fathom.* Don Saltero's coffee-house still looks as brisk as in Steele's time; Nell Gwynn's boudoir, still bearing her name, has become a gin temple, not inappropriately; in fine, Erasmus lodged with More in a spot not five hundred yards from this. We are encompassed with a cloud of witnesses, good, bad, indifferent."

Serious changes, no doubt, came over the district, more especially during the last decade; but, if these detracted from the charm that drew him thither, Carlyle of all residents had the slightest reason to complain, since to a great extent he had himself been, however unintentionally, their occasion. His name imparted a fresh lustre to the ancient suburb, and this unquestionably tended to increase the favour with which it was viewed by new settlers in the metropolis, more especially such as belonged to the literary or the artistic class. What Walter Scott did by his poems and romances for the rent-rolls of the Highland lairds, was done by its sage for property in Chelsea. So sensible of this were the local vestrymen, that they spoke of him with as much respect as if he had not been an author or a man of genius, and actually, in re-naming one of their finest squares, gave it that of Carlyle. Right in front of his house, though behind a high wall and having their entrance from an adjoining street, a huge block of Model Dwellings, almost as grim as Milbank Prison, had been reared; but Cheyne Row, amid all the growth of the surrounding population, still retained the monastic seclusion of a cathedral close, and put one in mind of a sleepy back street in some country town. For many years no small proportion of the stray passengers who might be seen sauntering on its pavement were people who had come, often from distant parts of the country, or even from the other side of the sea, to look at the dwelling-place of Carlyle; and usually they had some difficulty in realising that the narrow, three-storeyed, old-fashioned little house marked No. 5 could indeed be the place they had come so far to see. Its exceeding homeliness was only relieved by the marks which proclaimed it to be a relic of the reign of Anne; and those who were privileged to pass within found that the interior was not without a simple, old-world dignity often absent in the more pretentious structures of the Victorian age, while at the rear there was a large garden, with a fine feeling of antiquity in its red brick walls. For many years that garden was carefully tended by Mrs Carlyle, who planted in it primroses from Scotland—sent, as we have seen, by Sir George Sinclair all the way from Thurso—which still bloom there as each spring comes round. With all its seclusion and rusticity, the abode of Carlyle was near the heart of the great city. You may walk from it to Piccadilly or the Houses of Parliament in half an hour, to South Kensington and Hyde Park in less; and at the Pier close by at Old Battersea Bridge, beloved of Doré and Whistler, you find a brisk little steamer ready every fifteen minutes to take you to the Temple or to London Bridge. Carlyle knew what he was about when he chose his residence; and we do not wonder that he remained there through all the years of his London life. At one time, indeed, he did think of removing, as we learn from Miss Martineau, who, in her *Autobiography*, has left us one of the most pleasant glimpses of the Chelsea home. She described it as "the house which Carlyle was perpetually complaining of and threatening to leave, but where he is still to be found." She never believed that the Carlyles could flourish on that Chelsea clay, so close to the river, and earnestly entreated them to settle on a gravelly soil. Forth Thomas did go, on a fine black horse, in search of a rural hermitage, "with three maps of Great Britain and two of the World in his pocket, to explore the area within twenty miles of London;" but he came as he went; the lease, which had expired, was quietly renewed, and there, in spite of Miss Martineau's fears, he was spared to celebrate, within the old familiar walls, the eighty-fifth return of the anniversary of his birth.

When he first came hither, the recluse of Craigenputtoch, now a mature man of nearly forty, with habits chiefly formed among the mountains, felt it the strangest transition; "but one uses himself to all," as he remarked in the letter written at the time to Sir William Hamilton. "We have broken up our old settlement, and, after tumult enough, formed a new one here, under the most opposite conditions. Our upholsterers, with all their rubbish and clippings, are at length handsomely swept out of doors. I have got my little book-press set up, my table fixed firm in its place, and sit here awaiting what time and I, in our questionable wrestle, shall make out between us." One of the last things we should have looked for, from all that we have seen of the man, now happened. No doubt, one of the traditions of his boy-hood, picked up at Ecclefechan, speaks of a gift of oratory he displayed on a certain occasion, much to the astonishment of his father and all the neighbours; but Sartor on the platform is an apparition for which we are hardly prepared. In the summer of 1837, however, he actually stood forth in that character by delivering a series of six lectures on "German Literature" at Willis's Rooms, the first being given on Tuesday, the 2nd of May. The hall was crowded, yet the audience was correctly described by the few newspapers that took notice of the event as "select." Though his writings were familiar to the leaders of thought, he was as yet hardly known even by name to the great bulk of his countrymen. At that date he would have secured a much more com-posite audience at Boston or in any other New England town. The daily newspapers of London were as much in the dark about him as the mass of the people; and it is to the weekly *Spectator*, then edited by its founder Rintoul, who began life as a printer's boy at Dundee, and was therefore not ignorant of his great countryman, that we must turn for an account of the impression made by Carlyle as a lecturer. From the brief report given in the number of that journal for May 6, it appears that the opening lecture consisted of a history and character of the Germans, whom he described as the only genuine European people unmixed with strangers. The mere fact of the great, open, fertile country they inhabit never having been subdued, showed the masculine character of the race; indeed, the grand characteristic of the Teutonic intellect was *valour*, by which he meant, not mere animal courage, common to all races of men, but that cool, dogged, onward, indomitable perseverance, under good and evil repute, under circumstances untoward or propitious, by which alone great things are ultimately achieved. Among individual examples of this quality, he mentioned Kepler and his calculations, Milton and his *Paradise Lost.* Of national examples he gave the conquest of England, the settlement of America by the conquerors of England; the conquest of India, and the colonisation of the new continent of Australia by the same people. As to the manner of the lecturer, we are told by the same journal that, while "deficient in the mere mechanism of oratory," this minor defect was far more than counterbalanced by Carlyle's "perfect mastery of his subject, the originality of his manner, the perspicuity of his language, his simple but genuine eloquence, and his vigorous grasp of a large and difficult question." The opinion was also expressed that no person of taste or judgment could hear him without feeling that he was "a man of genius, deeply imbued with his great argument." Even the uncouth gossipmonger of the day, James Grant, from Elgin, was impressed by the strength of this strange new orator. "This course of lectures," says he, in his *Portraits of Public Characters*, "was well attended by the fashionables of the West End; and though they saw in his manner something exceedingly awkward, they could not fail to discern in his matter the impress of a mind of great originality and superior gifts." It is a fact not without significance, as illustrating the comparative smallness of the circle to which Carlyle's fame was yet confined in his own country, that even in the exceptionally enlightened *Examiner* and *Spectator* no

mention was made of the remaining lectures of the
series.   It is stated that he had prepared ample and
careful notes of the first of his lectures, intending to
do little more than read them ; but he very soon found
himself stumbling among them, when, casting them
aside, he proceeded extemporaneously, without trouble,
and much to the delight of his audience.   In the
following year, encouraged by the success of the ex-
perimental course, he gave a second series of lectures
at the Literary Institute, 17 Edward Street, Portman
Square ; his subject this time, "On the History of
Literature, or the Successive Periods of European Culture."   The first was delivered on Monday, April 30,
and they were continued on the Mcnday and Friday
of each succeeding week.   " He again extemporises,"
wrote Leigh Hunt in the *Examiner* ; " he does not read.
We doubted, on hearing Monday's lecture, whether he
would ever attain, in this way, the fluency as well as the
depth for which he ranks among the celebrated talkers in
private ; but Friday's discourse relieved us.   He strode
away like Ulysses himself, and had only to regret, in
common with his audience, the limits to which the
hour confined him.   He touched, however, in his
usual masterly way, what may be called the mountain-
tops of his subject—the principal men and themes.   We
had Troy, Persia, and Alexander ; Philip, 'a managing,
diagrammatic man.'   The Greeks in general, whose
character he compared with that of the French—the
Greek religion, which he looks upon as originating in
the worship of heroes, 'ultimately shaped by allegory,'
with destiny at the back of it (a great dumb, black
divinity that had no pity on them, and they knew not

what it was, only that it pitied neither gods nor men). Prometheus, 'a taciturn sort of personage,' who 'does not knowingly howl over any trouble;' Homer, whose individuality was undone by Wolff, in the year 1780, but whose aggregate (the Homeric poets) are unequalled by any subsequent poets in the world. Æschylus, 'a gigantic man,' not entirely civilised, whose poetry is 'as if the rocks of the sea had begun to speak to us, and tell us what they had been thinking of from eternity.' Sophocles, the harmoniser,—perhaps weakener of the musical strength of Æschylus,—and Euripides, its degenerator into scepticism and critical consciousness." In the third lecture he described the earliest character of Rome as consisting in a spirit of steady agricultural thrift, a quality which he considered "the germ of all other virtues." This thrifty faculty in the Romans became turned into the steady spirit of conquest, for which they soon grew famous,— all "by method" and "the spirit of the practical." The ordinary objection to the early Romans, as thieves and robbers, was very shallow. They were only a tribe of a superior character, gradually, and of necessity, forcing the consequences of their better knowledge upon the people around them. The Carthaginians he considered, in comparison with the Romans, as a mere set of money-hunters, "with a Jewish pertinacity" affecting their whole character. In the concluding lecture, a large portion of which was autobiographical, he described the effect which "Werterism" had upon his own mind, and the antidote he found to that morbid sentimentalism in the other writings of Goethe. He found in *Wilhelm Meister* that the letters of several young persons who had written for information about how to attain happiness, were tossed aside unanswered, and this struck him as very strange, seeing that a "recipe for happiness" was just the thing that he wanted, and had at that time been anxiously seeking. The seriousness of Goethe's character convinced him that there was some deep meaning in this which was worth inquiring after, and at last he began to perceive that happiness was not the right thing to seek; that man has nothing to do with happiness, but with the discharge of the work given him to do. The spiritual perfection of his nature, a mystic and nameless aim, which no man could explain,—and it were better left unexplained,—though they were lonely, pitiable, who had not glimpses of it,—which heroic martyr spirits of old times had called "the cross of Christ," and which Goethe himself had called "the worship of sorrow;" this, he began to apprehend, was the true object of search, and the proper end and aim of life. It must ever be a source of regret to the students of Carlyle's writings that, while the reporters of the London press were, in that summer of 1838, busy preserving every word of the orations of men who are already forgotten, this poor fragment is all that has come down to us of a series of lectures which would have thrown so much light on the story of Carlyle's spiritual life.

"The Revolutions of Modern Europe" was the title of a third course, also given at the Edward Street lecture-hall, in 1839; and in a notice of the second lecture, which had for its subject "Protestantism, Faith in the Bible, Luther, Knox, and Gustavus Adolphus," Leigh Hunt gave a characteristically vivid picture, both of the lecturer and his audience; the latter, as in the previous seasons, including ladies as well as gentlemen. Hunt's

notice is specially worthy of mark, from the felicitous
description of the orator's style given in the first two
lines; the epithets apply to everything Carlyle has written,
and, as an accurate characterisation of his style, we think it
has never been surpassed, or even equalled. "There is
frequently a noble homeliness," wrote Hunt, "a passionate simplicity and familiarity of speech, in the language
of Mr Carlyle, which gives startling effect to his sincerity,
and is evidently received by his audience, especially the
fashionable part of it (as one may know by the increased
silence), with a feeling that would smile if it could, but
which is fairly dashed into a submission, grateful for the
novelty and the excitement, by the hard force of the very
blows of truth. Thus, in describing the 'lie' which the
Papal tyranny had become by dint of its own obvious
disbelief and worldliness, he said it had come to be 'one
of the most melancholy spectacles which so august a
thing (as any sovereign representative of a faith) could
possibly offer. None but hypocrites and formalists have
any longer anything to do with such an anomaly. Good
men get out of it. It is quite a secondary kind of man
that gets at the head of it. If the world be a lie, and
everything present and future a juggle, then *that* may be
a truth, but not otherwise. It must be altered, *a thing
like that.*' The effect of hearty convictions like these,
uttered in such simple, truthful words, and with the
flavour of a Scottish accent (as if some Puritan had come
to life again, liberalised by German philosophy, and his
own intense reflections and experience) can be duly
appreciated only by those who see it. Every manly face
among the audience seems to knit its lips, out of a
severity of sympathy, whether it would or no; and all

the pretty church-and-state bonnets seem to thrill through all their ribbons."

In 1840, came what was unfortunately to prove the last series of all—the six lectures "On Heroes, Hero-Worship, and the Heroic in History," which, alone of the four courses, were published in a printed form, and became more immediately popular than any of his previous works. But they vexed the righteous soul of poor James Grant,* a bitter defender of a narrow orthodoxy, who, for many years, united in his own person the functions of editor of the newspaper organ of the publicans and defender of the Christian Faith, on the principle, we suppose, expressed by Burns, that "whisky and religion gang thegither." This eminently spiritual personage wanted to know if "any living man could point to a single practical passage" in any of Carlyle's lectures, and proclaimed Carlyle himself "but a phantasm" and his teachings utterly valueless. Mr Grant was also shocked by Carlyle's delivery. "In so far as his mere manner is concerned, I can scarcely bestow on him a word of commendation. There is something in his manner which, if I may use a rather quaint term, must seem very uncouth to London audiences of the most respectable class, accustomed as they are to the polished deportment which is usually exhibited in Willis's or the Hanover Rooms. When he enters the room, and pro-

---

* This singular character, while editing a daily paper devoted to the interests of the Pothouses of London, and which was, at the time we speak of, the organ also of the Prize Ring, assured a friend that he made it a point of conscience to write and publish one religious book per annum, to preserve his soul from the secularising influence of his professional life! His favourite theme in these soul-saving exercises was the "Glories of Heaven."

ceeds to the sort of rostrum whence he delivers his lectures, he is, according to the usual practice in such cases, generally received with applause; but he very rarely takes any more notice of the mark of approbation thus bestowed upon him, than if he were altogether unconscious of it.　And the same seeming want of respect for his audience, or, at any rate, the same disregard for what I believe he considers the troublesome forms of politeness, is visible at the commencement of his lecture. Having ascended his desk, he gives a hearty rub to his hands, and plunges at once into his subject.　He reads very closely, which, indeed, must be expected, considering the nature of the topics which he undertakes to discuss. He is not prodigal of gesture with his arms or body; but there is something in his eye and countenance which indicates great earnestness of purpose, and the most intense interest in his subject.　You can almost fancy, in some of his more enthusiastic and energetic moments, that you see his inmost soul in his face.　At times, indeed very often, he so unnaturally distorts his features, as to give to his countenance a very unpleasant expression.　On such occasions you would imagine that he was suddenly seized with some violent paroxysms of pain. He is one of the most ungraceful speakers I have ever heard address a public assemblage of persons.　In addition to the awkwardness of his general manner, he 'makes mouths,' which would of themselves be sufficient to mar the agreeableness of his delivery. And his manner of speaking, and the ungracefulness of his gesticulation, are greatly aggravated by his strong Scotch accent.　Even to the generality of Scotch-men his pronunciation is harsh in no ordinary degree.

Need I say, then, what it must be to an English ear?"
The polished critic, though himself a Caledonian, could
not away with that Scotch accent. "I was present
some months ago, during the delivery of a speech by
Mr Carlyle at a meeting held in the Freemasons' Tavern,
for the purpose of forming a metropolitan library; and
though that speech did not occupy in its delivery more
than five minutes, he made use of some of the most
extraordinary phraseology I ever heard employed by a
human being. He made use of the expression 'this
London,' which he pronounced "this Loondun,' four or
five times—a phrase which grated grievously on the ears
even of those of Mr Carlyle's own countrymen who were
present, and which must have sounded doubly harsh in
the ears of an Englishman, considering the singularly
broad Scotch accent with which he spoke." What
probably increased the sensitiveness of Mr Grant's ear
was the circumstance, darkly hinted in the close of the
sketch, that "a good deal of uncertainty" prevailed as
to the lecturer's religious opinions — in fact, it was
whispered that he was a Deist. However, we have to
thank this grotesque Scotch gossiper for being the instrument of letting us know that the series on "Hero-
Worship" was the best-attended of all the four courses of
lectures, the audience numbering, on the average, three
hundred, these being, for the most part, persons of rank and
wealth, "as the number of carriages testified." It would
appear that Carlyle had only consented to lecture at the
urgent solicitation of many friends and admirers; and,
though he stuck manfully to his bargain, when the last of
the four courses he undertook to deliver was completed,
he gave it to be clearly understood that never more

should he renew the experiment. Not that it had been a failure, so far as either he himself or his friends were concerned—the very reverse was the case; his public speech more than realised the highest expectations, and the audiences went on increasing every season. In after years he was frequently solicited to appear again on the platform; invitations to lecture came from America, as well as from provincial towns of England and Scotland, but he stedfastly adhered to his determination never again to adopt that mode of utterance. As was indicated in the touching farewell at the close of his final lecture, he had found that there was "much pain in the business," though a little pleasure also; but the pain, no doubt, greatly preponderated. Though the æsthetic Publican's Editor and Defender of Christian Orthodoxy had been scandalised by Carlyle's glaring want of politeness in not bowing *a la* Turveydrop to his auditors when they gave him a cheer, there was assuredly the most delicate courtesy — may we not also add, a modest and thankful spirit beautiful to contemplate— in the last words Carlyle uttered as a public lecturer: " With six months, instead of six days, we might have done better (with the subject). I promised to break ground on it; I know not whether I have even managed to do that. I have had to tear it up in the rudest manner in order to get into it at all. Often enough, with these abrupt utterances thrown-out, isolated, un-explained, has your tolerance been put to the trial. Tolerance, patient candour, all-hoping favour and kind-ness, which I will not speak of at present. The accom-plished and distinguished, the beautiful, the wise, some-thing of what is best in England, have listened patiently to my rude words. With many feelings, I heartily thank you all; and say, Good be with you all!" As we listen to the echo of that grateful valedictory strain, that has come over the interval of forty years with its thrill as of sweetest music unspent, we conclude that the critic who pronounced the lecturer "uncouth" simply succeeded—as so many censors do—in describing himself.

No one who has heard Carlyle talk in private requires to be told that he was a born orator. Nor can any such have failed to wish at times that he had further prosecuted the lecturing experiment; the one reflection that modifies this wish being that, if he had done so, we might have been deprived of some of the great historical works which he has left as a legacy to the ages. Habituating himself to public speaking, we can imagine Carlyle swaying the multitude even as it was ruled by the voice of John Knox; and it might have saved Carlyle from some mistakes if he had been brought face to face with his scholars. On the other hand, we remember the fate that overtook the friend of his youth, carried off his feet by the intoxication of triumphs as an orator; and we are content with the decision that Sartor formed in 1840, and from which he never swerved. Once in conversation in Edinburgh with Alexander Scott, the Principal of Owens College, who happened at the time to be lecturing at the Philosophical Institution, he asked his old friend how he liked the work, adding, "When I had to give my lectures on Hero-Worship, I felt as if I were going to be hanged." Though that was his feeling, it by no means proves him to have been unfit for the business of orator; since many of the greatest orators in the world have shared this experience, and indeed have never suc-

ceeded in shaking off the wretched sensation, down to
the very last. It may be worth adding that amongst
those who heard Carlyle lecture in 1838 was a brilliant
young lawyer from the United States, who subsequently
rose to distinction as Senator Sumner. "I heard Carlyle lecture the other day," writes he, in one of his
letters; "he seemed like an inspired boy; truth and
thoughts that made one move on the benches came
from his apparently unconscious mind, couched in the
most grotesque style, and yet condensed to a degree of
intensity, if I may so write." In confirmation of the view
we take of Carlyle as an orator, let us cite the evidence
of a second American witness, Margaret Fuller Ossoli.
That remarkable woman did not hear him lecture, but she
had the privilege of listening to his conversation. "His
talk," she says, writing in 1846, "is an amazement and a
splendour scarcely to be faced with steady eyes. He
does not converse, only harangues. It is the usual misfortune of such marked men that they cannot allow other
minds room to breathe and show themselves in their
atmosphere, and thus miss the refreshment and instruction which the greatest never cease to need from the
experience of the humblest. Carlyle allows no one a
chance, but bears down all opposition, not only by his
wit and onset of words, resistless in their sharpness as so
many bayonets, but by actual physical superiority, raising
his voice and rushing on his opponent with a torrent of
sounds. This is not in the least from unwillingness to
allow freedom to others. On the contrary, no man would
more enjoy a manly resistance to his thought. But it is
the nature of a mind accustomed to follow out its own
impulse as the hawk its prey, and which knows not how

to stop in the chase. Carlyle, indeed, is arrogant and overbearing; but in his arrogance there is no littleness, no self-love. It is the heroic arrogance of some old Scandinavian conqueror; it is his nature, and the untameable impulse that has given him power to crush the dragons. You do not love him, perhaps, nor revere; and perhaps, also, he would only laugh at you if you did; but you like him heartily, and like to see him, the powerful smith, the Siegfried, melting all the old iron in his furnace till it glows to a sunset red, and burns you if you senselessly go too near. He seems to me quite isolated, lonely as the desert; yet never was a man more fitted to prize a man, could he find one to match his mood. He finds them, but only in the past. He sings rather than talks. He pours upon you a kind of satirical, heroical, critical poem, with regular cadences, and generally catching up, near the beginning, some singular epithet, which serves as a refrain when his song is full. He sometimes stops a minute to laugh at himself, then begins anew with fresh vigour; for all the spirits he is driving before him seem to him as Fata Morganas, ugly masks, in fact, if he can but make them turn about; but he laughs that they seem to others such dainty Ariels."

Among the eminent auditors of Carlyle, besides those already named, who have left on record their impressions of the lectures, was Bunsen, who describes them as "very striking, rugged thoughts, not ready made up for any political or religious system; thrown at people's heads, by which most of his audience are sadly startled." Robert Browning was also a charmed listener; and so was Macready the actor at the lecture on "The Hero as

Prophet," of which he says that it was delivered with "a fervour and eloquence that only complete conviction of truth could give." The great tragedian adds that he was "charmed, carried away" by the lecturer. Crabbe Robinson, of course, was there; and of one lecture in particular we find him testifying that "it gave great satisfaction, for it had uncommon thoughts, and was delivered with unusual animation."

Lecturing was not the only new channel into which the talents of Carlyle were now directed under the stimulating influence, and by the literary conveniences, of the metropolis. Long before he left Scotland, and in consequence of a suggestion he first heard from the lips of his mother, he had been contemplating the political and religious conflict of the seventeenth century as a subject suitable for his pen; but now the idea which had been haunting his mind took a somewhat new form. He entered upon those wider studies of the subject which afterwards bore good fruit in the work that finally enabled England to regain the lost image of her Uncrowned King, which had been so foully defaced, beyond all recognition, by sectarian bigots of the preceding times. The biography of Cromwell, however, was a work that was yet to cost him years of strenuous toil; and before it saw the light several other books of its author were issued from the press. In 1837 appeared *The French Revolution, a History*—notable, in the first place, on this account, that it was the first book which bore on its title-page the name of Thomas Carlyle; worthy of special mark, moreover, because of its being also the first that straightway sent that name sounding through every nook and corner of Great Britain. We find opinion still curiously divided both as to its merits and the sort of impression it made at first upon the public mind. Some assert that it did not prove at once successful. " The incongruities," says one of these people, "monstrosities of style, and the author's disdain for what an admirer called the ' feudalities of literature ' struck all readers, and it was only some of them who thought much more of the intrinsic beauty of the jewel than of the strange setting." There is plenty of evidence, however, to shew that the immediate popularity of the book was great. One of the leading critics, no doubt, expressed the opinion that " it would be an interesting book were it well translated into English ; " but sneers like this could not hinder it from being both widely and keenly relished, not only on account of the intensity of its feeling and its depth of thought, but also for the graphic force and splendour of its style. It was certainly hailed by all who possessed critical discernment as the greatest historical poem in the language ; nor did they fail to recognise the fact that, while it was a prose poem, it was at the same time characterised by marvellous accuracy in its statement of facts. Landor hailed it with enthusiasm as the best book published in his time, and recognised the coming of a new literary potentate. Sir William Hamilton got hold of the book about three o'clock in the afternoon, and was so captivated with it that he could not lay it aside until he had finished the three volumes at four o'clock next morning. Charles Dickens was in the habit of reading it through twice every year ; and when he published his *Tale of Two Cities*, he said it had grown out of a hope to add something to the popular and picturesque means of understanding the terrible times of the French Revolution, "though," he added, "no one can hope to add any-thing to the philosophy of Mr Carlyle's wonderful book." Thomas Erskine of Linlathen hastened to send a copy to his friend Guizot; and, at Erskine's instigation, it was read by Dr Macleod Campbell, who deemed it valuable on account of its taking larger and deeper views of the events which it records than has been generally taken, though he thought there was "much to get over as to style and manner" in the book. This last remark was delicious, coming from such a source, Campbell having been the very worst stylist that ever wrote, even among Scottish theologians; in fact, the worthy man could not be said to have a style at all. Miss Mitford, of *Our Village*, had been told by Carlyle's admirers that this was his great work. "Perhaps it may be," said the little lady, "only I am quite convinced that nobody who did not know the story previously would gain the slightest idea of it from Mr Carlyle's three volumes, and that is not my theory of a history." John Stuart Mill, like Landor and Sir William Hamilton, did not agree with Miss Mitford, for he declared that "no work of greater genius, either historical or poetical, had been produced in this country for many years;" and in his *Autobiography* he points to the article in which he expressed this opinion as one of two conspicuous cases in which good was done by his daring to take a prompt initiative. "I believe," he says, "that the early success and reputation of Carlyle's *French Revolution* were considerably accelerated by what I wrote about it in the Review. Immediately on its publication, and before the commonplace critics, all whose rules and modes of judgment it set at defiance, had time to preoccupy the public with their disapproval of it, I wrote and published a review of the book, hailing it as one of those productions of genius which are above all rules, and are a law to themselves." Mill did not ascribe the impression produced to any particular merit in his *Westminster* article, for he did not think its execution good; anybody, in a position to be read, who had expressed the same opinion at the same precise time, and had made any tolerable statement of the just grounds for it, would, he thought, have produced the same effect. How great that effect was may be judged by the fact that the *Times* declared its readiness, "after perusing the whole of this extraordinary work, to allow, almost to their fullest extent, the high qualities with which Mr Carlyle's idolators endow him." Mr Mill certainly owed the book a good turn, for, though he makes no allusion to the circumstance, he had been the unintentional instrument of delaying its publication and of adding enormously to the toil involved in the production of the book. At one time he had himself a half-formed intention of writing a History of the French Revolution; and, when he learned that Carlyle was engaged on the subject, he handed over his collections to him, which, he tells us, proved "very useful." This naturally led to Mr Mill obtaining the loan of the manuscript of the second volume of Carlyle's work soon after it had been completed; and he carried the treasure to Mrs Taylor, the lady who subsequently became his wife. On retiring for the night, with culpable heedlessness she left the manuscript open on her study table, from which it accidentally fell on to the floor; and next morning an equally heedless domestic, imagining it to be waste paper, kindled the

fire with it !* Mr Mill, as those who knew the man may
fancy, was dreadfully mortified at this tragic mishap ; but
the victim took the accident, when he first heard of it,
with admirable composure, and actually succeeded by
and by in reproducing the volume, almost entirely from
memory—so firmly fixed was the form of the magnificent
narrative in the mind of its author. Mrs Carlyle, however, always entertained the opinion that the re-written
volume was not equal to the original ; and, taking all
things into account, we can well believe that she
was right. One version of the story, credited to Mrs
Carlyle, says it was Mr Mill's cook who burned
the book. "She had occasion to bake some cakes,
and finding the precious manuscript lying about, she
concluded that she might turn it to good account, and
accordingly, partly as fuel, and partly as lining for the
cake tins, she used up the whole of the manuscript."
It may have been Mrs Taylor's cook who did this ; it
certainly was not Mr Mill's. "Mr Carlyle never keeps
notes," said Mrs Carlyle, "but gets all his materials
ready, works till he has everything in his head, and then
winds it out like silk from a reel." Horrified at the
accident, Mr Mill and Mrs Taylor called on the great
historian. "Such a thing never happened before," said
Mr Mill. "Yes, though," answered Mr Carlyle, "Newton
and his dog Diamond." "True, but Newton went mad

---

* A similar fiery mishap befell De Quincey, whose *Daughters of
Lebanon*, printed at the close of the *Confessions*, is but a fragment,
owing to the accidental destruction by fire of five or six of the
dreams and noon-day visions. They were burned in a sudden confla-
gration which arose from a spark of a candle falling unobserved
amongst a large-pile of papers in a bedroom, when De Quincey was
alone and reading.

over it." "Well, well, we shall hardly be so bad as that," said Carlyle; and he soon afterwards began again at the beginning, scarcely saying a word about his misfortune at the time, but afterwards, as the work progressed, grumbling about it often. Another, and a fuller, version of the story is given by our American friend, Milburn, as it was related to him by Carlyle himself; though the report seems to us to have a little of the blind preacher in it as well as the genuine article. "A sad story, enough, sir; and one that always makes me shudder to think of. I had finished the second volume, and, as it lay in manuscript, a friend desired that he might have the reading of it; and it was committed to his care. He professed himself greatly delighted with the perusal, and confided it to a friend of his own, who had some curiosity to see it as well. This person sat up, as he said, perusing it far into the wee hours of the morning; and at length recollecting himself [herself?], surprised at the flight of time, laid the manuscript carelessly upon the library table, and hied to bed. There it lay, a loose heap of rubbish, fit only for the waste-paper basket, or for the grate. So Betty, the housemaid, thought when she came to light the library fire in the morning. Looking round for something suitable for her purpose, and finding nothing better than it, she thrust it into the grate, and applying the match, up the chimney with a sparkle and roar went *The French Revolution;* thus ending in smoke and soot, as the great transaction itself did more than half a century ago: At first they forbore to tell me the evil tidings; but at length I heard the dismal story, and I was as a man staggered by a heavy blow. I was as a man beside myself, for there was scarcely a page of

manuscript left. I sat down at the table, and strove to
collect my thoughts and to commence the work again.
I filled page after page, but ran the pen over every line
as the page was finished. Thus was it, sir, for many a
weary day; until at length, as I sat by the window, half-
hearted and dejected, my eye wandered along over acres
of roofs, I saw a man standing upon a scaffold engaged in
building a wall—the wall of a house. With his trowel
he'd lay a great splash of mortar upon the last layer, and
then brick after brick would be deposited upon this,
striking each with the butt of his trowel, as if to give it
his benediction and farewell; and all the while singing
or whistling as blithe as a lark. And in my spleen I
said within myself, ' Poor fool! how canst thou be so
merry under such a bile-spotted atmosphere as this,
and everything rushing into the regions of the inane?'
And then I bethought me, and I said to myself, ' Poor
fool thou, rather, that sittest here by the window whining
and complaining! What if thy house of cards falls? Is
the universe wrecked for that? The man yonder builds
a house that shall be a home perhaps for generations.
Men will be born in it, wedded in it, and buried from it;
and the voice of weeping and of mirth shall be heard
within its walls; and mayhap true valour, prudence, and
faith shall be nursed by its hearthstone. Man! symbol
of eternity imprisoned into time! it is not thy works,
which are all mortal, infinitely little, and the greatest no
greater than the least, but only the spirit thou workest in
which can have worth or continuance! Up, then, at thy
work, and be cheerful!' So I arose and washed my face,
and felt that my head was anointed, and gave myself to
relaxation—to what they call ' light literature.' I read

nothing but novels for weeks. I was surrounded by heaps of rubbish and chaff. I read all the novels of that person who was once a captain in the royal navy—and an extraordinary ornament he must have been to it;* the man that wrote stories about dogs that had their tails cut off, and about people in search of their fathers, and it seemed to me that of all the extraordinary dunces that had figured upon this planet, he must certainly bear the palm from every one save the readers of his books. And thus refreshed I took heart of grace again, applied me to my work, and in course of time *The French Revolution* got finished, as all things must, sooner or later."

Already this incident of the burnt manuscript has generated almost as many mythical contradictory tales as if it had happened centuries ago. Since Carlyle's death

---

* This and other portions of Milburn's report are confirmed by another writer, who, referring to a statement in *Chambers's Journal*, that Carlyle told Thomas Aird he considered the second effort better than the first, says :—"This is just the contrary of Carlyle's account made some four years since to the writer of this note. Sitting one evening in the drawing room of the house in Great Cheyne Row, myself and Carlyle were in conversation upon general subjects, when I remarked, 'I have heard that the manuscript of the *French Revolution* was destroyed before going to the printers. Was that so?' Carlyle—'Ay, ay, it was so.' Myself—'What did you do under the circumstances?' Carlyle—'For three days and nights I could neither eat nor sleep, but was like a daft man.' Myself—'But what did you do at last?' Carlyle—'Well, I just went away into the country;' and here he burst into a fit of loud laughter, and then said, 'I did nothing for three months but read Marryat's novels;' and after a serious pause he remarked, 'I set to and wrote it all over again;' but in a melancholy tone concluded, 'I dinna think its the same; no, I dinna think it's the same.'" Mr R. H. Horne says :— "Mr Mill was naturally in very great distress at the irreparable loss, and Mr Carlyle was seen doing his utmost to console and comfort him. Such nobility of heart and fortitude of mind deserve to be recorded in all histories of English literature, and elsewhere."

we have been told by leading journalists that it was the manuscript of the first volume to which the disaster befell, and that what became of it was never exactly known. " Mrs Taylor," according to the *Times*, "left it for some days on her writing table; when wanted, it could nowhere be found ; and the most probable explanation of its disappearance was the suggestion that a servant had used the manuscript to light the fire. Carlyle at once set to work to reproduce from his notes the lost volume. He swiftly finished his task, but he always thought that the first draft was the best." Another journal, labouring under the same misconception as to its being the initial volume that was destroyed, says : " The author bravely passed the matter off with some soothing pleasantry, and sat down and re-wrote the whole piece, page by page, from memory. It was a terrible effort, but the struggle brought its reward, for of the three volumes it has often been noticed there is none that can match with the first for intensity of feeling, concentration of thought, directness of statement, and compressed wealth of picturesque description." Thus each authority has a quite different story to tell ; yet the perplexed reader is not without consolation when he finds the obvious fiction furnishing a good moral which the fact refuses to yield.

CHAPTER XIII.

ENTERS THE FIELD OF CONTEMPORARY POLITICS—HIS
"CHARTISM"—THE STUDENT'S VOCATION—HIS "HERO-
WORSHIP"—GODWIN'S IDEA—"PAST AND PRESENT"
—MAZZINI'S ESSAY—CARLYLE'S DEFENCE OF THE
EXILE—SWINBURNE AND MACLEOD CAMPBELL—THE
"LATTER-DAY PAMPHLETS."

WITH the lectures and the collection of the multitudinous
materials for a history of the French Revolution, to say
nothing of the passing through the press of *Sartor* and
the arranging of the first English edition of the *Miscellanies*—a vigilant eye being meanwhile kept on Cromwell and the great Puritan struggle—it might be supposed that these opening years at Chelsea were sufficiently crowded with work.   But before the close of
1839 we find the diligent worker, now at the very height
of his productive power, breaking ground in quite a new
direction by the publication of his little volume on
Chartism, which was issued from the press of James
Fraser.   True, it may be described as a pamphlet
rather than a book ; and it partook of the character
of journalistic work, discussing the political questions of
the day.   To very many of his warmest admirers,
brought bitter disappointment—such as afterwards came
to his orthodox readers, in ecstacies over his *Cromwell*
when that apparently Calvinistic biography was suc-

ceeded by the *Life of John Sterling*, a bombshell which suddenly turned their joy into mourning. Close students of *Sartor* had fancied that the man who wrote it was a Radical Reformer; and so he was, doubtless, but not in their sense. On none of the movements in which they were then engaged with a view to heal the diseases of the body politic, did he bestow the slightest word of encouragement; on the contrary, he spoke of them all—their demands for an extended suffrage, and other popular agitations—with absolute contempt. Its assault upon the governing classes was too strong to win for *Chartism* the approval of the Tory press; and the maxims laid down in it, distinctly favouring a despotic rule as hard and mechanical as that of the Pharaohs, were condemned with entire unanimity by the Liberal journals. Both parties were at one in regarding the somewhat sulphurous little book as totally unpractical in its character. Now, however, while we detect in those fiery pages the germs of a theory of government that is antagonistic to our Constitutional system, even the staunchest Radical must admit that two, if not three, beneficial ideas of great practical importance were by that book first forced upon the attention of the public, two at least of them taking root with ultimate production of good fruit that we are happily enjoying, or about to enjoy, to-day. The most prominent of these three ideas came at once to be formulated under the title of the Condition of England Question, which doubtless had its origin in the indignant appeals of that pamphlet. The two fundamental remedies for the most pressing national wants on which Carlyle insisted were Universal Education and General Emigration. He lived to see that his advocacy of the former had not been in vain ; but his notions with respect to the latter have not yet been permitted to enter what is called, in the cant language of our day, the domain of practical politics. The Adminstrative Reform movement, unhappily abortive, and which still remains to be taken up in right earnest, may also be said to date its birth from Carlyle's first raid into the field of politics. The "strong government" theory which he then promulgated was afterwards illustrated and enforced in forms that gave pain to all friends of Constitutional freedom ; and a young poet of our time has attempted in one of his prose essays to account for the obvious degradation of Mr Carlyle's genius, as displayed in his later manifestoes, by laying down the principle that no student can enter the field of contemporary thought and action without incurring such a loss of sanity and power. It is the business of the student, this writer contends, to stand apart from the turmoil of his time—to seek, not contemporary but eternal truth ; he is to regard the heavens, not to delve in the earth : and unless he preserves this attitude of isolation, we are told that he is doomed to sink to the level of the bawling throng. We may be allowed to question the validity of this theory of the student's vocation when we look back to the days of Milton, the deepest thinker of his time and one of our two greatest poets, yet the right-hand man of Cromwell ; when we see Dante not only going on embassies, but so mixing himself with the affairs of Florence as to secure banishment ; when we call to mind the part played in politics by John Knox, who, far from being weakened by his active leadership in that stormy time, set a mark on his nation that cannot be effaced till that nation has ceased to be. Emerson, whom this essayist admires for his power of self-isolation, has certainly shown no want of sympathy with the public movements of his age and nation. Though it has been the fashion to call him "the Hermit of Concord," he has never been backward in throwing himself into contemporary conflicts. Indeed, he has been more of a public man in America than Carlyle ever was in England. In the controversy which almost rent his country in twain he took a steady and consistent part, so that when the strife came to a close, and the victory had been won, his was the pen chosen to write the victor's hymn of praise for Emancipation :—

> " Pay ransom to the owner !
>   Fill the cup to the brim !
> Who is the owner?   The slave is owner,
> And always was.   Pay *him !*"

With all deference to Mr Robert Buchanan, we are constrained, by the experience of the past as well as by the fundamental principles on which society is based, to decline acceptance of his postulate. The student, to do his highest work, must not withdraw himself from that conflict of which "only God and the angels can be the spectators." Not a few of our best men of thought at this moment, as in the past, are robust men of action. The author of the *Reign of Law*, is he not the most powerful orator in the House of Lords and an active administrator? Mr Gladstone, like the late Lord Derby, is one of our most accomplished scholars. John Stuart Mill's too brief presence in the Parliamentary arena, and his constant political activity out of it, inflicted no injury on the powerful mind or on the calm temper of that philosopher. It is not in his descent to mingle in the conflicts of his own generation that we shall find the clue to any weakness in the teachings of Carlyle; and even those who most lamented the attitude in which he often stood in relation to the political questions of his day, cannot think less of him for taking his share in the endeavours to ameliorate the condition of his fellow-men.

A more favourable reception awaited his next book, *On Heroes, Hero-Worship, and the Heroic in History*, also issued from Fraser's press, in 1841. It was simply a report, with a few emendations and additions, of his fourth course of lectures. Though Grant asserted that they were closely read, the truth is, they were purely extemporaneous—delivered without a fragment of written notes. The immediate popularity of the volume was proved by its passing speedily through some half-dozen editions; nor was its success confined to England, for, besides having a great run in the United States, it was soon translated both into French and German. We suspect it was the only one of his works, in addition to *The French Revolution*, so honoured in France. This was at once the fullest and clearest exposition that its author had yet published of his social, political, and philosophical creed. The ideas hastily indicated in the pamphlet on *Chartism* were wrought out more carefully; and the central principle illustrated on every page was that hero-worship with which Carlyle's name came to be most of all associated in the minds of men. " Great men," he said, "are the fire pillars in this dark pilgrimage of mankind; they stand as heavenly signs, ever-living witnesses of what has been, prophetic tokens of what may still be, the revealed embodied possibilities of human nature." Sentences like these had a fair look and a subtle seductive power; but the theory to which they gave such eloquent expression was one that could not bear the critical inspection to which the style might safely be subjected. It conducted to the conclusion that the millions are a mere brute mass, and that not in them, but in a few select individuals of a gifted sort alone is to be found the Spirit of God and all hope of progress in the world. This was not perceived at first by many readers on whom the book laid hold by reason of its wealth of curious biographic lore, its vivid portraits of great men, its generous ardour, and the passionate glow of its rhetoric. Of course, there is truth in very much that Carlyle said about heroes; but the exaggeration of that truth was sure to bring a heavy accumulation of errors in its train. It led to a scorn of Constitutional methods of government, and to a belief only in the " Heaven-born chief," in whom we also might believe, if our instructor had only been good enough to tell us of any machinery whereby to secure him, apart from the plan of counting heads, or " noses," as he contemptuously phrased it. It led of necessity to such monstrous beliefs as—that slavery is the natural condition of labour; that the morally diseased and the hopelessly weak are objects only of contempt and scorn, for whom let there be no toleration, no pity; that there is no majesty in a united people seeking to be purified and ennobled by the means of freedom; and that social order is incompatible with an indefinite number of distinct individual wills. The leading position in Carlyle's system, that intellect guarantees morality—in other words, that able man and good man are synonymous terms, and that the stupid are the only criminals—is a theory which he may have got from Godwin.

In 1843, from the press of Chapman & Hall, who were henceforth his publishers to the end, there was issued *Past and Present*, in which was given a graphic picture of the manners and morals of the twelfth century, as represented by Abbot Samson of St Edmundsbury; this picture being contrasted with the England of to-day, its condition "one of the most ominous ever seen in the world—full of wealth in every kind, yet dying of inanition." The author foresees, however, a happy haven, "to which all revolutions are driving us—that of hero-kings, and a world not unheroic." The present state of our own country is painted in the most sombre colours; we have an aristocracy either unable or unwilling to govern, a parliament elected by bribery, which starts with a lie in its mouth, and prefers profitless talk to indis-pensable work, and Captains of Industry whose connection with their workmen is that of buccaniers and Choctaw Indians. As a volume of historical etchings, executed with loving patience, at once accurate in their details and marvellously vivid, this work possesses imperishable interest and value; while, in its scathing exposure of the rotten condition of modern society, there is only too much truth. The book produced a profound impression on many minds, nor is its force yet spent; but one of the most significant incidents connected with its publication was the appearance of an essay "On the Genius and Tendency of the Writings of Thomas Carlyle," in the *British and Foreign Review* for October 1843. To an Italian exile in England, curiously enough, must be ascribed the merit of having been the first to detect what is perhaps the cardinal defect in the writings of Carlyle. Joseph Mazzini, the writer of the essay, penetrated to the heart of many subjects with such a keen discernment of what was unperceived by others that now, when we turn to his collected Essays, we are amazed at the number of instances in which he anticipated the laggard judgment of his fellows. There is an almost prophetic force in many of his speculations, and the accuracy of his insight was equal to its swiftness. More truly than his friend at Chelsea, the apostle of Italian Unity was a Seer. In that elaborate critique on Carlyle, written thirty-seven years ago, he hit the blot which no other student had then discovered. At that date, and even down to a much later period, the majority of readers were in the habit of regarding Carlyle as a foe to the aristocratic order of things which had so long dominated Europe, and a friend to the Democratic movement that received its first grand impulse from the French Revolution. The author of *Sartor* was nothing if not destructive. Small reverence had he for old-established institutions. His fierce attacks on many of these gave immense satisfaction to thousands in whose hearts the revolutionary spirit was stirring. In Herr Teufelsdröckh they beheld as they imagined, one of the most vigorous allies who had ever come to help on the good cause. And the Tories were of the same opinion, beholding in this strange new writer, not a friend, but an enemy. The stranger from Italy, however, did not share this delusion. He clearly saw what would have made the English critics in the two opposite political camps change their estimate of Carlyle, if they could but have got a glimpse of it. The merit of the discovery is seen to be all the greater when we recall the circumstance that the two men were personal friends, and that Carlyle, according to his wont, had been kind to the poor exile. Gratitude and liking for the man who was always glad to see and talk with him might have tended, one would suppose, to make Mazzini as blind to Carlyle's defect as all the English and American critics, still more readers, then seemed to be. But it was not so. Perhaps the vagaries of Carlyle's often inconsequent and self-contradictory talk in private may have assisted to put the Italian on his guard when studying his writings. Perhaps the fact that he was a foreigner made him more keenly watchful and dis-criminative because less carried away by admiration and wonder at the force and beauty of the rhetoric. Or, more likely still, the perception that Carlyle, though kind to him as a human being, had not the slight-est faith in his mission or his plans, but looked out with a sceptical, half-pitying, half-amused eye upon these, may have bred distrust in the bosom of the patriot.*

---

* Not without significance is this paragraph in Margaret Fuller's account,—most admirable, we doubt not, for its fidelity to truth as well as its vivacity,—of her meetings with Carlyle. He and his wife came to pass an evening with the American stranger. "Unluckily Mazzini was with us, whose society, when he was there alone, I enjoyed more than any one. He is a beauteous and pure music; also, he is a dear friend of Mrs Carlyle, but his being there gave the conversation a turn to 'progress' and ideal subjects, and Carlyle was fluent in invectives on all our 'rose-water imbecilities.' We all felt distant from him; and Mazzini, after some vain efforts to remonstrate, became very sad. Mrs Carlyle said to me, 'These are but opinions to Carlyle; but to Mazzini, who has given his all, and helped to bring his friends to the scaffold, in pursuit of such objects, it is a matter of life and death.' All Carlyle's talk that evening was a defence of mere force,—success the test of right ;—if people would not behave well, put collars round their necks ;—find a hero, and let them be his slaves, &c. It was very Titanic, and anti-celestial. I wish the last evening had been more melodious." One is almost

Be these things as they may, this much is certain, that Mazzini did not fall into the snare which had caught everybody else. "Mr Carlyle," he wrote, "comprehends only the individual, the true sense of the unity of the human race escapes him."* Here was a fundamental source of weakness—a root from which evil was sure to spring; for the man who is destitute of faith in humanity as a whole, can never be an efficient helper in the cause of true progress. "He sympathises with all men," continues Mazzini, "but it is with the separate life of each, and not with their collective life. He readily looks at every man as the representative, the incarnation, in a manner, of an idea; he does not believe in 'a supreme idea' represented progressively by the development of mankind taken as a whole. . . . He weaves and unweaves his web like Penelope; he preaches by turns life and nothingness; he wearies out the powers of his readers by continually carrying them from heaven to hell, from hell to heaven. Ardent, and almost menacing, upon the ground of ideas, he becomes timid and sceptical as soon as he is engaged on that of their application. He desires to progress, but shews hostility to all who strive to progress. Give him the past, something which has triumphed, and he will see in it all that there is to see, more than others are able to see. Bring the object near to him, and as with Dante's souls in the *Inferno*, his

---

tempted by such a recital to make an application he did not contemplate of one of Carlyle's sayings, reported by Lord Folkestone, that "there is nothing so sad as to hear a man tell lies beautifully."

* *Life and Writings of Joseph Mazzini*, iv. 75. London. 1867. There are two essays on Carlyle in this volume, the one devoted to a general review of his writings and genius, the other a critique of the *History of the French Revolution*.

vision, his faculty of penetration, is clouded." The essay must ever be regarded by English students as the most impressive monument of the rare insight of the man without whom we should not have witnessed the unification of Italy. Carlyle deemed him a visionary, cherishing " rose-water imbecilities;" but this mighty restorer of the greatest nation of antiquity, saw more clearly into Carlyle. His diagnosis detected, with unerring precision, what was at this date a concealed disease. The exile's essay remains, down to the present hour, the most valuable criticism that has been written on the subject.

Yet, after all, Carlyle appreciated, indeed loved Mazzini—a fact strangely overlooked by Mr Swinburne, the too ardent worshipper of the Italian patriot, in his recent letter to the Parisian democrats. The English poet, though Carlyle was " not one of his friends," reminds them of the service he " rendered to the English, if not to the French, in writing his unequalled and powerful book on the Revolution."* He invites them also to bear in mind

---

* If Dr Macleod Campbell rightly interpreted the tendency and use of this book, it is hardly one for which Mr Swinburne should give thanks. That eminent Scottish divine, by his countrymen regarded as an advanced Liberal in theology, so much so that they expelled him from their synagogue, but who was severely Conservative in politics, was delighted with Carlyle's *French Revolution* because it was so full of warning to the Radicals, both of England and the Continent. " Awful indeed," he exclaimed, " is the blindness of the movement party, with the example afforded to them of the impracticability of the theory of the people the sovereign, and of the hollowness of that seeming equality and brotherhood which is not the fellowship of a life in which all call God Father ; but which begins with shutting out the Father, and contrives a brotherhood in an outward and visible equality ; like that of sons who first killed their father, impatient of distributing to them of his goods severally as he willed, and then, in their jealousy of each other, and incapa-

the fact that he "always and everywhere branded with his contempt the Empire of Napoleon the Last, while many other Englishmen, to their everlasting shame, have prostrated themselves before Nero the Little." Mr Swinburne might likewise, and not inappropriately, have recalled the tribute to Mazzini spontaneously rendered in the hour of need by Carlyle, at the time when the dastardly as well as illegal opening of the exile's letters in the English Post Office was engaging the attention of Parliament and of an outraged nation. The *Times* happened then to say that it knew and cared nothing about Mazzini, but that even if he were "the most worthless and the most vicious creature in the world," that would not justify the tampering with his correspondence. Carlyle at once wrote to the leading journal, to testify that Mazzini was "very far indeed from being contemptible — none farther, or very few of living men. I have had," he continued, "the honour to know Mr Mazzini for a series of years; and, whatever I may think of his practical insight and skill in worldly affairs, I can with great freedom testify to all men that he, if I have ever seen one such, is a man of genius and virtue, a man of sterling veracity, humanity, and nobleness of mind; one of those rare men, numerable unfortunately but as units in this world, who are worthy to be called martyr-souls; who, in silence, piously in their

---

city of enjoying each what the other had, made, as robbers, equal distribution of the spoil of their dead father's wealth. Such was the French *brotherhood without a Father.*" Because the story told by Carlyle corresponded so exactly with what Dr Campbell anticipated as to the course of things in Britain, he was gladdened by the book, and in his letters of 1838 we find him earnestly commending it to others.

daily life, understand and practise what is meant by that. . . . Whether the extraneous Austrian Emperor and miserable old chimera of a Pope shall maintain themselves in Italy, or be obliged to decamp from Italy, is not a question in the least vital to Englishmen. But it is a question vital to us that sealed letters in an English postoffice be, as we all fancied they were, respected as things sacred; that opening of men's letters, a practice near of kin to picking men's pockets, and to other still viler and far fataler forms of scoundrelism, be not resorted to in England, except in cases of the very last extremity. When some new gunpowder plot may be in the wind, some doubledyed high treason, or imminent national wreck not avoidable otherwise, then let us open letters— not till then. To all Austrian Kaisers and such like, in their time of trouble, let us answer, as our fathers from of old have answered :—Not by such means is help here for you." It does not lessen the moral beauty of this letter to remember that it was written on the 18th of June 1844, only some nine months after the publication of Mazzini's essay.

The political creed of Carlyle found its ultimate and most violent expression in the *Latter-Day Pamphlets*, published during 1850 in numbers, entitled respectively *The Present Time, Downing Street, New Downing Street, Parliament*, and *Stump Oratory*. The attacks made in these against the " immeasurable democracy," which was characterised as " monstrous, loud, blatant, and inarticulate as the voice of chaos," at length opened the eyes of the English people to that defect in Carlyle's teaching which Mazzini had detected at the very outset. A few articles, published in the *Examiner* and *Spectator* in

1848, had given some indication of what was coming, so that the consternation among his friends at the wild reactionary outburst was not so great as it must otherwise have been. In spite of this preparation, however, they were saddened by the tones of almost savage scorn and mockery which pervaded the new book. The newspaper tentatives had been offensive enough; but in these pamphlets the writer was simply outrageous. His voice had risen to an angry scream—the harshest discords now grated upon the ear in place of the tender melodies that had diffused through all his previous writings a charm such as we feel in listening to the song of birds. He who had sounded the praises of Ebenezer Elliott in the *Edinburgh*, who was the author of the vindication of Burns, and, above all, who wrote the story of *Sartor*, was now furnishing ammunition to the slaveholders of America and giving comfort to European tyrants like Bomba of Naples. It was not possible that any but the advocates of Reaction could rejoice over such a sad spectacle as this. No truer, and assuredly no gentler, expression was given to the feeling of the friends of progress than the one penned, in sorrow, and not at all in anger, by the occupant of that Astronomical chair at Glasgow for which Carlyle was once a candidate. "It is," wrote Prof. Nichol, "as if he who had led us so far on the way had himself lapsed backward into the Everlasting No." More, and worse, than mere loss of temper was marring what used to be the perfect expression. "The shadow of a dreary fatalism," said Nichol, "seems to pass over his mind." But there was at least one consolation. To use a fine figure of his own, this wrath was but the inverted image of his yearning love. Men might call him the Apostle of Despair, and sneer at him as a fatalist; but "he is not at rest in his fatalism," as one remarked who knew him well and loved him much, "and while he resists it, it is not fatalism."

The book which closed the series of political studies begun more than ten years before was widely read, but found few sympathisers. Almost everywhere, indeed, it was condemned as the useless rhapsody of a tyro in politics. The public journals spoke of him as a recluse and a mere student, unacquainted with affairs, who could not, therefore, be expected to understand practical politics. They complained that, while he was so good at pointing out defects, he seemed incapable of suggesting remedies; and he was told that, though his motives might not tend in that direction, he was yet practically doing what in him lay to establish the savage doctrine, that Might is Right, which looks upon the world as a jungle, and men as beasts of prey. There was only too much truth in these censures; but, while we lament that there should have been any, the extent and intensity of the popular disapproval suggests one consolatory reflection. The man who persisted during ten weary years in publishing political theories that hardly any fellow-mortal approved, and which many of his oldest and best friends severely condemned, or received with a sad silence that he probably felt more keenly than he would have done trenchant rebuke, proves at any rate that he was free from the slightest taint of popularity-hunting. He would not stoop to court applause; nor would he swerve for an instant from what he believed to be the path of duty though the things he wrote only brought upon him the execrations of the multitude and—what was harder to bear—the mute protest of disappointed friends, accentuated by the occasional expression of approval in quarters from which only condemnation could have given comfort to a friend of humanity.   However mistaken, then, his views may have been, they were those of an independent, fearless spirit, who was ready to sacrifice in behalf of what he believed to be the truth even the esteem of his countrymen.

It should not be overlooked that, though as a whole the literary character of the *Latter-Day Pamphlets* is not up to the mark of his other works, they contain amidst their wildest rhapsodies not a few passages of singular force and beauty.   It has been said with justice that "even his stormiest and most 'Titanic' outbursts will generally bear analysis, and be found to err in nothing but redundancy of expression, an error due to his intense desire to force his whole meaning upon his readers." *

The monthly periodical which he was wont to designate the "sand magazine," and which would seem never to have regarded him with a favourable eye, probably perceiving that he was essentially a Democrat, was one of the foremost to assail him for the alleged want of practicality in his writings.   "Mr Carlyle," said *Blackwood*, "an astute and trenchant critic might, with show of justice, remark, assumes to be the reformer and castigator of his age—a reformer in philosophy, in politics, and religion—denouncing its *mechanical* method of thinking, deploring its utter want of *faith*, and threatening political society, obstinately deaf to the voice of wisdom, with the retributive horrors of repeated revolutions ; and

---

* *The Athenæum*, Feb. 12, 1881.

yet neither in philosophy, in religion, nor in politics, has Mr Carlyle any distinct dogma, creed, or constitution to promulgate. He is anything but a man of practical ability. Setting aside his style for the present, let us see whether he has ever, in the course of his life, thrown out a single hint which could be useful to his own generation, or profitable to those who may come after. If he could originate any such hint, he does not possess the power of embodying it in distinct language. Can any living man point to a single practical passage in any of these volumes ? If not, what is the practical value of Mr Carlyle's writings? What is Mr Carlyle himself but a Phantasm, of the species he is pleased to denounce ? " This objection, often repeated then and since in many quarters, has been replied to since Carlyle's death by Mr Leslie Stephen. "Some writers complain," he says, "that Carlyle did not advance any new doctrine, or succeed in persuading the world of its truth. His life failed, it is suggested, in so far as he did not make any large body of converts with an accepted code of belief. But here, as it seems to me, the criticism becomes irrelevant. No one will dispute that Carlyle taught a strongly marked and highly characteristic creed, though not one easily packed into a definite set of logical formulæ. If there was no particular novelty in his theories, that was his very contention. His aim was to utter the truths which had been the strength and the animating principle of great and good men in all ages. He was not to move us, like a scientific discoverer, by proclaiming novelties, but to utter his protest in behoof of the permanent truths, obscured in the struggle between conflicting dogmas, and drowned in the anarchical shrieks of contending parties.

He succeeded in so far as he impressed the emotions and the imagination of his fellows, not in so far as he made known to them any new doctrine."* Some would frame the reply to the complaint in a different fashion from that adopted by Mr Stephen, for it has been contended that Carlyle's political teachings were in the highest degree practical, and led almost immediately to important beneficial results, with a promise of yet accomplishing more good for the community. Writing in 1855, Thomas Ballantyne said :—"The general recognition, during the last twelve months, of the truth of what he was condemned for saying in 1850, may in some degree console Mr Carlyle for the abuse which was heaped upon him at the former period." And there can be no question that, besides originating the Administrative Reform movement, which is here, we presume, alluded to by Ballantyne, it was he who likewise caused the "condition of the people" to become a subject of much wider and deeper interest to men of all political parties than it had ever been before. Party distinctions have not yet ceased, nor is it likely that they will ever be obliterated; but, since the appearance of Carlyle's political writings, there has been a remarkable development of the sentiment which tends to bring together men of the most diverse political opinions in concerted action, with a view to the promotion of the social and domestic welfare of the people. It is, perhaps, no exaggeration to say that these endeavours to extinguish pauperism, ignorance, and crime—to elevate the masses of our toiling poor by securing for them better homes and encouraging better habits—received a mighty im-

---

* *Cornhill Magazine* for March 1881.

petus from, if they were not indeed originated by, the *Latter-Day Pamphlets*, and the two kindred works by which these were preceded. "The essential truth that pervaded their teachings, even in their frenzy, is now recognised. Again has the testimony of the solitary thinker passed into a commonplace of universal thought; while in Social Science Congresses, and a multitude of kindred agencies, individual or collective, we have in a very great measure, at least, the up-springing of seed sown long ago, amid wonder and scorn, by Thomas Carlyle."*

---

* *The Christian Spectator*, 1859.

CHAPTER XIV.

HAPPILY Carlyle did not devote the whole of his time,
even during the period that witnessed the publication of
his political works, to the consideration of contemporary
affairs. On the contrary, the greater part of that decade
was bestowed on the production of books which furnished
fuller scope for the development of the powers with
which he had been endowed, and which he had cultivated
with sedulous care during the years of his protracted
preparation. In particular, he had been working out a
grand idea which was doubly attractive to him on account
of its giving an opportunity for the expression of his
reflections on the great spiritual and political conflict of
the seventeenth century, and, at the same time, of fulfilling a purpose dictated by filial piety. The seed-thought
planted in his mind, years before, by his noble peasant
mother, at length bore fruit in the modestly-named work,
Oliver Cromwell's Letters and Speeches ; with Elucidations,
which appeared in the December of 1845. Not long

before his death, John Sterling had said, in a letter to Carlyle, "It is, as you say, your destiny to write about Cromwell; and you will make a book of him, at which the ears of our grandchildren will tingle." The work had this effect upon the generation by whom it was first read. Not only did it confirm the intuition of that simple-hearted and clear-sighted woman, but for whom the book might never have been written; it brought well-nigh the whole of the English people round from the opposite opinion to the view which she had reached in her secluded home in Annandale. No such revolution of public sentiment on a great historical question of primary magnitude was ever effected before by any single book; and the revolution was almost as instantaneous as it was conclusive. Is it needful to recall the evil work which sectarian malignity had combined with political malice to effect in blasting the reputation of Oliver Cromwell? There is no baser deed recorded in the history of England than the desecration, not merely of his tomb, but of that body which had been the temple of so noble a spirit—torn from its grave at Westminster by impious hands at the Restoration, and, after nameless indignities, thrown headless into a trench under the gallows at Tyburn. The unhallowed temper which wrought that infamy had survived through the succeeding century, and even entered our own. It was still actively existent when Carlyle sat down to write the biography of the Protector. Petty scribblers, incompetent, even had they been industrious, contented themselves with indolently echoing the slanders invented by the sacrilegious desecrators of the grave; nor was David Hume, though he professed to be a lover of truth, one whit better in respect to veracity on this subject than the Grub Street throng—if possible he was worse. The extent to which the truth had been, not merely obscured, but obliterated, may be estimated by the fact that even a large proportion of the Nonconformists of England had suffered themselves to be hoodwinked into acceptance of the view of the Protector which had its origin in the malice of their own, as well as his, enemies.* Not that efforts had been wanting on the part of several historical students to render justice to Cromwell's memory before Carlyle addressed himself to the task. It should never be forgotten, that Lord John Russell (the name he bore at the time he performed this work, and by which we best like to remember him) was the first writer of the century who put into print anything approaching an

---

* Never can we forget the shock it gave us when, nearly twenty years after the publication of Carlyle's biography, we found even in Cromwell's own county of Huntingdon, certain benighted natives of that region—"scene of a moral as well as a physical denudation," as one of the most distinguished of its living sons once described it to us—who had failed to get rid of the notion that the Protector was one of the most diabolical of human beings, and responsible even for the evil deeds wrought by the earlier Cromwell who became Earl of Essex. Hard as it may be to believe the story, it is nevertheless a fact that, even at the recent date we speak of, the occupant of the old house at Huntingdon, in which Cromwell was born, would, when pilgrims from America came to see it, cause them to be conducted to certain mean offices at the rear of the building as the place most intimately associated with his birth! The only great man the town or shire has produced, his name is to this hour treated with contempt by a section of the population; though by the great majority of the people in the Fen Country the story of "the Farmer of St Ives," and what he did for England and the world, is rightly deemed the grandest of all their local associations. But they have not yet dared to raise a statue in his honour on the soil from which he sprang, and a proposal, made a few years ago, to erect some such memorial in connection with the chief Nonconformist place of worship in the county town, has not been carried out.

honest and impartial estimate of the merits of the Protector. Before his view appeared, all the references to Cromwell, as we have already said, were but repetitions of the calumnies invented by the partisan writers of the Restoration period; if any author ventured to say a word in praise of certain acts of the Protector, they were careful to water down their rare deviations into eulogy with qualifications that tended to make his character, as a whole, that of a deep-dyed villain. In 1840 a painstaking and conscientious Nonconformist divine, Dr Robert Vaughan, the founder and first editor of the *British Quarterly Review*, in a historical work written by him for the Society for the Diffusion of Useful Knowledge, gave the world some true glimpses of the hero of the Commonwealth. He had been preceded, eight years earlier, by Lord Nugent in his *Memorials of Hampden ;* and earlier still, in 1828, Macaulay, in his essay on *Hallam's Constitutional History*, had startled the readers of the *Edinburgh Review* with a panegyric on the ruler whom he described as the greatest soldier of his age and the most statesman-like of English princes. Two years before Macaulay dared this splendid act of high courage, William Godwin, in his original survey of the Protectorate period, had furnished materials for arriving at something like a fair conception of Cromwell's character. But it is a remarkable fact that twenty years earlier than Carlyle, nineteen years before Vaughan, eleven years before Lord Nugent, seven years before Macaulay, and five before Godwin, Lord John Russell, truly reflecting the noble spirit of the house of Bedford, had written thus manfully and discriminatingly of the Protector :—" Cromwell did much for his country. He augmented her naval glory, and made her name formidable to all the legitimate Sovereigns to whom his birth was a subject of derision. The smile on their faces was checked by the terror in their hearts. He made use of this wholesome intimidation to secure the liberty of foreign Protestants, and before he died he perceived the danger to Europe from the growth of the French power, which he thenceforth determined to restrain. At home he held the balance, upon the whole, evenly and steadily; he gave no sect the preponderance of State favour." This testimony was printed in its author's *Essay on the History of the English Government*, published in 1821; and though in the subsequent editions of the work many alterations and omissions were made, not one word was ever withdrawn or modified of the passage eulogising the Protector. While we bear these facts in mind, however, it remains true that the work of restoring Cromwell's reputation in a really effective manner was yet to be accomplished. These pioneers had but barely broken ground on the subject; and the impression made by their united work was inadequate to the thorough vindication of the great ruler whose memory had been so foully traduced. When Carlyle's biography appeared, the work was done. It for ever rescued one of the noblest spirits ever given to England from all the accumulated misrepresentations that had gathered around his name. Once for all, it placed a faithful portrait of the great soldier, patriot, and statesman before the eyes of the world.

It has been justly observed that few can form any idea of the amount of labour that was involved in the performance of this task—how many thousands of books, how many tens of thousands of pamphlets, of tracts, of old newspapers, had to be perused, compared, excerpted, before this could be accomplished. As in all his previous historical essays, and also in his biographical articles, including the fine miniature portrait of the Protector given four years earlier than his great book in *Heroes and Hero-Worship*, Carlyle had not now based any of his conclusions respecting the character he pourtrayed on the intuitions vouchsafed to a vivid imagination. Far from that, they were the result of the most patient investigation of the right materials, pursued with a diligence that was never exceeded by any German Dryasdust, and informed with the discrimination of the philosopher and that imaginative power of the true poet which penetrates to the essence of a man's character and shows what he really was. With what fidelity he touched even the very minutest accessories of his subject, the mere external drapery, so to speak, of his central theme, the student of his *Cromwell* may learn if he happens to be a resident for years in any of the localities connected with the Protector's life. He will find that the very smallest note on some old house, such as the Biggen Malten at Ramsey, one of the oldest seats of the Cromwell family, or on the discursive, sleepy river Ouse where it lazily creeps (we cannot say of this river that it ever runs) past the market-town of St Ives, or on some quite subordinate local person who turns up by accident in a letter of the Protector's, are all as strictly accurate as if the writer had dwelt for a lifetime in the places he describes. In many parts of the book, in as the descriptions of the Battle of Dunbar or of the Protector's Death-Bed, the biography becomes a poem, and one of the most thrilling sort; but it would be a prodigious mistake to suppose

that it is not also trustworthy history, written by one of
the most exact, patient, conscientious, and common sense
of all our historians, who would spend laborious days and
defy the " Museum headache " in order to verify a significant name or date, and who would not deflect a hair's
breadth from what he knew to be the truth to gain all the
rhetorical points in the world.   His mode of doing historical work was quite original.   He unites the familiar
style of characteristic detail pursued by Plutarch and Boswell with a power of generalization that has never been
excelled; and it has certainly not been the least of his
many services to the age, that besides vindicating Cromwell's memory, he has revolutionized this branch of literature, having been the chief inspirer of that new order of
workmen from whom we have received such vital additions to our historical library as Mr Froude's *England*
and Mr Motley's *Dutch Republic,* such biographies as Mr
Masson's *Milton,* Mr Spedding's *Bacon,* Dean Stanley's
Arnold, and Principal Tulloch's *Leaders of the Reformation,* works in some of which we find the conscientious
industry combined with not a little of the imaginative
and literary power of the master.

How many hundreds of headaches at the British
Museum that work on Cromwell must have cost Carlyle !
It was this " Museum headache," as he dolefully called
it, and which was really a most serious affliction, that led
him to take part in the movement incidentally referred to
by Gossip Grant, for the establishment of a great library
in London that should contain all the best books of
reference, and from which the subscribers might procure
a plentiful supply of books to use at their own homes.   It
may be remembered that, on the death of the late Lord

Clarendon, who had occupied the post for several years, Carlyle was elected president of the London Library. But comparatively few were aware how appropriate that appointment was. The institution was in reality a child of his own. At the British Museum he had, like many other literary workers, found the inconveniences interfering so seriously with work that he went there as seldom as he could help, for we find him confessing that he was " rather a thin-skinned sort of student," and he was always afflicted when he did go with that wretched " Museum headache." Thus it came about that in 1840, desiring to see a good reference library founded where he might feel more at his ease, and get a bundle of books home with him when he desired to make a leisurely survey of any, he set some younger men of his acquaintance to work to start such an institution ; and the result was the London Library. The most of these young friends, we may note, passed away from earth before Carlyle : for they included John Forster, the editor of the *Examiner* and biographer of Goldsmith; William Dougal Christie, C.B.,* the biographer

---

* It was to Mr Christie, an old friend of Charles Buller's, as well as of Mr Buller's illustrious tutor, that we owed the privilege of our introduction to Carlyle ; and we have before us a little note scribbled in pencil on one of the days of June, 1870, when Carlyle was very poorly in health, that we cannot resist giving here :— " Dear Christie,—My hand is very unwilling, mutinous even, but I compel it to act,—in pencil. I have lately read a life of Dryden which seemed to me done with rigorous fidelity. Yours always, T. C." The *Life of Dryden* here referred to is the one prefixed to the Globe edition of that poet, edited by Mr Christie ; and it is indeed worthy of this characteristic commendation. Those who have read Mr Christie's sketch of " Glorious John " will recognise the exceeding felicity of the phrase applied to it by Carlyle. We may also add that when the *Life of the First Earl of Shaftesbury* appeared, Carlyle expressed to ourselves the opinion that it was the

of the First Earl of Shaftesbury and editor of Dryden ; and Mr Spedding, the editor of Bacon. Still, though he transferred his allegiance from the British Museum to the Library in St James's Square, it must not be supposed that he did not continue to make an extensive use of the former ; and in his evidence before a Royal Commission he testified to the exceeding value of its library. He was specially emphatic when he spoke of the Thomasson Collection of Tracts, as furnishing splendid materials for history. "They are called the King's pamphlets," he said, "and in value, I believe, the whole world could not parallel them. If you were to take all the collections of works on the Civil War, of which I have ever heard notice, I believe you would not get a set of works so valuable as those." Mr Robert Cowtan, one of the assistant librarians at the Museum, in a volume relating to the old libraries in the institution, says he heard, quite incidentally, from a lady who attended the Reading Room about 1850, that she used to receive the most gallant attentions from Mr Carlyle whenever she met him at the Museum. These attentions were not on account of any personal acquaintance, but were simply rendered to her as a lady engaged in literary investigations. Mr Cowtan, in the same book, relates with honest pride how he had the honour of looking out from the Thomasson Collection referred to by Carlyle in his Parliamentary evidence many of the Tracts that were used by the illustrious historian for his *Cromwell.* Carlyle, we may here

---

most faithful and complete view of the period to which it relates ever written. This judgment he embodied in a letter of some length, which, being got in loan by a certain noble lord, was unfortunately lost in its re-transmission through the post.

note, was one of several men of letters who about 1847 entered the lists against Mr Panizzi's management of the Museum, and whose complaints led to a Parliamentary investigation which issued in many decided reforms being effected. Amongst the complainants was another Scotsman, Mr George Lillie Craik, editor of the *Pictorial History of England.* Mr Payne Collier, the oldest literary man now alive in England—for he was born in 1789—also joined in the assault upon the administration of the Museum.

Though by some his *Cromwell* is regarded as Carlyle's historical masterpiece, a view which may be defended on religious rather than on literary grounds, while comparatively few deny that it is one of the most satisfactory and valuable of all the contributions ever made to English history, it has not escaped adverse criticism. In the first of the published letters to her friend, Mr Boner, the little authoress of *Our Village,* writing in the same month in which the book was published, said : " The most important book has been Carlyle's *Cromwell,* in which the mutual jargon of the biographer and his subject is very curious. Never was such English seen. The Lord Protector comes much nearer to speaking plain than his historian." In another letter to Boner, who was a warm admirer of Carlyle, Miss Mitford returns to the attack : " After you have read more of him, you will like him less. I am quite sure that your fine taste will be repelled by the horrible coarseness of some of his nicknames in the Cromwell book. He is constantly talking of flunkeyism, and trades upon half-a-dozen cant words of that order." There is a grain of truth in this complaint about the nicknames. We can-

not help thinking that poor Dryasdust fares rather hardly
at his hands; and there is a sharp point in the question we
have seen put somewhere—Would not Sir Walter Scott,
who invented the name "Dryasdust" in his kindly
humour, have been ashamed to play upon it so often
and so long as Carlyle (who merely picked it up) has
done? That its occasional introduction is exceedingly
effective, cannot be denied; but there are times when
its reappearance, instead of being humorous, is simply
tiresome. What other historian is so much in the habit
of assailing his authorities in anything like the same
truculent fashion? In reply to this, it may be urged, that
comparatively few previous historians have worked with
the same, almost preternatural, minuteness of investigation, so that their tempers were not likely to be tried to
the same extent as his. Nor is this all that must be
taken into consideration; for is there any other instance
of the union of the archæological spirit, as we find it in
him, with the poetic? and how was it possible for a
high-strung nervous organisation like his to go through
the terrible drudgery to which he was constrained by
his acutely active conscience, and his passion for
truth, without a great deal of irritation, which had, of
necessity, to find vent in a way characteristic of the
man? He went through more serious hard work in
writing a page than little Miss Mitford would have in
writing a volume, for he never applied an epithet which
he could not have justified by a hundred facts, hidden
away, it might be, in dusty, cobwebbed corners, from the
view of all other men. Writers like Miss Mitford, or
even Walter Scott, on the other hand, could pepper their
"copy" with epithets without a thought of anything but

how they would sound. We need not wonder, then, why the easy-writing people should have condemned Carlyle for his abuse of Dryasdust. They had not taken the trouble to be as much in Dryasdust's company; else they also might have got into the habit of abusing him quite as much as Carlyle did. To a visitor from Australia, Mr David Buchanan, he once remarked that no one would credit the prodigious labour he had undergone before he even began to write *Cromwell.* He said he laboured to gain almost as intimate a knowledge of the man he was going to write about as he had of himself; and this was only to be attained by a minute examination and close study of every letter and document that had ever emanated from him, and an intimate knowledge of all the circumstances under which he acted, the events by which he was controlled or impelled to action, and the men who acted with him and against him, as also every detail respecting the circumstances and surroundings of the position or situation. All this knowledge, he said, was only to be got at by enormous labour, and was valuable when attained only as it was made use of with intelligence and insight. An incidental illustration of the profound sense he had of the value of all expedients for escaping the society of Dryasdust, is furnished in the letter he sent to the historian of Dumbartonshire, when that gentleman brought out the first edition of his useful compilation, *The Annals of Our Time.* Carlyle hastened to give Mr Irving's book a good word. " To fish up," said he, " and extract or extricate from the boundless overflowing ' Mother of Dead Dogs,' with judicious clearness, the millionth part of something like *historical* which may be floating past (999,999 facts mere putrescence, unsavoury or even poisonous more or less), especially if you indicate, too, *where* the authentic account of that was to be had—this I have often thought would be an incalculable service for serious readers of the present and still more of the future generations. I exhort you to continue at the work and bring it to more and more perfection."

Some other censors have complained, that the attempt to convert the garments of men and their outward peculiarities into historical portraits has been exaggerated in this and the other historical writings of Carlyle. These critics speak of him contemptuously, as belonging to the school called by M. Rigault, *les Gobelins de la Littérature*, from their servile attempts to imitate painting. But it will generally be found, we believe, on careful inquiry, that the stress he laid on the garment, or the external peculiarity, was well considered, and had more reason in it than some people might imagine. "His shrewdness," we are told by a competent witness, "especially in judging of character from small indications, was extraordinary. He once denounced, as a scoundrel, a man of business, who, at the time, was in the best repute, and who, shortly afterwards, turned out to deserve all that had been said against him. 'How,' he was asked, 'did you find him out, Mr Carlyle?' 'Oh,' said he, 'I saw rogue in the twist of the false hip of him as he went out at the door.' He was once asked what he thought of a new acquaintance whom he had seen for a few minutes. 'I should call him a willowy sort of a man.' The unspeakable felicity of the epithet could be shown only by an unwarrantable breach of confidence."* Nor must it be for-

---

* *St. James's Gazette Newspaper*, Feb. 5, 1881.

gotten, that his picturesque touches were never sham expedients for covering slightness of work. "No one denies," says Mr Leslie Stephen, "that, whatever the accuracy of the colouring in his historical studies, they at least imply the most thoroughgoing and conscientious labour. If Dryasdust does not invest Cromwell or Frederick with the same brilliant lights as Carlyle, he admits fully that Carlyle has not scamped the part of the work upon which Dryasdust most prides himself. At worst, he can only complain that the poetical creator is rather ungrateful in his way of speaking of the labours by which he has profited. It is, indeed, a subsidiary pleasure, in reading all Carlyle's writings, to feel that the artist is always backed up by the conscientious workman."

When he was a young Fellow of Magdalen, just turned thirty, Dr J. B. Mozley contributed to the *Christian Remembrancer* for 1846 a criticism on Carlyle's *Cromwell* which, in spite of its High Church rancour and juvenile hardihood of assertion, is still worthy of being read. It has been included in the first of two volumes of *Essays, Historical and Theological*, published (in 1878) since Canon Mozley's lamented death. The writer who saw in Strafford "as noble a man as ever England produced," and who regarded Laud with unqualified admiration, of course pictures Cromwell as a monstrous crocodile— "mighty, but unseemly; tremendous, but vile;" and no effort is spared to expose the weak points of the bio- grapher as well as those of his Puritan hero. Though the essay overshoots the mark by its blind sectarian passion, Mozley was too clever a man to fail in detecting some real blemishes which mar the Protector's biography; and perhaps one of his most effective hits was that in which he hurls his sarcasm at the vague and oracular utterances of the northern seer. " Mr Carlyle's Reality," says the critic, " is a magnificent abstraction ; it refuses to be caught and grasped, and will give no account of itself for the satisfaction of sublunary and practical curiosity. It wages an eternal war with shadows ; it is a disperser of phantoms ; lies flee before it ; formulæ shudder at its approach. This is all we know of its nature and its characteristics. It carries on a great aerial battle nobody knows where ; and teaches with sublime infallibility nobody knows what." Of all the adverse criticisms of *Cromwell* that we have seen, this is perhaps the only one that succeeds in scoring a point against the book.

The immediate success of the work was greater than that which had attended any of its author's previous productions. A new edition was called for before many weeks after the first was published ; and a third edition, in four volumes, appeared in 1849, containing large additions in the shape of letters of Cromwell, and other matter throwing light on his biography. The book has left little indeed for others to do in the delineation of that massive figure, and all subsequent writers who have had occasion to pourtray Cromwell have shown their good sense by carefully abstaining from entering into competition with Carlyle. His friend Mr Masson, in his great work on the *Life and Times of Milton*, may have brought into a clearer light certain elements of Cromwell's character which Carlyle overlooked ; but he does not claim for his picture of the Protector aught else than a subordinate position, and when he arrives in his narrative at such an incident as the Battle of Dunbar, he contents himself with a brief statement of the main facts, referring the reader to "the one full, grand, and ever-memorable account" given by his illustrious predecessor. Even had the political writings of Carlyle been productive of infinitely worse results in the direction of strengthening despotic ideas than they really were, he might well have been forgiven by the friends of freedom on account of the service he rendered to the cause of religious and civil liberty when he restored the image of Cromwell, freed from dust and defilement, to the admiring gaze of the English people. That old name immediately became a new watchword with the party of reform ; and, whether he meant it or not, Carlyle was, through his biography of Oliver, henceforth enrolled among the most powerful of the progressive forces of his age. The spirit of the book was at once transfused into the veins of modern England, and became part of the very life blood of the nation. The words of Cromwell and of his biographer were repeated in thousands of pulpits and on every platform, and potent were they in promoting many a good cause. Nor has the force of the book been exhausted yet ; it still goes on working like leaven, making the great "uncrowned King of England" the promoter of righteousness and freedom in our own century even as he was in that century which had him in the flesh to fight its battles at Naseby and Dunbar.

It is pleasant to recall the fact that, on his visit to the field of Naseby for the purpose of being able to describe the site of the battle, Carlyle was accompanied thither by Dr Arnold. The meeting of the two distinguished historians was fated to be their last as well as their first; for Arnold died within six short weeks of the happy time

when he received Carlyle as his honoured guest.   It was on
Friday, 13th May 1842, that Carlyle went down to Rugby
by express invitation ; and on the following day host and
guest together explored the battlefield.   Carlyle left the
schoolhouse expressing the hope that it might "long continue to be what was to him one of the rarest sights in
the world—a temple of industrious peace."   This visit gave
great delight to Dr Arnold, who had long cherished a
high reverence for Carlyle, and was proud of having
received such a guest under his roof.   During the few
weeks that intervened between that visit and Arnold's
departure from earth, he continued full of the subject,
talking joyously with successive visitors about the pilgrimage to Naseby with Carlyle.

CHAPTER XV.

MANY were ready to say with Macaulay, "We have a
kindness for Mr Leigh Hunt." But it seems strange, on
the first view of it, that the old companion of Shelley
should have found one of his staunchest friends in
Thomas Carlyle. He was an ex-newspaper editor who
had been in prison for libel, though no doubt the Prince
Regent deserved all that the *Examiner* said about him,
and much more; his writings had a vivacity that gave
many readers an impression of levity; he was as ignorant
of the ways of the business world as a child, as destitute
of decision of character as Hamlet; and he was always
struggling with pecuniary difficulties, from which he had
to be rescued periodically by the help of friends. Holding
a religious creed that ignored all the stern facts of human
experience, he was an Apostle of Cheerfulness whose
gospel was calculated to make any serious spirit, with a
sense of realities, somewhat sad; and he was described in
old age by one of his acquaintances as "the grey-headed

boy." Yet the man who by some people had been designated the Apostle of Despair took Leigh Hunt to
his heart and cherished him there with a warmth
that made the words of Macaulay in praise of Hunt
seem cold. The strong-willed, prudent, thrifty, self-
dependent Sartor, who was supposed to have no patience
with the weak and wayward, regarded this light and
airy being with deep and tender affection. One cause of
the seemingly incongruous connection, so far as Carlyle
was concerned, may be traced to a feature of his
character which no one has described with so much
felicity as Leigh Hunt himself. "I believe," wrote the
latter, "that what Mr Carlyle loves better than his fault-
finding, with all its eloquence, is the face of any human
creature that looks suffering, and loving, and sincere ; and
I believe further, that if the fellow-creature were suffering
only, and neither loving nor sincere, but had come to a
pass of agony in this life which put him at the mercies
of some good man for some last help and consolation
towards his grave, even at the risk of loss to repute, and
a sure amount of pain and vexation, that man, if the
groan reached him in its forlornness, would be Thomas
Carlyle." We have already seen that it was Hunt who
wrote the first, as it still remains the best, of all the really
appreciative descriptions of Carlyle's literary style ; this
paragraph in his *Autobiography* proves that he understood
the man as well as he understood his writings. It was to
him a constant delight to expatiate on what he so happily
designated "Carlyle's paramount humanity."* That

---

* When Leigh Hunt died, the *Spectator* said : "We have smiters
and denunciators out of number ; the glowing and generous dogma-
tism of Carlyle has called up a host of imitators, who, while quite

humanity must have been powerfully appealed to by the misfortunes of Hunt—the cruel slanders that had been heaped upon his devoted head by hireling partisans both in Edinburgh and London, more especially in the Scottish capital, and the poverty that perpetually dogged his footsteps, causing his exquisite powers, both as poet and essayist, to be monopolised by hack-work, for which the pay was often wretched, and never liberal. There was something pathetic in the spectacle of the poet, who had written the *Story of Rimini*, condemned to the drudgery of writing gossip for the newspapers, which, even in old age, he was often obliged to hawk about among the editors before he could get a customer; and the pathos must have been deepened, rather than modified, especially to such an onlooker as Carlyle, by the meek, sunny, hopeful, uncomplaining spirit with which the victim bore it all. Nor would the sympathy of the earnest worker be lessened as he noted that, with all his seeming levity, Hunt was a genuine solid man of letters, of vast and richly varied culture, with a literary taste and insight such as no other journalist of his generation possessed; as sober and industrious as he was accomplished; and who might have accumulated riches if it had not been for his painstaking conscientious care in securing perfect accuracy of statement and the most exquisite form possible for even the most trivial bit of work that he undertook.* So that, after all, there was

---

as positive as their master, possess neither his brain nor his heart : let us also accept and reverence the Apostle of Charity—the man whose poems and essays were all written in the anticipation of a Future of love and wisdom, such as many have dreamt of, but few believed in and worked for with such constancy as he."

* "The immense amount of labour," says his eldest son, speaking

no mystery in the friendship which the grim hermit from Nithsdale conceived at first and cherished ever afterwards for this sunny-hearted creature, who, in some respects closely resembling himself, was yet in others as far removed from him as one human being could be from another.

In *Leigh Hunt's London Journal* (1834-5) the dawn of Carlyle's genius had been hailed with intensest appreciation by an editor quick to perceive merit wherever he found it, and who, to his credit, did not allow the attacks upon himself which had appeared in the Edinburgh organ of the Tories to cool the ardour of his enthusiasm when a new star rose in the northern sky.*   Turning to the two

---

of his father's *London Journal,* " which he bestowed, particularly in searching out every point to elucidate and to verify, involved an outlay of time and of money that could scarcely be returned even by a large and certainly not by a limited sale. The expenditure in time, exertion, and health was thus constantly in excess of the returns. For by far the largest proportion of the labours, all that which simply negatived or failed to elucidate, instead of verifying, remained unseen by the public, but was as conscientiously and arduously gone through as the similar portion which resulted in print." Though unperceived by the mass of general readers, it was clearly seen by Carlyle—of that we may rest assured ; and hence, even had there been no other qualities to recommend the worker, Carlyle would have held him in high esteem.

* A Scottish reader cannot glance over the file of Leigh Hunt's miscellany without being greatly struck by the constant recurrence of helpful, sympathetic words in favour of Scottish authors, some of the number till then quite unknown to southern readers, and just emerging into view in their native country. No sooner, for example, had Hugh Miller's first book, the *Legends and Scenes of the North of Scotland,* made its appearance, than Hunt hastened to give long extracts from the book, at the same time expressing the confident opinion—which the world has since seen amply verified—that the stonemason of Cromarty was a "remarkable man, who will infallibly be well known." He earnestly exhorted the young author to set about making a second volume without delay, and adds :—"He is

volumes of Hunt's charming miscellany (would that we had such a magazine to-day!), we find the 19th number (Wednesday, August 6, 1834) giving the place of honour to an article on Goethe in which Carlyle is introduced to the notice of Hunt's readers. It opens with some objections to the German poet's plan of life, in taking no notice of the politics and public events of his time, and in refusing to busy himself with the hopes of the world and the advancement of society. Goethe's enemies said that he thought in this matter for expedience' sake, and because he happened to be comfortably situated, and, therefore, had no personal interest in change. As we might expect, while of too kindly a nature to echo this serious charge, Hunt did not, by any means, approve the poet's theory.

'Old Mortality' come to life again in a younger and nobler shape; but his own pages will rescue the designation from its applicability. Mr Miller, it seems, is, or has been a common stonemason, and itinerant architect of tombs; and from 'cogitations in those shades' he has issued forth a writer of pretensions that would have been little expected from such a beginning, though (singularly enough—unless it is an Irishism to say so) not without its special precedent in this remarkable age; for Mr Allan Cunningham was of the same trade. But Mr Miller, besides a poetical imagination, though not yet exhibited in verse, has great depth of reflection; and his style is so choice, pregnant, and exceedingly like an educated one, that if itself betrays it in any respect to be otherwise, it is by that very excess; as Theophrastus was known not to have been born in Attica, by his too Attic nicety." It is significant to note the patient and loving care with which Leigh Hunt, not content with these liberal, but thoroughly just, words of praise, is at pains to italicise all the gems of thought and expression in the extracts given from the stonemason's book. As we read these characterisations of new authors, so independent and generous in their spirit, so unconventional and courageous, and always so just, we feel inclined to say that there was at that time but one other man of letters in London who could have written them; and that was the friend of Leigh Hunt who had just the other day pitched his tent in Cheyne Row.

But he has hardly begun his argument against it, when he suddenly breaks off: "We had written thus far, when, having become further acquainted with the *Character-istics*"—Carlyle's essay in the *Edinburgh*, the one that finally severed his connection with that Review—"in the intervals of our writing, our feelings of respect and admiration for Goethe have been so increased, that we must plainly confess we cannot proceed in the same strain of objection to him." On another page of the same number, an extract is printed from Carlyle's *Specimens of German Romances*, the editor praising the translator's "masterly criticism" of Richter's genius, "which we have read twice over for the mere pleasure received from the force and abundance of the thinking." In the 23rd number, Hunt reprints that magnificent passage, which we have already given, from Carlyle's article on "German Literature," in which he demonstrated, to use Hunt's felicitous title, that "the perception of beauty and nobleness is not a matter of rank." In the 34th number there is a long passage, with similar complimentary allusion to Carlyle as the author, from the famous essay on Burns; and in the 42nd, Hunt gives a portion of Carlyle's tribute to Charles Buller, with a characteristic note, in which he says: "It may be as well to add, considering the prevailing tone of this magazine, that the article from which the following passage is taken, is written in sober earnest— we need not·add, how well." Ever and anon choice paragraphs are inserted from the essays of Carlyle, always with their author's name appended, instead of that of the Review in which they had appeared; and to Carlyle's translation of *Wilhelm Meister*, we find him giving "our reason, our imagination, our tears." The pleasant miscellany had not a long life, for it expired in the last month of 1835. Fifteen years afterwards, on December 7, 1850, there appeared a new *Leigh Hunt's Journal*, also, alas! short-lived, for it was discontinued on the 29th March 1851. It is fondly remembered, we doubt not, by some of our readers who have now reached or passed middle age; and these do not need to be reminded that this delightful periodical contained three articles from the pen of Carlyle, entitled, "Two Hundred and Fifty Years Ago (from a Waste-Paper Bag of T. Carlyle)." The introductory paper had for its title, "Hollies of Haughton;" the second, "Croydon Races;" the third and last, "Sir Thomas Dutton and Sir John Hatton Cheek." These sketches have been reprinted in their author's *Miscellanies*. But in Leigh Hunt's old periodical, in which we find those frequent friendly allusions to Carlyle, there is an anonymous poem which, although no one has ever called attention to it, seems to us as if it may possibly have been a contribution from the editor's friend in Cheyne Row. When it first met our eye, casually glancing over the time-stained yellow pages of the treasured volume, two verses at once stood out with amazing distinctness as bearing the impress of no common hand, and our first thought was, Can this be Carlyle? The more closely we have looked into the matter the stronger has the feeling of probability grown, until it is now beginning to assume with us the shape of a settled conviction; at all events, be our guess right or wrong, we shall venture to lay the poem before our readers, so that they may be in a position to judge for themselves. The piece is contained in the 30th number of *Leigh Hunt's London Journal*, issued on Wednesday, Oct. 22, 1834, by which time, it will be observed, Carlyle was fixed in Cheyne Row, where he had Leigh Hunt as a frequent visitor. The poem runs thus :—

DRUMWHINN BRIDGE,

OVER THE RIVER ORR—BUILT 1832.

Meek autumn midnight glancing,
  The stars above hold sway,
I bend, in muse advancing,
  To lonesome Orr my way.

Its rush in drowsy even ·
  Can make the waste less dead ;
Short pause beneath void Heaven,
  Then back again to bed !

Hoho ! 'mong deserts moory,
  See here the craftsman's hand ;
Vain now, bleak Orr, thy fury,
  On whinstone arch I stand.

Dull Orr, thou moorland river
  By man's eye rarely seen,
Thou gushest on for ever,
  And wert while earth has been.

There o'er thy crags and gravel,
  Thou sing'st an unknown song,
In tongue no clerks unravel !
  Thou'st sung it long and long.

From Being's Source it bounded,
  The morn when time began ;
Since thro' this moor has sounded,
  Unheard or heard of man.

That day they crossed the Jordan,
  When Hebrew trumpets rang,
Thy wave no foot was fording,
  Yet here in moor it sang.

And I, while thou'st meandered,
  Was not, have come to be,
Apart so long have wandered,
  This moment meet with thee.

> Old Orr, thou mystic water!
>   No Ganges holier is;
> *That* was Creation's daughter,
>   What was it fashioned *this?*
>
> The whinstone Bridge is builded,
>   Will hang a hundred year;
> When bridge to time has yielded,
>   The brook will still be here.
>
> Farewell, poor moorland river:
>   We parted and we met;
> Thy journeyings are for ever,
>   Mine art not ended yet.

November, 1832.

The two verses that stood out so vividly had recalled to us a familiar passage in that charming picture of Carlyle's child-life at Ecclefechan which is to be found in the opening pages of the second book of *Sartor.* " Already in the youthful Gneschen, with all his outward stillness, there may have been manifest an inward vivacity that promised much; symptoms of a spirit singularly open, thoughtful, almost poetical. Thus, to say nothing of his Suppers on the Orchard-wall, and other phenomena of that earlier period, have many readers of these pages stumbled, in their twelfth year, on such reflections as the following? 'It struck me much, as I sat by the Kuhbach, one silent noontide, and watched it flowing, gurgling, to think *how this same streamlet had flowed and gurgled, through all changes of weather and of fortune, from beyond the earliest date of History. Yes, probably on the morning when Joshua forded Jordan;* even as at the mid-day when Cæsar, doubtless with difficulty, swam the Nile, yet kept his *Commentaries* dry,—*this little Kuhbach, assiduous as Tiber, Eurotas or Siloa, was murmuring on across the wilderness, as yet unnamed,*

unseen : here, too, as in the Euphrates and the Ganges,
is a vein or veinlet of the grand World-circulation of
Waters, which, with its atmospheric arteries, has lasted
and lasts simply with the World. Thou fool! Nature
alone is antique, and the oldest art a mushroom ; that
idle crag thou sittest on is six thousand years of age.'
In which little thought, as in a little fountain, may there
not lie the beginning of those well-nigh unutterable medi-
tations on the grandeur and mystery of Time, and its
relation to Eternity, which play such a part in this Philosophy of Clothes?" The book in which this passage
occurs had been completed in 1831, but was lying in a
private drawer at Craigenputtoch (when not in the hands
of the astonished publishers' "tasters") at the time the
above poem was written—not being able to get itself into
print till *Fraser* opened a door for it in 1833. Then the
Orr Water, be it noted, is a moorland stream that flows
through at least one parish, if not more, marching with
that of Dunscore, the parish in which Carlyle was residing when the bridge of Drumwhinn was built. With this
fact we must link the curious coincidence that, while the
poem bears to have been written on one of the opening
days of November 1832, it only made its appearance in
print in the October of 1834, not much more than three
months after Carlyle had set up his " little book-press "
in the house in Cheyne Row, and when Leigh Hunt, we
know, was often with him, no doubt speaking at times of
his new venture, his *London Journal* having been started
in April, and probably suggesting the propriety of Carlyle
giving him a contribution for its pages. That there was
no good reason for refusing such a request will be all the
more obvious when we mention that the periodical,

besides having Leigh Hunt, his friend, for its conductor, numbered among its contributors such writers as Walter Savage Landor and William Hazlitt. Could there be anything more natural than that Carlyle, thus solicited, should give him the little poem? That such a manuscript was likely to be lying in his drawer at the time is a theory seen to be quite tenable when we mark the dates prefixed to the small collection of poetical "Fractions," as he calls them, included in the second appendix to the first volume of his *Miscellaneous Essays.* These dates show that the seven pieces of verse there published were written between 1823 and 1833, so that he had not given up trying his hand at rhyme when Drumwhinn Bridge was built. We have thus marshalled some of the points, both in the internal and the external evidence, conducting us to the conclusion that this anonymous poem was probably the work of Carlyle; nor have we yet exhausted all the features of the case that tend in the same direction. Apart from the fact that a notable portion of the poem is simply a paraphrase of the sentences we have cited from *Sartor,* reproducing the very same allusions to the Jordan and its passage by the Israelites, together with mention of the Ganges, is not the whole spirit of the piece Carlylean to the very core? What said the Laird of Craigenputtoch to Emerson on that August day in 1833 as they walked and talked among the hills, looking up at Criffel and down into Wordsworth's country? "Christ died on the tree; that built Dunscore kirk yonder; that brought you and me together. Time has only a relative existence." So in the poem, there is at least a kindred thought:—

> From Being's Source it bounded
>   The morn when time began;
> Since through this moor has sounded,
>   Unheard or heard of man.
>
> That day they crossed the Jordan,
>   When Hebrew trumpets rang,
> *Thy* wave no foot was fording,
>   Yet here in moor it sang.
>
> And I, while thou'st meandered,
>   Was not, have come to be,
> Apart so long have wandered,
>   This moment meet with thee.

And who that stood on the whinstone arch over that moorland river in that remote corner of Scotland in the November of 1832 could it have been if it was not the dweller at Craigenputtoch, the Mystic,* who was heard to sing on this wise :—

> Old Orr, thou mystic water !
>   No Ganges holier is ;
> *That* was Creation's daughter,
>   What was it fashioned *this ?*

The very italics are significant, as any one may see who marks Carlyle's corresponding use of them in his acknowledged poem, entitled, " The Beetle ;" nor will the capital

---

* " I attempted, in the beginning of 1831, to embody in a series of articles, headed ' The Spirit of the Age,' some of my new opinions, and especially to point out in the character of the present age the anomalies and evil characteristics of the transition from a system of opinions which had worn out to another only in process of being formed.   The only effect which I know to have been produced by them was that Carlyle, then living in a secluded part of Scotland, read them in his solitude, and saying to himself (as he afterwards told me), ' Here is a new Mystic,' inquired on coming to London that autumn respecting their authorship ; an inquiry which was the immediate cause of our being personally acquainted.   .   .   .   He soon found out that I was not ' another Mystic.' "—*Autobiography by John Stuart Mill.*

letters that are employed pass unobserved by any careful student of Carlyle's writings. In addition to all which considerations, we must likewise note the extreme simplicity of the title; the homeliness yet dignity of the diction, conveying great thoughts in the very simplest language; the characteristic allusion to "the craftsman's hand," and to the tongue "no clerks unravel;" the "hundred *year*" in the penultimate verse; and the humorously tender farewell in the last to the "poor moorland river." If this be not the workmanship of Carlyle, all we can say is, that no author ever came nearer it; and, be it his or not, the reader will, perhaps, kindly excuse our intrusion of the certainly noteworthy little poem when we recall attention to the fact that, both by subject and date, it does at least have some reference to the memorable sojourn of Carlyle among the hills of Galloway.

Both in Leigh Hunt's *Autobiography*, 1850, and his *Correspondence*, 1862, tokens abound of the intimate friendship that subsisted between Hunt and Carlyle. Their acquaintance began in the February of 1832, when the elder of the two men sent a copy of his *Christianism* to the writer of "Characteristics." By the 20th of the above-named month, Carlyle, then lodging in London, was inviting Hunt to tea, as the means of their first meeting; and on the 20th of November, the month in which "Drumwhinn Bridge" was composed, Carlyle was writing from Craigenputtoch urging Hunt to "come hither and see us when you want to rusticate a month," adding, "Is that for ever impossible?"—as it really was with the hard-driven poet and journalist, whose circumstances were always embarrassed, so much so that on more than one occasion he was literally without bread, and obliged to write to friends to get his books sold, that he might have something to eat. The pressure was sorest upon him from 1834 to 1840; his difficulties had been increasing in that very year when Carlyle pressed him to visit Nithsdale, and bad as they were then they became infinitely worse after he had moved from the New Road to Chelsea, which he seems to have done shortly before Carlyle's settlement in Cheyne Row. Hunt lived in the immediately adjoining street, and Carlyle had only too frequent occasion to know in detail the troubles that were almost daily perplexing his unfortunate neighbour. Yet it was in the very midst of those miseries that such incidents would occur as the one of which Mr R. H. Horne, the poet, gives such an amusing account in his *New Spirit of the Age*, 1844. At a little gathering, shortly after the publication of *Hero-Worship*, the conversation turned on the heroism of man, Leigh Hunt, as was his wont, taking the bright side, with most musical talk of the islands of the blest and the Millennium that was surely hastening, Carlyle dropping heavy tree-trunks of philosophical doubt across his friend's pleasant stream. "But the unmitigated Hunt never ceased his overflowing anticipations, nor the saturnine Carlyle his infinite demurs to those finite flourishings. The opponents were so well matched that it was quite clear the contest would never come to an end. But the night was far advanced, and the party broke up. Leaving the close room, they suddenly found themselves in presence of a brilliant starlight night. 'There,' shouted Hunt, 'look up there, look at that glorious harmony, that sings with infinite voices an eternal song of Hope in the soul of man.'

Carlyle looked up. They all remained silent to hear what he would say. Out of the silence came a few low-toned words, in a broad Scotch accent. 'Eh! it's a sair sicht!'" In 1840 Hunt left Chelsea, but the fraternal ministrations of Carlyle did not cease; and when at length in 1847 the poor old poet got a pension from the Queen of £200 a year, at the instance of Lord John Russell, one of the most active promoters of the movement that secured this provision was Carlyle, who drew up a paper in which the claims of Leigh Hunt were set forth in a manner which would have made refusal even by an unsympathetic Minister impossible. The first paragraph of the Memoranda ran thus: "That Mr Hunt is a man of the most indisputedly superior worth; a *Man of Genius* in a very strict sense of that word, and in all the senses which it bears or implies; of brilliant varied gifts, of graceful fertility, of clearness, lovingness, truthfulness; of childlike open character; also of most pure and even exemplary private deportment; a man who can be other than *loved* only by those who have not seen him, or seen him from a distance through a false medium." The statement also contained the following notable passages:—"That his services in the cause of reform, as Founder and long as Editor of the *Examiner* newspaper; as Poet, Essayist, Public Teacher in all ways open to him, are great and evident: few now living in this kingdom, perhaps, could boast of greater. That his sufferings in that same cause have also been great; legal prosecution and penalty (not dishonourable to him; nay, honourable, were the whole truth known, as it will one day be): unlegal obloquy and calumny through the Tory Press;— perhaps a greater quantity of baseness, persevering, im-

placable calumny, than any other living writer has undergone. Which long course of hostility (nearly the cruellest
conceivable, had it not been carried on in half, or almost
total misconception) may be regarded as the beginning of
his other worst distresses, and a main cause of them, down
to this day." Carlyle added, that Leigh Hunt, though toiling continually "with passionate diligence," had hardly
been able to provide for the day that was passing over him,
and that none of his distresses had arisen from wasteful-
ness, since he was a man of humble wishes, who could
live with dignity on little, "but from crosses of what is
called Fortune, from injustice of other men, from inexperience of his own, and a guileless trustfulness of nature,
the thing and things that have made him unsuccessful"
making him, "in reality, *more* loveable." The memoranda closed with a fine compliment to Lord John Russell,
as an English minister, "in whom great part of England
recognises (with surprise at such a novelty) a man of
insight, fidelity, and decision." When Leigh Hunt
published his *Autobiography*, one of the first to congratulate him was his faithful friend in Cheyne Row, who
declared it to be "an excellent good book, by far the best
of the autobiographic kind I remember to have read in
the English language ; and, indeed, except it be Boswell's
of Johnson, I do not know where we have such a picture
drawn of a human life." Carlyle added, that the book
had been "like a written exercise of devotion" to him ;
he had "not assisted at any sermon, liturgy, or litany,
this long while," that had had so religious an effect upon
him. "Adieu, dear Hunt," he says, in the closing paragraph of his letter ; "you must let me use this familiarity,
for I am now an old fellow too, as well as you." No-

where do we see the great heart of Carlyle more beautifully displayed than in the story of his relations with that old Reformer, of whom it has been justly said that, long before Reform was popular, "he wielded one of the most vigorous lances in the forlorn hope of Liberals," and who yet was one of the gentlest of mankind, as he was also the sunniest, most graceful, and refined of all the essayists of the Victorian age.

The magnanimity of Carlyle was, we have reason to believe, not less apparent in his relationship with another distinguished contemporary who has already been named as an intimate friend, though in some important respects there was even a greater difference, both as to temperament and opinion, between the two than existed in the case we have just pictured. In his *Autobiography* we find John Stuart Mill declaring, in the sadly extravagant yet profoundly touching eulogy of his wife, that she was more a poet than Carlyle, and more a thinker than Mill himself—that her mind and nature included Carlyle's, and "infinitely more." There is a generous recognition of Carlyle's literary power and of the influence exercised by his writings upon Mill ;* but the latter says nothing

---

* "The good his writings did me," says Mill, "was not as philosophy to instruct, but as poetry to animate. . . . We never approached much nearer to each other's modes of thought than we were in the first years of our acquaintance. I did not, however, deem myself a competent judge of Carlyle. I felt that he was a poet, and that I was not ; that he was a man of intuition, which I was not ; and that as such, he not only saw many things long before me, which I could, only when they were pointed out to me, hobble after and prove, but that it was highly probable he could see many things which were not visible to me even after they were pointed out. I knew that I could not see round him, and could never be certain that I saw over him ; and I never presumed to judge him

as to the cessation of their personal friendship. That took place suddenly at the time of Mill's marriage to Mrs Taylor, in 1851. Mill, we believe, was chiefly if not wholly responsible for the breach, though this was probably the result of the influence exercised over him by another. An innocent joke about the marriage of the philosopher had come to the ears of Mill, carried to him by some " candid friend ;" and immediately he ceased to be a visitor at the house in Cheyne Row, where for years he had been a constant and always welcome guest. This gave extreme pain to the warm-hearted Carlyle, as well as to his wife, who from that hour never heard any reason given for the course of conduct which Mill had deemed it fitting to pursue. We have been told by one who knew both men intimately, and who most deeply regretted the estrangement, that Carlyle and his wife devised a kindly scheme to invite Mr and Mrs Mill to dinner at Cheyne Row, in order that the old amicable relationship might be restored. Carlyle sallied forth one morning to give the invitation in person, but near the India House was passed by Mill on the pavement in such a cold, resolute, unmistakeable fashion that the " cut " went to his heart, and he returned, disconsolate, with his kindly purpose unfulfilled.

How many humbler men of letters could bear witness to the truth of the testimony given in such an impressive form by Leigh Hunt, as to Carlyle's warmth of heart! The case of the still-surviving Thomas Cooper, the old Chartist leader, is but one example of many more that might be cited; and the mention of his name, as well as

---

with any definiteness, until he was interpreted to me by one greatly the superior of us both "—that is, by Mrs Mill !

of those that have gone before, suggests the reflection that, if Carlyle's political sentiments frequently gave pain to the friends of Reform, he seems, somehow, all along to have had an exceedingly warm side to Reformers. The poem written by Cooper in jail, *The Purgatory of Suicides*, he dedicated to Carlyle, from whom he received in return a kind letter, and subsequently many substantial tokens of friendly consideration. " I owe many benefits to Mr Carlyle," he says in the Autobiography published by him in 1872. " Not only richly directoral thoughts in conversation, but deeds of *substantial* kindness. Twice he put a five-pound note into my hand, when I was in difficulties ; and told me, with a look of grave humour, that if I could not pay him again, he would not hang me. Just after I sent him the copy of my Prison Rhyme, he put it into the hands of a young, vigorous, inquiring intelligence who had called to pay him a reverential visit at Chelsea. The new reader of my book sought me out and made me his friend. That is twenty-six years ago, and our friendship has continued and strengthened, and has never stiffened into patronage on the one side, or sunk into servility on the other—although my friend has now become ' Right Honourable,' and is the Vice-President of ' Her Majesty's Most Honourable Privy Council.' " It was at Carlyle's house that an incident occurred which Mr Cooper puts on record, because of the previous want of kindness which another Mr Forster had exhibited. " My novel of *The Family Feud*," he says, " drew a handsome critique in the *Examiner* from Mr John Forster— for a wonder ! I may as well tell how it came about. I went to 5 Cheyne Row, Chelsea, one evening, with the intent of spending a couple of hours with my illustrious friend Thomas Carlyle. But I had not been with him more than half-an-hour when Mr John Forster was announced. I met him without any high degree of pleasure. And although there was no treat on earth I could have desired more than to listen to the interchange of thought between two such intellects as those of Carlyle and John Forster, —I felt inclined, with the remembrance of the past, to 'cut my stick!' And I certainly should have decamped hastily, had it not been for an incident worth mentioning. A loaded truck stopped at the street door—there was a loud knock—and the maid-servant ran up stairs, breath-less, to say that a huge parcel had been brought. Mr Carlyle seemed all wonder and muttered, 'A huge parcel! *what* huge parcel?—but I'll come down and see.' And, somehow or other, we all went down to see—for there was a large wooden case, evidently containing a picture. A hammer and a chisel were soon brought, and I offered to take them, and open the case—but, no! my illustrious friend would open it himself. 'It's doubtless the picture from that old Landor,' said he; and he worked away vigorously with his implements till there was revealed a very noble picture indeed, with its fine gilded frame. It was a portrait of David Hume, in full dress—the dress he is said always to have worn when he sat down to write: so strangely were his polished style and his full dress associated. 'Only think of that old Landor sending me this!' broke out Carlyle again and again, as we all stood gazing on the portrait with admiration. This incident served to 'break the ice' so far that I joined a little in the conversation that followed; and when Mr Carlyle quitted the room to fetch a book he wanted to show his friend, Mr John Forster said to me, in a marked tone,

'You have just had a novel published by Routledge—do you happen to know whether a copy has been sent to the *Examiner?*' I replied that I did not know; but I would inquire. 'Take care that it is addressed to me, will you?' said Mr Forster; 'you understand what I mean? Take care that it is addressed to me personally'—and he nodded and smiled. 'Thank you, sir,' said I; 'I will address a copy to you, myself'—for I thought I did understand what he meant. I rose to go soon after, and my illustrious friend, with the perfect kindness he has always shown me, would go with me to the street door to say 'good night.' So I whispered to him, in the passage, and requested him to strengthen the good intent there seemed to lie in John Forster's mind towards me. Carlyle gave me one of his humorous smiles, and squeezed my hand, as an assurance that I might depend upon him. And so the favourable critique on my *Family Feud* appeared in the *Examiner*."

CHAPTER XVI.

HIS NEWSPAPER ARTICLES—INTEREST IN THE TEMPERANCE MOVEMENT—SUPPORTS THE PERMISSIVE BILL—CONTEMPT FOR THE FOURTH ESTATE—FRIENDSHIP WITH JOURNALISTS—THOMAS BALLÀNTYNE—HIS AMERICAN INTERVIEWERS—BURLESQUES OF HIS STYLE.

"OF all priesthoods, aristocracies, governing classes at present extant in the world, there is no class comparable for importance to that priesthood of the writers of books." When he penned this sentence, Carlyle included in the modern priesthood the writers for the newspapers; indeed he gave them an honourable place on his list. "The writers of newspapers, pamphlets, books, these are the real, working, effective Church of a modern country." But the young man who had arrived at this revolutionary conclusion, was not destined to do much for the Fourth Estate—except abuse it in such a wholesale and vituperative style, as no other public personage of his generation ventured to adopt. Had he been born a little later into the world, it is possible he might not have escaped being drawn into the vortex of journalism; but its attractive power was not in Carlyle's youthful days what it has since become—so the peril was one easily avoided. Poor as the pecuniary reward of the pedagogue might be in a country town on the Border or in Fife, it was perhaps as good as any the student could have got by contributing even to a metropolitan journal; as for the country papers in the opening quarter of the century, they were generally edited by the printer with a pastepot and a pair of scissors. That Carlyle had early formed a plan of life, with which the incessant distractions of the journalist's career would not have harmonised, has, we trust, been made sufficiently clear at the outset of our narrative; but it may be questioned if he would have rested content with hack-work for Dr Brewster, had the Edinburgh newspapers of that time been able to afford the scope for his talents, and the respectable pecuniary rewards which they are able to give to a brilliant young writer to-day. The lightest bits of press work executed by Carlyle at the beginning of his career as man of letters, were the couple of book notices he wrote for that *New Edinburgh*, which was not permitted to grow old; and we hear of nothing in the way of contributions to the newspapers till we arrive at the year of Charles Buller's death, and no more after that till the appearance of the series of articles which heralded the *Latter-Day Pamphlets*. The number of these contributions was six in all. The first appeared in the *Examiner* on March 4, 1848, and the last in the same journal of December 2 of the same year. "Louis Philippe" was the theme of the former article; the latter was the tribute to the writer's old pupil. On April 29, he printed in the *Examiner* an article on "Repeal of the Union;" and on May 13 there came three articles at a rush—two in the *Spectator* and one in the *Examiner*. The titles of these ran thus:—"Ireland and the British Chief Governor," "Irish Regiments (of the New Era)," and "Leglislating for Ireland." None of the six articles has been reprinted in the *Mis-

cellanies, and only the obituary notice of Buller is familiar to the reading public of to-day. Beyond a few letters, all of them that we remember addressed to the *Times*, Mr Carlyle has since 1848 contributed nothing to the newspapers. More than once the temptation to write for them has been put in his way; a case occurred some twelve years ago, when a provincial daily journal was said to have offered him a thousand guineas if he would write for it a description of the Derby Day, to which his name should be appended. Of course he was not caught by this golden bait; indeed, years before it was held out, he had given up contributing even to the magazines and reviews, for, about 1853, we remember being told by the then secretary of the Scottish Temperance League (Mr Robert Rae, now of London), how he had called at Chelsea upon Carlyle, with a view to prevail upon him to write something for the *Scottish Review*—a shilling quarterly the League was then publishing. This was the first occasion on which we happened to hear mention made of a fact that has now for some years been familiar enough to at least one section of the public—how Mr Carlyle was profoundly interested in the temperance question. He entered heartily into conversation with Mr Rae on the subject, perceiving at a glance, we doubt not, the sincerity and earnestness of his visitor. He was greedy of information about the progress of the work the League had in hand, and felt so much sympathy with it, that he would have written an article for the *Scottish Review* but for the fact that he had already refused similar applications from old friends, magazine and review editors, in London. Besides, were he to contribute an article, he added, there would be no end to the applications that would flow in upon him from other quarters; so, reluctantly, he had to say no.

Here it may be noted that, in the early days of the temperance movement, when some of its old pioneers in the Chelsea region held large open-air meetings, Carlyle was a frequent and attentive listener. When a Permissive Bill Association was formed in the district, its promoters felt encouraged by this token of sympathy with their work to invite him to attend the first public meeting; and, though he was unable to accept the invitation, he sent a reply that gave them great encouragement and tended much to strengthen the force of their agitation. "My complete conviction," he said, writing on 18th April 1872, "goes, and for long years has gone, with yours in regard to that matter; and it is one of my most earnest and urgent public wishes that such Bill do become law." They then asked him to accept the presidency of their society, and, in declining the honour in a courteous and kindly note, he said, "From the bottom of my heart I wish you success, complete and speedy." They had sent him a bundle of their literature; "the pamphlets," he told them, "shall be turned to account, though I myself require no argument or evidence farther on this disgraceful subject." It was indeed one that had long engaged his thoughts; in his *Chartism* perhaps the fiercest of all his bursts of indignation occurred in his Dantean picture of a certain class of the Glasgow operatives. "Be it with reason or unreason," he there wrote, "too surely they do in verity find the time all out of joint; this world for them no home, but a dingy prison-house of reckless unthrift, rebellion, rancour, indignation against themselves and against all men. Is it a green, flowery world, with azure everlasting sky stretched over it, the work and government of a God; or a murky, simmering Tophet, of copperas-fumes, cotton-fuz, gin-riot, wrath and toil, created by a Demon, governed by a Demon? The sum of their wretchedness, merited or unmerited, welters, huge, dark, and baleful, like a Dantean Hell, visible there in the statistics of Gin; Gin, justly named the most authentic incarnation of the Infernal Principle in our times, too indisputably an incarnation; Gin, the black throat into which wretchedness of every sort, communicating itself by calling on Delirium to help it, whirls down; abdication of the power to think or resolve, as too painful now, on the part of men whose lot of all others would require thought and resolution; liquid Madness sold at tenpence the quartern, all the products of which are and must be, like its origin, mad, miserable, ruinous, and that only!" Carlyle's appeal to the working-men electors doubtless led to the conversion of not a few of the long-deluded victims: "No man oppresses thee, O free and independent franchiser; but does not this stupid pewter-pot oppress thee? No son of Adam can bid thee come or go; but this absurd pot of heavy-wet, this can and does! Thou art the thrall, not of Cedric the Saxon, but of thy own brutal appetites and this scoured dish of liquor; and thou pratest of thy *liberty?* Thou entire blockhead!"

Years after the interview with the representative of the Scottish League he did indeed, in one or two instances, depart from the rule he had laid down for himself as we shall hereafter see, by giving Professor Masson a couple of articles for *Macmillan*, and by handing to another esteemed friend, Mr William Allingham, then the editor of *Fraser*, the two last historical essays he was ever to publish. But for the newspapers he never did any work beyond the six articles of 1848. Indeed, he often professed a great contempt for them. To the Rev. Joseph Cook, the Boston Monday lecturer, he said, "We must destroy the faith of the public in the newspapers." The Fifeshire editor, Mr Hodgson, tells us that, when he was introduced to the aged philosopher by Provost Swan of Kirkcaldy, Carlyle burst out in invectives against the newspaper profession, declaring it to be "mean and demoralising." To Charles Boner, long the German correspondent of a leading London daily, he spoke in the same truculent fashion. We have heard of his saying more than once that he never read the papers, as they contained only "gutter-water;" but it sometimes struck those who enjoyed the privilege of conversing with him that he had a singularly extensive acquaintance with the passing events of the day for a man who gave no heed to the morning paper, and who only glanced now and then into "a weekly print called *Public Opinion*, which somebody was good enough to send him regularly." Still, as in his relations to Reform and its advocates, so was it here: whatever he might be pleased to say or to write about the Fourth Estate, he was, from the commencement to the close of his career, on the very friendliest terms with gentlemen (and ladies, too—Miss Martineau, for example) whose main work in the world consisted in writing for the papers. Quite a crowd of journalists, such as Leigh Hunt and Thomas Aird, John Forster and David Masson, were included in the innermost circle of his friends; and how kind, considerate, and helpful he was to a still larger number of less distinguished members of the press, scores at least could personally testify. As we have already shewn, he was a good friend to Thomas Cooper, who was a newspaper man; and nothing could exceed his kindness to Thomas Ballantyne, the quondam Paisley weaver who rose to be editor of the *Manchester Times*, and who subsequently started a short-lived journal in London under the ill-fated title of *The Statesman* (to which, somehow, misfortune seems ever to cling). William Maccall, at one time the conductor of the *Critic*, and, like Ballantyne, hailing originally from Carlyle's own south-western district of Scotland, was also honoured with his friendship. To Ballantyne he gave permission to make a volume of extracts from his writings, prefaced with a brief biographical memoir; and he likewise counselled him to write an autobiography, on which Ballantyne was, we believe, engaged, when death cut short his labours in the August of 1871, at the age of 65. An earnest and sincere man, gifted with a fine taste in literature, he was also an ardent politician, and as such closely associated with Cobden and Bright in the Free Trade struggle. In later years he enjoyed the personal acquaintance of Lord Palmerston and the Earl of Clarendon; but he will be remembered as having for thirty years been on terms of affectionate intimacy with Thomas Carlyle. It was amusing, however, to note that even when he was speaking in his kindliest vein of these journalistic friends, Carlyle would almost always contrive to get in his stereotyped sneer at the newspaper. Thus, in his *Life of John Sterling*, he speaks slightingly even of the *Athenæum* and the *Times*, saying of the former that, after it passed out of Sterling's hands into those of Mr Dilke, it took root, and "still bears fruit according to its kind." In 1861, when he sent a letter to the leading journal in favour of a subscription to help the family of Inspector Braidwood, who had perished while discharging his duty at a great fire, he almost apologised for being aware from the newspaper accounts of the tragic end of the brave fireman. He knew nothing of the matter, he explained, " but what everybody knew, and a great deal less than every reader of the newspapers knows." As if he personally never read the newspapers at all! In 1870, when poor Ballantyne published what proved to be his last book, *Essays in Mosaic*, Carlyle was asked to say a word in its favour which might be inserted in the preface. "I have long recognised in Mr Ballantyne," wrote Carlyle, " a real talent for excerpting significant passages from books, magazines, newspapers (that contain *any* such), and for presenting them in lucid arrangement, and in their most interesting and readable form." The sneer is put in the parenthesis; but we ought, perhaps, to call it Carlyle's little joke, rather than a sneer. If such a remark were made in earnest it would be simply foolish. Even Dr Johnson confessed that he never picked up a newspaper in which he did not find something worth remembering; and if that was true of the newspaper in its feeble infantine state, how much more justly applicable would the remark be to-day !

One of the reasons for a dislike that deepened with the advancing years may, perhaps, be found in the very questionable habit some of his American visitors had, of sending home, to newspapers in their own country, reports, often imperfect and misleading, of conversations they had been permitted to have with him in Cheyne Row.

These, of course, soon found their way back to the old country, and were generally reproduced in British journals. Not seldom they caused him profound annoyance, especially when the reported talk happened to relate, as it frequently did, to the political and social condition of the United States. In once reporting to a Cincinnatti paper a strong expression of Carlyle's resentment of the liberties thus taken by some of his American visitors, Mr Moncure Conway said : "Carlyle feels, as do those who have been in the habit of listening to his conversation through many years, that no chance expressions during an hour or two ought to be held up as representing his full opinions on the great subjects involved in the political and social tendencies of America. He is, indeed, opposed to democracy, and he looks upon the two leading Anglo-Saxon nations, America and England, as going, one close after the other, upon the wrong path. And that is about as much as Carlyle's casual American visitors get from him. If, however, they should be able to hear all sides of the question within his view, they would find that he regards both countries as destined to pass through the democratic or negative phase of development, to a condition of social order which the most radical Republican or Democrat would probably regard as a nobler ideal than his own. At no time has Carlyle's deep interest in all that concerns America failed. As he respects the German longing for unity, so, even while withholding his sympathy from the North in our late civil war, as to its purpose, I have often heard him pay a tribute to its love for the Union. The determination of the Americans to defend that Union did not fail to excite his admiration, and in his address in Edinburgh he named America as among 'the greatest nations.' His knowledge about America is also far beyond that even of the most educated Americans. I have often been amazed at the exceeding minuteness of his acquaintance with the whole history of America, from the date of its discovery —its settlement, progress, the rise of its cities, its pioneers, soldiers, literary men. I have known him entertain a room full of educated Americans with facts and anecdotes about their own country, which one and all afterwards confessed had been utterly unknown to them. He speaks in touching terms of the way in which America first took him up, and of the fact that the first book of his own that he ever saw was sent him from America with a good sum of money for writing it. And he still speaks of Emerson as 'the clearest intellect now on the planet.'"

A second irritant that sometimes added vehemence to his fulminations against the newspaper press was the disrelish he had for the imitations of his style that occasionally found their way into the public journals. Even when these were good-natured as well as clever, he seemed unable to regard them with equanimity; and when they could neither be called kindly nor clever, they made him very angry. Once, well on to twenty years ago, he was made excessively indignant by a smart defence of a notorious criminal, written in Carlylese, which appeared in a Glasgow print. The writer of this rather gruesome *jeu d'esprit* had reproduced so happily some of the most striking characteristics of his style that even intelligent students of his writings were at first imposed upon.*

---

* In one of the earliest of the *Glasgow University Albums*, published a quarter of a century ago, appeared the first of a series of extremely clever imitations of Carlyle by the same hand. The per-

Carlyle's attention was called to it by a gentleman in the neighbourhood of Edinburgh, who either wanted to know if the article was genuine, or wished to make Carlyle acquainted with the fact that many people in Scotland were accepting the production as his own. From the gruff reply, it was evident that the Master failed to appreciate the joke, and that he was very angry indeed with the too apt pupil. Even in 1874, when our Fifeshire editor conversed with him at Provost Swan's, he had not forgotten that old bit of Glasgow Carlylese. "I mentioned the name of one (St Andrews) Professor," Mr Hodgson informs us, "with the primary object of introducing that of the Professor's son. The Professor's name he had not heard, but that of the son was somewhere embedded in his memory. It was connected with a letter in a Glasgow newspaper, the *Morning Journal*, about the Sandyford murder. The gentleman

---

petrator, it is only right to add, has since done much sound literary work, both in prose and verse, including a graceful memoir of his friend Alexander Smith. He has also written an essay "On Mill and Carlyle," containing what he entitles "An Occasional Discourse on Saurteig, by Smelfungus," prefaced with the remark, "In the little extravaganza I need not formally disclaim an offensive intention to Mr Carlyle, a man whom I entirely honour, and, though with only a modified belief in him as a prophet, consider him simply our greatest man of letters now living." The happiest of all the imitations of Carlyle's manner is that by Mr Russell Lowell in the introduction to the *Biglow Papers;* and we are told that one, almost equally felicitous, appeared in an early number of Mr Miall's *Nonconformist,* "which caused great joy to some who took it for a veritable utterance of Carlyle himself, and a proof that he had enlisted himself under what then appeared the Quixotic banner of a true religious freedom!" Much more unendurable to Carlyle than these professed burlesques must have been the mountain of books in which he was imitated by writers who had no humorous intention to excuse their folly.

I refer to warmly espoused the cause of Jessie M'Lachlan, the person convicted, and—a master of Mr Carlyle's style —wrote a letter as if from Mr Carlyle himself in which the woman's case was zealously vindicated. ' Yes,' said Mr Carlyle to me, ' I remember now; some rawboned blockhead mixed my name up with that parcel of lies and crime; but didn't he do some honest work after ?'" That Carlyle was not so indifferent to the contents of the newspapers as one might have supposed, is indicated by what follows in Mr Hodgson's narrative :—" It was an easy transition from this to the Crieff murder, and to the jurors who recommended the convict to mercy. His gleaming satire blighted the whole proceedings as a sham and a lie, in which the jurors and the murderer had shares alike. He has such a contempt for the flash sentimentality which is at the bottom of what jurors usually do in name of mercy, that the intimation to him that fifteen of the ' Palladium' with one of their favourites had just figured on the gallows would evoke merely a fleeting smile of contemptuous gratification." Let us hope that this somewhat sanguinary editor's interpretation of the great man's talk was, in this instance, a shade stronger than it ought to have been. "It is absolutely necessary to Carlyle's conception of social order and stable government," adds his Fife interpreter, " that the gallows in these days should be in constant operation, and I, for one, am an ardent believer in that doctrine." Of course, the people who talk in this fashion never contemplate the inclusion of themselves among the individuals requiring to be " worked off" by the beneficent Calcraft.

CHAPTER XVII.

THE "LIFE OF STERLING"—SECRET OF ITS POPULARITY—
ITS GRAND DEFECT—MACLEOD CAMPBELL'S CRITICISM
—STERLING'S ESSAY ON CARLYLE—THE "LIFE OF
FREDERICK"—ANECDOTES OF ITS PRODUCTION—ITS
MERITS AND DEFECTS—CARLYLE'S SOJOURN IN GER-
MANY—VISIT FROM THE EMPRESS OF GERMANY—
ACCEPTS THE "ORDER FOR MERIT."

IT was in the same epoch of his life during which he
published the political pamphlets and his *Cromwell*, that
Carlyle also prepared a small biography, which, though it
gave pain to not a few readers on account of the manner
in which it treated the highest of all themes, was yet
universally regarded, in respect to its form, as the most
exquisite work of its class produced in this generation.
That first feeling, instead of wearing off, has been deepened with each succeeding year; and there are many,
whose judgment is entitled to respect, ready at this
moment, with unqualified confidence, to pronounce *The
Life of John Sterling* unrivalled among all the brief
biographies extant in our language—an opinion on behalf of which there is much to be said. The subject of
the book, though he tried his hand at several things, was,
according to Carlyle's view of him, appointed by nature
for a poet; and he had barely passed the age of Burns
and Byron when he was summoned from earth, not only
" released from his toils before the hottest of the day,"

but before his proper work had really begun. It was in 1844 that he died, at the age of thirty-eight. The memoir by Carlyle appeared in 1851. Sterling had committed the care of his literary character and printed writings to Archdeacon Hare and Carlyle, to do for both what they judged fittest ; and, after consultation between the joint-executors, it was agreed that the Archdeacon should edit the writings and write the Life. To this Carlyle consented all the more gladly, no doubt, on account of the conclusion to which he had come, that no biography at all was needed in this case, not even according to the world's usages. Sterling's " character was not supremely original, neither was his fate in the world wonderful. Why had not No Biography, and the privilege of all the weary, been his lot ?" Yet he who asked this question decided eventually that poor Sterling, having already been made the subject of one biography, should have a second too. The worthy Archdeacon had treated Sterling as a clergyman merely, whereas the whole of Sterling's clerical life had been confined to exactly eight months. " But he was a man, and had relation to the Universe, for eight-and-thirty years." Respect for the truth demanded a second biography ; and, without the slightest disrespect to Mr Hare, readers have reason to be glad that he fell into the professional blunder which secured for the world a new Life of his old curate by Carlyle. Of course, fault was found with the latter by some for the more than implied reflection on the good Archdeacon ; but Carlyle believed that he had " a commission " for doing this bit of work " higher than the world's, the dictate of Nature herself," and he would therefore have been to blame had he failed to obey the behest.

R

Yet we do not believe that it is the main purpose the author had in view which gives to Carlyle's little book its chief interest and popularity, nor even its highest and permanent value. Describing that literary Conservatism of his uncle which caused Lord Macaulay to neglect the writings of his greatest contemporary,* Mr Trevelyan

---

* It was certainly not because of entire ignorance of his writings that Macaulay abstained from reading Carlyle's works. He had, of course, read all the articles contributed by him to the *Edinburgh Review*, including the one on Burns. The judgment he had formed of them is indicated in one of his letters to Macvey Napier, of date February 1832, in which he says : " As to Carlyle, he might as well write in Irving's unknown tongue at once. The *Sun* newspaper, with delicious absurdity, attributes his article to Lord Brougham." Alas, it was not the poor *Sun* alone that was in darkness. In a letter to Leigh Hunt, Macaulay described Carlyle as "a man of talents, though absurdly overpraised by some of his admirers "—a phrase that lets in a little light on the writer's frame of mind ; perhaps he felt the praise to be not quite so absurd as he affected to consider it. " I believe," adds Macaulay, "though I do not know, that he ceased to write (for the *Edinburgh Review*), because the oddities of his diction, and his new words, compounded *à la Teutonique*, drew such strong remonstrances from Napier." This from the counsellor of Napier, and the man who had written telling the worthy editor that Carlyle "might as well write in Irving's un-known tongue at once ! " Macaulay's unfavourable estimate of Carlyle was not likely to be modified by the advice the latter gave to a friend who was in feeble health, and which somehow got into all the papers, to confine his reading to "the latest volume of Macaulay's *History*, or any other new novel." They met once at the same dinner table, when Carlyle was astonished by the fluent talk of the brilliant Whig orator, and wondered who he was ; he remarked of him afterwards that he seemed "a decent sort of fellow, who looked as if he had been reared on oatmeal." It is worth while, by the way, comparing Carlyle's estimate of Leigh Hunt, to whom he had personally ministered for years, with that formed by Macaulay, as given in Mr Trevelyan's *Life*, ii. 476. The "Cynic" of Chelsea contrasts favourably in this matter with the Whig his-torian, who, though of the same political colour as the struggling poet, seems to have been content to get his knowledge of Leigh Hunt and his difficulties at second hand.

expresses regret " that one who so keenly relished the exquisite trifling of Plato should never have tasted the description of Coleridge's talk in the *Life of John Sterling*, —a passage which yields to nothing of its own class in the *Protagoras* or the *Symposium ;*" and were the passage here so justly lauded, along with the vivid portrait of Sterling's father, the " Thunderer " of the *Times*, and a few other pieces of its drapery withdrawn from the book, it is to be feared that the volume would instantly be deposed from the high position in the esteem of the reading public which it now occupies. For one who goes to it that he may study the main subject of the work, a score, probably, are attracted by what we may term its subordinate features, and especially by the masterly delineations of Coleridge and that astonishing unsuccessful ex-farmer of Bute who found his niche at last, after many wanderings, in Printing House Square.

When we turn to the problem of Sterling's life, as it is unfolded by the biographer, the impression made is much less satisfactory. If the Archdeacon's biography was imperfect in one direction, Carlyle's is no less imperfect in another. In the former, as an able and by no means narrow-minded critic pointed out some years ago in the *Christian Spectator*, there are a host of Sterling's letters concerning such topics as the Divine Nature, Revelation, Moral Evil, the Evidences of Christianity, Miracles, and other matters on which it is generally thought important to have settled views. " But in one sentence Carlyle contemptuously dismisses all these discussions ! They were ' immeasurable dust whirlwinds,' which while they lasted only blinded poor Sterling's eyes and made him miserable. It was not until he ceased to inquire into these matters, got out of their range, acted as though the question had no interest for him, and dedicated himself to a ' life's work ' of quite another description, that he could cheerfully hope and live.　That life's work appears to have been the composition of divers elegant tales, sketches, feebler poetry already forgotten, and fierce criticism, which, however, will scarcely be remembered. Surely Sterling was living more nobly, when, in the very atmosphere of the questions scouted by Carlyle, he was devoting himself, under the guidance of his other friend, Mr Hare, to the bodies and spirits of men, as curate in a country parish."　A reply to this may no doubt be suggested, to the effect that Sterling was out of his proper sphere altogether as a clergyman, and that the religious discussions referred to were shallow insincerities, from which nothing real could possibly come.　Carlyle, it may be urged, saw in Sterling a reflection of himself, with this difference only, that Sterling being weaker, had gone on to the pulpit, for which he had no vocation at all, since "artist, not saint, was the real bent of his being ;" hence the scorn that is poured, like lava, on the utterly untenable position which Sterling had endeavoured to occupy. This interpretation would lead to a more favourable estimate of the biography ; but one other blot seems to have been hit by Dr Macleod Campbell, who confessed that, while there was certainly much in the book which had struck him as very beautiful, he had closed it with much more regret than admiration.　To his friend Erskine of Linlathen he wrote : "It is very beautiful—most artistic. It has also the higher interest of making the man Carlyle more known to me, and as a *brother* man.　Yet for all this I have scarcely ever, if ever, read a book that has cost me so much pain." This, because it seemed as if Carlyle, by his superior mental force, had deliberately led Sterling astray and then rejoiced in his triumph. " I cannot but feel," said this critic, " that there is an unmistakable self-magnifying tone in the book, and that his joy over Sterling is a most painful, and, I would add, most instructive contrast to Paul's joy over Timothy."

The volume throws many side-lights on Carlyle's own life—the external as well as the inner. We have a description, for example, of his first meeting with Sterling, an accidental one, in Mr Mill's room at the India House; we are told how Sterling's mother, "essentially and even professedly Scotch," took to Mrs Carlyle "with a most kind maternal relation;" and we learn how Carlyle was moved by the first review article on himself and his writings. It was Sterling who wrote the essay, and it appeared in the *Wesiminster* in 1839. It has been reprinted in Hare's edition of Sterling's works. " What its effect on the public was I knew not, and know not; but remember well, and may here be permitted to acknowledge, the deep silent joy, not of a weak or ignoble nature, which it gave to myself in my then mood and situation; as it well might. The first generous human recognition, expressed with heroic emphasis, and clear conviction visible amid its fiery exaggeration, that one's poor battle in this world is not quite a mad and futile, that it is perhaps a worthy and manful one, which will come to something yet: this fact is a memorable one in every history; and for me Sterling, often enough the stiff gainsayer in our private communings, was the doer of this. The thought burnt in me like a lamp, for several days." There is also printed in the biography a long letter from Sterling to Carlyle, in which he reviews *Sartor*, classifying it with the " Rhapsodico-Reflective " order of books, and placing it, for " depth and fervour of feeling, and in power of serious eloquence," far above the masterpieces of Rabelais, Montaigne, Sterne, and Swift.

Carlyle had now reached his 56th year; and it was at this age that he addressed himself to the task of writing what was destined, so far as bulk at least is concerned, to be his greatest book. *The History of Frederick the Great*, completed in six volumes, forming nearly a third part of all that he has written, represented the labour of upwards of fourteen years. The first two volumes were published in 1858, the third and fourth in 1862, and the last instalment of the gigantic work early in 1865. As a monument of patient industry, it has no parallel among the productions of the English press by contemporary authors; but it may be questioned whether such patience and such industry might not have been better employed. One cannot help hoping it is true, as we have been told, that Carlyle once remarked to a friend, " I never was admitted much to Frederick's confidence, and I never cared very much about him." We only wish this feeling had found a more definite expression in the book itself, whereby much adverse criticism, and not a little misunderstanding of Carlyle's real attitude towards the author of that Devil's dance known as the Seven Years' War—the royal highwayman who stole Silesia—might have been prevented. By many, and more especially by all his brother-Scotsmen, it must ever be regarded as a calamity both to Carlyle's reputation and to his own country, that, instead of crowning the magnificent edifice reared by his literary skill and industry with a book that seems to deify one of the vilest characters in the whole range of history, he did not rather devote the third and closing period of his active life to the fulfilment of another task which he had contemplated at the outset of his career. We are still destitute of such a History as would have made for ever legible to all mankind the "heaven-inspired seer and heroic leader of men," John Knox, even as Carlyle has succeeded in picturing the great Puritan statesman and soldier of England. The struggle led by Knox was in itself a great one, apart altogether from its hero—"nearly unique in that section of European history," is Carlyle's own deliberate verdict on the battle that was fought in his native North for the highest cause. "Scottish Puritanism seems to me distinctly the noblest and completest form that the grand Sixteenth Century Reformation anywhere assumed. We may say also that it has been by far the most widely fruitful form." Such was Carlyle's solemn declaration towards the very close of his life; and, in giving it, he had to lament the fact that the chief historian of the struggle is a writer "cold as ice to all that is highest in the meaning of this pheno-menon." Surely it must have been with a pang of self-reproach that Carlyle chronicled this mournful fact. The half, or even a third, of the time which he had devoted to Frederick of Prussia might have sufficed to furnish the world with a history of Knox and the Scottish Reformation that would have been by far the greatest and most precious book in the literature of Scotland. Feeling this strongly while the book on Frederick was being written, our regret is deepened now that the hope of getting a worthy and all-sufficing work on Knox and Scotland is for ever gone, since the man who alone could have produced it is lying in his grave; and the regret necessarily intensifies the sentiment of hostility with which, even apart from the unworthiness of its central figure, we should be compelled to approach the *Life of Frederick.* Yet it would be unfair to allow this to blind us to its unquestioned merits as a history, or to the marvellous patience and conscientious labour of which it is the monument. For the sake of describing his last hero-king, as Dean Stanley truly said, Carlyle " almost made himself a soldier* and a statesman." We are told that as the work in its earlier phases foreshadowed the dimensions to which it must extend, he had a special study prepared at the top of his house, whose walls and shelves were exclu-

---

* The eulogy of Sir Charles Napier, the hero of Scinde, which Carlyle addressed to Sir W. Napier, in a letter of date May 12, 1856, gave a description of that hero's battle pieces that is applicable to those he was himself writing at the time. Sir William had sent Carlyle a copy of his *History of the Administration of Scinde,* and, after reading the book, Carlyle says :—" The narrative moves on with strong, weighty step, like a marching phalanx, with a gleam of clear steel in it—shears down the opponent objects and tramples them out of sight in a very potent manner. The writer, it is evident, had in him a lively, glowing image, complete in all its parts, of the transaction to be told ; and that is his grand secret of giving the reader so lively a conception of it. I was surprised to find how much I had carried away with me, even of the Hill campaign and of Trukkee itself; though without a map the attempt to understand such a thing seemed to me desperate at first." Of Napier's volume, Carlyle further says :—" It is a book which every living Englishman would be the better for reading—for studying diligently till he saw into it, till he recognised and believed the high and tragic phenomenon set forth there ! A book which may be called ' profitable ' in the old Scripture sense ; profitable for reproof, for correction and admoni- tion, for great sorrow, yet for ' building up in righteousness ' too—in heroic, manful endeavour to do well, and not ill, in one's time and place. One feels it a kind of possession to know that one has had such a fellow-citizen and contemporary in these evil days."

sively devoted to the subject. "There must have been near two thousand books in this room, every one of which was in some way connected with that subject, and the walls not occupied by books were covered with pictures representing Frederick or his battles. He seemed for years indeed to be possessed by the man about whom he was writing. There was no labour he would not undergo to find the exact fact on each point, however trivial it might seem to others." His search after accurate information involved an amount of toil which, if it were fully described, would appear incredible. Even in Germany, whither he went to hunt up materials and visit certain localities, we have heard him say that the obstacles which barred his path were almost insurmountable; it was with the utmost difficulty he could secure any authentic information, for example, as to the uniform worn by a German infantry soldier in Frederick's time. He only got this bit of information at last, after wasting many days in futile inquiries, and no end of toil in digging among the records at Berlin. No public man in Germany to whom he applied could either give him the desired information or tell him where it was to be got.* It was in 1858 that Carlyle went to Germany, and, in addition to many other places famous in the wars of Frederick, he visited Zarndorff, Leuthen, Liegnitz, Sorr Mollwitz,

---

* Once, in conversation with a visitor on this subject, he also remarked on the general ignorance of historical matters that existed even among the class in London who pass for sages and oracles. He said he scarcely ever put a question to these people that they could answer, and as he had always some questions to put, if they saw him coming along the street, they turned off (this accompanied with a genuine Annandale guffaw) in another direction to avoid a fresh exposure of their ignorance.

and Prague. The vivid descriptions of the battles of Chotusitz and Dettingen owe very much to this journey. But he did not go back to Germany. On an April day in 1862 when Charles Boner looked in at Cheyne Row he found Carlyle " sitting in dressing-gown and slippers looking over the proofs of *Frederick*, Mrs Carlyle sitting on the sofa by the fire ;" and Carlyle told him he should not pay another visit to Germany. " As long as he was there he could get nothing fit for a Christian man to eat ; no bed big enough to sleep in. The bedsteads always too short, and like a trough. Once, to his surprise, the mattress was too long for the bed, and so he lay all night with it arched like a saddle in the middle. There were no curtains, and in the hotels people stamped overhead, and tramped past his door all night. He had not slept all the seven weeks he was in Germany, and felt the worse for it, he verily believed, up to the present day." It was during this visit to the Fatherland that Carlyle uttered the characteristic sarcasm against some of Goethe's critics that George Lewes has reported, with so much gusto, in his Life of the German poet. At a dinner party in Berlin some were complaining of Goethe's want of religion. " For some time Carlyle sat quiet, but not patient, while certain pietists were throwing up their eyes, and regretting that so great a genius ! so godlike a genius ! should not have more purely devoted himself to the service of Christian truth, and should have had so little, etc., etc. Carlyle sat grim, ominously silent, his hands impatiently twisting his napkin, until at last he broke silence, and in his slow, emphatic way, said, ' Meine Herren, did you never hear the story of that man who vilified the sun because it would not light his cigar?' This bombshell completely silenced the enemy's fire."

The fact that *The Life of Frederick* has got packed into it what we may truly designate a complete political history of the eighteenth century, the overflowing richness of its humour, the hundreds of biographical vignettes executed as only Carlyle could do such work, are features that give it a permanent interest and value, whatever we may think of its philosophy; and he who is at pains to study the volumes will probably be inclined to agree with the verdict that in none of Carlyle's works is more genius discernible, and that it gives an insight into modern history such as is to be found in no other book. But the reader must also have perceived that it is marred by many serious defects. It is the most crotchetty of all Carlyle's works. It abounds in fresh nicknames, refrains, and other peculiarities of diction, in addition to all the old ones, that become tiresome when so often repeated. " Whole pages," as an acute critic has remarked, " are written in a species of crabbed shorthand; the speech of ordinary mortals is abandoned; and sometimes we can detect in the writer a sense of weariness and a desire to tumble out in any fashion the multitude of somewhat dreary facts which he had collected." The truth is that Carlyle, as he frequently told his friends, entered on the task of writing this book reluctantly, simply from a feeling that he had a call to do it; and he used to add that, if he had foreseen the difficulties, he would never have begun it. Even so early as 1858 he had got very sick of the business; for when he was the guest of Varnhagen von Ense in Germany, he told his host that this " Friedrich " was " the poorest, most troublesome, and arduous piece of work he had ever undertaken." There was no satisfaction in it at all, he said; only labour and sorrow. "What the devil had I to do with your Frederick?" As to which Von Ense, who records the conversation in his *Tagebücher*, cynically observes, "It must have cost him unheard of labour to understand Frederick—if he does understand him." To friends at home he was wont to say that "he had tried to put some humanity into Frederick, but found it hard work." He has himself, in a letter to Sir George Sinclair, described the winding-up of the performance as almost more than he could accomplish; and from Mrs Carlyle's letter to Sir George, given on a previous page, it would appear that he had hardly one day's good health or one night of sound sleep during the whole of the years in which he was engaged upon the gigantic work. He refreshed himself for the completion of his arduous task by a visit to Thurso Castle, where he was for some weeks the guest of Sir George Sinclair, and derived much benefit from the rest and change of scene. Before making that visit he wrote, under date 31st July, 1860, "You need not reckon me quite an *invalid* after all. My sleeping faculty has returned, or is evidently returning, to the old imperfect degree; but my work, but my head!—In short, I was seldom in my life more worn out to utter weariness; or had more need of lying down for a little rest, under hopeful conditions." Writing to Sir George on 15th April, 1863, we find him saying: "I am still kept overwhelmingly busy here; my strength slowly diminishing, my work progressing still more slowly,—my heart really almost broken. In some six or eight months,—surely not longer than eight,—I hope to have at last done: it will be the gladdest day I have seen for ten years back, pretty much the one glad day! I have still half a volume to do; still a furious struggle, and *tour-de-force*, as there have been many, to wind matters up reasonably in half a volume. But this is the *last*, if I can but do it; and if health hold out in any fair measure, I always hope I can."

The first effect of the book in England was to weaken its author's moral influence, for the Christian conscience of the country revolted against its teaching, and was shocked by the pictures of Frederick and his father. It was only as the book receded from view, and its author's previous writings were reverted to, that the painful impression wore off. That feeling was only too well founded. Though he did not magnify Frederick, in whom Force without Righteousness was incarnate, as he had magnified Cromwell, it cannot be denied that he treats this unspeakable monster with a deference to which he was in no way entitled; and at times it would almost appear as if he loved him for his unendurable brutality, while he has actually the hardihood to charge other historians with injustice in not recognising the candour with which Frederick owned that his seizure of Silesia was one of the greatest crimes ever perpetrated.* That

---

* Dr Peter Bayne, who has published more than one essay on Carlyle's writings, says :—" It took nine acres to furnish a grave for the dead of one battle out of those which Frederick fought with a view to robbing his neighbour and making people talk about him. Many years before the appearance of Mr Carlyle's *Life of Frederick*, Lord Macaulay wrote an essay on that hero. After careful study of Mr Carlyle's volumes, we are prepared to affirm that Macaulay is right in his estimate of the man, and that Mr Carlyle's ingenious and elaborate eulogy does not render it necessary to qualify in any essential particular his Lordship's verdict."

such a cynical confession of wickedness should modify
the feeling of righteous indignation against the criminal,
still more that it should be a bar against the sternest
reprobation, is a monstrous theory, which, were it applied
practically in judicial proceedings, would enable thousands of the worst criminals to escape. In the most
explicit terms, Carlyle reproduces the abominable doctrine
of Hobbes, when, justifying his hero's seizure of Silesia,
he exclaims, "Just rights! What are rights never so just
which you cannot make valid? The world is full of such.
If you have rights, and can assert them into facts, do it;
that is worth doing." It may be said that here he means
by Mights simply that which is Possible; or, in other
words, that he wants his readers to be content with what
they can get—good advice, doubtless, when it is put in a
proper form, but, as here enunciated, certainly liable to
misconstruction that may produce results of deadliest
evil. An author is bound to consider the meaning which
is likely to be attached to his words; and ambiguity, of
which the slaveholder and the despot can avail themselves to justify their systems, with all their accompanying
horrors, is criminal in any writer. The typical sentence
we have cited is one of many Satan might quote, to suit
his own ends; and, so far as we can see their meaning, he
need not trouble himself to put a forced construction on
the words. Carlyle, in penning these unfortunate sentences, seems to have forgotten that where there are no
Rights there can be no Duties; and that was a pertinent
question which the acute and earnest author of *Henry
Holbeach* addressed to him: "Do you, I ask, refuse to
acknowledge the idea of Rights? Then you shan't have
the other word to sport with. Give it back directly, and

take your place in the Infernal Cohort, under the old Black Flag *that we know.*"

The book is a great favourite in Germany, and it made Carlyle doubly dear to the people of that country. Well might they be grateful to this illustrious Scotsman, who had devoted two of the three epochs of his working life to the exposition of their national literature and history. When the Empress of Germany was in England in the May of 1872 she personally communicated to Carlyle a flattering message from the Emperor thanking him for his *Life of Frederick ;* and in 1873, on the death of Manzoni, he was presented with the Prussian " Order for Merit." Some people were foolish enough to feel, and even to express, surprise when Carlyle declined the Grand Cross of the Bath, offered in 1875 through Mr Disraeli, the more especially as he had not long before accepted the *Ordre pour le Mérite.* They overlooked several important facts, which led others to rejoice that the English honour had been rejected. In the first place, it was ludicrously inadequate—Carlyle ought to have had long before a seat in the House of Lords ; secondly, it came too late. Goethe was only 27 years of age when Karl August made him a member of the Privy Council. To offer Carlyle a G.C.B. at 80 was almost worse than to leave him in the evening of his life, as he had been left during his working days, without recognition from the State to which he had rendered such splendid service. He consulted the dignity of letters as well as his own personal honour when he declined to accept the tardy and insignificant decoration. There were in his native Scotland country gentlemen under forty who had for years been called " Right Honourables " by grace of the monarch who had suffered her greatest Scottish subject to spend all his years of arduous toil without one token of favour. As respects the honour that came from Germany, well might Carlyle accept that; not only had it come more timeously, it was of far higher significance and value. The *Ordre pour le Mérite* is not given by the Sovereign or the Minister, but by the Knights of the Order themselves, the King only confirming their choice. The number of the Knights is strictly limited (there are no more than 30 German and 30 Foreign Knights), so that every Knight knows who will be his peers. Not even Bismarck is a Knight of this Order. Moltke was elected, but simply as the representative of military science; nor does he rank higher in this Order than did Bunsen, the representative of physical science, or Ranke the historian.

CHAPTER XVIII.

ALMOST immediately after the completion of what was
destined to be Carlyle's last literary work of importance,
came an honour that, of all things the world had to offer,
was perhaps the one most likely to be grateful to his
heart. In the previous decade an attempt had been
made by some of his admirers among the students at
Edinburgh University to secure his nomination for the
office of Lord Rector; but the few adventurous spirits of
1856 discovered that they were before their time. They
were obliged to yield to objections which few who made
them would care to see recalled to-day. Ten years later
the tide had turned; and a second endeavour, made in
the November of 1865, was crowned with triumphant
success. By a majority—the largest on record—of 657
against 310, he was elected Lord Rector in preference to
Mr Disraeli.* There have been few such days even in

---

* Twice before his election by his own University he had been
invited to allow himself to be nominated for the office of Lord
Rector, once by students in the University of Glasgow, and once by
those of Aberdeen; but both of these invitations he had declined.

Edinburgh as that Easter Monday, the 2d of April 1866, on which he delivered his Inaugural Address in the Music Hall before an audience that included, not only his young constituents, but many people from distant parts of the country, and even from foreign shores, attracted thither by the prospect of witnessing Carlyle's reception in the capital of his native land.   It was his first appearance as a public speaker since he gave his lectures on Hero-Worship twenty-six years before.   Like those lectures his address was a purely extemporaneous utterance, delivered conversationally and without a single note; and, as must have been expected by those who really knew the man, there was in it a singular mellowness of thought and feeling, admirably reflected in the homely language in which it was couched, and the fine flashes of humour and sarcasm by which it was irradiated.   The main subject of his discourse was "The Choice of Books;" and the chief lessons he had to enforce were to avoid cram, to be pains-taking, diligent, and patient in the acquisition of know-ledge.   With remarkable emphasis he insisted on the vital distinction between knowledge and hypothesis.   The hypothetical and the known are never confounded with-out loss to man, loss of strength, loss of truth, for is not truth the soul's strength?   He protested against the notion that a University is the place where a man is to be fitted for the special work of a profession; its function, he contended, is to prepare a man for mastering any science by teaching him the method of all.   There were but two points trenching on politics in the address, and one was the quotation from Machiavelli of the statement —with which he evidently agreed himself, though he refrained from asking assent to it—that the history of

Rome shows that a democracy could not permanently exist without the occasional intervention of a Dictator. The other was a declaration of the necessity for recognising the hereditary principle in government, if there is to be "any fixity in things." Proclaiming anew his old doctrine no the virtue of Silence, he lamented that "the first nations in the world—the English and the American—are going all away into wind and tongue." One hearer from London declared that it was worth coming all the way in the rain in the Sunday night train were it only to have heard Carlyle utter the final sentence of his penultimate paragraph, "There is a nobler ambition than the gaining of all California, or the getting of all the suffrages that are on the planet just now!" One of his last words counselled the students to take care of their health; the old word for "holy" in the German language, *heilig*, also means "healthy." He also exhorted them to read Knox's *History of the Reformation*, "a glorious book," full of humour and of "the sunniest glimpses of things;" and there was hearty laughter when he advised them to "keep out of literature, as a general rule." He had talked for an hour and a half. At times his eye kindled, and the eloquent blood flamed up the speaker's cheek; the occasional drolleries came out with an inexpressible voice and look; as for the fiery bursts, they took shape in grand tones, the impression made deeper, not by raising, but by lowering the voice. Alexander Smith, the poet, who was secretary to the University, wrote the most vivid sketch of the proceedings; it is included in his *Last Leaves*. He describes Carlyle's voice as "a soft, downy voice," with "not a tone in it of the shrill, fierce kind that one would expect it to be in reading the

Latter-Day Pamphlets."   Time and labour seemed to have dealt tenderly with Carlyle; "his face had not yet lost the country bronze which he brought up with him from Drumfriesshire as a student fifty-six years ago." His hair was yet almost dark; his moustache and short beard were iron grey; his eyes, wide, melancholy, sorrowful; altogether in his aspect there was something aboriginal, as of a piece of unhewn granite. "I am not ashamed to confess," wrote the author of *Dreamthorp*, "that I felt moved towards him, as I do not think I could have felt moved towards any other living man." Before the address several gentlemen, including Professors Huxley and Tyndall, received the honorary degree of LL.D. The Senatus had offered to "cap" the new Lord Rector; but he laughed it off, saying that he had a brother who was already a Doctor, and that if two Dr Carlyles should appear at the gate of Paradise, mistakes might arise. His old friend, Erskine of Linlathen, was one of the recipients of the degree; but this good man wrote soon after to a friend, "Of course nobody calls me Dr, except for fun." Carlyle was Mr Erskine's guest during this visit to Edinburgh; and when the address was well achieved (says Dr Hanna, in his memoir of Erskine), and it was found that the Lord Rector was none the worse, but rather the better for the deliverance, the host invited two or three intimate friends to meet him at dinner. Sir William Stirling Maxwell, "with nice tact, gave such turn to the conversation as allowed fullest scope to the sage who has praised silence so well, but fortunately does not practise it." Released from his burden, Carlyle was in excellent spirits, and discoursed in his most genial mood of his old Dumfriesshire remembrances, of the fate of James IV., and other matters of Scottish history, and of the Emperor Napoleon, of whom he was no admirer.

In one of his little songs, thrown off nearly forty years before, he had pictured life as " a thawing iceboard on a sea with sunny shore." There had come to him a gleam of sunshine, lighting up what on the whole had been a sombre pathway through the world; and it was at this very hour, while the echo yet lingered in his ears of those joyous greetings that assured him how warm was the place he had in the heart of young Scotland, that the ground, in a moment, seemed to melt away from beneath his feet. He had just received what, in one sense, might be called the crowning honour of his life; it was followed, with tragic swiftness, by his greatest grief. He had gone from Edinburgh to Dumfriesshire to visit his relations on his way home to London; and on the 17th of April we find him writing from Scotsbrig, his brother's (as it had been before his father's) farm at Ecclefechan, to Mr Erskine. " This is almost the first day I have had any composure," he said; " and I cannot but write you a little word of gratitude, to Mrs Stirling (Erskine's sister) and you, for your cordial reception of me in my late ship-wrecked state, and your unwearied patience with me, during the whole of the late adventure. Now that it is all comfortably over, and a thing to look thankfully back upon, there is no feature of it prettier to me than that your kind chamber in the wall should have been my safe lodging-place, and that there, with the very clock silenced for me, I should have been so affectionately sheltered. Thanks for this, as for the crown of a long series of kind-nesses, precious to remember for the rest of my days."

He adds how he sprained his ankle a week ago, but that it is mending ; and how he has written a little word to Lady Ruthven, and was still busy penning notes when he ought rather to be " in the woods of Springkell " on his " solitary rides of meditation." Finally, it was his purpose to be at home on " Monday next—from Dumfries, my penult and one remaining shift."*

Before next Monday came, that home had been for ever darkened. On Saturday, April 21, Mrs Carlyle was taking her usual drive in Hyde Park, about four o'clock, when her little favourite dog, trotting by the side of her brougham, was run over by a carriage. She was greatly alarmed, though the dog had not been seriously hurt. She lifted it into the carriage, and the coachman drove on. Not receiving any call or direction from his mistress, he stopped the carriage and discovered her, as he thought, in a fit. He at once drove to St George's Hospital, which was near at hand. Here it was discovered that she must have been dead for some little time. The bright, loving spirit that had walked by the side of our Pilgrim, sustaining his sad heart at every step of his journey for forty years, was gone.

A year afterwards Erskine of Linlathen, a still older

---

* For this and other extracts in the present chapter, including what very many must regard as the most precious letter of Carlyle's they have ever seen, we are indebted to the *Letters of Thomas Erskine of Linlathen,* edited by William Hanna, D.D. Edinburgh : David Douglas. 1877. This book, which contains other letters from the same source, no student of Carlyle ought to overlook ; it brings us into close acquaintance with the character of Carlyle's most intimate Scottish friend through life—the man to whom he opened with least reserve the secret workings and the deepest thoughts and aspirations of his spirit.

man, was also left alone in the world by the death of his last surviving sister. Carlyle was one of the first to hasten with words of sympathy. "Alas! what can writing do in such a case? The inexorable stroke has fallen; the sore heart has to carry on its own unfathomable dialogue with the Eternities and their gloomy Fact; all speech in it, from the friendliest sympathiser, is apt to be vain, or worse. Under your quiet words in that little note there is legible to me a depth of violent grief and bereavement, which seems to enjoin silence rather. We knew the beautiful soul that has departed, the love that had united you and Her from the beginnings of existence, —and how desolate and sad the scene now is for him who is left solitary. Ah me! ah me! Yesterday gone a twelvemonth (31st March 1866, *Saturday* by the day of the week) was the day I arrived at your door in Edinburgh, and was met by that friendliest of Hostesses and you; three days before I had left at the door of this room one dearer and kinder than all the earth to me, whom I was not to behold again: what a change for you since then, what a change for me! Change *after* change following upon both of us—upon you especially! It is the saddest feature of old age that the old man has to see himself daily grow more lonely; reduced to commune with the inarticulate Eternities and the Loved Ones now unresponsive who have preceded him thither. Well, well; there is a blessedness in this too, if we take it well. There is a grandeur in it, if also an extent of sombre sadness, which is new to one; nor is hope quite wanting— nor the clear conviction that those whom *we* would most screen from sore pain and misery are now safe and at rest. It lifts one to real kingship withal, *real* for the first time in this scene of things. Courage, my friend; let us endure patiently and act piously to the end."

On the Wednesday following her death, the body was conveyed from London to Haddington for interment, and the funeral took place on Thursday afternoon. Carlyle, who had hastened to London immediately on receipt of the solemn message, was accompanied to Haddington by his brother, Dr Carlyle, Mr John Forster, and the Hon. Mr Twistleton. The funeral *cortége* was followed on foot by a large number of local gentlemen who had known Mrs Carlyle and her father. The grave lies in the centre of the ruined roofless choir of the old Abbey Church of Haddington. In accordance with the Scottish custom, there was no service read. Carlyle threw a handful of earth on the coffin after it had been lowered into the grave. On the tombstone, which already recorded the names of her parents, this additional inscription was placed by Carlyle:—" Here likewise now rests Jane Welsh Carlyle, spouse of Thomas Carlyle, Chelsea, London. She was born at Haddington, 14th July 1801; only child of the above John Welsh and of Grace Welsh, Caplegill, Dumfriesshire, his wife. In her bright existence she had more sorrows than are common, but also a soft invincibility, a capacity of discernment, and a noble loyalty of heart which are rare. For 40 years she was the true and loving helpmate of her husband, and by act and word unweariedly forwarded him as none else could in all of worthy that he did or attempted. She died at London 21st April 1866, suddenly snatched away from him, and the light of his life as if gone out."

Surely one of the tenderest and most heart-moving, as it was also, we believe, one of the truest, inscriptions ever placed by a husband over the grave of a departed wife. It would not be saying too much—has not the most competent witness said it himself in these words?—that but for this woman the greater part of the work that has made her husband's name tower above all others in his century · might never have been done. It was no small matter that her little fortune made him independent of the drudgery that had hitherto repressed the ardour of his spirit, and circumscribed the bounds of his literary efforts; it was in the years immediately succeeding his marriage that he produced the essay on *Burns*, his *Characteristics*, and, above all, *Sartor*. That dowry enabled him to face London life and the biography of Cromwell—an experiment no poor man, nailed to hack-work for daily bread, could possibly have dared. Thus he was set on the road to fortune. Nor was it the small but sufficient material provision she brought that constituted the whole, or even the best part, of the help. Many a poor man, especially of the literary and professional class, has had cause to rue the day that tied him to a rich wife. Selfish, purse-proud, exigeant, ever remembering the original disparity of their worldly fortunes—all the more, perhaps, if her own has been trivial—she has been an instrument to drag him down. But Jane Welsh was a woman of good sense, of culture, of heart, capable of appreciating her husband's powers, and who gave him the reverential devotion of her entire being and life. Thrice-happy Sartor to secure such a prize! Every kind of needed help came to him with her—cheerfulness to sustain his spirit in its darkest hours; self-abnegation without limit, to endure the tempest of his anger and even his days of distempered gloom; the thrifty diligence that made her perfect mistress of the humblest work in the kitchen, the taste that made each apartment of the dwelling fit for any peer of the realm to enter; an intellect that seemed to many who knew them both scarcely inferior to his own,* with powers as a conversationalist that some, Margaret Fuller for example, no mean judge, deemed superior;—never, surely, was man happier in his wife. But for this woman, the world, perhaps, might never have got the greatest works of Thomas Carlyle.

She had always cherished the memory of her native town. After her father's death, and her mother's removal to Templand, near Thornhill, she often visited her uncle Benjamin, who succeeded to her father's practice. She continued to take a deep interest in some of the old people of the place, helping the poor whom she had known in former days. It is in connection with one of these humble Haddington friends of her youth, one brought specially close to her by the most intimate domestic association, that there emerges into view a little story of great beauty and significance. Many years have elapsed since we happened one day to hear, in Edinburgh, through a friend who had quite accidentally made the discovery, that there was a poor old woman in the neighbourhood of that city, who was visited by Carlyle every

---

* "Before *Maud* was printed," says a writer in *Chambers's Journal*, "Tennyson used to come and read it aloud to her, and ask her what she thought of it. Her reply the first time was, 'I think it is perfect *stuff!*' Slightly discouraged by this remark, the Laureate read it once more; upon which Mrs Carlyle remarked: 'It sounds better this time;' and on being read to her the third time she was obliged to confess that she liked it very much. This little incident shews how Tennyson must have valued her clear judgment and excellent taste."

summer when he came to Scotland, and to whose comfort he ministered with the greatest generosity, and at the same time, with almost reverential delicacy. It did not surprise us to hear the story, or rather the little fragment of a story, that thus reached our ears ; but the curiosity naturally excited was not satisfied until the publication of the second volume of the *Letters of Thomas Erskine of Linlathen*, in 1877. On opening that delightful book, almost the first thing that met our eye was the interpretation of the story. The old woman's name was Mrs Braid, and she had been a nurse of Mrs Carlyle. She was often visited by the Laird of Linlathen. Referring to the hero on whom Carlyle was then at work, "this weary Fritz," Erskine says, "I would much rather be honest Mrs Braid selling flour and bacon, and lovingly bearing the burden of her bed-rid son." In the January of 1868, Carlyle writes to Erskine, "I owe you many thanks for that pious little visit you have made to Greenend and poor Betty. Often had I thought of asking you to do such a thing for me by some opportunity, but, in the new sad circumstances, never had the face. Now that the ice is broken, let me hope you will from time to time continue, and on the whole, keep yourself and me in some kind of mutual visibility with poor Betty, so long as we are all spared to continue here. The world has not many shrines to a devout man at present, and perhaps in our own section of it there are few objects holding more authentically of Heaven and an unseen 'better world,' than the pious, loving soul, and patient heavy-laden life of this poor old venerable woman. The love of human creatures, one to another, where it is true and unchange-able, often strikes me as a strange fact in their poor history, a kind of perpetual Gospel, revealing itself in them; sad, solemn, beautiful, the heart and mother of all that can, in any way, ennoble their otherwise mean and contemptible existence in this world." In the following year, 1869, he writes: "I am very thankful that you went to see poor Betty; she is one of the most venerable human figures now known to me in the world. I called there, the first thing after my bit of surgery, in the neighbourhood, end of July last; I seemed to have only one other *visit* to make in all Scotland,—and I made only *one.* The sight of poor Betty, mournful as it is, and full of mournfullest memories to me, always does me good. So far as I could any way learn, she is well enough in her humble thrifty *economics*, etc. : if otherwise at any time, I believe you understand that help from this quarter would be a *sacred* duty to me."

They were weary days in Cheyne Row that followed the great loss. "I am very idle here," he writes in the January of 1868, "very solitary, which I find to be oftenest less miserable to me than the common society that offers. Except Froude almost alone, whom I see once a week, there is hardly anybody whose talk, always polite, clear, sharp, and sincere, does me any considerable good." It was a great evil to him, he added, that he had no work, at least none worth calling by the name. "I am too weak, too languid, too sad of heart, too unfit for any work, in fact to care sufficiently for any object left me in the world, to think of grappling round it and coercing it by work. A most sorry dog-kennel it oftenest all seems to me, and wise words, if one even had them, to be only thrown away on it. Basta-basta, I for most part say of it, and look with longings towards the still country where at last we and our loved ones shall be together again." At the time he wrote this letter his sister, Mrs Aitken of Dumfries, had been with him for two months, "to help us," he says, "through the dark hollow of the year." Lady Ashburton, who had been a great friend of Mrs Carlyle's, was never weary of ministering to the disconsolate widowed one. It is to this period of his life that we owe one of the most solemn and pathetic, and also one of the most comforting of all his letters that we have yet been privileged to see. Writing on the 12th February, 1869, to Erskine, he says : " I was most agreeably surprised by the sight of your handwriting again, so kind, so welcome ! The letters are as firm and honestly distinct as ever ;— the mind too, in spite of its frail *environments*, as clear, *plumb-up*, calmly expectant, as in the best days : right so ; *so* be it with us all, till we quit this dim sojourn, now grown so lonely to us, and our change come ! 'Our Father which art in heaven, Hallowed be Thy name, Thy will be done ;'—what else can we say ? The other night, in my sleepless tossings about, which were growing more and more miserable, these words, that brief and grand Prayer, came strangely into my mind, with an altogether new emphasis ; as if *written*, and shining for me in mild pure splendour, on the black bosom of the Night there ; when I, as it were, *read* them word by word,—with a sudden check to my imperfect wanderings, with a sudden softness of composure which was much unexpected. Not for perhaps thirty or forty years had I once formally repeated that Prayer; nay, I never felt before how intensely the voice of Man's soul it is ; the inmost aspiration of all that is high and pious in poor Human nature ; right worthy to be recommended with an 'After this manner pray ye.'" Then he adds: "I am still able to walk, though I do it on compulsion merely, and without pleasure except as in work *done*. It is a great sorrow that *you* now get fatigued so soon, and have not your old privilege in this respect;—I only hope you perhaps do not quite so indispensably need it as I; with me it is the key to *sleep*, and in fact the one medicine (often ineffectual, and now gradually oftener) that I ever could discover for this poor clay tabernacle of mine. I still keep working, after a weak sort; but can now do little, often almost nothing;—all my little 'work' is henceforth *private* (as I calculate); a setting of my poor house in order; which I would fain finish *in time*, and occasionally fear I shan't."

It was in one of these sombre closing years that a movement was begun, in his wife's native town, to erect a memorial to her ancestor John Knox, who also was born there; and, though Carlyle had been disappointed not long before with the failure of a similar scheme at Edinburgh in which he had taken part, he gave his hearty support to this new endeavour, while by no means sanguine as to its success. At the outset he subscribed £25, with the promise of more if the details were successfully carried out; on the score of failing health he declined to join the committee, but furnished practical suggestions as to its formation, proposing, for one thing, that Mr Froude should be invited to act on it—a hint that was promptly improved, and to which the distinguished historian gave his cordial consent. The memorial was to take the form of a school, and this led Carlyle to refer, in his letter, to the days when Edward Irving was a teacher in Haddington. He hoped the school, when established on the new basis, would be worthy of its ancient fame. "If the site of the new school," he said, in a letter dictated by him on the 15th February 1875, "was on the ground on which Knox is known to have actually walked, it would beyond all things give the building a memorial character. In regard to 'ornamentation,' of which there was some mention in an article in the *Scotsman*, the best architect to be found anywhere ought to be employed;—a man who would keep before his eyes the fact that Knox never in his life said or did anything untrue or insincere ;—and that the Parish School, or 'National Monument' (or whatever name it may be called), sacred to his memory, should be scrupulously preserved from every species of meaningless and 'unveracious ornamentation." In a postscript he suggested that "the people of Haddington would do a really good work by marking, by a simple obelisk and a good oak tree, the site of the house in which Knox's Father lived, which Mr Laing, in his Preface to Knox's Work, says is discoverable." After the building was begun, and on learning that arrangements had been made for giving the institution the character of a grammar school, he showed his entire approval by doubling his subscription, and sent a cheque for £50. In the last interview which one of his Haddington acquaintances, Colonel Davidson, had with Carlyle, only a few months before his death, he inquired after the welfare of the school, and expressed pleasure on hearing of its success. It is satisfactory to know that the suggestion for marking the house of Knox's birth with an oak tree has been acted on ; some day soon the obelisk should be placed there too, with the words of Carlyle inscribed upon it. We may add that, although he had in one of his *Latter-Day*

Pamphlets denounced the "brazen images" erected to unworthy men, the whole of which he would have melted at once and turned into warming-pans, he did not by any means object to the erection of worthily-executed statues of veritable heroes. In 1856 he became an honorary member of the committee for the erection of the Wallace Monument on the Abbey Craig. In 1870 he expressed his willingness to subscribe his "bit of contribution" to a Bruce Monument at Stirling; and in a letter to the secretary he said: "Dr Gregory's Inscription is very good, but besides mentioning the year of Bannockburn it surely would be an obvious improvement to give the *day* of the *month* (and even of the week, if that latter is indubitably known)." The author of both these patriotic schemes was the Rev. Charles Rogers, the Scottish genealogist and antiquary, who had been visited with severe criticism on account of his management of the Wallace Monument affair ; and the fact that Carlyle always kept a pretty sharp eye on what was appearing in the Scottish journals is amusingly illustrated in the letter to Dr Rogers, of date 25th June 1870, with respect to the proposed Bruce Monument; the closing sentence expresses "sincere wishes" for the success of the plan, "*un*troubled in this instance." It remains to be noted that Carlyle was also a supporter, both by pen and purse, of the Bruce Monument that has lately been erected at Lochmaben. He took a specially warm interest in that scheme—no doubt on account, to some extent, of his feeling of local attachment as a Dumfriesshire man, and also as a member of a family that had first settled in Annandale six hundred years ago under the wing of the progenitors of the Bruce.

After the death no summer passed, as long as health allowed, in which Carlyle did not go to Haddington to visit the grave, and also the house in which his wife had spent her early years, and under whose roof they had first met. It was with a feeling of sympathetic awe that the inhabitants of the ancient town who were familiar with his aspect would see the venerable pilgrim revisiting these shrines of his heart. "He liked to go alone," we are told, "and if unobserved he used to walk up the passage which led from the street to the house in which his wife had lived before their marriage, and to look into the little garden, which was perhaps the centre of many sweet and sad memories." On an autumn day of 1880 a stranger from America made a pilgrimage to the graveyard at Haddington to see the burial-place of Mrs Carlyle. "Mr Carlyle," said the sexton, as he pointed to the stone, "comes here from London now and then to see the grave. He is a gaunt, shaggy, weird kind of an old man, looking very old the last time he was here. He is to be brought here to be buried with his wife. He comes here lonesome and alone. When he visits the wife's grave, his niece keeps him company to the gate ; but he leaves her there, and she stays there for him. The last time he was here, I got sight of him, and he was bowed down under his white hairs, and took his way up by that ruined wall of the old cathedral, and around there and in here by the gateway, and he tottered up here to this spot." Softly spake the gravedigger and paused. Softer still, in the dialect of the Lothians, he proceeded : "And he stood here awhile in the grass, and then kneeled down and stayed on his knees at the grave ; then he bent over and I saw him kiss the ground ; ay, he kissed it again and

T

again ; and he kept kneeling, and it was a long time before he arose and tottered out of the cathedral and wandered through the graveyard to the gate where his niece stood waiting for him."

CHAPTER XIX.

AT his first meeting with John Sterling, in the February of 1834, the conversation turned, amongst other things, on the Negroes, and Carlyle noticed that Sterling's views had not "advanced" into the stage of his own on that subject. A happy thing for Sterling, we should say, since Carlyle had already arrived at the conclusion that an "engagement for life," his euphemism for slavery, was really better than "one from day to day." Sterling, the infatuated creature, thought "the Negroes themselves should be consulted as to that!"—the manifest absurdity of which Carlyle marks in his account of the colloquy with a contemptuous point of exclamation. It was in John Stuart Mill's private room at the India House that the meeting took place, and he perhaps recalled that conversation about the Nigger in after days. Carlyle expounded his anti-Negro views, with brutal frankness, in the *Latter-Day Pamphlets*, where he declared, "I never thought the rights of negroes worth much discussing in any form ;" and he adhered to them to the last.	In the September of 1874, when Mr Hodgson, the Cupar editor, mentioned the news in the day's papers of the lawless Southern whites having driven Governor Kellogg from his seat at New Orleans and illegally possessed themselves of the government, Carlyle said he was in no way surprised, save that the conflict had been so long of coming, adding that "the man who is seventy-nine years of age (his own age at the time) has not seventeen minutes to spare for the entire negro race." That was in perfect harmony with the bitterly scornful words he had, with unhappy consistency, employed on this subject from the first. "Lord John Russell is able to comfort us with the fact that the negroes are doing very well." "Our beautiful black darlings are at least happy, with little labour except to the teeth, which surely in those excellent horse jaws of theirs will not fail." "Quashee will get himself made a slave again, and with beneficent whip will be compelled to work."*	We care not to quote the worst of the words he wrote, of some of which we hesitate not to say that they were a disgrace to the writer's manhood.

It was this theory as to the Negro that caused Carlyle,

---

* An honoured friend of ours, whose name is known and esteemed in all the Protestant churches of England and America, once, on a visit to Jamaica, got into conversation with an old negro, a man of long-established character and piety, on the attacks which Carlyle had made upon his race. He knew of them, but had not seen them. While they were being repeated in detail, the negro, who was of a noble and venerable aspect, drew himself up with dignity, and some other tokens of natural resentment ; but when the tale was finished, his countenance relaxed into its usual benignity, as he replied, "Me pity Massa Carlyle, sir, and *me forgive him !*"—as sublime a sentiment in its way, we take it, as ever fell from the lips even of a peasant-saint in Dumfriesshire.

at the time of the Civil War in America, to espouse the side of the South; and his fierce invectives no doubt led many of his countrymen to take the same side. The *American Iliad in a Nutshell*, of date May 3, 1863, published in *Macmillan's Magazine*, represented the conflict as simply a dreadful fight between Peter of the North and Paul of the South as to whether they should "hire" their servants for life—a singular meaning to put into the word hire—or by the month or year; and the little squib, a really silly as well as sad document, closed with a jeering reference to the want of success that had attended the Northern armies. Within a few weeks the course of events took the sting out of this cruel sneer. At that very moment thousands in England were protesting that Peter of the North cared nothing for the slave—another opinion that was falsified by the issue; but it betrayed a singular ignorance on the part of Carlyle, in spite of what Mr Conway has told us about his marvellous mastery of American history and topography, that he failed to perceive the primary purpose of the War, which resulted not only in Emancipation, but also in the preservation of the threatened Union. He was not afflicted with the same blindness during the struggle that took place, at a later date, between Germany and France— clearly he saw and approved the effort of the former to regain her lost provinces; but in this instance there was no Nigger to obscure his vision.

Something even worse than the abortive little nutshell iliad was to come. Fidelity to the truth, and the duty of pointing out a fundamental error in his political writings, alone could constrain us to record the fact, that the year of his great private grief also witnessed, what we conceive

to be, the greatest mistake of Carlyle's life. That year
had not ended when, amidst the sorrowful regrets of
many of his sincerest friends and admirers, he hastened
to welcome and justify Governor Eyre on the return of
the latter, red-handed, from such outrage and slaughter
in a British Colony, as almost rivalled the worst deeds
of the Spaniards in Jamaica, and which even a Roman
pro-consul would have blushed to own. In giving comfort to the enemy of the murdered Gordon, and the
author of a massacre in which more lives were taken than
in Jefferies' Bloody Assize, he was not the only distinguished man of letters in England who went astray; for
the committee of Eyre's defenders, on which he early
enrolled his name, and to whose funds he subscribed £5,
could also boast of having in its membership, Tennyson,
Ruskin, and Kingsley. The Romans, though they were
Pagans, had a moral standard which forbade a triumph to
the victor in a civil war; but Kingsley, the Christian
minister, sat at the festive board at Southampton, at
which Eyre was entertained when he arrived in England,
spattered with the blood of his fellow-subjects.* Ruskin
headed the Defence Fund with a subscription of £100,
explaining that, in doing so, he had sacrificed a summer

---

* Mr Kingsley was personally connected with the West Indian
planter interest, through family relationship, which no doubt ac-
counted, in part, at least, for this true friend of the English poor having
so little regard for the lives of the negroes of Jamaica. Speaking of
the Jamaica Massacre, which his grace condemned, at a meeting in
Glasgow, on the 27th January, 1868, the Duke of Argyll said :
"Several of my earliest and dearest friends were connected with
West India property, and through West India property, with the
slave trade ; and I have observed that, even to this very day—ay,
to the second and to the third generation of those who held slaves—
there is a comparative coolness on the subject of slavery."

journey to Switzerland, where he had much wanted to go, "not only for health's sake, but to examine the junctions of the Molasse sandstones and nagelfluh with the Alpine limestone, in order to complete some notes he meant to publish next spring on the geology of the Great Northern Swiss Valley." Carlyle acted as one of the two vice-presidents of "The Eyre Defence and Aid Fund," his colleague being Sir Roderick Murchison, and the president the Earl of Shrewsbury. Next to these names the most distinguished on the committee were Earl Manvers, Sir Thomas Gladstone, Professor Tyndall, John William Kaye, Viscount Melville, Lord Gordon Lennox, and Henry Kingsley.* Carlyle went out of his usual course by presiding at the first two meetings of the committee, which were held at No. 9 Waterloo Place, Pall Mall, the first on the 29th August, 1866, the second on the 5th September. On the first occasion, he said, he

---

* It may be worth while to note some of the names of "The Jamaica Committee," which undertook the duty, after it had been finally declined by the Government, of prosecuting Mr Eyre and his subordinates for acts committed by them in the so-called rebellion in Jamaica, and especially for the illegal execution of Mr Gordon. Mr John Stuart Mill, M.P., was chairman, and the committee included John Bright, Thomas Hughes, M.P., W. E. Baxter, M.P., Charles Gilpin, M.P., Professor Fawcett, M.P., Joseph Cowen, M.P., Duncan M'Laren, M.P., Professors Cairnes, Goldwin Smith, Francis W. Newman, Thorold Rogers, J. J. Tayler, and Beesly, Herbert Spencer, Edward Miall, Sir Wilfrid Lawson, Frederick Harrison, Humphrey Sandwith, and Titus Salt. In the circulars of the committee presided over by Carlyle the proceedings of the above-named gentlemen were denounced as "un-English and disgraceful." Carlyle himself verbally described them as a "noisy" clique, and Ruskin said he was glad to make any sacrifice to shew his "much more than disrespect for the Jamaica Committee." So foolish may even the greatest intellects become, when blinded by the passion of the distempered partisan.

"considered that the committee should be presided over by some nobleman of power and influence. As he, however, considered it to be a solemn public duty on the part of every man who believed that Governor Eyre had quelled the insurrection in Jamaica, and saved that island, to come forward and boldly proclaim such to be his opinion, he would gladly consent to take the chair at the present meeting." After speeches by a West India merchant and Mr S. C. Hall, the editor of the *Art Journal*, the latter of whom expressed the belief that the prosecution of Eyre would never be attempted, Carlyle said he "considered that it would be advisable to meet the wishes of all well affected parties, and he therefore proposed that the title of the Fund be altered from 'The Eyre Testimonial and Defence Fund' to 'The Eyre Defence and Aid Fund.' In his opinion the amount of money subscribed, though an important, was by no means the most important point. The main object of the committee ought to be to attack resolutely, by all fair methods, the fallacy (for such he could not but believe it to be) that these noisy denunciations of Mr Eyre, were the deliberate voice of the people of England, or did at all express England's opinion about Mr Eyre." The vote of thanks to Carlyle for presiding was proposed by a captain of the 10th Hussars, and seconded by a captain of the Royal Navy. At the second meeting, at which Mr Ruskin denounced the threat to prosecute Eyre as "the cry of a nation, blinded by its avarice to all true valour and virtue," Carlyle said he was "glad to find that no less than twenty-five new names had been added" to the committee during the week, and that "subscriptions were flowing in from all quarters." At the third meeting, though he did not preside, Carlyle was again present, and, with "very great pleasure," accepted the post of vice-chairman. The reports of what he was doing brought upon him a flood of correspondence, much of it by no means complimentary, which he "could not afford to read, much less to answer;" and, as "his one answer to all such correspondence from without," he caused a letter to be published, in which he eulogised Eyre as "a just, humane, and valiant man, faithful to his trusts everywhere, and with no ordinary faculty of executing them," and declared that "penalty and clamour are not the things this Governor merits from any of us, but honour and thanks, and wise *imitation* (I will further say), should similar emergencies rise, on the great scale or on the small, in whatever *we* are governing." The nature of the work thus commended for universal imitation can only be appreciated by recalling a few of its salient features. Four Hundred and Fifty innocent negro peasants of Jamaica, many of whom would have shed the last drop of their blood in defence of the British Crown, had been slain in cold blood, in batches of ten and twenty per diem; Six Hundred other inhabitants of the island, from the aged matron of seventy to the young boy of twelve, and including some pregnant women, had been stripped naked and flogged with a new instrument of torture made of piano-wire; and One Thousand Homes had been robbed and burned by the soldiery! As if this were not enough, Eyre sanctioned an Act, the effect of which was to confiscate the provision grounds belonging to the widows and orphans of those who had been executed. Nothing like it had occurred in British history since "the bloody Claverhouse" and the Highland Host desolated the south-western shires of Scotland in the Covenanting days. The Massacre of Glencoe was the merest trifle to the Jamaica Massacre of 1865. Very many of the Jamaica victims were, like Gordon, members of Christian churches; one of them was a white girl, the daughter of a missionary—she was stripped and flogged with the piano-wire cat.*

Carlyle's too famous letter, most admirable as to its form—each sentence gleaming flashes as of cold steel— had no words too contemptuous to apply to the men who were denouncing the Massacre. "The clamour," he said, was "disgraceful to the good sense of England; and if it rested on any depth of conviction, and were not rather (as I always flatter myself it is) a thing of rumour and hearsay, of repetition and reverberation, mostly from the teeth outward, I should consider it of evil omen to the country, and to its highest interests, in these times." England, he continued, had never been wont to spend its sympathy on "miserable mad seditions, especially of this inhuman and half-brutish type;" and he "flattered"

---

* For detailed and authoritative proof of all these statements, see the Report of the Royal Commission; Charge by Lord Chief Justice Cockburn in the case of Nelson and Brand; and what Mr (now Lord) Cardwell so truly designated "those ghastly volumes," the Jamaica Blue Books of the period. These documents may be commended to the attention of the Rev. Gavin Carlyle, who, in some pleasant reminiscences of his great namesake, refers to his own father, "now a venerable missionary in Jamaica, a year younger than Carlyle himself." It appears from the son's statement, that his father, "though the greatest friend of the negroes," took Eyre's part. "A friend sent Carlyle one of his letters on the subject, and he sent it back with great delight, saying, it was just what he would have expected from the good sense of his old friend." Praise from the greatest enemy of the Negro could hardly be pleasant to "the greatest friend of the negroes" in Jamaica.

himself that it had not changed, "not yet quite; but that certain loose superficial portions of it have become a great deal louder, and not any wiser, than they formerly used to be." In conclusion, he hoped that, by the "wise effort and persistence" of the committee he had joined, "a blind and disgraceful act of public injustice might be prevented, and an egregious folly as well." Betaking himself to an obscure nook of England, where he received the shelter of justices who refused to commit him for trial, the ex-Governor contrived to elude what an honourable man, accused of a great crime yet conscious of his innocence, is always anxious to obtain. Market-Drayton, the birthplace of Clive, was the hiding-place of this modern hero, this "just, humane, and valiant" man, extolled by Carlyle. If the panegyric had been well-founded, the Governor would have hastened to secure a fair trial by a jury of his countrymen; but, instead of justifying the praises bestowed upon him by his friends, he resorted to every possible artifice in order to escape the necessity of submitting his conduct to a judicial tribunal. One of the guiltiest of his subordinates, Colonel Hobbs, had committed suicide by throwing himself into the sea on the homeward voyage; but two others also deeply implicated, Lieutenant Brand and Colonel Nelson, committed for trial by a London magistrate, were set free by a grand jury whose members went in the teeth of what has been regarded as the noblest charge delivered by the greatest Chief Justice of our century. But that charge remains; and as long as it continues to be read men will see how grievously Carlyle had gone astray. According to the doctrines laid down by Cockburn, the hanging of Gordon was murder, and martial law, as interpreted in Jamaica, a thing utterly foreign to our institutions and without the faintest sanction in the principles of English jurisprudence. The Charge was hailed by the great bulk of the nation with profound satisfaction; and this feeling went on deepening when the country received the report of the Royal Commission sent out to Jamaica, and subsequently heard that the new Governor of the island, Sir John Grant, was swiftly carrying out the very reforms for advocating which Gordon had been executed without trial. A few faint attempts were made by a few friends of the degraded Governor to have him restored to the public service or placed on the pension list; but the moral sense of the country revolted from these proposals, and there is now no danger of their being again renewed.

Both from individuals and organs of public opinion entitled to respectful attention there came expostulation and reproof. By the leading journal of his native country, a newspaper neither then nor at any other part of its history obnoxious to the charge of being weakly humanitarian, Carlyle was reminded that no man alive should have less sympathy and less admiration for Governor Eyre than he. "If his teaching about the value and nobleness of energy is to be kept from doing harm and not good," said the *Scotsman*, "it must be fenced by this strenuous provision, that energy shall be guided and tempered by justice." That he failed to see this did not, however, surprise those who were best acquainted with his works. "It is curious," wrote the author of *Tom Brown's Schooldays*, to an American journal, "how the test of the treatment of inferior races divided men in our time more keenly and subtly than any other. I never now can really depend upon an Englishman's political faith until I know how he felt about your rebellion, or how he is feeling about this outbreak of ours in Jamaica. The foremost men on the wrong side with us are Carlyle, Ruskin, and Kingsley. Our people are calling them renegades, but this is not fair. The only one to whom the name can with even *prima facie* fairness be given, is Kingsley. Carlyle has been a power-worshipper and a despiser of freedom any time this twenty-five years. Reverence him as one does, and must, there is no denying this. Ruskin has been the captive of Carlyle's bow and spear for the last ten years, or nearly that. He is intensely clear, keen, and narrow; can never see more than one side, and is as bigoted a hero-worshipper, both in the good and evil sense, as his great master. He is fond now of saying, ' I am a King's man, not a mob's man,' including tyrant in his term King, and people in his term mob."* The *Daily News* accurately interpreted the feeling of thousands, when it lamented the deterioration of moral sentiment in Carlyle. " The generous enthusiasm, the poetic insight, the pure, if austere, morals, the blended hope and sadness of an earnest temperament which glowed in his earlier pages, live in his later writings only as half-extinguished fires under the smouldering ashes. Personally one of the kindest of men, Mr Carlyle has cultivated an intellectual taste for bloodshed—a literary lust of carnage. He has become, by sedulous self-indulgence, voluptuous in cruelty. Like old Lear, in

* In 1880, when a candidate for the Lord Rectorship of Glasgow University, in opposition to Mr Bright, Mr Ruskin wrote that Carlyle and he were now the only two King's men left in the kingdom !

his madness, he threatens to quit the stage, muttering 'Kill—kill—kill.'" The question arose in many minds, as they read Carlyle's diatribes, if John Stuart Mill is "superficial," who, then, in England is profound? and they pointed to the calm and lucid explanation of the part he was taking in the controversy which Mr Mill had given in Parliament, with all the quiet dignity and force of argument becoming a philosopher. The idea of justice was involved; but in his pamphlet on *Model Prisons*, Carlyle, when asked for a definition of justice, had only declaimed in eloquent language. Not so Mr Mill, who had been at pains in his writings to define it with precision, and whose action was the outcome of his serious thought — of fundamental principles reached by the exercise of reason. Carlyle did not reason; ruled by rhetoric and his emotions, he set reason at defiance. One remark of an able writer who mixed in the fray seems worthy of preservation for permanent use :—" While the men whose eloquent writings, wherein are often found episodes of tender, touching pathos, and noble, generous sentiment, are yet disfigured with a passionateness and one-sidedness truly startling, have ranked themselves with the supporters of Mr Eyre; the men of calmness, of patient thought, and of industrious investigation have decidedly pronounced against him. On his side—we have hot and intemperate feeling; against him—cool, calm, collected thought."

That these remonstrances were of no avail in modifying the aversion to the negro which Carlyle had so long cherished was made apparent in the following year, 1867, by the publication in *Macmillan* of what might be called the last of the *Latter-Day Pamphlets*. Its title was

Shooting Niagara ; and After. While the primary purpose of the essay was to assail the Reform Bill of Mr Disraeli, a statesman he had always viewed with distrust, it included a reproduction of the little American Iliad. The great conflict in the United States was over, but even yet he failed to apprehend its purport. In the previous year, while the case of the Jamaica Massacre was pending, Emerson had been astonished and distressed, telling his friends that " Carlyle was losing himself;" and this assault upon the American form of government, with its violent expressions of contempt, both for the liberated negro and the Republic, deepened the regret felt by his oldest friends on the other side of the sea. " The Almighty Maker," said Carlyle, in this latest manifesto, with a confidence in his own knowledge of the Divine purpose which he would have called fanatical in another man, "has appointed the nigger to be a servant," and the American War, having been undertaken to set him free from servitude, was a war against Heaven's decree. Moreover, it was a war against an eternal law of human society, which demands that servantship shall not be on the nomadic principle at the rate of so many shillings a day, but upon the principle of a contract for life. In other words, slavery is the natural condition of labour ; and that for the white man as well as the black. Mr Moncure Conway, the sincerity of whose anti-slavery feeling was attested by the liberation of his own slaves long before the War, assures us that Carlyle took the wrong side, not because his sympathies were with the oppressors, but because he was misled as to the facts of the case by the stories told him by slaveowners concerning their patriarchal arcadia in the South.

"An American lady whose noble son had died amid great renown in the Northern ranks, sent to Carlyle the memorial volume of the Harvard students who had fallen in the war, containing their letters, their biographies, and an account of their thoughts and deeds during ·that great struggle for liberty. The old man read that book from first page to last, and some time afterwards, when that American lady came to see him in person, he grasped her hand, and, even with tears, said, 'I have been mistaken.'" It is a pity Carlyle himself did not make his change of view known to the world. He certainly owed this reparation to a public whom he had done so much to mislead.*

As respects our own country, he declared that it had been "drowned in hypocrisy, lying to steep in the Devil's Pickle, for the last two hundred years;" and what with this new Reform Bill of "traitorous politicians," the Charge of Chief Justice Cockburn on martial law, and the throwing of Governor Eyre by the Ministry out of the window to a "knot of nigger-philanthropists," he believed the consummation was at hand. He had only one hope, and that lay in "our aristocracy," whom he described as "a body of brave men and of beautifully

---

* Some of the public journals persistently refused to accept Carlyle's political teachings as meant to be serious. He had made merry at those who expected a Millennium from extension of the suffrage, declaring that all the Millenniums he ever heard of heretofore were to be preceded by a chaining of the devil for a thousand years. "Sound doctrine," replied one of his amused critics, "and Mr Carlyle may as well begin the operation at Chelsea." Another replied, "We like to be told by Mr Carlyle that we are all going to the devil, because he clothes the gloomy intimation in such fantastic garments, and makes our future state so picturesque, that it ceases to be terrible."

polite women," "noble souls," "of high stoicism," and all manner of virtues. A somewhat different picture this from the one he drew of the aristocracy in *Past and Present;* indicating also a change since that day in the October of 1831 when he wrote from London to Macvey Napier, "This is the day when the Lords are to *reject* the Reform Bill. The poor Lords can only accelerate (by perhaps a century) their own otherwise inevitable enough abolition; that is the worst they can do; the people and their purposes are no longer dependent on them." As a politician, he had changed during the interval of fifty years; and to some people it will seem that the change was not one for the better.

CHAPTER XX.

THERE remained now only two other occasions on which
Carlyle was to feel a necessity laid upon him to acquaint
the public with his views on the question of the day. In
the autumn of 1870 his friends had observed a great
improvement in his health and spirits, which seemed to
be rising in consequence of the Prussian victories in the
war with France. He was almost daily at his club, the
Athenæum, freely and joyously conversing with its
habitués on the great European topic of the hour; and
the exultant strain of his talk was, perhaps, not mode-
rated by the fact that a large proportion of the men he
met retained a keen sympathy with France, even though
many of them rejoiced to see the Empire of the Third
Napoleon rushing to its justly-merited doom. Carlyle's
exuberant feeling was expressed in a letter published by
the *Weimar Gazette* in October; the epistle had been

handed to that journal by the private friend in Germany to whom it was addressed. Of course, it gave profound satisfaction to the victorious nation, and made the name of Goethe's British expositor dearer than ever to the German people. This letter was succeeded in November by a long manifesto, addressed to his own countrymen through the *Times*, which proved that the writer's power in the minatory line had not by any means abated on account of advancing years. It was imperatively necessary, said this new proclamation, that France, which had proved herself not only unfit to guide others, but which "is swallowed up in oceans of vanity and all sorts of mendacity, not only of the conscious, but, what is far worse, also of the unconscious sort, should be dethroned from her seeming primacy in Europe." This work Germany, under the guidance of Bismarck, was about to achieve. In doing it she was not only vindicating for herself the position to which she was entitled, but she was also paying off France for all the miseries and mischiefs wrought upon her by the latter country during the last four hundred years. She must recover the territory stolen from her by France, and restore Alsace and Lorraine to a reconstituted Germany, or as much of the latter at least as would serve for a secure boundary-fence between the two countries. In the efforts of the French to defend themselves, he saw nothing admirable. They are a vile race, altogether given over to lies, and the father of lies—all their patriotism vanity, vapouring, and idle gesticulating. In contrast with them, the English public were summoned to look admiringly at "that noble, patient, deep, pious, and solid Germany." It was to Carlyle "the hopefullest public fact" that had occurred

in his time that such a people " should be at length
welded into a nation and become Queen of the Continent, instead of vapouring, vain-glorious, gesticulating,
quarrelsome, restless, and over-sensitive France." The
letter was manifestly one-sided, and lacking in the quality
of solid, comprehensive judgment. Carlyle's historical
review of the quarrels between France and Germany for
four hundred years introduced a principle, which, if
universally acted on, would plunge the whole world into
war, and, as one of the most incisive of his critics, who
was also a warm personal friend, told him, " wipe civil-
isation from the face of Europe with a sponge of blood."
Did not his own book on the French Revolution show
that, if Germany had suffered at the hands of France
four centuries ago, France had been plunged into twenty
years of war at a time much nearer our own by the
iniquitous assaults of Germany? Besides, to speak of
Germany as equivalent to Prussia, involved a false
assumption. The wrongs (if wrongs they were) inflicted
by France on Germany really fell upon Austria, for there
was then no kingdom of Prussia in existence. The rise
of Prussia dates from the seizure of Silesia by Frederick;
her claim to represent the rights and avenge the wrongs
of Austria and the old German Empire is that of a
burglar.*　　As to Carlyle's furious contempt for the

---

* By no writer was the historical argument against Carlyle's
manifesto more effectively presented than by Dr Peter Bayne, who,
the son-in-law of a Prussian general, spoke from an intimate personal
acquaintance with Prussia and her history. In the latest edition of
his first book, *The Christian Life*, Dr Bayne gives a prefatory essay,
analysing the general teaching of Carlyle, and pointing out what he
conceives to be its fundamental errors.

French Government of Defence, it was suggested that "if, instead of acting with signal moderation, they had shown the maniacal energy of the Government of the Reign of Terror, and set fifty guillotines spouting blood, he might have spoken of them with more respect." Objectionable as Carlyle's letter seemed to be in so many respects, even at the time of its publication, when the general joy at the fall of the author of the *coup d'état* led multitudes to rank themselves on the side of Germany, it is now, after the lapse of a decade, seen even more plainly to be untenable. The argument was unjust to France; and its sympathy for Germany, based on sentimental rather than equitable grounds, was also distasteful to lovers of freedom, since it rested in no slight degree on Carlyle's satisfaction with the absence among the Germans of those political virtues which the English people justly value in themselves.

An amusing episode in connection with Carlyle's enthusiastic devotion to the cause of Germany was the imposition successfully practised on him by an astute son of the Fatherland, Robert Waldmüller-Duboc by name, who, in the December of 1870, sent to Carlyle a little book of verse, called "The Thousand Years' Oak of Alsace," with an inscription indicating that the author of the volume was in the German army, then engaged in the siege of Paris. Carlyle hastened to send an acknowledgment of the "beautiful little blue book," the contents of which he praised lavishly as "betokening in the writer a delicate, affectionate, poetic, and gifted human brother, well skilled in literary composition—not to speak of still higher things." As a matter of fact, we are assured by

competent judges, who have read Herr Waldmüller's
verses, that they are thin and feeble, with a thread of
attempted satire running through them that does not tend
to hilarity in the reader's mind.   But Carlyle imagined
they were written by a German soldier, which led him
to see in the book merits nobody else could discover.
"That a soul capable of such work should now date to
me from 'Le Vert Galant,' and the heart of a great and
terrible World-event, supremely beneficent and yet supremely terrible, upon which all Europe is waiting with
abated breath, is another circumstance which adds im-
mensely to the interest of the kind gift for me; and I
may well keep the little book in careful preservation as a
memorial to me of what will be memorable to all the
world for another 'thousand years.'   I wished much to
convey some hint of my feeling to you, as at once a
writer of such a piece, and the worker and fighter in such
a world; and I try to contrive some way of doing so.
Alas! my wishes can do little for you or for your valiant
comrades, nobly fronting the storms of war and of winter;
but if this ever reach you, let it be an assurance that I do
in my heart praise you (and might even in a sort, if I
were a German and still young, envy you), and that no
man, in Germany or out of it, more deeply applauds the
heroic, invincible bearing of your comrades and you, or
more entirely wishes and augurs a glorious result to it at
the appointed hour.   My faith is that a *good* genius does
guide you, that Heaven itself approves what you are
doing, that in the end Victory is sure to you.   Accept
an old man's blessing; continue to quit yourselves like
men, and in that case expect that a *good* issue is
beyond the reach of Fortune and her inconstancies.

God be with you, dear sir, with you and your brave brethren in arms."

Alas! this valiant and heroic, as well as delicate and gifted young warrior turned out to be no warrior at all, but a mere newspaper correspondent!—a fact which must have considerably disgusted Carlyle, if it ever came to his knowledge. But Herr Waldmüller-Duboc, who at once handed the epistle to Mr Archibald Forbes as a serviceable "sensation" for his next morning's letter, had the satisfaction of seeing it duly telegraphed to London, where it appeared next morning (January 11, 1871) in the very largest type—the characteristically smart preface of Mr Forbes, who of course did not "peach" upon the provider of the copy, opening with the startling words, "Thomas Carlyle on the foreposts! The Sage of Chelsea among the besiegers of Paris!" It was a good stroke of business for Herr Waldmüller-Duboc. It also threw what he himself would have called "a straggle" of illumination on the emotional nature of Herr Waldmüller-Duboc's victim. We must add that the strong enthusiasm for Germany which beat in the heart of Carlyle did not exclude a tender sympathy for the sufferings entailed upon the French; and to a lady actively employed in London furthering the French Relief Fund he sent "a little ear of corn to join with the charitable harvest you are reaping, which I trust will be abundant for the sake of those poor Frenchwomen whom with all my heart I pity as you do."

In the November of 1876, when he was within a few days of his eighty-first birthday, a warlike speech delivered at the Guildhall by Lord Beaconsfield provoked a brief

letter to the *Times* from Carlyle, assailing the policy on
the Eastern Question of "our miraculous Premier," and
denouncing "the unspeakable Turk."   Never in the
political history of our time did two little phrases perform
such effective service ; and, as this letter was to be the
last its writer should address to his fellow-countrymen, it
is pleasant to think that it was the one, of all his political
manifestoes, that gave the widest and most intense satisfaction.   That it contributed in a degree quite dispropor-
tioned to the length of the epistle in hastening the down-
fall of Lord Beaconsfield's Administration, has been
admitted on every hand.   That political leader had at no
time been a favourite of his.   In 1867, in a conversation
with a visitor from Australia on the public men of
England, "he seized hold of Disraeli and ridiculed him
with a bitterness of sarcasm, and a force and vigour of
expression, which made me feel," says the narrator, "I
was listening to an intellectual giant.   He then assailed,
fiercely, the lords and gentlemen who have so long
allowed themselves to be led by such a man, mentioning
the circumstance of Disraeli having winked his eye to a
large Edinburgh audience, as he informed it of the
process of 'education' to which he had subjected the
aforesaid lords and gentlemen in the matter of Reform.
He was full of fun and satiric humour while handling
Disraeli, and seemed to be utterly unable to get over the
monstrous anomaly of all the great lords and gentlemen
suffering themselves to be led by this notorious political
juggler.   He literally dissected poor Mr Disraeli with a
sharp, incisive power, and an amazing knowledge of the
anatomy of his subject, which was striking and entertaining in the highest degree."   So in Fifeshire in 1874, to

its Tory editor, when they got on politics, "Mr Disraeli was the first politician who fell in his way, and him he executed in a noose—you could almost see him dangling from the ceiling. Mr Disraeli was 'a clever trickster,' who 'could not look facts in the face.'" The phrase, "He whom men call Dizzy," was originated by Carlyle; and he could hardly contain himself in private conversation when the name was mentioned. This life-long feeling of antagonism found its culminating public expression in the scornful declaration which he threw in the teeth of the Guildhall orator, when he declared that it was "impossible for any Minister or Prime Minister that exists among us" to undertake a war against Russia on behalf of the Turk. "It is evident to me that this would be nothing short of insanity," he continued. He would give the Turk "something very different from war on his behalf." The Turk "must *quam primam* turn his face to the eastward; forever quit the side of the Hellespont, and give up his arrogant ideas of governing anybody but himself." In the main, this last letter of Carlyle was on the side of truth, justice, and humanity—it was a wise as well as a potent word of advice to the British people; yet it evinced an undue sympathy with the despotic drill imposed by their government on the Russian people, and the general result of the argument did not seem to harmonise altogether with certain memorable words about Mahomet and Islamism which Carlyle had uttered on a London platform thirty-six years before. If the word spoken by Mahomet was really invested, as Carlyle then argued, with Heavenly power, how had it come about that the followers of Mahomet had sunk to depths that were "unspeakable," and were, of all the governing powers in Europe, alone beyond reclamation? During the year that followed the publication of the "miraculous Premier" epistle, one would here and there come across bills posted on dead walls, and even in railway trains and cabins of steamers, entitled "Thomas Carlyle's Query," which asked, "I wonder how long John Bull is going to allow a miserable Jew to dance on his belly?"

It has been urged by some that, notwithstanding all the appearances to the contrary, Carlyle's sympathies were essentially democratic; and those who hold this opinion might point to the last political act of his life as a symbol of the alleged fact. Dean Stanley was his friend; but, though the Dean was the author of the scheme, and sought to carry it into effect with almost passionate ardour, Carlyle at once authorised the attaching of his signature to the memorial against the desecration of Westminster Abbey by the intrusion into it of a monument in honour of the unhappy Prince Imperial. The moral influence of this act was made all the more emphatic by a hasty declaration on the part of Dean Stanley, that the signature must be a forgery. The Dean was apparently unacquainted with the handwriting of Carlyle's niece, and also unaware of the fact, familiar enough to his intimate friends, that Carlyle had not for a long while been able to use his pen.

Amongst the replies to Carlyle's last letter, perhaps the least pleasant was one issued in pamphlet form by Mr Swinburne. It professed to have the Eastern Question for its theme, but that was manifestly no more than a peg on which the writer contrived to hang a violent personal attack on Carlyle. This pamphlet recalled an incident, which was probably its motive, of 1874, when Carlyle's opinion of the author of *Chastelard*, given in conversation to Emerson, on the last visit of the Concord sage to England, found its way into the American journals. The truth of the estimate was much in excess of the refinement of the language in which it was expressed; and Mr Swinburne wrote a passionate reply, in which he described the words of Carlyle as "the sewerage of Sodom," adding that "a foul mouth is ill matched with a white beard." Emerson he pictured as "a gap-toothed and hoary-headed ape, carried first into notice on the shoulder of Carlyle, and who now, in his dotage, spits and chatters from a dirtier perch of his own finding and fouling." It was no doubt true that Carlyle, in 1841, had edited the first English edition of his American friend's essays, to which he prefixed a characteristic eulogy of their author; but Emerson hardly needed this to make him known to the world, as the English poet's irate and unedifying assault seemed to imply. The figure used by Carlyle to describe Mr Swinburne was not a nice one; but it expressed the loathing excited within him by a school of versifiers who have imported into England the worst vices of effeminate sensualists who in France degrade the name of poet. The exclusion of drinking songs, and worse, from Miss Mary Carlyle Aitken's selection of *Scottish Song*, published in 1874 in the Golden Treasury Series, may be ascribed with some confidence to the influence of her uncle. It was, perhaps, the same guidance that caused only three of Sir Walter Scott's compositions to be given. To the last Carlyle clung to the depreciatory estimate of the author of *Waverley* which he had expressed, with almost an excess of frankness, in that early essay wherein he asserted that Scott had never been inspired with one idea, purpose, instinct, or tendency that was worthy of the name of great, having nothing to recommend him, indeed, but a "healthy, manly nature" that made him the equal of William Cobbett.　The essay on Scott contains some of its author's noblest teaching; but for what he said against Sir Walter there are many, in his native land and elsewhere, who have never been able to forgive Carlyle.　It was an essay, however, which Erskine of Linlathen never wearied in praising; Madame Vinet thought it admirable; and so did Sir George Cornewall Lewis, to whom also Scott's aims appeared "low and vulgar," and his views of literature "sordid."　By no writer has the favourable estimate of Scott been more earnestly or more effectively enforced than by Mr Gladstone.　The curious fact deserves to be put upon record that the great Free Church leader, Dr Candlish, was prepared to nominate Carlyle as the man of all others who, in his opinion, ought to preside at the Scott Centenary Celebration in Edinburgh in 1871.　Much to his own relief, however, Carlyle was not called to this ceremony, and, indeed, he could not well have presided at such a festival after the candid judgment of Sir Walter and his work which he published in the *Westminster Review* in 1838, and from which he never afterwards swerved.　But the attitude in which Candlish stood to Carlyle on this occasion was a pleasing and hopeful sign of the times.　Even theologians noted for their "soundness" in the faith were now regarding the Sage of Chelsea with less suspicion and more respect.　We ought not to forget, however, that

Dr Chalmers had long before this date declared that Carlyle, by his firm grasp of the religious sentiment, had done more than any other man of his time to " vindicate and bring to light the Augustan age of Christianity in England."

Carlyle has told how, on the eightieth, which was also the last, birthday of Goethe, it was celebrated by an outward ceremony of a peculiar kind, "wherein, too, it is to be hoped, might be some inward meaning and sincerity." It fell on the 28th of August 1831, and on that day the sage of Weimar received a graceful compliment from fifteen Englishmen. As a token of their veneration, they presented the poet with a highly-wrought seal, on which, amidst tasteful carving and emblematic embossing, stood these words, engraven on a gold belt, along with the date—" To the German Master : From Friends in England." This seal was designed, as before noted, by Mrs Carlyle ; and a letter accompanied the gift, written by her husband, which expressed in touching language the reverence felt by the donors "as the spiritually taught towards their spiritual teacher."

It is Saturday, the 4th of December 1875 ; and now it is Carlyle, the disciple and first British expositor of Goethe, who has completed the eightieth year of his earthly pilgrimage. It was not inappropriate that the first tribute should arrive at Cheyne Row in the morning, in the shape of a telegram from Berlin, subscribed by ten of the most distinguished professors and politicians of Germany, the list headed by the historian Leopold von Ranke, who himself was within a few days of completing his eightieth year. These Germans thanked Carlyle, "the champion of Germanic freedom of thought and moral integrity," for having done so much to promote cordial relations between the English and German nations. The second tribute came at a later hour of the day from British friends. Along with a gold medal, of exquisite design, the workmanship of his friend J. E. Boehm, bearing on one side a portrait of the patriarch, there was a quiet and kindly letter of congratulation; both were simply handed in at the door of his dwelling, the mode of presentation deemed most congenial to Carlyle's feelings, besides being in accord with the wholesome British aversion to all theatrical display in connection with the solemn realities of life. "Not a few," said the letter, "of the voices which would have been dearest to you to hear to-day are silent in death. There may perhaps be some compensation in the assurance of the reverent sympathy and affectionate gratitude of many thousands of living men and women throughout the British Islands and elsewhere, who have derived delight and inspiration from the noble series of your writings, and who have noted also how powerfully the world has been influenced by your great personal example. A whole generation has elapsed since you described for us the hero as a Man of Letters. We congratulate you and ourselves on the spacious fulness of years which has enabled you to sustain this rare dignity among mankind in all its possible splendour and completeness. It is a matter for general rejoicing that a teacher whose genius and achievements have lent radiance to his time still dwells amidst us; and our hope is that you may yet long continue in fair health, to feel how much you are loved and honoured, and to rest in the retrospect of a brave and illustrious life."* Of the medal, an engraved representation of which we are privileged to lay before our readers (*see page* 321), silver and bronze copies were struck for the use of the subscribers, with a few for presentation to public institutions; the copy sent for Carlyle's acceptance was in gold.

In the opening months of the same year which brought this beautiful and solemn tribute at its close, the wonderful old man had published what was to be his penultimate work. Without the slightest preliminary notice, the January number of his first friend in time of need, *Fraser's Magazine*, gave the initial instalment of the *Early Kings of Norway;* and the brilliant little series

---

* This document was subscribed by the following friends:—Thomas Aird, William Allingham, Alex. Bain, Thos. S. Baynes, John S. Blackie, J. E. Boehm, W. Boxall, Wm. Brodie, R.S.A.; John Brown, M.D.; Robert Browning, John Caird, Edward Caird, H. Calderwood, Lewis Campbell, Robert Carruthers, Edwin Chadwick, Fred. Chapman, Henry Cole, Thomas Constable, Archibald Constable, Henry Cowper, George Lillie Craik, D. M. Craik, Francis Cunningham, Charles Darwin, Erasmus Darwin, J. Llewelyn Davies, James Donaldson, David Douglas, Edward Dowden, George Eliot, Edward Fitzgerald, Percy Fitzgerald, Robert Flint, John Forster, W. E. Forster, Robert Were Fox, A. C. Fraser, Richard Garnett, Ad. Gifford, John Gordon, A. Grant, John Richard Green, Alex. B. Grosart, George Grove, William Hanna, R. Palmer Harding, T. Duffus Hardy, Frederick Harrison, Robert Herdman, R.S.A.; W. B. Hodgson, Jos. D. Hooker, Robert Horn, Thomas Hughes, Thos. H. Huxley, Alexander Ireland, William Jack, R. C. Jebb, David Laing, Samuel Lawrence, Arthur Laurenson, W. E. H. Lecky, G. H. Lewes, J. Norman Lockyer, John Lubbock, E. L. Lushington, Godfrey Lushington, Vernon Lushington, Lyttelton, Æ. J. J. Mackay, Alexander Macmillan, Henry S. Maine, Theodore Martin, Helena Faucit Martin, Harriet Martineau, David Masson, William Stirling Maxwell, Henry Morley, John Morley, Chas. Edward Mudie, F. Max Muller, Charles Neaves, M. O. W. Oliphant,

of anonymous sketches were carried on and completed in the February and March numbers. Three years after their appearance, the editor of the magazine incidentally referred to the curious circumstance that, when these papers appeared, only one of the critics detected the authorship; and we may be permitted to claim whatever of credit belongs to that exception, though to us it was indeed a marvel, not merely that we stood alone in this matter, but that every person whom we were able to consult had grave doubts on the subject, even the most intelligent regarding the sketches as no more than a good imitation of the master's style. To us it seemed that but one hand in England could have penned even the brief business-like, preliminary statement as to the original sources from which the substance of the notes had been derived. Some of the critics ascribed the work to Mr Froude; and when the belief we hazarded was at length confirmed, the same guides hastened to express the opinion that the work exhibited signs of senility. Unfortunately for them it soon transpired that, instead of being a product of the author's old age, it had in reality been written many years before he handed the manuscript for publication to his friend Mr Allingham, at that time

---

Eliza Andrews Orme, Richard Owen, Noel Paton, W. F. Pollock, Richard Quain, M.D. ; Henry Reeve, Mary Rich, Alexander Russel, J. R. Seeley, W. Y. Sellar, Henry Sidgwick, Samuel Spalding, James Spedding, W. Spottiswoode, Arthur Penrhyn Stanley, J. F. Stephen, Leslie Stephen, J. Hutchison Stirling, Susan Stirling, Patrick D. Swan, Tom Taylor, W. Cowper-Temple, A. Tennyson, Anne Isabella Thackeray, W. H. Thompson, George Otto Trevelyan, Anthony Trollope, John Tulloch, John Tyndall, J. Veitch, G. S. Venables, A. W. Ward, Hensleigh Wedgwood, F. E. Hensleigh Wedgwood, W. Aldis Wright.

the able editor of *Fraser*. In the same year he published in the same magazine a paper which, unlike the Norse sketches, had been newly written. *The Portraits of John Knox* was the last fruit off the old tree; and the vivid sketch of the great Reformer from the pen of the venerable octogenarian proved that his hand had lost none of its cunning, while it deepened the sorrow that this vignette was all we were ever to get from that hand on the same subject.

By permission, from the Medal by J. E. Boehm, Esq., A.R.A.

CHAPTER XXI.

IT was in one of the opening years of the last decade of
his life that we enjoyed the privilege of first meeting
Carlyle. On entering that presence, in the drawing-room
upstairs where he sat reading a newly-issued number of the
Quarterly, the feeling, we are free to confess, was one of
almost pained surprise. It was hard to realise that this
could indeed be Thomas Carlyle. Not because he was
so much more feeble in his physical aspect than we had
expected to find him, with one shoulder so much raised
as to amount to a deformity; but because that aspect
was likewise so very homely, the air so rustic and
peasant-like, not to say uncouth. When, some time
afterwards, we opened the newly-published Memoirs of
George Ticknor, we could understand how it came to
pass that the dandiacal person from Boston who met
Carlyle upwards of forty years ago, when he was known
merely as a contributor to the magazines and reviews,
described him in his journal as "a vulgar-looking little

man." That was, beyond question, the impression any person, taking a merely superficial look, would have carried away. What we saw was simply such a face and form as we had come across hundreds of times in the glens and on the moorlands of Western Scotland—mending a feal dyke, seeing to the sheep, or hoeing potatoes in a cottage kailyard by the roadside. Met with in any one of these positions, he would have seemed in his natural place; only a keen inspection could have suggested the suspicion to any passer-by that there was something out of or beyond the ordinary run of peasants in this man. Surely no other cultured Scotsman ever went through the world with so little change of the external appearance and air that he had before leaving the cottage of his birth. At no period of his life, from all that we have been able to make out from conversations with his sister and others who had known him well, was Robert Burns so much of the rustic in appearance, deportment, or speech; and yet Carlyle was a student from his earliest days, mixed for years in the best society of Edinburgh before he was thirty, got a highly cultivated lady for his wife, and an estate along with her, while for upwards of forty years he had been the intellectual leader in the Great Metropolis — latterly such a potentate in the literary world of the nineteenth as Johnson was in that of the eighteenth century, and even a little more. There is something profoundly significant in the tenacity with which Carlyle must have resisted those social influences that usually rub off the provincial angularities and impart at least an external polish. That tenacity was in keeping with one of the root principles of his teaching, and reflected, perhaps to an exaggerated extent, his abhor-

rence of mere seeming—his detestation of shams. To
the last his mother always spoke of him as "Oor Tam;"
so also spoke at least one of his sisters, a farmer's wife;
and any Scotsman meeting him, even in his latter days,
could have no difficulty in understanding why that was
the habit of those who knew him best. In manner he
had preserved the strongly-marked characteristics of his
youth and his family; we question if he deflected a hair's
breadth from one of these even when he was being
ministered to in her castle by the kindly Countess who
watched over his health after the death of his wife; or
even when he was received, in 1869, by Queen Victoria
at the Deanery of Westminster; or when he was receiving
the Empress of Germany in his own house in Cheyne
Row. A bit of native granite, verily, must this man be,
who, after some forty years of London life, mingling
in the best and most polished circles, courted by the
loftiest in station, with the wife of an earl to send him
his daily loaf of bread from her own kitchen, because it
had been found to answer best with his weak digestion,
and carrying him off to her castle on the breezy cliffs of
Kent whenever he seemed in need of a breath of sea air,
with even an Empress calling at his abode in Cheyne
Row, should still bear about with him, in his general
aspect, air, and accent, nay, in his very modes of speech,
the unmistakable marks of the obscure Annandale
village in which he was born. Tenacity of will in all
this beyond anything we ever saw or have read of in
books. Old·age had bowed him down and shrivelled up
the once full and vigorous form; but he never could
have answered to those descriptions which represent him
as tall and stately. Old folks at Thornhill, who remem-

ber well the days when he and Mrs Carlyle used to visit Mrs Welsh on their way to and from Craigenputtoch and Edinburgh, had told us that he was not a tall man—about five feet seven or eight is the figure they give; and their recollections, in some instances exceedingly vivid, must be in accordance, we suspect, with the fact. Our friend Mr Thomas Lawrie, the well-known picture-dealer in Glasgow, famous as an angler and a walking encyclo-pædia of good stories about Burns and Carlyle, and many other Dumfriesshire worthies, is one of the surviving natives of Thornhill who came into close contact with the Laird of Craigenputtoch when he was visiting at his mother-in-law's. Carlyle in those days struck the homely people of the little upland town as "a bit of a dandy." He was always dressed in a nice shooting-jacket, the cloth a fashionable "mixture" not familiar to the rustic populations, and the jacket well made by a city tailor; the "philosophy of clothes" evidently studied practically by young Sartor in those early years of his married life, if Mr Lawrie's recollection may be trusted, as we think it may. The young folks would stay with Mrs Welsh for a few days each time they passed, either going to or coming back from Edinburgh; and, "to put aff his time," Carlyle would enter into familiar chat with Lawrie, who was then a house-painter in his native parish, while the young man was at work on Mrs Welsh's premises at Templand. It was that lady who gave any importance he then had (in the estimation of the Thornhill people) to Carlyle. She was a true lady, in every way; very fine-looking, with an impressive air and carriage, yet kind and motherly to all who dwelt under her roof, or came about the farm. When a young man of the village, Mr Lawrie's brother, came home, as it was thought, in a decline, Mrs Welsh took kind motherly notice of him, inviting him to walk up to the farm every morning, to get "a drink of warm milk frae the same coo"—the mile he had to travel and the milk would do him good; he did get better, and the cure was ascribed to Mrs Welsh, perhaps justly. "If Carlyle hadna' been married to Mrs Welsh's dochter, he wadna' been muckle thocht o' at Thornhill." Forty-five years ago an old lecturer on physiognomy came to that region, and astonished the good folks of the countryside by what he said concerning the changes that came over the countenance of each individual in the course of his life. Mr Lawrie can never look at one of the current photographs of Carlyle without thinking of that old lecturer; for he never saw so striking an illustration of the truth of his saying. "No doubt, the beard has made a great difference in him, as in so many other people; but the change is indeed astonishing, and the shaggy eyebrows especially make him appear an altogether different man from what he looked at Thornhill."*

The weight of more than seventy years is resting upon him on this day that finds us sitting by his side in the drawing-room of the old house in Cheyne Row; but, though his body has become decrepid, his mind is still

---

* Here we may note Mr Lawrie's testimony that Gilfillan's picture of Craigenputtoch, cited on a previous page, is, as we suspected, wholly absurd; instead of being wild and weird, it is "a bonny place," with "a wee bit burn" making it lively, and much good arable land about, smiling in the summmer and autumn with excellent crops. Such is the report, at all events, of Mr Lawrie. Templand, Mrs Welsh's residence, we may add, is what the Scotch call "a genteel farm-house" in the parish of Closeburn, about a mile from Thornhill. Mrs Welsh's father farmed Morton Mains, in the parish of Morton, which lies in the same portion of Nithsdale.

bright and powerful, and the touch of country bronze in his complexion, the rosy tint on his cheek, the red velvetty winter-apple hue, together with the fire that yet flashes from his bright blue eye, proclaim that there is still a fount of vigorous life left in the aged pilgrim. It is the eye that makes the chief charm of this strange, rugged countenance ; its glance at once so keen, as quick to mark external objects as it was that morning he entered Annan town by his father's side a child of ten, as piercing as when he spake with Coleridge at Highgate, and yet so sad, wistful, and tender, with a far-away look, as if the object on which he gazed was in another world. There is a wonderful contrast between the other features of the countenance and that eye of Carlyle's ; together, they reflect the contrast in his character and his writings. Apart from the eye the face has a hard, stern, cold, even forbidding aspect, such as we might associate with the Scot who has found a not uncongenial sphere on a West Indian plantation, carving his way to success by the use of the " beneficent whip ;" but in the eye there is a depth of tenderness that wells up like the light in a clear, deep pool among the mountains. This face reads the strange riddle of its owner's books ; we see in it the author of *Frederick* and of *Sartor*, of the harsh, discordant, denunciations of the poor negro in the *Latter-Day Pamphlets*, and of those Letters to Erskine that might have been written in the Isle of Patmos by St John.

That new number of the *Quarterly* which we found him reading, paper-knife in hand, was the one that contained an article, not yet forgotten, by Dr Carpenter on the subject of Spiritualism ; and a reference to the essay set him off in a fashion that soon decided his identity, if for the first few minutes a doubt existed on that head. There was no other man in the world competent to pour forth such a withering blast of scorn but Thomas Carlyle. He wondered what the world was coming to when even educated people and the leaders of society were becoming believers in this foul superstition—this abominable new invention of the Evil one. And then he recounted some of the facts stated in the article, warmly praising Dr Carpenter for the masterly way in which he had treated the subject. It was in the course of the conversation on this repulsive phenomenon of Spiritualism that we first heard from his own lips a kindred assault on the Darwinian philosophy, concerning which he spoke in such a way as led us to accept as authentic a report we first met with in a transatlantic journal, a few years afterwards, of a conversation an American visitor had had with him, and which proved that the faith in which he was nurtured at his mother's knee in the old Dumfriesshire home had not lost its hold upon Carlyle. To the American he had said : " A good sort of man is this Mr Darwin, and well meaning, but with very little intellect. Ah, it's a sad, a terrible thing to see nigh a whole generation of men and women, professing to be cultivated, looking around in a purblind fashion, and finding no God in this universe. I suppose it is a reaction from the reign of cant and hollow pretence, professing to believe what in fact they do not believe. And this is what we have got to. All things from frog-spawn ; the gospel of dirt the order of the day. The older I grow—and I now stand on the brink of eternity—the more comes back to me the sentence in the Catechism which I learned when a child, and the fuller and deeper it becomes. ' What is the chief end of man? To glorify God, and enjoy him for-ever.' No gospel of dirt, teaching that men have descended from frogs, through monkeys, can ever set that aside." These words were in harmony with what Carlyle had, at the same period, said to a friend of our own, to whom he confessed, in most touching language, that he was seeking his way back to the simple faith of his childhood, convinced that there was more in that than in all the wisdom of the *illuminati*. On one of the opening days of 1877 we published the report by the American visitor in a Scottish journal, from which it found its way into the London newspapers, where it was erroneously given as an extract from a letter written by Carlyle, this statement being the invention of some blun-dering sub-editor. Immediately, the erroneous assertion that Carlyle had written such an epistle was denied, " on the best authority," by a correspondent of the *Times*, under-stood to be Mr Lecky, the historian ;" but the controversy that ensued placed it beyond a doubt that the words were an authentic report of an actual conversation. One and another witness stepped into the arena to testify that they also had heard Carlyle use almost precisely the same language. One witness related, on the authority of Lady Ashburton, how at her house the conversation, on one occasion, turned on the theory of Evolution. Carlyle took no part in it, but at length, a pause occurring, he exclaimed, " Gentlemen, you are well pleased to trace your descent from a tadpole and an ape, but I would exclaim with David, ' Lord, Thou hast made me but a little lower than the angels.' " Mr Andrew James Symington, the poet and essayist, wrote : " I can vouch for having heard the same or similar sentiments from the

Sage of Chelsea, whose reverence for the God of the Bible is so deep and true that, to his thinking, it is far too sacred to be much spoken about. On one occasion, in particular, I heard him remark that the short, simple, but sublime account of Creation, given in the first chapter of Genesis, was in advance of all theories, for it was God's truth, and, as such, the only key to the mystery; that it ought to satisfy the *savans,* who in any case would never find out any other, although they might dream about it. Then, alluding to the Development hypothesis, waxing warm, and, at the same time, bringing his hand down on the table with a thump like the sledgehammer of Thor, he emphatically added—'I have no patience whatever with these gorilla damnifications of humanity!'"*

A friend of ours, also an old friend of Carlyle's, and, we may add, one of the most intimate English friends of Emerson, having lately printed, for private circulation, a most complete Bibliography of Leigh Hunt, Hazlitt, and Charles Lamb, this book was spoken of, Carlyle saying he had got a copy, and praising it as a "most piously-executed piece of work," worthy of all commendation, though it struck us, from an incidental remark, that it was the portion of the book relating to Leigh Hunt that had possessed the greatest interest and charm for Carlyle. This was proved almost immediately. As we had noted that he nowhere speaks of the gentle "Elia," though he

---

* We do not wish it to be supposed that we sympathise with these expressions against the Darwinian theory and its supporters; for, whatever the nature and tendencies of that theory may be, it must not be forgotten—as Carlyle seemed to forget—that many who accept the doctrine of Evolution, concerning which we here say nothing, are Christian believers, and that, too, of a much more definite type than Carlyle himself could be said to be.

has written so kindly of Leigh Hunt and other contemporaries of Lamb, we ventured to ask him if he had much personal acquaintance with the latter. The quality of Mr Carlyle's own humour made us suspect that we should probably hear little to Lamb's advantage; and this suspicion was all the stronger when we reflected that the personal habits of "Elia" must have made him a distasteful object to the sober and correct-living Scot, who, as Wordsworth has so finely indicated, preserved in his life at least the severe purity of Calvinism, however far he might have departed from the Calvinistic creed in his speculative system. "What makes you ask—what interest have you in Lamb?" "I like his humour." "Humour —he had no humour." We mildly submitted our belief that he had. "You are mistaken—it was only a thin streak of Cockney wit;" this phrase uttered with a shrill shout expressive of ineffable contempt; and then the speaker added, "I dare say you must have known some —I have known scores of Scotch moorland farmers, who for *humour* could have blown Lamb into the zenith!" The pictorial effect of this figure, delivered in a high Annandale key, especially when the speaker came to the last clause of the sentence, it is impossible for print to convey—the listener saw poor Lamb spinning off into space, propelled thither by the contemptuous kick of a lusty Dandie Dinmont, in hodden grey, from the moors of Galloway or Ayrshire.

"The only thing really humorous about Lamb," he continued, "was his personal appearance. His suit of rusty black, his spindle-shanks, his knee-breeches, the bit ribbons fleein' at the knees o' him : indeed he was humour personified !" this last clause again in the high key, making the figure effective and mirth-compelling to a degree. And then he told us how the first occasion on which he met "the puir drucken body" was at Enfield, in 1829, at the house of a most respectable lady. It was the forenoon; but Lamb, who had been "tasting" before he came, immediately demanded gin, and because he could not get it, "kicked up a terrible row." Moral disgust at poor "Elia's" misconduct was evidently at the root of the feeling of antipathy evinced by Carlyle in speaking of his humour. Lamb was not a humourist because he got drunk, and because he demanded gin in the forenoon at a lady's house.

Then we were told, as an example of Lamb's Cockney wit, how at Enfield, on the same occasion, he had expressed his regret that the Royalists had not taken Milton's head off at the Restoration. That was one of the bright remarks which he invariably fired off whenever he met anybody for the first time; Carlyle had often afterwards heard him repeat it. At Enfield he gave it for Carlyle's benefit, to astonish the stranger from Scotland. "But Lamb was a Liberal," we remarked; "he could not have wished such a fate for Milton?" "Ah, you don't see his point; he wished the Royalists had taken Milton's head off in order that they might have damned themselves to all eternity!" Then, *sotte voce*, Carlyle added, "Puir silly cratur!"

Moral disgust, however, with a strong dash of the Scottish Philistine in it, was perhaps not the only cause of the dislike; we suspect the ethereal quality of Lamb's humour was distasteful to the old Viking, who relished something of a more robust, not to say a coarser, order. Bulwer Lytton speaks of Lamb as one of those rare favourites of the Graces on whom the gift of *charm* is bestowed ; but the charm was assuredly not felt by Carlyle, whatever the cause may have been. In the same essay, Bulwer Lytton says : " As Scott's humour is that of a novelist, and therefore objective, so Lamb's is that of an essayist, and eminently subjective. All that he knows or observes in the world of books or men becomes absorbed in the single life of his own mind, and is reproduced as part and parcel of Charles Lamb. If thus he does not create imaginary characters, Caleb Balderstones and Major Dalgettys, he calls up, completes, and leaves to the admiration of all time a character which, as a personification of humour, is a higher being than even Scott has imagined, viz., that of Charles Lamb himself. Nor is there in the whole world of humorous creation an image more beautiful in its combinations of mirth and pathos. In the embodiment of humour, as it actually lived amongst us in this man, there is a dignity equal to that with which Cervantes elevates our delight in his ideal creation. Quixote is not more essentially a gentleman than Lamb."

In spite of the stain of gin, we must confess that we prefer to look upon poor "Elia " as personified humour in Lytton's sense, rather than in Carlyle's ; and when we recall the story of Lamb's devotion to his sister Mary, in which there is a pathetic grandeur that rises to the sublime, we can only marvel that it failed to correct what we believe to be a singularly false estimate of that bright and charming creature concerning whom the most classical of modern poets exclaimed :—

> " Few are the spirits of the glorified
> I'd spring to earlier at the gate of Heaven."

That same day the talk turned to one of whom Carlyle
was sure to speak more sympathetically; and, in spite of
the emotion (not of a pleasant sort) excited within us by
what we conceived to be the almost abominable injustice
done to Lamb, it was with hushed heart that we listened
to the friend of Edward Irving, as he spoke of that old
companion of his youth. How often we had read the
survivor's tribute to Irving! We felt it was no small
privilege to hear him now speaking on the same theme.
It has been stated by Mrs Oliphant, in her *Life of Irving*,
that the subject of that work claimed kindred with the
Howies of Lochgoin, and was proud of the connection
with that old Covenanting family, to which belonged John
Howie, author of the *Scots Worthies*.* We asked Carlyle
if he knew whether there was any truth in the statement.
He replied that this claim of kinship with the Howies
was one which he well remembered Irving to have cherished with satisfaction, if not with pride. Then he proceeded to relate an anecdote which he had been told
more than forty years before by an old Glasgow friend of
Irving's, and of his own, the late William Graham,
"a most worthy man," which not only went to confirm

---

* The old Martyrologist was a moorland farmer in Ayrshire, and
his farm of Lochgoin, which is held to-day by a grandson, has been
occupied by the family for six hundred years. The Howies are,
indeed, believed to have been Waldensian refugees, who fled from
their country to Scotland in the great Papal persecution of the
twelfth century, and who settled at Lochgoin. Through all the
subsequent generations they have remained, in the land of their
adoption, faithful to the venerable traditions of their house; and in
the Covenanting struggle they came to the front among the suffering
witnesses for the truth, their moorland dwelling having been twelve
times "harried" by the spoiler, and on several occasions burned to
the ground.

the fact that Irving believed he was a kinsman of the martyrologist, but which also threw a quaint light both on Irving and the family of Lochgoin. When Irving was settled at Glasgow as the assistant of Dr Chalmers, he resolved to make a pilgrimage to Lochgoin, not only that he might look upon the scene of so many stirring events in the Covenanting history, but in order to make the acquaintance of those whom he believed to be his kindred. Accordingly, he first of all took a public coach, which carried him on his journey—to the village of Eagelsham in the Mearns—the district where Professor Wilson spent most of his boyhood, and which he has described in the early chapters of the *Recreations of Christopher North*. From the village Irving was obliged to make the rest of his pilgrimage on foot. Not only was there no conveyance, but the greater part of the way was over a wild moor, abounding in black tracts of marshy soil, across which no vehicle had ever ventured to pass. It was dark when the great preacher arrived at the door of the little farmhouse—then, as for many a year after, a poor thatched hut of one storey, such as the English tourist views to-day with amazement when he has penetrated into the glens of the Western Highlands. Irving could hear that the family were engaged at evening worship, "the Books," Carlyle called it, as he told the story, before retiring for the night. Gently he lifted the latch, and entered on tiptoe the homely kitchen, lighted only by a turf fire. The members of the household were on their knees, and in the dim light the stranger sought the nearest vacant space, and—"we may be sure, with much pious emotion," said Carlyle—knelt with his kindred. With closed eyes he bent his head over what seemed at first to be a chair or stool ; but in a little while a genial warmth began to be diffused from this object, which he could not understand ; by and by it became hotter still, and in a little while the heat was so strong he could endure it no longer.　Opening his eyes, and steadily surveying the object, he discerned, through the gloom, that he had been kneeling over a huge pot, but recently withdrawn from the fire, and containing the supper for the pigs !　At this point, Carlyle broke into hearty laughter ; and then, resuming, he told how, when the service was ended, Irving received a hearty welcome from the good man of the house, who was a son of the martyrologist,* and spent a happy night under the humble roof where so many generations of godly men and women had practised that "plain living and high thinking" which has contributed so mightily to make Scotland what it is.　This was a story evidently much to Carlyle's liking ; and it is impossible to reproduce on paper the graphic touches of the narrative as it fell from his lips, especially the account of the journey over the black bogs surrounding Lochgoin, and the reverential manner in which he described Irving's pious delight on finding his supposed kindred so well employed when he reached their house in the "gloaming."　But was Irving really connected with the Howies ? we inquired.　Carlyle knew nothing about that.　Might it not be through his mother that he was related ?　"His

---

* Many years after that visit we found Irving's *Orations of Judgment to Come* in the library at Lochgoin, and read the volume with wonder and awe, on the moor close by—our first meeting with Carlyle's leal-hearted friend.　On the fly-leaf was an inscription by the author, shewing that he had sent the book as a present to his old host, the son of the martyrologist.

mother!" exclaimed Carlyle, "no, no: his mother was a Lowther; she was a Cumberland woman."* He added that when Irving wanted a thing to be true, he was almost sure to find some reason for believing it.

Of the author of the *Scots Worthies* and the book by which he is best known, Carlyle spoke with profound respect. "A simple, earnest, fine old man," he said, "who had written, in his own homely way, one of the best books on the religious history of Scotland." Since he came to London he had given away many copies of it to English friends who wished to understand that history— a subject on which many of them were wofully in the dark. He had given Mr Froude a copy, to let him see what kind of men there had been in the kingdom of Scotland.

From the Covenanters and the moors of Ayrshire our talk on this occasion passed, by association of ideas, to an old seat of the Cromwell family in Huntingdonshire with which we happened to have somewhat intimate personal relations. "What sort of folk are the Fen farmers?" inquired Carlyle. Many of them, we replied, were very much of the same stamp as their forefathers who fought with Cromwell, and with whom he had some acquaintance, we replied; and then, we fear not without

---

* The Rev. Gavin Carlyle, a nephew of Edward Irving, and editor of his collected works, informs us that Irving's mother once wrote to him of Carlyle as "uncouth." He wrote back that if Carlyle lived, he would be one of the greatest men in England. With this we may bracket an inedited anecdote, which proves the constant loyalty of Irving to his friend. The late Dr Kirkwood, a well-known Secession minister, was in London on a visit at the time of Carlyle's settlement in Cheyne Row, and, in conversation with Irving, the talk turned on the new-comer. "Carlyle," exclaimed Irving, "will revolutionise the literature of England!"

a touch of malice, we told a story of one, a good friend
of our own, who had sacrificed a farm rather than vote
at the previous Parliamentary election against his conscience. "More fool he!" cried Carlyle, in his very
loudest key. "And was it to put Gladstone in that he
did that?" We replied in the affirmative. "Gladstone!"
he exclaimed, with a snort of contempt, "and that
Heaven-born Minister of War, Mr Cardwell! Froude
tells me they have, perhaps, a dozen guns and six
howitzers that could fire in the event of a war!" We
suggested that there might be as much conscience in a
man going to the poll for Gladstone, in the teeth of land-
lord intimidation, as there was in his ancestor fighting at
Naseby or Dunbar. We even ventured to go a little
farther, and to question the soundness of the theory
which seemed to confine the service of God by Englishmen to the seventeenth century, as if He had not quite
as much to do with the nineteenth; but the response to
this was the reverse of satisfactory. The biographer of
Cromwell refused to be drawn out on this delicate point.
But there was no end to his glorifying of the Germans,
who were at that time completing their victory over
France. His estimate of the French Generals in the war
was exceedingly contemptuous; even Macmahon came
in for a satirical lashing of the utmost severity. A friend
who was present at this conversation, and who, from long
official experience, was informed on the subject above the
mark of most men, afterwards assured us that Carlyle,
whom he had known intimately for upwards of thirty
years, was talking on these war topics very much at
random, and without exact information about the men
whom he held up to scorn. Bismarck was the god of his

idolatry; all the other politicians in Europe were the merest "windbags," he the only genuine article in that line. Against the friend above-mentioned, he maintained that the influence of a great united Germany would be peaceful, though an observation with which he backed up this opinion scarcely seemed to support it. The very name German, he said, indicated that he had always been distinguished for his warlike character and success in arms. He is the *guerre*-man, that is, the *war*-man. " It's just the same word we have in Scotland, ' I'll *gar* ye do't.' " * And so he went on pointing out how *guarantee*, and probably the word *war* itself, came from the same root. Yet the German, he would have it, was radically one of the most peaceful of human beings—the very last to pick a quarrel; but when driven to it, he will also be the last to yield.

---

* This might serve as Carlyle's motto. His theory put Erskine of Linlathen in mind of old Sir Harry Moncreiff's saying, that we need men who will " mak' us for to know it," and who will also " mak' us for to do it."

CHAPTER XXII.

CARLYLE was a thorough Scot. He clung, with a fond
and almost passionate tenacity, to more than the dialect
and accent of his "own stern Motherland." Never was
there a man who preserved everywhere, and to the last, the
mint-mark of the place of his nativity as he did. Not even
honest Allan Cunningham may be named as approaching him in this respect. It was not only the quaint
but musical speech of Annandale that he carried about
with him during the whole of his earthly pilgrimage; in
mind and heart—in all the essential qualities of his being
—he bore the stamp of that south-western region of Scotland that will be known to coming generations as pre-
eminently the Land of Carlyle. London he selected as
his place of residence simply for its convenience as a
literary workshop. In the forty-seven years that followed
his settlement in Cheyne Row hardly a summer passed
in which he did not revisit his native district. Even
after his mother was gone, he never failed to look in

upon his brothers and sisters at their respective homes, taking an interest in their domestic welfare and preserving fresh and vigorous the recollections of his childhood. One nephew he took away to push his fortune in the metropolis, in the house of his own publishers; and when his wife was suddenly snatched from his side it was a sister's child that he asked to come and keep house for him in the distant wilderness where he dwelt. One other sister, married to a farmer in a bleak upland part of their native district, he tried to make more comfortable by endeavours, often renewed, to get a belt of trees to grow round her mountain home; but all the efforts of " oor Tam" proved futile—the young trees he brought, or sent, never came to anything, the place was so exposed and the soil so uncongenial. To Dumfriesshire he would have latterly returned altogether, he told his friend Thomas Aird, but for the fear that he might become intellectually torpid away from the society to which he had become accustomed, and which can only be procured in the great city. Those who enjoyed the privilege of visiting Carlyle, especially if they were fellow-countrymen, can testify how vivid were his reminiscences of his early days at Ecclefechan and Annan, and how he liked nothing better than to hear of the old companions of his boyhood. That the talk was good, though occasionally a little bitter and stinging in its characterisations, when he got on the subject of the worthies he had known in his youth, need not be told to those who have read his graphic picture of the "steel-grey" peasant-prophet, Dr Lawson of Selkirk. When a West Country humourist like the late John Kelso Hunter published his autobiography, no reader enjoyed it more than Carlyle, and he praised that book of genuine homespun, in no stinted measure, for its "good humour and canny shrewdness," and especially "for the pleasant way in which it had reminded him of what he himself knew so well long ago." He liked its "subdued vein of just satire," too, which ran through it, he said, "like a suspicion of good cognac in a wholesome tumbler of new milk." He was greatly pleased when we told him that his letter to Hunter had been the chief means of sending a large edition of the quaint cobbler-artist's *Retrospect* over the world, and that Hunter had pocketed the largest sum ever got by the author of any volume published in the West of Scotland. "He deserves it," said Carlyle; "there was truth, and humour too, in that book of the Cobbler's—I mind it well." In 1859, when the Scottish people were celebrating the Centenary of Burns's birth, he gave hearty support, both by pen and purse, to the fund for the Misses Begg, the nieces of the poet. "Could all the eloquence," he wrote, "that will be uttered over the world on the 25th next, or even all the tavern bills that will be incurred, but convert themselves into solid cash for those two interesting persons, what a sum were there of benefit received, and of loss avoided, to all the parties concerned! I think, at least, the question ought to be everywhere put, pointedly, yet with due politeness, wherever in Scotland, or elsewhere, there is an assemblage of men met to express their admiration, tragic pity, &c., for Burns, what amount of money they will give to save from indigence these two nieces of Burns? The answer, virtual answer, which this question got in 1842, threw rather a dismal light to me on such assemblages; but they ought to be tried again, with more direct emphasis; and very shame will perhaps force them to do something towards saving indigent merit on the one hand, and saving on the other what is too truly a frightful (though eloquent) expenditure of pavement to a certain locality we have all heard of!" This letter contributed in no slight degree to secure the success with which the effort was crowned. With the London Scots, however, of the toddy-drinking and rhetorical species, who prove their patriotism chiefly at taverns, he would have nothing to do. They tried, more than once, to catch him for the presidential chair, but they never succeeded. In 1870, one of their number published a letter, wherein he gave an account, not meant to be amusing, of how he and three other compatriots got up the London dinner in celebration of the Burns Centenary, at which James Hannay presided. Two of the originators of the scheme (thought to be so great a scheme that years afterwards there was actually a printed controversy as to who started it) were deputed to wait, most likely appointed themselves to wait, upon Carlyle at his Chelsea home, to see if *he* would take the chair! " We might as well have stayed at home, however," was their lugubrious report. His attachment to the land of his birth was too deep and tender to admit of such a degradation—for, to a man of his nature, it would have been nothing short of that—a speech about Scotland and Burns, at a convival gathering in a tavern, by Thomas Carlyle, being a phenomenon simply inconceivable.

Though he did not patronise their "kirks" to any appreciable extent, having, indeed, usually a small congregation of his own to minister to at his own house on the Sundays, he was on friendly terms with a few of the Presbyterian clergy. When Alexander J. Scott, afterwards the Principal of Owens College at Manchester, was minister of the Presbyterian Church at Woolwich, he was in constant intercourse with Carlyle. In the July of 1838 we find Erskine of Linlathen closing a letter to Scott with the sentence: "Remember me lovingly to the Carlyles and Maurice." When Scott, in 1848, became a candidate for the Chair of English Literature in University College, Carlyle commended him as a man "long and intimately known to him," and " of great, solid, and original powers of mind; of a pure, high, and earnest character; whose rare merits the whole world, if at length the fit arena were conceded to him, might yet well come to recognise." For some twenty years the Chelsea Presbyterians had for their pastor a severely orthodox, but personally genial, sailor-like Scotsman, the Rev. Thomas Alexander, whose theological standpoint may be guessed from the fact that it was he who wrote an attack on *Good Words* in the *Record* which made some little stir at the time in the "religious world," and is referred to in Norman Macleod's biography. Though Mr Alexander was a Presbyterian of the most antique type, advocating stern adherence to the well-trod paths in which the Covenanting fathers travelled, he was on excellent terms with his neighbour in Cheyne Row; and when he died very suddenly, and under most distressing circumstances, in 1872, Carlyle sent a touching letter of condolence to Dr Hogg, one of the elders of the congregation, which was read at the funeral. Next Sunday Carlyle attended the church, and listened to the funeral sermon, which was preached by Dr Oswald Dykes, a native of his own county of Dumfries. At the sale of poor Alexander's library, the article that excited the most interest and the keenest bidding was a scrap of notepaper, mounted in an ebony frame, on which was written in its author's "kenspeckle" caligraphy a versicle by Carlyle. The minister had applied for a subscription towards building schools in connection with the church, and this was the reply he got :—

> " Rev. T. Alexander, with many regards.
>
>> " There was a Piper had a Cow,
>> And he had nocht to give her ;
>> He took his pipes and play'd a spring,
>> And bade the Cow consider.
>> The Cow consider'd wi' hersel'
>> That mirth wad never fill her :
>> ' Gie me a pickle ait strae,
>> And sell your wind for siller.'
>
> "Chelsea, 3d Feb. 1870. T. CARLYLE."

The minister did not get the expected subscription at the time ; but, by playfully threatening to have the verse lithographed for sale, he succeeded in his object. A second kindred versicle, escaped from the custody of some lady's album, runs thus :—

> " Simon Brodie had a cow ;
>> He lost his cow, and he could na find her,
>> When he had done what man could do,
>> The cow cam' hame, and her tail behind her.
>
> "Chelsea, 23 Jan. 1849. T. CARLYLE."

Both of these trifles remind one of the old rhymes that used to be current at the firesides of the Scottish Lowland peasantry before the newspaper had come, to banish, not only the chap-books, but also a vernacular literature, mostly in verse, that never found its way into print until the few lingering fragments were gathered by the antiquary in our own day. A third Presbyterian minister of London who had ready access to Carlyle was his namesake, the Rev. Gavin Carlyle, the nephew of his old friend Edward Irving. To him Carlyle once spoke of his old kinsman, Dr Carlyle, of Inveresk, as a "pot-walloping Sadducee;" and, talking of his college days at Edinburgh, he described one of the professors in the Theological Hall, as having "a face red like the setting sun on a misty day—such a man speaking of the ethereal and the heavenly!" Of the Presbyterian ministers in Scotland who have left records of their meetings with Carlyle, the most prominent were Dr Chalmers and George Gilfillan. The latter writes in 1845 :—"Carlyle's excellent mother still lives, and we had the pleasure of meeting her lately in the company of her illustrious son, and beautiful it was to see his profound and tender regard, and her motherly and yearning reverence, to hear her fine old Covenanting accents concerting with his transcendental tones." Gilfillan adds that "it was worth a thousand homilies to hear Carlyle, as we were privileged to do, talking for four miles of moonlit road, with his earnest, sagacious voice, of religion, baring ever and anon his head as if in worship amid the warm, slumberous August air." When Gilfillan wrote his first *Gallery of Literary Portraits*, in which there was an article on Carlyle's *French Revolution*, pitched on a key of rapturous admiration, the recipient of the praise wrote to Thomas Aird, in whose paper at Dumfries the article first appeared :—"It is a noble panegyric; a picture painted by a poet, which means with me a man of insight and of heart, decisive, sharp of outline, in hues borrowed from the sun. It is rare to find one's self so mirrored in a brother's soul."

One of the longest of Mr Carlyle's later visits to Scotland was made in the autumn of 1871. It extended over several months; and towards the close of October he returned to Cheyne Row much invigorated in health, having greatly enjoyed the sojourn in his native country. In the autumn of 1874 he made another protracted stay in the North, residing for a time at Portobello for the sea-bathing and on account of its proximity to Edinburgh, and afterwards, accompanied by his brother the Doctor, and his niece, passing over to Fife, where he was the guest for several weeks of his old pupil, Provost Swan of Kirkcaldy. He drove about a great deal in the pleasant little "Kingdom," as the Fife people love to designate their county; and one day, Thursday, September 17, was devoted to St Andrews. While sauntering among the tombs that surround the ruins of the ancient Cathedral, a lady observed that he was about to pass one noteworthy grave without perceiving it. She therefore ventured to say to him, "This is Samuel Rutherford's grave." He bowed and thanked her, and, having read the inscription on the tombstone, said, "Ah! he was a deep thinker." On another day he visited a school on the Links at Kirkcaldy, and the master, anxious to show the children at their best before their distinguished visitor, set them to sing. Carlyle asked that they should sing something by Burns; but the master not having practised the children in Burns, had to excuse himself and them as well as he could. Carlyle left exclaiming, "Scotch children singing, and not taught Burns's songs! Oh, dear me!" Every morning he walked before breakfast to Seafield Tower, a distance of a mile and a half, to enjoy a bathe in the sea; and after breakfast he sallied forth armed with a long clay pipe into the grounds surrounding the mansion of his host. "A most inveterate smoker Mr Carlyle is," said the local chronicler, "and has been since he was here sixty years ago." This statement is confirmed by a story current at Cannes, whither he went one season to be under the care of Dr Franks. "I'll do anything, Doctor, ye tell me," was his first remark; "but ye maunna stop my pipe!" In the garden behind his house in Cheyne Row, in the summer time, under an awning, there was a table with a canister of tobacco and a supply of pipes, whither he always betook himself, with his guests, after six o'clock tea; and to any stranger he was almost sure to preface the smoke with a denunciation of the Government for laying "a tax of some hundreds per cent. upon the poor man's pipe, while the rich man's glass of wine pays scarcely one-tenth of this impost." He felt somewhat comforted by the thought that the amount of tobacco smuggled into England is about as great as the quantity that pays the duty, which some one had told him was actually the case; "the Smuggler," said he, "is the Lord Almighty of the Chancellor of the Exchequer, saying to him, 'Thus far shalt thou go, and no farther, and here shall thy proud waves be stayed.'"

It was during one of these visits to his native country that he spent a few days near the little Stirlingshire village of Balfron. During his stay his hostess had occasion to send her butler to the bank to get a cheque cashed. The banker, a gentleman of literary tastes, said he would himself call presently with the cash, and shortly afterwards proceeded to fulfil his self-imposed mission. On the road he met the lady, out taking a walk with her venerable guest. Carlyle turned aside to view the scenery while the banker addressed the lady, explaining how, as she had so distinguished a visitor, he could not resist taking the liberty of coming up, in the hope that he might have the great honour of seeing her guest. Thereupon Carlyle, who had heard all that was passing, turned round, and, addressing the hero-worshipper in his most sarcastic tone, said, "Weel, noo that you are here, be sure and tak' a gude look at him! Be sure that you'll ken him the next time you see him!" The poor banker was glad to get out of the great man's presence as quickly as possible.* The coachman who daily drove Carlyle out in Stirlingshire that year, kept a careful record of all the places and distances. He was suffered to pass no mansion or scene of a striking character, without giving a complete account of it to the lively octogenarian; and when he happened to be in ignorance as to its name, etc., he was obliged to pull up and receive an elaborate rebuke for his unpardonable ignorance. One evening, in another part of the country, Carlyle was present at a social party, where the old homely custom of calling on each member of the company for a song, or, failing that, a story, was observed. A learned minister of the Kirk, who, under a veil of the most perfect pastoral gravity, carries a rich fund of quaint humour, sang the old ballad, "Oor gude-

---

* A kindred story is current in Chelsea. While Carlyle was one morning taking his customary walk, a well dressed man approached him, with the question, "Are you really the great Thomas Carlyle, author of the *French Revolution?*" "I am Thomas Carlyle," was the reply, "and I have written a history of the French Revolution." "Indeed! Pray pardon a stranger for speaking to you; but I was *so* anxious to have a look at you." "Look on, man!" quoth the philosopher, as he resumed his walk; "look on! it will do me no harm, and you no good."

man cam' hame at e'en, and hame cam' he," and gave the piece with a *naïveté* which charmed the sage, who asked to have it over again. Many a year had passed since he last heard the song, and it touched the spring of old memories. A few days afterwards he met the reverend vocalist on a country road, and gave his hearty greeting as they neared each other by merrily chanting the first line of his song. It seems to have been the clergy of the Establishment he came most into contact with during these visits to Scotland; he thought the Secession Kirk was not now what it had been in his young days, and as for the other great Presbyterian denomination, his favourite formula when describing it was, " That compendium of all righteousness, the Free Kirk !" From which we may infer that he had no excessive liking for it.

He was in his 84th year when he paid his last visit to his native country; and on this occasion he went thither for the purpose of being present at the marriage of the niece who had acted as his amanuensis and housekeeper during the whole of his widowed life. The bridegroom was one of her Canadian cousins, Mr Alexander Carlyle, B.A., of Bield, Brentfield, Ontario. The marriage ceremony, which took place on August 21, 1879, according to the Scottish custom, was performed in the house of the bride's father, Mr James Aitken, of The Hill, Dumfries, always one of his homes when he visited Scotland; and after the ceremony Carlyle, who was in excellent health and spirits, entered into conversation with the officiating clergyman, the Rev. James A. Campbell, parish minister of Troqueer, remarking, with tears, that he felt grateful to Almighty God for having spared him so many years. He also spoke of the work of John Knox, and of his being monumentally commemorated.   Mr Campbell was deeply impressed with the Christian earnestness of the illustrious veteran.   The newly-married pair took up their residence at Chelsea under the same roof with their venerated relative.   He had become so habituated to the gentle ministrations of his niece that her departure from the home which her presence had brightened for upwards of twelve years was a simple impossibility.   Before his death there was, to the great delight of the old man, another Thomas Carlyle in the Chelsea home.

CHAPTER XXIII.

MANY are the stories, humorous and pathetic, that cluster
round No. 5 Cheyne Row. One of the prettiest is that
relating to Leigh Hunt's graceful little poem, "Jenny
Kissed Me!" Poor Hunt had come one day in hot
haste to the Carlyles, to tell them of some rare bit of
good fortune that had just happened either to himself or
them; whereupon Mrs Carlyle sprang from her chair,
threw her arms about the old poet's neck, and gave him
a cordial kiss; hence the poem. That Carlyle was
exceedingly sensitive to noise has been already attested
by the fact that at Edinburgh the Erskines were obliged
to stop the clock in his chamber while he was thinking
out his Rectorial address. In the graphic sketch of
Carlyle in his London home in the *Englische Charak-
terbilder*, Berlin, 1860, by Dr Frederick Althaus, one of
the German translators of Carlyle's *Frederick*, an account
is given of the historian's workshop—a large noise-proof
chamber forming the top storey of the house, which he
built specially for the purpose of securing quiet and

freedom from interruption. A lady residing close by kept Cochin China fowls, whose crowing was such a nuisance that Carlyle sent in a complaint. But the message of the philosopher only moved her to indignation. "Why," she exclaimed, "the fowls only crow four times a day, and how can Mr Carlyle be seriously annoyed at that?" "The lady forgets," was his rejoinder, "the pain I suffer in *waiting* for those four crows." Like Dean Swift, Christopher North, Charles Dickens, and some other eminent men of letters, Carlyle was a great nocturnal pedestrian before the infirmities of old age crept upon him. His favourite beat was the riverside district in which he dwelt; he carried an enormous stick on these occasions, and walked with his eyes fixed on the ground. He kept to this habit all through the time of the garotting panic, though friends warned him that the *History of Frederick*, on which he was then engaged, might be suddenly cut short some night if he did not give up his midnight rambles. This walking was his specific for procuring sleep. Mr Ruskin once sent a letter to the papers on the subject of the alleged bad manners of the English people, as compared with those of the continental nations; and he stated, as an illustration of this, that Carlyle could not walk out in the streets of Chelsea without being subjected to insult by the "roughs" of that region. Carlyle at once wrote to say that there was no truth in the allegation; in fact, he penned no fewer than three notes contradicting the report, an exhibition of candour that did not pass without comment, especially among those who could recall the time when Carlyle was wont to sally forth on horseback every Wednesday to enjoy a ride on Denmark Hill with his friend and worshipper. Not a little slanderous tattle used to appear in the papers about him. In 1870 he was pictured by some one as absolutely alone in his house at Chelsea, deserted by everybody on account of his wretched temper; the truth being that he was not in town at all, but in the country, the guest of his good friend Lady Ashburton. Mr Ruskin, the slanderers said, was the longest suffering, but he also had been compelled to give up his visits to Cheyne Row. Ruskin had been there every other day till Carlyle left town for a change of air, rendered necessary by the weak state of his health during the severe winter of 1869-70. All who visited Carlyle at the time when these reports were current invariably found him in his most amiable mood. This was especially the case in the spring of 1871, when the first volume of the "people's edition" of his collected writings made its appearance. It was to have been published on the 15th of March; but the orders poured in to such an unexpected extent, that the publishers could not supply them all at the date originally fixed; hence they had to delay the issue. The demand for the book, especially in Scotland, was beyond all their calculations, and indeed something quite unprecedented. Carlyle's surprise and his gratitude for this widespread interest in his writings among the working classes were, we had reason to know, most profound.

Of the more purely literary anecdotes, one of the best used to be told with inimitable point by Dickens. The self-confident editor of a certain weekly paper was present at a dinner-party, and had enunciated some weighty opinion on the subject under discussion, wrapping it up in a small parcel and laying it by on a shelf as if done with for ever—and a dead silence ensued. This silence, to the astonishment of all, was broken by Carlyle looking across the table at the editor, in a dreamy way, and saying as though to himself, but in perfectly audible tones, "Eh, but you're a puir cratur, a puir, wratched, meeserable cratur!" Then, with a sigh, he relapsed into silence. To a popular young novelist, the writer of some Scottish stories, who had called upon him, he said, "When are you going to begin some honest, genuine work?" To another popular author, of the flippant Cockney sort, a wit, he said, "And when, sir, do you bring out the Comic Bible?" It has been said that at first Carlyle sent his manuscript to the printer without making any corrections on the first words that came, but that, happening to see the interlineated "copy" of a distinguished contemporary, he changed his plan and also took to making emendations, almost on the scale of a Balzac. We have the authority of Miss Martineau, however, for a statement that does not harmonise with this story. She tells how almost every other word was altered in Carlyle's proofs. One day he went to the office to urge on the printer. "Why, sir," said the latter, " you really are so very hard upon us with your corrections. They take so much time, you see!" Carlyle replied that he had been accustomed to this sort of thing—he had got works printed in Scotland, and ——." "Yes, indeed, sir," interrupted the printer, " we are aware of that. We have a man here from Edinburgh, and when he took up a bit of your copy he dropped it as if it had burnt his fingers, and cried out, ' Lord have mercy! have you got that man to print for? Lord knows when we shall get done—with all his corrections!'" On the question of Copyright he thought much and wrote not a little. As early as 1839, indeed, he presented a petition to Parliament on the subject of the Copyright Bill then engaging the attention of the Legislature; it was in this document he described himself, with characteristic preference for simple, homely phrase, as a "Writer of Books." It is amusing to read the answers which he gave to Joseph Hume, in the Commission upon the British Museum, on the subject of the selection of books. "But what you might think a bad book I might think a good one," was the substance of Mr Hume's questions to the sage, who was for stark naked despotism in this matter. Carlyle would allow a book of which he personally disapproved "a run for its life," but he would shoot it down if he could. Mr Hume was quite unable to produce any impression upon him, and the subject dropped.

Carlyle felt a little annoyed at a West-End bootmaker, who lithographed a note of commendation which he had received from the author of *Sartor*, and used it as an advertisement; the sage was troubled with corns, and having been induced to give this tradesman a trial, found such relief in using his boots that he felt constrained to send him a compliment along with the next order, never dreaming of the purpose to which it would be turned. He was vexed at first, but afterwards laughed, disdainfully, when the subject came up, though he would usually add some praise of the man's skill from an experience of him six times repeated. He was better satisfied with the paragraph which appeared in the papers telling about a tanner whose manufacture was rèmarkable for its excellence, and who explained the matter by saying, " If I had not read Carlyle, I should never have made my leather so good." This story pleased him very much— more so, perhaps, than the most glowing panegyric on his works that had ever appeared in print.

Perhaps the last public meeting Carlyle attended was one in St James's Hall, when Mr Ralston, who has done so much to familiarize English readers with the literature of Russia, lectured on " Stories for Children of All Ages." The sage came and went leaning on the arm of Mr William Allingham. He was always very fond of children, and used to carry a supply of sweets in his pocket to give to the bairns about his own door at Chelsea. To the last he continued to sneer at novel-writing, expressing contempt even for the masterpieces of George Eliot, whose *Adam Bede* he pronounced " simply dull ;" and at no time did he ever lose an opportunity of condemning verse, of which he had been intolerant for at leasty forty years. He had advised even Mrs Browning " to say rather than to sing," when she sent him one of her earliest books ; and there was more than a grain of truth in Miss Mitford's sneer, that he kept a set form of a letter to send to all the poets, great and small. The publication of one of these letters a few years ago provoked a great controversy, and Mr Russell Lowell expressed his belief that Carlyle has no artistic sense of form or rhythm, scarcely of proportion, and that therefore he looks on verse with contempt as something barbarous—as a savage ornament which a higher refinement will abolish as it has abolished tatooing and nose-rings. Mr Lowell admits that he has a conceptive imagination vigorous beyond any in his generation, with a mastery of language equalled only by

the greatest poets, but holds that he is altogether destitute of the plastic imagination, the shaping faculty. But
it would be a great mistake to suppose that he has no
soul for genuine poetry. Who has shown a more profound appreciation of lyrical compositions than he? No
writer has more completely exhibited what goes to form
the essence of a song. That aphorism of Fletcher of
Saltoun's, "Let me make the songs of a people, and you
shall make its laws," has been so very frequently cited
that it has grown stale; but the first man to quote it was
Carlyle.

When poor Ernest Jones, the Chartist leader, was
denouncing the established authorities in the presence
of Carlyle, the latter shook his head and told him that,
"had the Chartist leaders been living in the days of
Christ, He would have sent the unclean spirits into
them, instead of into the swine of the Gergesenes, and
so we should have happily got rid of them." One day,
in the company of some clerical friends, he said "he
would build a wood and leather man to reason as well as
most country parsons." One evening, at a small literary
gathering, a lady, famous for her "muslin theology," was
bewailing the wickedness of the Jews in not receiving our
Saviour, and ended her diatribe by expressing regret that
He had not appeared in our own time. "How delighted,"
said she, "we should all be to throw our doors open to
Him, and listen to His divine precepts! Don't you
think so, Mr Carlyle?" Thus appealed to, he replied,
"No, madam, I don't. I think that, had He come very
fashionably dressed, with plenty of money, and preaching
doctrines palatable to the higher orders, I might have
had the honour of receiving from you a card of invita-

tion, on the back of which would be written, 'To meet our Saviour;' but if he had come uttering His sublime precepts, and denouncing the Pharisees, and associating with the Publicans and lower orders, as He did, you would have treated Him much as the Jews did, and have cried out, 'Take Him to Newgate and hang Him!'" He admitted, however, that Lord Houghton would probably invite Him to breakfast. Once, while staying at a country house, Carlyle was requested to conduct family worship; he readily complied, and, as soon as the household had assembled, began reading the Book of Job, which he read right through to the end. "I call the Book of Job," he writes, "apart from all theories about it, one of the grandest things ever written with a pen." One evening, during his visit to Provost Swan at Kirkcaldy, on returning from his afternoon siesta to the family sitting room, he sat down with a Bible in his hand, and, as the cloth for tea was being laid, audibly repeated the last hymn in the Scottish collection of hymns, the one beginning—

> " The hour of my departure's come,
> I hear the voice that calls me home ;
> At last, O Lord, let trouble cease,
> And let thy servant die in peace."

There were surprised listeners to all this; but having re-read, audibly too, one or two of the verses, he, still heeding no one, turned the pages of the book, and silently perused some passages in the stately chapters of Job.

On the day he heard of Mazzini's death, he said to Mr Moncure Conway, who is, in our opinion, the most successful of all who have tried their hand at reporting

Carlyle's talk, "I remember well when he sat for the first time on the seat there, thirty-six years ago. A more beautiful person I never beheld, with his soft flashing eyes and face full of intelligence. He had great talent— certainly the only acquaintance of mine of anything like equal intellect who ever became entangled in what seemed to me hopeless visions. He was rather silent, spoke chiefly in French, though he spoke good English even then, notwithstanding a strong accent. It was plain he might have taken a high rank in literature. He wrote well, as it was—sometimes ·for the love of it, at others when he wanted a little money; but he never wrote what he might have done had he devoted himself to that kind of work. He had fine tastes, particularly in music. But he gave himself up as a martyr and sacrifice to his aims for Italy. He lived almost in squalor. His health was poor from the first; but he took no care of it. He used to smoke a great deal, and drink coffee with bread crumbled in it; but hardly gave any attention to his food. His mother used to send him money; but he gave it away. When she died, she left him as much as two hundred pounds a year—all she had; but it went to Italian beggars. His mother was the only member of his family who stuck to him. His father soon turned his back on his son. His only sister married a strict Roman Catholic, and she herself became too strict to have any- thing to do with him. He did see her once or twice; but the interviews were too painful to be repeated. He desired, I am told, to see her again when he was dying; but she declined. Poor Mazzini! I could not have any sympathy whatever with many of his views and hopes. He used to come here and talk about the 'solidarity of peoples'; and when he found that I was less and less interested in such things, he had yet another attraction than myself which brought him to us. But he found that *she* also by no means entered into his opinions, and his visits became fewer. But we always esteemed him. He was a very religious soul. When I first knew him he reverenced Dante chiefly, if not exclusively. When his letters were opened at the post-office here, Mazzini became, for the first time, known to the English people. There was great indignation at an English government taking the side of the Austrian against Italian patriots; and Mazzini was much sought for, invited to dinners, and all that. But he did not want the dinners. He went to but few places. He formed an intimacy with the Ashursts, which did him great good—gave him a kind of home-circle for the rest of his life in England. At last it has come to an end. I went to see him just before he left London for the last time, passed an hour, and came away feeling that I should never see him again. And so it is. The papers and people have gone blubbering away over him—the very papers and people that denounced him during life, seeing nothing of the excellence that was in him. They now praise him without any perception of his defects. Poor Mazzini! After all, he succeeded. He died receiving the homage of the people, and seeing Italy united, with Rome for its capital. Well, one may be glad he has succeeded. We wait to see whether Italy will make anything great out of what she has got. We wait." The *Athenæum* has told us, since Carlyle's death, of an extant document connected with the renting, by Mazzini, of a house in York Buildings, Chelsea, before the letter-opening year. Mrs Carlyle had negotiated the matter, and Carlyle signed the agreement as poor Mazzini's witness.

In 1857 Carlyle was appointed a trustee of the National Portrait Gallery, on the death of the Earl of Ellesmere. From Harvard University he received and accepted the degree of LL.D. a few years ago. In 1868 he was elected president of the Edinburgh Philosophical Institution, in succession to Lord Brougham, who had succeeded Macaulay; and this office he held till his death. Though unable to appear publicly before the members, he hardly ever was in Edinburgh without visiting their rooms, and never failed to express cordial approbation of the work that was being done by the society. He was also a patron of the Chelsea Literary Institute, which had its head quarters in the Vestry Hall in King's Road, close by his own residence; and he was on the Commission of the Peace for Dumfriesshire. We may add that copies of a letter exist in which he describes his interview with Her Majesty at the Deanery of Westminster in 1869.

From the sometimes authentic reports of American "interviewers," a conception may be formed of the life that was led by the wonderful old man in those years when he sat waiting and longing for the day of his release. Dr Cuyler, the American preacher, who visited Carlyle in 1873, stated that not an article seemed to have been changed in the house since his previous visit in 1842. Carlyle was attired in a long blue woollen gown, reaching down to his feet; his grey hair was in an uncombed mop on his head; his clear, blue eye was still sharp and piercing, and a bright tinge of red was on his thin cheek. He reminded this visitor of an old alchymist. He was still able to talk with his wonted vigour, and commenced at once, after a few inquiries about Longfellow, Bryant, and other American friends, a most characteristic discourse on the degeneracy of this age of delusions and impostures. With great vehemence he declared that " England has gone clean down into an abominable and damnable cesspool of lies, and shoddies, and shams !" The first of these which he specified were the swindling joint-stock companies, and new schemes for turning everything into gold. " Abominable contrivances for turning commerce and trade into a villainous *rouge et noir.*" So he continued to talk, on occasion, through most of the years of his last decade; it was not till the dawn of 1880 that he was bereft of his extraordinary powers as a conversationalist. The last picture we have of him is from the pen of a Scottish schoolboy, one of the sons of the late Alexander Munro, the sculptor, who died young in 1871. The boys, being at school at Charterhouse, went to see their father's old friend in the May of 1880, and one of them wrote home an account of their visit. They were led up the stair with the heavy wooden balustrade into the " well-lighted, cheerful-looking room," with the little old picture of Cromwell on the wall and the sketch by Mrs Carlyle of her Haddington home on the mantelpiece—the room in which Carlyle had passed the most of his time since he gave up working fourteen years before. Nothing could be more touching than the picture drawn by the boy, a grandson, we may note, of the late Dr Robert Carruthers, the accomplished journalist, of Inverness. " The maid went forward and said something to Carlyle, and left the room. He was sitting before a fire in an armchair, propped up with pillows, with his feet on a stool, and looked much older than I had expected. The lower part of his face was covered with a rather shaggy beard, almost quite white. His eyes were bright blue, but looked filmy from age. He had on a sort of coloured night-cap, and a long gown reaching to his ankles, and slippers on his feet. A rest attached to the arm of his chair supported a book before him. I could not quite see the name, but I think it was Channing's works. Leaning against the fireplace was a long clay pipe, and there was a slight smell of tobacco in the room. We advanced and shook hands, and he invited us to sit down, and began, I think, by asking where we were living. He talked of our father affectionately, speaking in a low tone as if to himself, and stopping now and then for a moment and sighing. He mentioned the last time they met, and said one took a long walk to see the other (I could not catch which), 'and then he went away to Cannes and died,' and he paused and sighed. 'And your grandfather, he is dead too.' He said he had done much good work, and written several books of reference, mentioning particularly his having explained who the people mentioned in Boswell's *Life of Johnson* were. All this was in a low tone, and rather confused and broken, so I cannot put it clearly down. He said he liked my grandfather very much. I said I thought every one did. He agreed, and spoke very highly of him as a 'most amiable man.' He asked what I was going to be. I said I was not sure, but I thought of going to college for the present. He asked something of which I only caught the words 'good scholars.' I said I hoped we should turn out so. He said there could be no doubt about it, if we only kept fast to what is right and true, and we certainly ought to, as the sons of such a respectable man. He strongly exhorted us to be always perfectly true and open, not deceiving ourselves or others, adding something about the common habits of deceit. He went on, 'I am near the end of my course, and the sooner the better is my own feeling.' He said he still reads a little, but has not many books he cares to read now, and is 'continually disturbed by foolish interruptions from people who do not know the value of an old man's leisure.' His hands were very thin and wasted; he showed us how they shook and trembled unless he rested them on something, and said they were failing him from weakness. He asked, 'Where did you say you were staying, and what are you doing there?' I told him we were at Bromley for our holidays, which ended on Thursday, when we returned to school. He asked if we were at school at Bromley. I told him we were at Charterhouse. 'Well, I'll just bid you good-bye.' We shook hands. He asked our names. He could not quite hear Henry's at first. 'I am a little deaf, but I can hear well enough talking,' or words to that effect. 'I wish you God's blessing, good-bye.' We shook hands once more and went away. I was not at all shy. He seemed such a venerable old man, and so worn and old looking that I was very much affected. Our visit was on Tuesday, May 18, 1880, at about 2 P.M."

That summer of 1880 was the longest and loveliest that had visited our island within the memory of living men; but it was the first that found Carlyle unable to leave town for his accustomed holiday. He had seen his native north for the last time. For more than a year, indeed, he had been visibly failing fast. The Chelsea people missed him from their streets; his morning walk by the riverside had became infrequent, and each time he did appear, his form was more bowed, his step feebler. Instead of going out every day, he was compelled to make it each alternate day; then twice a week was as much as he could bear; at last, not at all. For months his airing had been taken in a bath chair. The breaking up, spread over more than ten years, of a most active and vigorous constitution, had been almost imperceptible in its slow, successive, certain stages; but it was now evident that the end was drawing nigh. Once in the summer time it was thought he would die, and for several days his life hung in the balance; and when the winter came, with an Arctic rigour as exceptional as the length and beauty of the preceding summer, the thoughts of many turned to the old man in Cheyne Row. They wondered how he was faring as they saw so many of the aged dropping down at their own doors; and when his 85th birthday arrived, these thoughts were concentrated still more on the venerable pilgrim. He was now obliged to remain in his room, unable even to go down stairs; and at length, on one of the days of January, we learned that the severity of the season was proving too much for his diminished vital powers, and that he was slowly sinking. Even in the midst of the keen political excitement over that weary Irish problem, which he had discussed half a century before, thousands turned each morning, as they opened the newspaper, first of all to the bulletin from his physician, Dr Maclagan; the nation waited by that bed-side as if the peasant's son had been a king,—which, in very truth, he was. Even on the other side of the sea, in that great Republic of the West, which had hailed the dawn of his genius before it was recognised in his own country, each day's report was looked for not less eagerly;

while Germany waited for the tidings as if he had been one of her own sons. Generally the news was, that he had passed a quiet night, and that his general condition remained the same. Thus was it for many days. On Thursday morning, the 3d of February, the doctor found him in a drowsy state, moaning now and then in his sleep. He was almost pulseless, and in such an extremely exhausted condition that it was feared the heart's action might cease at any moment. So he continued till five o'clock on Friday evening, when he became unconscious, his respiration being extremely feeble, and the heart's action barely perceptible. Thus he lingered through the night; and on the morning of Saturday, the 5th, about half-past eight o'clock, he breathed his last. During the previous thirty-six hours he had suffered no pain. Dr Maclagan was in attendance when the end was drawing nigh, but medical skill was of no avail. His niece, the constant companion of all his widowed years, and who had been to him as the most loving of daughters, was with him to the last. He had suffered from no organic disease; his life had gradually burnt itself out, and he died from a general failure of vital power.

Next day, in Westminster Abbey, Dean Stanley told his congregation of "one tender expression—one plaintive yet manful thought—written but three or four years ago," that had not yet reached the public eye; and which it was grateful, most of all in such an hour, to hear—though it took by surprise no one who really knew Carlyle. "Three nights ago, stepping out after midnight and looking up at the stars, which were clear and numerous, it struck me with a strange new kind of feeling. 'In a little while I shall have seen you also for the last time. God Almighty's own Theatre of Immensity, the Infinite made palpable and visible to me. That also will be closed, flung to in my face, and I shall never behold it any more.' The thought of this eternal deprivation, even of this, though this is such a nothing in comparison, was sad and painful to me. And then a second feeling rose in me: What if Omnipotence, that has developed in me those pieties, those reverences, and infinite affections, should actually have said, 'Yes, poor mortals, such of you as have gone so far shall be permitted to go further. Hope; despair not. God's will, God's will, not ours, be done.'"

CHAPTER XXIV.

THE "PAUSE OF SORROWFUL STILLNESS"—TRIBUTES OF
THE PRESS AND THE PULPIT—THE FUNERAL—HIS
BEQUEST OF CRAIGENPUTTOCH : THE JOHN WELSH
BURSARIES—PERVERSION OF TRUSTS—HIS INFLUENCE
ON LITERATURE AND ON LIFE—HIS RELATION TO
CHRISTIANITY—THE SELF-DISCIPLINE OF HIS LIFE—
HIS LETTERS.

THE world, it was truly said by the chief reflector of the
feeling of England, seemed duller and colder, that one
grey old man at Chelsea had faded away from among us.
As another powerful journal remarked, it was a striking
testimony to the greatness of Carlyle's position, that men
were almost as much impressed by the tidings of his
death as if he had been taken in the midst of his career.
His work had been finished nearly fifteen years before—
no more was expected from him ; yet every educated
Briton, and even many of the manual toilers in our
nation, felt that they had lost something by the disappearance of a writer to whom they owed so much. He had
passed away in a season of almost fierce political conflict,
but for the moment even the leaders in the strife became
oblivious of its heats and distractions—there had come,
as one of these leaders finely remarked, "a pause of
sorrowful stillness" in the minds of all men. At the
recollection of the brave old worker who had gone to his

rest, of his noble character, of his magnificent work, "the battles of the hour seemed but pale skirmishes." Nor did the fact pass unnoted, that while the parliamentary government of which he had said so many hard things was in the very crisis of one of its most trying struggles, he was gently sinking away from it all, setting out on the voyage to the still country, "where, beyond these voices, there is peace."

Never was the press of Great Britain more unanimous than in the testimony which it bore respecting Thomas Carlyle. On all hands, by the organs of every political party and of every church, it was conceded that he had been the greatest and most heroic man of letters of our time, and that he had left his traces more deeply than any single Englishman on the moral character of the nineteenth century. The organ of the fashionable world of London pointed to the humble station in which he was born as an incitement to ambition. The son of a small Scottish farmer, he had died regretted and mourned by an entire nation. The representative of the most advanced Liberalism contended that he had never been an idolator of mere brute, selfish force, for he placed Cromwell above Napoleon; he believed in the divinity of strength, but only in the strength which is strong in rectitude and self-denying in labour. His cynicism had nothing in common with the cynicism of this materialistic age; his stern Hebraism scorned the modern Hellenists, and it was impossible that he could be the prophet of modern aristocracies. The Scottish journals mourned the departure of "the greatest Scotsman of his genera-tion," one worthy to be ranked with John Knox and Robert Burns, in some respects to be placed above even

them ; and pointed with pardonable pride to his personal
character, fruit of the wholesome training in that peasant-
home of Annandale, as constituting perhaps the truest'
element of his greatness. The people of the little land
that lies north the Tweed might be excused if they felt
their hearts swell as they read in the most influential
organ of British public opinion, that their newly-departed
compatriot was a man who had educated himself in the art
of plain living and high thinking, before he presumed to
educate others, and who, when he had become famous,
as while he was obscure, never taught the world lessons
which he had not first made part of his own being.

As was to be expected, the press of Germany vied with
that of Britain in doing honour to the memory of Carlyle, as also did the press of England's daughter, the
Great Republic across the sea, generously forgiving
the many hard words he had used in speaking of her.
The press of Italy did not fail to render justice to the old
friend of Mazzini, praising him both as a writer and as
a man; from France alone came the one discordant
note. There the Republican journalists reciprocated
the feeling of dislike with which he had viewed their
country; their verdict was distinctly unfavourable, and
obviously coloured by political resentment. They de-
fined him as "a Scotchman of an age anterior to
Burns, a Scot of the Covenant and Old Testament," who
judged Diderot and Danton according to the Covenanters'
standard ; and declared that nothing could be looked for
from a man who took his standpoint on the Cromwellian
dictatorship in criticising parliamentarism, industrialism,
and all that is great and small in modern civilization.
" Hero-worship and hatred of French sensualism blinded

Carlyle. He was original and vigorous, but too fantastic and archaic to merit the name of a great thinker." The most favourable estimate was pronounced by the chief organ of the Clericals, which, while deploring the contempt felt for the Latin races by this " Cromwellian Roundhead of the nineteenth century," praised him for " his implacable antagonism to that modern state of society in which falsehood, hypocrisy, scepticism, and stupid frivolities are more and more taking the place of the chain of sentiments and ideas which links earth to heaven." The marvels of industry did not awe him, the progress of humanity he did not place in the triumphs of matter; in his eyes a man was a man only on condition of being a tabernacle of the living God.

In hundreds of pulpits, on both sides of the Border, by preachers of the two Established Churches and of nearly all the Nonconformist communions as well, the life and writings of Carlyle were made the subject of discourse; and the conclusion almost unanimously reached was, that he had been the greatest moral teacher of this generation. At Oxford, in 1840, Professor Sewell said to his students: " Pantheism is invading this country in a great variety of modes, and in particular a man named Carlyle, who writes in a grotesque and striking manner, has introduced it in a most objectionable form." Not even in the most orthodox pulpits of his native country was such language as this uttered when he passed away. Even the rigid representatives of the least advanced section of the " Compendium of all Righteousness" had nothing but good to say of him. " No greater preacher of righteousness ever lived in modern times," said the minister of old St Giles's Church at Edinburgh; and in the same city one of the most thoughtful representatives of Nonconformity spoke of him as not the least of the many great men God had given to "the small and manly Scottish nation," and stated, as a fact of his own spiritual experience, that in some of his most troubled hours he had derived more aid from *Sartor* than from any other book save the Bible. " It is said he did not attend church or chapel, which, if true, as it is only partially, need not be marvelled at, when it is considered what both church and chapel have done to drive such men away from their doors." One preacher at Dundee took it to be a hopeful sign that the orthodox were not without hope that Carlyle may have found his way into Heaven. Those who cherished the hope were not trespassing far into the realm of Christian faith and hope. " Pity the heaven," he said, " that has no room for men like Carlyle. Pity the hell that got him, so far, at least, as its own peace and stability were concerned. Iniquity would not find much rest there with Carlyle's eyes upon it." Another preacher on the banks of the Tay described him as a man of blameless life, clearly gifted with the spirit and gifts of Isaiah and Ezekiel ; and yet there was no Church that would have admitted him to its ministry, or even to its membership. He had turned away from all ecclesiastical bodies, that, like Paul, he might go unto the Gentiles and preach to God's wider Church scattered throughout the world. The best men in the ecclesiastical bodies, however, did not turn away from him. The Dean of Durham publicly suggested, within a day or two of his death, that a Carlyle Scholarship should be established at Newcastle in honour of the man whose works were familiar, he knew, to so many of the sons of toil on the busy banks

of the Tyne ; and the Rector of Chelsea came forward
with a proposal to have Mr Boehm's statue of their sage
erected on the Thames Embankment at the end of the
quiet little street that will henceforth be a shrine visited
by pilgrims from every quarter of the world.

Though Dean Stanley offered a grave in the Abbey, it
was the universal expectation that Carlyle would be laid
beside his wife at Haddington. But on the eve of the
funeral it transpired, as the inner circle of his friends had
known for years, that he was, by his own wish, to find his
grave with his kindred in that province of Scotland where
he had been born and nurtured. This harmonised with
all that we knew of his character. It was the last impressive illustration of the fact, urged by the Parisian journals
as a complaint, that Carlyle was a Scot of the Old Testament. Though he declared to John Sterling that the
old Jew stars have now gone out, he was himself a
standing proof that they are by no means extinguished.
This was exemplified in many ways, even in the very
writings that seemed to superficial readers destructive of
the religious cult and the sacred traditions that had so
long dominated the life of the Scottish nation ; and now
we saw it confirmed by the Hebrew-like desire that he
should be laid, after life's fitful fever, in the " auld
kirkyard " in the village of his birth, where his fathers
sleep. On the evening of Wednesday, February 9, the
body was removed from Chelsea to Euston Square, and
left for the North by the 9 o'clock train, accompanied
by Mr Alexander Carlyle, B.A., and his wife. The
arrangements, in accordance with the express desire of
the deceased to have his obsequies conducted in the
most private and simple manner, had been kept so secret

that the body passed unobserved through the streets of London from Cheyne Row to Euston; and even next day at Ecclefechan, only the villagers and a few newspaper men who had travelled thither almost on a peradventure, were present to witness the touchingly simple funeral procession as it moved slowly along the snow-covered country road from the railway station to the graveyard. The mourners were Mr James Carlyle, late of Scotsbrig, brother of Carlyle; Mr James Carlyle, jun., Newlands; Mr John Carlyle, Pingle, Middlebie; Mr Alexander Carlyle, B.A., London; Mr J. C. Austin, The Gill, Annan, nephews; Mr James Aitken, The Hill, Dumfries, a brother-in-law; Mr John Aitken, The Hill, Dumfries; Mr Alex. Welsh, merchant, Liverpool, a cousin of the late Mrs Carlyle; Captain Henry F. Wall, Liverpool; as also Professor Tyndall, Mr J. A. Froude, and Mr W. E. H. Lecky, who had travelled from London to attend the funeral of their deceased friend. Mr Russell Lowell, the American Ambassador, had been invited, but was unavoidably absent. A few gentlemen connected with the district were also in the churchyard; the villagers, who had shut their shops and left off work, gathered, in their ordinary attire, in clusters by the roadside, while the younger portion of the inhabitants watched the interment from the churchyard wall, a score or so of women, with little coloured shawls thrown round their shoulders to protect themselves from the cold, standing at the side of the gate. The muffled bell in the schoolhouse tower was rung slowly; when the hearse drew up at the churchyard gate, about twenty-five minutes to one o'clock, the spectators reverently took off their hats and remained uncovered until the coffin was carried to the grave. At this moment

a sharp shower of sleet fell, but before the coffin had been
laid upon the trestles the sun shone through the clouds
and sent a gleam into the open grave. According to the
Scottish custom, there was no religious ceremonial. It
was with difficulty the relatives could restrain their
emotion, and Mr Froude, Professor Tyndall, and Mr
Lecky all seemed deeply moved. Mrs A. Carlyle, the
niece, was in the churchyard, though her presence was
unknown to the spectators. Several beautiful wreaths
were laid upon the coffin, and choice flowers thrown
into the tomb; the transient gleam of sunlight that
had suddenly pierced the dull leaden skies sparkled
on the flowers and on the polished oak of the coffin
wet with the rain. Never before had so great a man
so simple a funeral. An old woman in the crowd at
the gate told how Carlyle himself had pointed out to
her, two summers before, the place in his family "lair"
where he intended he should be laid. Carlyle's grave is
in the centre, his kindred lying on each side of him.
Nearest to him on one side is his mother; on the other
side his brother John, the translator of Dante, who died
in 1879. The lair is in the west corner of the kirkyard,
under the shadow of some bourtree bushes growing out
of the wall. It is surrounded by a stout railing, with no
ornamentation. Two plain stones bear the names of the
Carlyles who lie beneath; the record of Carlyle's mother,
from the pen of her illustrious first-born, tells how "she
brought" her husband "nine children, whereof four sons
and three daughters survive gratefully reverent of such a
father and such a mother." The kirkyard, enclosed on
one side by a stone wall, on the other three sides with a
thorn hedge, is not above a dozen yards square; its

hillocky surface is crowded with old tombstones, some falling forward and others backward among the long rank grass; it is one of the least lovely of the rustic burial-grounds in a land where sentiment does not much run in the direction of ornamenting the "cities of the dead." There is very little of an outlook on the surrounding country, just a glimpse to be got of a fir-covered hill on one hand, and of the Roman camp on Burnswork Hill, on the other; but from Carlyle's grave you can see the house in which he was born, only a stone-throw distant. That Border land has long been rich in memorials of the distinguished dead; but henceforth it must attract even a greater throng of pilgrims to its soil, for now in addition to the tombs of Robert Burns, the Ettrick Shepherd, and Thomas Aird, it has the grave of its greatest son, Thomas Carlyle.

Before the month in which he died was ended, it became known that Carlyle, while he yet occupied the office of Lord Rector, in 1867, had executed a deed bequeathing to the University of Edinburgh the estate of Craigenputtoch which his wife had brought him, for the endowment of ten bursaries in the Faculty of Arts, to be called the "John Welsh Bursaries," in honour of his wife's father and forefathers. The "deed of mortification," read at a meeting of the Senatus on the last Saturday of February, is perhaps the most remarkable document of the kind that was ever written—a revelation of the mind and heart of the testator singularly impressive and touching; the terms in which it is expressed rising to a solemn and lofty pitch of genuine eloquence that must secure for it an enduring place among the most precious of its author's literary remains. It opens with a tribute to his "late dear, magnanimous, much-loving, and to me inestimable wife." It was for her sake, and in memory of "her constant nobleness and piety towards him (her father) and towards me," that Carlyle, "with whatever piety is in me," bequeathed to Edinburgh University "this Craigenputtoch, which was theirs and hers." Such was the main motive of the bequest; but Carlyle also had a wish to help "the young heroic soul struggling for what is highest," and very characteristic is the provision that the bursaries should "always be given, on solemnly strict and faithful trial, to the worthiest; or if (what in practice can never happen, though it illustrates my intention) the claims of two were absolutely equal, and could not be settled by further trial, preference is to fall in favour of the more unrecommended and unfriended." To this Carlyle adds the solemn monition: "Under penalties graver than I, or any highest mortal, can pretend to impose, but which I can never doubt—as the law of eternal justice, inexorably valid, whether noticed or unnoticed, pervades all corners of space and of time— are very sure to be punctually exacted if incurred, this is to be the perpetual rule for the Senatus in deciding." We are here reminded of an incident that occurred when he accompanied Emerson on their pilgrimage to Stonehenge during his American friend's second visit to England. Just before entering Winchester, they stopped at the Church of Saint Cross, and, after looking through the quaint antiquity, demanded the piece of bread and the draught of beer, which the founder, Henry de Blois, in 1136, commanded should be given to every one who should ask it at the gate. They got both from the old couple who take care of the church; but "this hospitality of seven hundred years' standing did not hinder Carlyle from pronouncing a malediction on the priest who receives £2,000 a year, that were meant for the poor, and spends a pittance on this small beer and crumbs." Such maladministration of sacred trusts always roused his deepest indignation; and never more than when the endowments so perverted by unscrupulous trustees had been left for educational purposes. When Mr W. C. Bennett published a pamphlet in 1853 exposing such a case in connection with Roan's School at Greenwich, Carlyle wrote thanking him: "I hope you will completely achieve the reform of that scandalous mismanagement, to the benefit of this and future generations; and cannot but wish there were such a preacher in every locality where such an abuse insults mankind;—a rather frequent case, I believe, in poor England just now." And, as Mr Bennett happened to be a song-writer, he added: "Such work (as the writing of the pamphlet) I continue to think, is much more melodiously 'Poetical' for a human soul than the best written verses are."

Of the ten John Welsh Bursaries, five are to be given absolutely and irrevocably for proficiency in Mathematics, Carlyle holding that proficiency therein is perennially the symptom, not only of steady application, but of a clear, methodic intellect," and that it offers, "in all epochs, good promise for all manner of arts and pursuits." The other five are to be given for proficiency in "classical learning," which also "gives good promise of a mind," though he is not quite so sure that it will continue to retain its present position as an instrument of culture; hence he leaves power to the Senatus of the University to change the destination of this part of the endowment, "in case of a change of its opinion on this point hereafter in the course of generations." The value of Craigenputtoch is at present £250 a year, likely to become £300. Each bursary will be tenable during the whole undergraduate course. Very beautiful are the closing words of the testator. "So may a little trace of help, to the young heroic soul struggling for what is highest, spring from this poor arrangement and bequest; may it run, forever if it can, as a thread of pure water from the Scottish rocks, tinkling into its little basin by the thirsty wayside, for those whom it veritably belongs to. Amen."

Many years have passed since the greatest thinker of America asserted that the influence of Carlyle might be traced in every new book; and one of the most powerful of our own essayists, far enough from being an unqualified admirer, acknowledges that the intellectual career of Carlyle "has exercised on many sides the profoundest sort of influence upon English feeling;" that "his influence in stimulating moral energy, in kindling enthusiasm for virtues worthy of enthusiasm, and in stirring a sense of the reality on the one hand, and the unreality on the other, of all that men can do or suffer, has not been surpassed by any teacher now living;" and that "whatever later teachers may have done in definitely shaping opinion, in giving specific form to sentiment, and in subjecting impulse to rational discipline, here was the friendly fire-bearer who first conveyed the Promethean spark, here the prophet who first smote the rock."* Even

---

* *Critical Miscellanies.* By John Morley. Pp. 195-6. London. 1871.

where a protest has to be lodged by the judgment against Carlyle's doctrines, our feelings are almost always enlisted in his favour by our faith in the sincerity of his purpose, the singular purity and earnestness of his life, and the depth of his genius, to say nothing of the force and beauty of that utterance which are almost always so great as to overbear disapproval of the thought he utters.

When we trace his influence on contemporary literature, we find that although Wordsworth denounced him as "a pest to the English tongue," he has done more than any other writer to exalt and bring to perfection prose composition. His style, by some objected to as German, was in reality his own, much more derived, as to its peculiarities, from Ecclefechan and the old Secession pulpit (whose cadence may often be detected in his loftiest flights) than from the authors of Germany, greatly as he was beholden to these, especially to Jean Paul. It is unrivalled for its simplicity, richness, clearness and strength, infinitely preferable to that conventional style which has so often served to conceal or give inadequate expression to thought. For this he substituted the plain-speaking of colloquial intercourse, not afraid of it even when it verged towards vulgarity. Despising the artificial and frigid phraseology of the schools, he has freely employed "the fresh and beautiful idioms of daily speech;" and if an author should wish his words to be as hooks, this merit at least cannot be denied to the words of Carlyle. The notion, that his style was affected and unintelligible (Dr Robert Chambers said it was " painfully studied "), arose from the fact that " every fresh experiment in language is ridiculed and disliked, unless it be a retrograde experiment "—also from the strangeness of a strong, independent, learned, humorous, and altogether human being daring to speak to the public in his own natural voice. If there is a pronounced mannerism in Carlyle's writings, it is only because he is true to his own pronounced individuality; there is not in it the slightest taint of affectation. His word is ever in harmony with the thought or feeling to be expressed. Indeed, you see his thoughts visibly shaping their vehicle as they rise in the author's mind. One of the first things you marked in conversing with him was, that he spoke exactly as he wrote. Though sternly patriotic in his temper, his style is cosmopolitan; he enriches his discourse with all that he has gathered in the field of the world's literature. In the same spirit, he uses many of the freedoms falsely supposed to be permissible only to the composers of verse, flashing out sudden bursts of homely laughter, or almost savage scorn, or tenderest pathos in quick succession, according to the theme and the varying mood of his mind; teaching some great truth by a familiar phrase of the market, or some sharp nickname either borrowed or manufactured from the talk of the street; taking, in short, the word or phrase that will best serve his turn, no matter whence it comes—from Annandale or from Hindostan. Edward Irving's prophecy he has fulfilled by revolutionising two departments of English literature, biography and history. As a historian he must be classed with the great masters who display a universal and impartial insight into the leading elements of the period with which they are dealing. And this he combines with the characteristic excellencies of the lesser lights who gain in vivid power by limiting the scope of their effort to the reproduction of that element with which they personally sympathise.

He unites the power of detachment, which is fair to all the actors in the story he has to tell, with the warm and enthusiastic personal interest and sympathy of conviction. He is too great a humourist to be a narrow and bitter partisan; too earnest in spirit to pourtray a struggle without taking a side. He sees something to love and pity in the hearts of all men; but he never allows this to blind him to the cause of righteousness and truth. He has powers of severe compression equal to those of the coldest of philosophical historians, being indeed altogether matchless in his use of what has been happily called the stenographic method; and yet he has carried the power of local painting to the very highest pitch. It is this union of the two styles of historical writing that explains the form which his work has assumed, and accounts for its so-called mannerisms.

As to his influence on religion and life, that is a more perplexing problem, and one that will probably continue to provoke as much controversy in the future as it has done in the past. That he has communicated a mighty impulse to the moral activity of his generation, is almost universally conceded. He has penetrated ingenuous souls with a reverence for the true and the just thing. He has also taught more impressively than any other writer in our language the sacredness of work. But we are far from accepting the evangel that is founded on Hero-Worship, concerning which it has been too truly said that it begins by placing certain select men on a superhuman pinnacle, and ends with wholesale shooting of the weak. With respect to his religious teaching, some have thought him a truer representative of Scottish Puritanism than even Hugh Miller; and there is not a little truth in the shrewd remark that, " in the same way as Dr Newman has been an indirect and powerful promoter of free thought in matters of religion, so has Carlyle played into the hands of religious bodies to whose views he has been ever utterly opposed." His position has certainly not been a consistent one. To a friend of ours who happened once to say that he held the same religious views as himself, Carlyle with some heat retorted, "*My* religious views! And who told you *what* my religious views are ?"* This question was as just in one point of view as it was touching in another ; for no one could possibly tell what he meant by his mysterious allusions to God and Eternity. We are not disposed to question the sincerity of feeling in that great heart which has now ceased to beat ; but it is to be feared that Carlyle was nearly as much in the dark as to his meaning as any of his readers. We are in hearty unison with the feeling of a friend, who has suggested that, on the subject of Christianity, Carlyle ought either to have said more— or less.

One lesson of Carlyle's life has been incidentally

---

* This reminds one of the saying of the First Earl of Shaftesbury, appropriated without acknowledgment in Lord Beaconsfield's *Endymion*, when his lordship remarked that "all sensible men are of the same religion." "And pray what is that ?" "Men of sense never tell," replied the Earl. The *St James's Gazette* says : "The reason why Carlyle did not state his views plainly and simply are obvious enough. In the first place, if he had done so sixty years ago, he would not only have lost all influence, but he would have starved. In the next place, he would have taken up the position which of all others was most unwelcome to him—namely, that of a rebel and revolutionist." What would become of the veracity on which Carlyle was always insisting, were this interpretation of his conduct a true one !

alluded to by his friend Professor Masson. The latter is pointing out the sad fact that most literary men do not see or scheme much farther than into the middle of next week, any more in what pertains to the conduct of their intellect than in their material concerns, so that life for them is but a series of disconnected efforts, having no real strategic unity. But there have been men, he says, who, at an early period of their lives, or at some period less early, have formed a resolution as to the direction of their activity for the rest of their lives, and have kept true in the main to their plans. Mr Masson cites the examples of Bacon, Gibbon, Milton, Hallam, and Wordsworth, and then adds :—" If among our still living British writers we would seek for one in whose life, reviewed as a whole hitherto, the same character of what may be called strategy, the same noble self-discipline on a large scale, is obvious with all the clearness of a historic fact of our time, whom should we name but Carlyle ?" This lesson is emphasized when we contrast the outcome of his well-planned life with the comparatively wasted lives of two of his most brilliant contemporaries. De Quincey did achieve marvellous things in spite of the absence of this strategy; but what might he not have done had he combined with his lofty genius a corresponding measure of self-discipline ? As for John Wilson, Scott and others declared he had a capacity that might make him, in literature, the very first man of his generation ; but, alas ! he did not do justice to his wonderful gifts, and was distanced in the race by inferior men who observed that stringent self-regulation which he failed to apply to his splendid powers.

How pleasant it is to recall the blameless nature of

Carlyle's private life, and the beautiful spirit which he exemplified not only within the domestic precinct, but also in all the social relationships, where he was ever the friendliest and most helpful of men. To the young in particular he was a loving and faithful monitor, ready at all times to bestow patient, earnest thought on the case of the very humblest youth who applied to him for advice as to the conduct of his life. When his multitudinous letters to young men and women who thus sought his counsel have been brought together, they will constitute a volume not only full of the richest practical wisdom, but also pervaded throughout by a tenderly sympathetic feeling such as was never equalled by any other of the world's philosophers. Had a Boswell been at work by his side to chronicle his matchless talk, the result would inevitably have eclipsed the *Johnson* which thus far stands without a rival in our literature ; and we are firmly convinced that the collection of Carlyle's Letters which is happily sure to appear some day, will make a book greater, both as to its literary interest and its enduring moral value, than even the poetic romance of *Sartor* or the greatest of his histories.

APPENDIX.

I.—THE PORTRAITS OF CARLYLE.

NO one has more eloquently vindicated the utility of trust-worthy portraits of great men than Carlyle. His last essay was on *The Portraits of John Knox*. Old Beza, in the dedication of his *Icones*, after avowing the delight he had in contemplating the face of any "heroic friend of Letters and of true Religion," proceeded to defend himself against any imputation of idolatry or image-worship ; but Carlyle declares the defence to be "superfluous." Any frequent visitor to the little house in Cheyne Row knew that its tenant had what most people would call a craze for portraits of great men.

1. DANIEL MACLISE was hardly the artist we should have selected to execute a portrait of Carlyle ; but to his pencil we are indebted for the earliest we have seen. Maclise was for many years a neighbour of Carlyle's, living but a few doors off, round the corner, at 4 Cheyne Walk—one of the houses facing the water. The portrait, a full-length, appeared in *Fraser's Magazine* for June 1833. So far as we are aware, this was the first portrait of Carlyle that had been taken. He was at that date in his thirty-eighth year. In the sketch he is leaning against a column, one hand supporting his head, the other holding his hat. The letterpress accompanying the

portrait was a bit of not very brilliant Carlylese by Maginn. "Here hast thou, O Reader!" he says, "the from-stone-printed effigies of Thomas Carlyle, the thunderwordoversetter of Herr Johann Wolfgang von Goethe. These fingers now in listless occupation supporting his head, or clutching that outward integument with which the head holds so singular a relation that those who philosophically examine, and with a fire-glance penetrate into the contents of the great majority of the orb-shaped knobs which form the upper extremity of man, know not with assured critic-craft to decide whether the hat was made to cover the head or the head erected as a peg to hang that upon—yea, these fingers have transferred some of the most harmonious and mystic passages—to the initiated, mild-shining, inaudible-light instinct—and to the uninitiated, dark and untransparent as the shadows of Eleusis —of those forty volumes of musical wisdom which are commonly known by the title of 'Goethe's Werke,' from the Fatherlandish dialect of High-Dutch to the Allgemeine-Mid-Lothianish of Auld Reekie." And so on. In 1835 Maclise executed a large cartoon etching of the writers in *Fraser*, and here we see the author of *Sartor* in the company of Maginn (who presides at the symposium), Southey, Proctor, Macnish, Coleridge, Hogg, Croker, Lockhart, D'Orsay, Thackeray, Ainsworth, Hook, Brewster, and others. He does not seem very much at home in the company; and his face is peepy and obscure. Carlyle was the last survivor of these Fraserians. Speaking of Maclise's portrait, Mr R. H. Hutton says:—"You see hardly anything characteristic but the bright eye and arched eyebrow, which seem to indicate a love of marvel; you certainly see nothing of that strong contempt for average life and eager craving after traces of force and grandeur, which have made Carlyle's countenance in later life the very type of a cynical mystic's, of the face of one yearning after hidden fires, and other earth-shaking powers, of which he could but seldom detect in the actual world even the trace. Maclise has not thrown any touch of ridicule into his sketch of Carlyle, unless he has made it just a little conceited and moony, though very like the later countenance, of course, in feature. Had he drawn him in later life, what a powerful picture he must have given."

2. COUNT D'ORSAY'S sketch was published in 1839 by Mitchell the printseller. It is much more characteristic of the artist than of the subject. " If Carlyle should ever relax his opinions upon society," says one critic, " and desire to go down to posterity as a fashionable personage, rather than as a stern moralist, this will be his favourite portrait. It was taken when no man of position was considered a dutiful sub-ject who did not wear a black satin stock and a Petersham coat." Even so lately as 1862 Carlyle continued to wear a stock—and a very stiff one, too—and could see no reason why everybody else should not be compelled to do the same. Charles Boner, who visited him in the above year, found Carlyle laughing at what the press and the public were saying about the soldiers' dress. They abused the stock. " Why, a stock was most comfortable ; the best neck-cover-ing a soldier could wear. He always wore a stock." There-fore, he did not see why soldiers were not to wear stocks, and resented indignantly the interference of the press in such matters. But not long after this colloquy with Mr Boner he departed widely from that old and certainly absurd fashion commemorated in the sketch of D'Orsay, who, by the way, was even a less appropriate artist to treat such a subject than Maclise.

3. SAMUEL LAURENCE painted a portrait about 1843, of which it has been said that it is " perhaps the most intellec-tual-looking of all the published likenesses ; the beetle-browed, stern figure presents to one's mind the very ideal of

a giant in thought." Mr Laurence, many years afterwards, executed a copy of the Somerville portrait of John Knox, which he agreed with Carlyle in accepting as the true representation of the Scottish Reformer. A reference to Mr Laurence will be found in Carlyle's Essay on the Knox Portraits.

4. In 1844 a good portrait appeared in the *New Spirit of the Age* (edited by R. H. Horne; 2 vols.) It is subscribed with the familiar "most faithfully yours, T. Carlyle." It seems to have been from a painting by ARMYTAGE. It still bears the younger look of Maclise's 1833 sketch, but with a touch more of the ripeness of years, yet with a look of hectic contemplativeness.

5. THE CAMBRIDGE LITHOGRAPH.—An esteemed friend possesses a striking portrait of which we have seen only the one copy. It is "drawn on stone" and "lithographed." The publisher is Roe of Cambridge. It is said to be "after a daguerrotype." It bears no date; but the copy we have seen was bought by its owner about twenty years ago. The face looks like that of a man of fifty years of age. There is no moustache or beard, and only a slight whisker. The hair is rather closely cut, and is brushed somewhat loosely down on the forehead. The face is almost a profile. The most striking features are the eye and the lips; the eye is heavy and melancholy, the lips are very firm and compressed. In the room in which we have seen this portrait there are companion lithographs of Maurice and Tennyson. It presents a striking contrast to the face of Maurice, with its firm yet sensitive mouth, and bright, hopeful look. Tennyson, on the other hand, has a perplexed, questioning, and half-timid look. Our friend who owns the portraits thinks that one might write under Tennyson, "The problem pondered;" under Carlyle, "The problem faced as insoluble;" under

Maurice, "The problem solved." Or, to put it in another way—"Before the Storm;" "In the Storm;" "After the Storm." But Maurice's face in the flesh bore traces that an inward conflict was still going on for the maintenance of his faith and hope. The portrait, however, is somewhat idealised, and gives rather the impression of calm and settled assurance. Another friend, now deceased, informed us that many years ago he was shown by a near relative of Carlyle a rather faded talbotype of the philosopher, and was then informed that it was taken by John Sterling, who in failing health amused himself by taking some pictures of his friends. Our friend's recollection of the picture corresponds with the description of the lithograph published by Roe of Cambridge. John Sterling's talbotype and the daguerrotype must have been about the same date. If the talbotype which our friend saw is still in existence, it must be altogether unique.

6. In 1857 there was a picture in the Royal Academy's Exhibition of "Mr and Mrs Carlyle at Home," by Mr ROBERT TAIT, the same "friendly Scottish artist" who is twice referred to in exceedingly complimentary terms in Carlyle's essay on *The Portraits of Knox*. It was Mr Tait who reported to Carlyle on the portrait of Knox in Glasgow University, and also on the bronze figure on the monument in Glasgow Necropolis. Mr Tait furthermore reported on the famous Somerville Portrait of the Reformer.

7. AN ANONYMOUS SKETCH.—In J. Camden Hotten's little volume, containing Carlyle's Rectorial Address, there is a portrait, engraved from a sketch taken, it is not said by whom, in 1859. It is not without a measure of fidelity, but must have been taken when the subject of the sketch was in one of his dullest moods.

8. BUST BY BEHNES.—A bust of Carlyle was modelled by
Behnes for the Crystal Palace Portrait Gallery. The short
biographical and critical notices in the catalogue—very able
they were, but in Carlyle's case rather disparaging—were
written by Samuel Phillips, author of *Caleb Stukely*, and for
many years literary critic to the *Times*.

9. Mr HERDMAN painted a portrait which was exhibited
in the Royal Academy's Exhibition of 1876. Good, both as
a painting and a likeness.

10. There is a medallion by WOOLNER, of which it is quite
unnecessary to say that it is in the highest degree artistic,
marked by grace and delicacy; but it is not a speaking
likeness.

11. Mr CRITTENDEN has executed a bust.

12. Mr J. E. BOEHM, A.R.A., the sculptor of the statue of
John Bunyan erected at Bedford, completed a fine statue of
Carlyle in 1876, from which the portrait facing title-page
is engraved. The venerable author is seated in an armchair, and the likeness is simply perfect. The statue, which
gave great satisfaction to its subject (and he was by no
means easy to please in such matters), was exhibited in the
Royal Academy, and it has been proposed by the Rev.
Gerald Blunt, rector of Chelsea, that the people of that parish
shall acquire the statue, and set it up on the Thames Embankment at the end of Cheyne Row. Mr Boehm is warmly
eulogised by Carlyle in the essay on *The Portraits of
Knox*, where it is declared that his judgment of painting and
knowledge of the history, styles, and epochs of it seemed to
the essayist far beyond that of any other man he had com-
muned with.

Mr MILLAIS·executed a portrait in 1879. It is a seated figure, the hands on the lap, one leg crossed on the other, with strongly-contrasted light and shade on the powerful, deeply-indented features, the ashy brownness of the complexion, and the whitish iron-grey of the stubbly beard and thick moustaches. This is thought by some to be the noblest of all the portraits.

14. Mr HOWARD, M.P., who lately succeeded his father in the representation of East Cumberland, and who is heir-presumptive to the Earldom of Carlisle, executed more than one striking sketch of the sage, who was his intimate friend. It was Mr Howard who acted with so much energy and enthusiasm as the secretary of the Eastern Question Association.

15. G. F. WATTS, R.A., has painted a portrait, which has been etched by M. RAJON. The artist's proofs, numbering 125 only, were sold at three prices—with remarques, at fifteen guineas; on Japanese paper, at six guineas; on Whatman paper, at five.

16. J. M. WHISTLER'S portrait, exhibited at the first Exhibition of the Grosvenor Gallery, but not a new work then, has been variously estimated. Some conceive it to be " one of the most acceptable achievements" of Mr Whistler; and it was said that Carlyle, at the time of its production, considered it the finest portrait of himself that had till then been painted. Others declared that it was " no more Carlyle than a lump of black anthracite is a glowing fire;" for our own part, we sympathise with the latter opinion. Carlyle is represented seated on a wicker-bottomed chair, dressed in black, with a brown cloak or shawl thrown over his knees, on the top of which rests his black wide-awake hat, his right hand leaning on a staff. This likeness was engraved on steel by Mr JOSEY in 1878.

17. A bust by Mr Wm. BRODIE, R.S.A., in the Exhibition of the Royal Scottish Academy in 1881, was bought by Mr John Leng, Kinbrae, Newport, the price being £150.

18. The latest portraits are nine or ten water-colour sketches from life by Mrs ALLINGHAM, done about two years ago. The artist, having the privilege of sitting frequently in his room, sketched him reading, smoking, sleeping, &c., and Carlyle pronounced the likenesses to be highly successful. They will probably be exhibited in the course of the season (1881).

ETCHINGS.—A series of etchings have for some time been in process of execution by Mr Howard Helmick. They are reproductions of authentic and unpublished portraits and sketches in the possession of the family; and, covering a period of about fifty years, they show Carlyle in the more intimate aspects of his home life—at ease in his garden and at work in his study. These etchings, six in number, will be issued by the Etchers' Society.

PHOTOGRAPHS.—For many years we have been so familiar with the photographs of Carlyle—of which there has been a greater variety provided than in the case of any other man of our time, not excepting even Mr Gladstone or Lord Beaconsfield—that it is surprising to be told that a considerable period elapsed before he could be induced to sit to a photographer. At first he professed a superlative contempt for the new art, but by and by saw reason to change his mind. When the *Critic* published a bibliographical memoir of Carlyle in 1859, he declined to assist them to the use of a good portrait; whereupon they published a shocking caricature, though they described it as a characteristic likeness, "the attitude in which he stands being one which his friends will recognise as that in which he will sometimes remain for hours, when earnestly engaged in the discussion of some absorbing question "—a statement as far from the truth as the portrait. Many of the photographs have been striking and powerful—some, indeed, painfully so. One of the most faithful likenesses is that taken by Mr Charles Watkins, of 34 Parliament Street, London, in which Carlyle is represented with his broad-brimmed felt hat on his head, casting the upper part of the face into shadow. It was one of the portraits taken by Messrs Elliot & Fry, of Baker Street, that had the honour of being engraved for the initial volume of the people's edition of Carlyle's writings. In the October of 1862 an admirable photograph was taken by Mr Vernon Heath, an engraving from which appeared in the *Illustrated London News*, February 19, 1881. An additional interest attaches to this portrait on account of its having been taken at the Grange, Lord Ashburton's place. Mr Heath writes : "Carlyle was then in the height of his vigour and power, and both he and his wife impressed me deeply. Towards the close of the week Bishop Wilberforce joined the party. Just think what it was to hear Carlyle and the Bishop in argument !—and that was my good fortune. There was one wet morning we amused ourselves with my camera, and it was then this portrait was taken." In 1874, on his visit to Kirkcaldy, in Fifeshire, Carlyle sat to Mr Patrick, of that town, who succeeded in producing a set of four (different positions) that were thought by Carlyle himself to be very successful. There is a strikingly faithful photograph taken in 1876 by F. Bruckmann, of 11 King Street, Covent Garden. A capital engraving from one of the photographs of Elliott & Fry appeared in the *Graphic* of April 30, 1870. It is a profile, and reproduces with admirable effect the keen-searching, sceptical, half-contemptuous and yet most pathetic weary look, which was probably the most habitual with its subject. A good portrait was published upwards of a dozen years ago in the *Illustrated London News*.

II.—THE CARLYLE FAMILY.

Of the father of Carlyle we have received an anecdote that helps to confirm the view of the old man given in our second chapter. After the death, in his eighty-second year, of the Rev. John Johnston, the Burgher minister of Ecclefechan, which took place May 28, 1812, there was considerable difficulty in procuring a successor. The congregation first called Mr John M'Kerrow, but the Synod appointed him to Bridge of Teith. Then they called Mr Robert Balmer, but he was sent to Berwick. Next, Mr Andrew Hay, who declined the call, and never got another. The fourth preacher called was a Mr B——, who was appointed by the Synod to East Campbell Street, Glasgow. During the negotiations with the last-named person, he had spoken a good deal about the stipend to be given, and contrasted the pecuniary provision offered by Ecclefechan—not to the advantage of the village —with what he could get in Glasgow. When this came out at a meeting of the Session, or of the Congregation, old Carlyle rose up, and, with a decisive sweep of his arm, said, "*Let the hireling go !*" His fellow-members at once acted on the advice. Our informant says this was a good proof of old Carlyle's insight into human character, as the minister he so summarily dismissed had a wide repute for being richly endowed with "saving knowledge," and worldly wisdom generally.

All Carlyle's brothers and sisters were distinguished by a decisive, strong character ; and of his surviving brother James, we have heard more than one of his acquaintances remark that, with Thomas's education, he might have been another of the same. His words seem to have double power in his mouth, and were always "clenching" when aught was under discussion. It was he who received the striking eulogy from the old parish roadman at Ecclefechan. "Been a long time in this neighbourhood ?" asked an American traveller on the outlook for a sight of the sage. "Been here a' ma days, sir." "Then you'll know the Carlyles?" "Weel that ; a ken the whole o' them. There was, let me see," he said, leaning on his shovel and pondering, "there was Jock, he was a kind o' throughither sort o' chap, a doctor, but no a bad fellow Jock—he's deid, man." "And there was Thomas?" said the inquirer eagerly. "Oh ay, of course, there's Tam—a useless munestruck chap that writes books and talks havers. Tam stays maistly up in London. There's naething in Tam. But man, there's Jamie owre in the New-lands—there's a chap for ye. He's the man o' that family ! Jamie tak's mair swine into Ecclefechan markets than ony ither farmer in the parish !"

Carlyle is survived by many near relatives, the most of whom are still resident in their native country, though others have emigrated to Canada, where more than one nephew has risen to a position of professional distinction. A nephew now farms Craigenputtoch, though he does not occupy the house where *Sartor* was written, being obliged to reside else-where, to be near schools for his children. In the mean time, the house is given up to a shepherd. Of all the members of his family, perhaps the one who most closely resembled Carlyle is his sister, Mrs Aitken, of Dumfries, the mother of the young lady who for so many years acted as the house-keeper of her uncle. We have heard Mrs Aitken described by those who are privileged with her acquaintance as a lady of remarkable intellectual power and a most brilliant con-versationalist, with quaint, bright forms of expression akin to those that lighten up the books of her illustrious brother. In addition to translating Dante's *Inferno*, Dr John Carlyle wrote several articles for the *Edinburgh Review* and other periodicals.

The name Carlyle is pronounced "Keryl" in Annandale. We have stated in the first chapter that Carlyle took a warm interest in the genealogy of his House. A reference to his genealogical inquiries will be found in *Sartor Resartus*, where we are told that Teufelsdröckh had written "long historical inquiries into the genealogy of the Futteral Family, here traced back as far as Henry the Fowler : the whole of which we pass over, not without silent astonishment." He was unquestionably proud of his name and ancestry. "For indeed," he says, "as Walter Shandy often insisted, there is much, nay almost all, in Names. The Name is the earliest Garment you wrap round the earth-visiting ME: to which it thenceforth cleaves, more tenaciously (for there are Names that have lasted nigh thirty centuries) than the very skin."

III.—DAVID HOPE OF GLASGOW.

The late Mr David Hope, merchant, Glasgow, who died an old bachelor, had a fine collection of letters written to him by Carlyle when they were young men. Mr Hope was a nephew of the old rector of the "Hinterschlag Academy" at Annan, and he and young Teufelsdröckh were great friends. Carlyle always made Hope's house in Windsor Place his home when he was in Glasgow. A friend, who once saw some of the letters, remembers that one had been written from the Highlands, where Carlyle was sojourning with a pupil. The closing passage of the epistle was an urgent cry: "Send the Tobacco, or there will be a famine in the land. We shall be obliged to use the coltsfoot leaves if you don't see to it. I am still the old complaining man, you see. 'Why should a living man complain?' Simply *because he's a fool.*"

INDEX.

EDINBURGH : PRINTED BY HOME & MACDONALD.